BERKLEY UK

THE PACK

Jason Starr is the author of nine previous novels and has won the Anthony Award and the Barry Award. He lives in Manhattan and is currently writing the sequel to *The Pack*. Visit his website at www.jasonstarr.com.

D1092986

The Pack

JASON STARR

BERKLEY UK

PENGUIN

BERKLEY UK

Published by the Penguin Group
Penguin Books Ltd, 80 Strand, London WC2R ORL, England
Penguin Group (USA) Inc., 375 Hudson Street, New York, New York 10014, USA
Penguin Group (Canada), 90 Eglinton Avenue East, Suite 700, Toronto, Ontario, Canada M4P 2Y3
(a division of Pearson Penguin Canada Inc.)
Penguin Ireland, 25 St Stephen's Green, Dublin 2, Ireland
(a division of Penguin Books Ltd)
Penguin Group (Australia), 250 Camberwell Road, Camberwell, Victoria 3124, Australia
(a division of Pearson Australia Group Pty Ltd)
Penguin Books India Pvt Ltd, 11 Community Centre, Panchsheel Park, New Delhi – 110 017, India
Penguin Group (NZ), 67 Apollo Drive, Rosedale, Auckland 0632, New Zealand
(a division of Pearson New Zealand Ltd)
Penguin Books (South Africa) (Pty) Ltd, Block D, Rosebank Office Park, 181 Jan Smuts Avenue,
Parktown North, Gauteng 2193, South Africa

Penguin Books Ltd, Registered Offices: 80 Strand, London WC2R ORL, England

www.penguin.com

First published in the United States of America by The Berkley Publishing Group 2011
First published in Great Britain by Berkley UK 2012
002

Printed in England by Clays Ltd, St Ives plc

ISBN: 978-0-241-95669-4

www.greenpenguin.co.uk

MIX
Paper from
responsible sources
FSC™ C018179

Penguin Books is committed to a sustainable
future for our business, our readers and our planet.
This book is made from Forest Stewardship
Council™ certified paper.

ALWAYS LEARNING   **PEARSON**

For Chynna

THE PACK

ONE

Simon Burns woke up feeling something nibbling on the back of his neck. He'd been having a dream where he was swimming in an ocean—maybe the Aegean, off Crete, where he'd never been. It had been a pleasant, relaxing dream until he felt the nibbling. Then his heart rate accelerated as he was convinced he was being attacked by a shark or something deadly, and when he woke up he instinctively sat up and nearly elbowed his wife, Alison, in the jaw.

"Hey," she said.

It took a few moments to register that he wasn't swimming in the Aegean and was in his apartment on Eighty-ninth and Columbus.

"Oh, sorry." His heart was still pounding.

Alison was sitting up, hugging him from behind, kissing the back of his neck. So much for a vicious shark attack.

"Bad dream?" she asked.

"Good and bad," he said.

"What was the bad part?"

"I thought you were a shark in Greece."

"A Greek shark, huh? I'm not that scary, am I?"

"It was only a dream."

She kissed him again under his jaw, then asked, "How do you feel?"

How do you feel? was their code for *Do you want to make love?* They'd been in a slump lately. No one's fault; they'd both been busy working full-time jobs, and when they came home they were with Jeremy until he went to sleep—some nights not until ten o'clock—and by then they were so zonked they usually crashed on the couch, watching TV. Dr. Hagan, their marriage counselor, had assigned them exercises to increase intimacy in their marriage—going on date nights, planning romantic getaways—but what with child care and work they hadn't had much time for any of that either.

"I'm feeling pretty good," Simon said, trying to get into the mood.

He kissed Alison on the lips, holding her head steady, and then she fell back onto the bed and he was on top of her, holding her hands. He tried not to get distracted, but it was hard not to. He glanced at the clock on the night table—seven forty-four. He was an account manager at a midtown ad agency, and he had a big client meeting in forty-six minutes. He tried to focus on making love, but he kept worrying about the meeting and the pending decision about a promotion, and replaying bits of random work conversations in his head.

"Is everything okay?" Alison asked.

"Fine," Simon said. "Why?"

"Never mind," she said.

Simon kissed her, moaning a little, and then his eyes shifted toward the night table: seven forty-five.

"Mommy!" Jeremy, their three-year-old, called from his room.

Alison gave Simon a look that asked, *Can you believe this?*

"Maybe he'll go back to sleep," Simon said.

They listened, didn't hear anything, and resumed making love, and then the alarm clock went off with what it played every morning—U2's "Beautiful Day."

"I guess bad timing comes in twos," Simon said.

"Mommy!" Jeremy called again.

"Coming, honey!" Alison said. Then she pulled up her panties and said in a frustrated tone, "This is so hard."

Simon, also out of bed, said, "It was just a little coitus interruptus."

"No, I mean all of this." She gestured with her hands, looking around the room. "Both of us working full-time, trying to squeeze in sex whenever we can. And I feel like we're missing Jeremy's whole childhood."

"Come on," Simon said. "I think you're being a little melodramatic now."

"You know what I mean," she said. "We get to spend, what, three or four hours a day with him? It's just not enough."

They'd been through this before. When Jeremy was born, Alison had considered leaving her job in pharmaceutical sales and trying to find something part-time, but when they crunched the numbers they realized they just couldn't swing it. They were barely getting by in Manhattan on two full-time salaries, and moving out of the city would be just as expensive when they factored in commuting costs and the need for two cars. So they'd decided to stay in the city and keep their jobs and hire a babysitter to take care of Jeremy on weekdays. The situation was hardly uncommon—most working parents in Manhattan had to hire babysitters, but it was especially rough when Jeremy had a learning leap and said a new grown-up word or learned a new trick in the playground. These were moments that parents could never get back.

"I'm just as frustrated as you are," Simon said. "If my promotion comes through, maybe you can switch to part-time or even quit. But until then, there's nothing we can do."

"I know, I know," Alison said. "I'm just saying, it's getting to be a drag, that's all."

Alison put on a long "Best Mommy in the World" T-shirt and left to attend to Jeremy.

Simon shaved and showered as quickly as he could, and then he came out to the dining room, finishing getting dressed, buttoning his shirt. Jeremy was in his booster seat having breakfast: Special K and a juice box.

"There's my big guy," Simon said. "Gimme a high five, kiddo."

He held up his hand and Jeremy slapped it and said, "High five."

"Thataboy," Simon said.

He glanced through the pass-through at Alison, who was unloading the dishwasher. He could tell she was still upset about their conversation, but there was nothing he could say to make it better, especially when he was already late for work.

He finished buttoning his shirt as he went into the closet and grabbed the first tie he saw—the navy one—and wrapped it loosely around his neck, then put on his suit jacket and grabbed his briefcase and headed back through the apartment.

The doorbell rang. Simon knew who it was before he answered it— Margaret, their babysitter.

"Hello, Simon, good morning to you."

Margaret was the third babysitter they'd had since Jeremy was born— Marianna had quit when she and her family moved back to Ecuador, and Linda had left to have her own child. It was weird that babysitters could afford to quit their jobs to take care of their own kids, but he and Alison couldn't, but then again the babysitters usually lived in the outer boroughs. If you wanted to live in Manhattan, in an apartment bigger than a studio, in a decent building, in a decent neighborhood, then you had to make sacrifices.

Margaret was by far the best babysitter they'd had. She was Jamaican, was in her forties, had two grown kids, and, most important, was great with Jeremy. She was patient and fun, and it was clear that she actually enjoyed the time she spent with him. Jeremy couldn't get enough of her. He talked about her all the time, sometimes asking for her on weekends and having crying fits when she went home at night. Though it was great that he had such a close connection with his babysitter, at times it was tough to take for Simon and especially for Alison. It reminded them of how much they were missing out on by having someone else raise their child.

"Yay, Margaret's here!" Jeremy said excitedly. He got up from the table and ran to Margaret and gave her a big hug.

"Come on, you have to finish your breakfast," Alison said.

Jeremy ignored her, saying to Margaret, "I want to show you the painting I made yesterday."

"Go ahead, finish your breakfast, listen to your mother now," Margaret said, and Jeremy immediately obeyed and returned to his seat.

Simon glanced at Alison and could tell how disappointed and hurt she felt, although she wasn't really showing it.

While Margaret tended to Jeremy, Alison returned to the dishwasher. Simon, rushing out, came up behind her and kissed her on the neck and whispered, "The vicious shark attacks again." This didn't even get a smile. He added, "Everything's going to be okay, sweetie, I promise." She remained deadpan. Then he said, "Hey, like Bono says, it's a beautiful day," and she almost smirked.

"Got you," he said.

"Yeah, you got me," she said.

Simon had been working for Smythe & O'Greeley, or S&O, for seven years. Previously he'd worked as a copywriter for a smaller agency, but he liked his current job better because he had more personal interaction with clients—that is, he got to entertain more. The promotion to senior account manager would give him more creative input, and it would be a nice change-up from what he'd been doing lately.

As Simon was swiping his card key to enter the S&O offices, Paul Kramer came up behind him and said, "Arriving early to kiss up to Tom, huh?"

Paul was a few years younger than Simon. Like Simon, he was an account manager being considered for the senior position. There were actually four candidates for the position from S&O and—rumor had it—a few candidates from outside the company. Simon felt he was in an excellent position to get the job because of his seniority—he'd been at S&O longer than any of the homegrown candidates, including Paul, who'd only been with the company for about a year—and because he was the most qualified for the position.

"No, I just have an early meeting," Simon said.

"With Tom?" Paul asked with a sly smile.

Tom Harrison was their boss.

"No, with a client," Simon said.

"Which client?" Paul asked.

Paul was still smirking, as if he were playing the role of someone who was competitive and catty about a promotion, though it was obvious that he *was* being competitive and catty.

"Dave Milligan from Deutsche Bank," Simon said.

"I believe you, I believe you," Paul said. "I guess."

Ugh, Simon hated office politics. He just wasn't very competitive by nature. Growing up, he'd never gotten very involved in organized sports and he didn't play on any teams in high school or college. Although he went out to bars with guys from the office to watch the big games on TV, he didn't watch sports at home, and he didn't really understand why winning and losing was so life-and-death to people. Getting petty with his co-workers seemed just as silly and counterproductive. Ultimately, wasn't everyone in the company on the same team anyway?

"Morning, Mark," Simon said to his assistant.

"Morning," Mark said. "The clients just got here, they're in the conference room. The bagels and coffee arrived and I told them you'd be right with them."

"That's great; thanks so much for taking care of all that," Simon said.

That was the mistake people made. If you got petty with people, it didn't get you anything in the end. Treat people with respect and good things happen. This philosophy had worked well for Simon throughout his career.

The meeting with Deutsche Bank went great. They were more than pleased with their current relationship with S&O and wanted to increase their expenditures for next quarter, and they wanted to discuss new campaigns for next year.

Buzzed from the positive meeting, Simon returned to his office. He was about to sit at his desk and start typing up some ideas for the proposal when Mark came in and said, "Tom was looking for you before."

"Thanks," Simon said. "Did he say what it was about?"

"No, but he wants you to meet with him in Joe McElroy's office right away."

"Great, thank you," Simon said.

Joe McElroy was an assistant in Human Resources. Simon figured this had to do with the promotion; maybe Tom wanted to give him the news in Joe's office because they needed to review the benefits package. Simon didn't want to get too far ahead of himself and jinx it, but it was hard not to get a little excited. He'd been working his butt off at this job for seven years, and it felt so great to finally get rewarded for his work. With the bump in income he could increase his contributions to his retirement fund and Jeremy's college fund and make occasional double payments on the mortgage. He could also take the family on vacations without feeling a financial crunch and, maybe in a year or two, if he got another promotion with higher pay or was able to switch to move up at another agency, Alison could quit her job and stay home with Jeremy by the time he started kindergarten.

When Simon entered, Tom was standing next to Joe in front of the desk. Tom was in his midforties, but twenty or so years in the stressful advertising business and countless martini lunches and happy hours made him look about ten years older. Joe was young, clean-cut, a few years out of college.

"Hey," Simon said.

Tom started to say something, maybe hello back, but Simon cut him off with: "So I've got some great news. Just got out of a meeting with Dave Milligan and Andrew Chin from Deutsche Bank. Looks like they're going to be expanding their expenditure with us big-time next quarter."

"Really? That's, um, great," Tom said, "but I—"

"I know, I'm psyched," Simon said. "I've been on these guys for months about this and I think I finally pushed them off the fence." He noticed that Tom seemed distracted, maybe upset about something. Simon asked, "Is everything okay?"

"No," Tom said. "I'm afraid not." He still wasn't making eye contact.

"If I didn't get the promotion, I understand," Simon said. "I know there were other candidates and only one of us can—"

"I'm sorry, but we're going to have to eliminate your position," Tom said.

There was silence, like the silence after an atom bomb is dropped.

"Excuse me?" Simon actually didn't understand what Tom had said; the words didn't make sense to him.

"I'm sorry," Tom said. "My hands are tied on this and I feel awful about it."

Simon had a dull, sickening feeling in his gut. He felt like Tom had sucker punched him, which in a way he had.

Joe said, "You can step outside now, Tom."

As Tom left the office he rested a hand on Simon's shoulder briefly and said, "I'm sorry."

Simon was still in a daze. Was this really happening?

Joe held out a folder for Simon to take and said, "This explains everything you need to know about your severance and benefits. . . ."

Joe's voice faded to white noise. Thoughts swirled in Simon's brain, and none of them made any sense. Looking at Joe, Simon felt like he was watching a silent movie in slow motion. Simon heard Joe say "be happy to run through it all with you" and "answer any questions you might have" and then the voice faded out again. Simon was amazed how cold Joe was, showing no emotion. Joe could have been alone in the room, talking to a wall.

Simon didn't remember leaving Joe's office. He was suddenly marching in the corridor, and then, it seemed like the next instant, he was in Tom's office, saying, "This is a joke, right? You're not actually firing me, right?"

Tom was sitting at his desk. Simon was so upset he was actually shaking.

"You shouldn't be in here," Tom said.

"Are you kidding me?" Simon said. "What the hell is going on here? Come on, just talk to me."

Tom took a deep breath, then said reluctantly, "Look, you know how it is these days. It's a numbers game, pure and simple."

"But at that performance review two weeks ago you said I'm doing an excellent job. Those were your exact words—'You're doing an excellent job, Simon.'"

Joe rushed into the office and said, "You're going to have to leave this office now, Mr. Burns."

"Mr. Burns?" Simon said to Joe. "Did you seriously just call me Mr. Burns?"

"Do what he says," Tom said.

"Come on, I'm begging you," Simon said to Tom. "I have a wife and a kid, and we have to pay a mortgage and maintenance and child care and—"

"I'm serious," Joe said. "You're not allowed to have this discussion."

"Why me?" Simon continued to Tom. "Why not somebody else? I mean Paul's been here, what, a year? Why not fire him?"

"This could affect your severance," Joe said.

"I mean you don't even talk to me?" Simon was getting angrier, raising his voice. "You don't even give me a chance to defend myself? After seven years? Seven goddamn years?"

"I'm sorry, Simon," Tom said.

"Please don't speak to him," Joe said to Tom.

"Oh, you're sorry," Simon said. "Oh, well, that makes things so much better. Tell me, tell me, tell me this." Simon knew he was losing control, but he kept going. "When did I ever, in seven years, when did I ever not deliver for you? Every project I've gotten to you on time, I've never missed a meeting. The only time I took a sick day in seven years was when my son had the goddamn swine flu."

"If you don't leave right now," Joe said to Simon, "I'll have to write this up."

"Look me in the eye," Simon said to Tom. "Look me in the eye and tell me you didn't have anything to do with this decision."

Tom's eyes shifted away, toward his computer monitor.

"Unbelievable," Simon said and marched out. He slammed the door for effect and the whole flimsy wall shook and he heard something in the office fall and glass shatter. He made it about halfway back to his desk, feeling dazed and numb, then turned and rushed back into Tom's office and said, "I'm sorry. I—I didn't mean to do that."

Now Tom looked pissed off, as he was bending over the broken picture frame, starting to pick up the biggest pieces of glass. He said, "Just go, Simon. It's over, okay?"

A heavyset security guard had entered the office and was standing next to Joe.

"I'm sorry," Joe said to Simon, "but you need to pack up your personal items and leave the building right away. Kevin will give you a hand."

Simon stood there for several seconds, feeling numb, and then he walked away. People in the office had stopped what they were doing, peering over their cubicles or looking up from their desks. Still in a fog, feeling like he was half there, Simon ignored everyone. Somehow he wound up in his office, packing a box with stuff as the security guard lingered near the door, but he didn't remember getting the box and he was barely aware of anything he was doing. At one point, Mark came over and said, "Hey, I'm really sorry, man," but Simon didn't answer him or even look over.

As he finished packing, the shock of being fired was starting to fade, and the anger was hitting full force. This was such total crap. He wasn't just some part-time employee or temp. He'd put in seven years of his life working for S&O, and this was how it was ending? What had Tom said,

We're going to have to eliminate your position? Have to, like it was ordained from God or something. After all these years, couldn't Tom at least have given him a heads-up, any kind of hint that this was coming down the pike? But, no, Tom hadn't said a word to him, though—Simon suddenly realized—there had been a few clues. Like that staff meeting two weeks ago Tom "forgot" to tell him about, or what about that time—when was it, late last week?—when Simon got on the elevator with Tom and Eric, one of the creative directors, and their conversation suddenly stopped? The more Simon thought about it, the more he realized there had been little, subtle clues all along, and maybe if he hadn't been so stressed out at work, and with his whole crazy schedule, he could've put the pieces of the puzzle together sooner and realized his job was in jeopardy.

Still, it was so spineless of Tom to just spring this on him. Yeah, like Simon was really supposed to believe that Tom's hands had been tied on this, that Tom had stood up for him with Andy Wallace and the other guys in management? If Andy had suggested letting Simon go, Tom had probably acquiesced right away. Or, more likely, it had been *Tom's* idea. Simon could imagine it so clearly now—Andy meeting with Tom and asking for a suggestion for who to let go—Paul or Simon—and Tom saying, "I think we should fire Simon."

Simon wished there were something he could do—go over Tom's head, file some kind of grievance—but he knew that whining about the situation would get him nowhere. People got fired all the time in advertising; it was par for the course. He'd been fortunate that, up until today, it had never happened to him. But it had definitely been a mistake slamming the door to Tom's office and breaking that picture frame. After all, he might need a recommendation.

Leaving the office was one of the most humiliating experiences of Simon's life. Although he didn't see anyone watching him, he knew *everyone* was watching him. This would be the highlight of their day— hell, their week. They'd tell their spouses and friends about how Simon Burns had been fired today and how he'd slammed his boss's door and broken a picture frame. Simon just wanted to get the hell out of there as fast as possible, but it seemed like it took minutes to get from his office to the elevators. He was trying to focus straight ahead and to be Zen, in the moment, but it was impossible to block out his thoughts. This was the first time he'd been fired from any job, he suddenly realized, and he was completely unprepared for the wild rush of emotions. He felt embarrassed, ashamed, like a total failure. He was also terrified, knowing there was no way he could pay the bills with some flimsy unemployment check. The job market was so tough there was no guarantee he could find a job this year, and he was going to have to burn through his savings just to pay the rent.

Walking up Broadway, Simon stepped off a curb when a traffic light had turned to DON'T WALK and a speeding cab almost hit him. He barely cared, though, as he continued uptown in a daze, feeling like his whole life had gone to hell.

TWO

Alison took the news much better than Simon had expected. He didn't want to break it to her over the phone, so he told her in person, when she got home from work and after Margaret left. At first she was upset and angry, calling Tom names and commiserating about how unfair it all was, especially the way it had gone down, but then she said, "You know, maybe this isn't such a bad thing."

She was on the couch and Simon was pacing. Jeremy was in his room playing with his train set.

"How isn't it bad?" Simon said. "We were barely getting by on two salaries and now we have one, and in this economy it could take months or longer before I find another job."

"Maybe you don't have to find a job," Alison said.

Simon stopped pacing and said, "You're kidding, right?" He knew she wasn't, so he continued, "How are we supposed to survive? Have you seen the bills lately? We can use my severance to pay off the credit card bills, it'll barely cover that, and then what? The mortgage is thirty-two hundred a month alone, then there's the maintenance, the bills, Margaret's salary—"

"We can fire Margaret," Alison said.

Now Simon knew what Alison was getting at. He said, "And how are we supposed to afford that? We were barely getting by on two salaries. All we'll have is your salary and my unemployment, and remember unemployment's taxable."

"We can cut back on expenses," Alison said. "Eat at home more, get rid of the premium cable channels, shop in bulk at Costco, not run the AC as much in the summer. If we cut corners and put our minds to it, I bet we can save five hundred bucks a month, easy."

"Five hundred dollars won't make a dent," Simon said.

"Maybe we can save a thousand," Alison said. "We can take more subways and buses, and I'll stop splurging on massages. I can even start buying my makeup at Rite Aid instead of Sephora."

"I still don't think the numbers are going to work out," Simon said.

"Okay, so maybe we'll have to dig into our savings for a while until we figure out how to get by. But I don't think we'll have to dig in as much as we think. And if we don't contribute to our Roths this year, we'll be able to replenish some of the money."

"Yeah, and what am I supposed to do?" Simon said. "Be a stay-at-home dad for the rest of my life?"

"Not the rest of your life," Alison said. "You can keep looking for work, but in a worst-case scenario, if you don't work for a year, maybe two years, until Jeremy starts kindergarten, it wouldn't be such a bad thing. Maybe you can do some freelancing, consulting from home, and meanwhile at least one of us would be with Jeremy during the day— that's the most important thing, right?"

Simon had to admit the idea made sense. Alison was doing well at her job, making a decent salary, and they could go on her health insurance. Besides, at least for right now, they didn't have any choice. Since Simon didn't have a current résumé ready it would probably be weeks before he could even start interviewing.

"I don't know," Simon said, "can you really see me as a stay-at-home dad?"

"A lot of men do it," Alison said. "My friend Julie's husband, Ron, stays home with his kids in Westchester, and I know a few people on Facebook whose husbands don't work. People have to do whatever they can these days to get by."

"But are you going to be happy?" Simon asked.

"I'll be happier than I am now," Alison said. "I mean, of course I'll wish I were the one staying home with him, but I'll get used to it, and I think it'll be better for us too. You've been so stressed out at work lately, it hasn't been great for the marriage. Maybe a break from working will help with everything, you know?"

Simon didn't like how she was vaguely blaming him for their marriage problems, but he didn't want to make an issue of this. If anything, it was a subject to possibly bring up during the next session with Dr. Hagan.

"Okay, I'm willing to give it a shot," he said.

For the rest of the evening, Alison seemed excited about the new plan, going on about the new schedule and suggestions of playgrounds, potential play dates, and free events around the city for Simon to take Jeremy to. Though Simon could understand why Alison thought it was great that Jeremy could be raised by one of his parents, he wasn't quite as giddy about it as she was. After all, today had been one of the worst days of his life. He'd been fired from his job and there was suddenly a dark cloud over his whole career. He didn't want a sympathy party, but a little sympathy would have been nice.

They did their nightly routine—Alison got Jeremy ready for bed and then Simon read him a bedtime story. When Jeremy fell asleep, Simon went down the hall to the master bedroom and saw Alison in bed using her laptop.

"There's so much for you guys to do around the city," she said, still in an upbeat mood. "I'm e-mailing you a whole list of things to do. This is going to be so great. You two are going to have such a great time together."

Simon went into the kitchen and poured a glass of Chardonnay from an open bottle in the fridge. He was hoping the wine would calm him down, help put this nightmare day behind him, but he was still tense when he returned to the living room. He turned on the TV—maybe to Comedy Central—and eventually fell asleep.

In the morning Simon had to fire Margaret. Alison had suggested calling her before she left her apartment in Queens, but Simon felt that would've been too harsh. Margaret had been Jeremy's babysitter for almost two years, and he felt she deserved to get the news in person.

Before Margaret arrived, Alison took Jeremy for a walk in his stroller so there would be less drama.

Margaret seemed to know something was wrong when she recognized the silence in the apartment and asked, "Where's Jeremy?"

Deciding not to beat around the bush, Simon said, "I'm sorry, we have to let you go."

He explained the situation—how he'd been fired himself yesterday and they simply couldn't afford to pay for a babysitter.

Margaret was teary eyed.

"Believe me, I know exactly what you're going through," Simon said. "I know a lot of people say that in these situations, but in this case it's true."

"I understand," Margaret said. "Where's Jeremy?"

"We thought it would be best if he wasn't here. But you can talk to him on the phone later and we'd love to have you over sometime for dinner."

"Thank you," Margaret said, "that would be nice."

She was taking the news with dignity; he had to give her that. She wasn't slamming doors and breaking picture frames.

When Margaret left, Simon paced the apartment. At first he was feeling bad for having to say good-bye to Margaret, who had become a part of their family, but then the sour feeling morphed into feeling bad about the way his job had ended. Yes, Tom had totally blindsided him and there had been a lot of hidden agendas and political backstabbing going on, but it had been a big mistake to leave the office the way he had. He felt humiliated, like he'd made a big fool of himself.

He opened his laptop and typed:

Dear Tom,

I want to apologize for the way things went down yesterday. The whole situation caught me off guard. I was in shock and wasn't really aware of my behavior. Obviously I regret my reaction and I'd be happy to pay to get the picture frame repaired. I'm still pretty shocked and upset, of course, but I understand that business is business and I hope we can make the best of a bad situation. How about we grab lunch or a drink, maybe next week sometime, and talk this thing through in person?

Sorry again about yesterday and looking forward to meeting up soon.

All best,
Simon

Simon read the note several times and thought he'd achieved the perfect tone. He liked that the note was respectful and apologetic, but not wimpy—a tough line to toe. He only made one change—"Dear Tom" to "Hi, Tom," going for a more friendly, casual opening. He read it again, liking it even more, then clicked send. He hoped the message would help mend fences with Tom or at least start a dialogue. The advertising world in Manhattan was a fishbowl, and the last thing that Simon needed was for word to get around that he was a troublemaker and that he'd left his job at S&O on bad terms.

Alison and Jeremy returned from their walk.

"Where's Margaret?" Jeremy asked.

He was a smart kid and noticed the major change in his daily routine.

Alison could probably tell how uncomfortable Simon was about breaking the news, so she jumped in and said, "Margaret's not going to be with you during the day. From now on Daddy's going to be with you during the day."

That was when the all-out fit started. Crying quickly evolved into uncontrollable wailing, kicking, and arm flailing. Alison had to get ready to go to work, and when she returned from the bedroom in a black designer suit and heels, her hair in a neat bun, pulling along a small suitcase with product samples, the fit was still going strong.

"I'm in a huge rush," she said to Simon at the door. "I have a meeting in fifteen minutes on Sixty-fourth and Mad and I can't be late. Ugh, sorry to leave you like this, but this just confirms we made the right decision—he was getting way too attached to her." She gave him a peck on the lips. "Call me later and let me know how the day is going. Good luck."

She left, and with a hysterical three-year-old in his arms, it suddenly hit Simon that this was his life now—he was officially a stay-at-home dad.

Simon tried to calm Jeremy with distractions. He suggested playing with books and games on his LeapFrog, but even an attempted bribe of Häagen-Dazs Amazon Valley Chocolate didn't work. There was just no reasoning with an out-of-control three-year-old. If the twos were terrible, then the threes were psychotic. If anything, Jeremy was getting *more* hysterical. All kids master the precise tone and level of screaming to drive their parents insane, and Jeremy was no exception. He'd always been a loud child—when he was born he was the loudest baby in the nursery—but now that he was a toddler his screaming was especially piercing and grating, at least to Simon's ears. Figuring some fresh air might help, Simon put him in his stroller—well, tried to. Jeremy, carrying on so badly he was virtually unreachable, kept arching his back and wouldn't let Simon strap him in. Although Simon was trying to stay in control, he realized he was screaming at his son. Then, deciding he'd had enough of this crap, he picked up the screeching kid in one hand and the stroller in the other and left the apartment.

Simon carried his hysterical son for three blocks. At Eighty-sixth Street, Jeremy was so exhausted from the fit that he finally went into his stroller. Simon was tired too and wished someone would wheel *him* around the city all day.

They went to the playground in Central Park at Eighty-first Street and Central Park West. Simon had been to this playground many times on Saturdays and Sundays, but it had a much different vibe during the week. On weekends there were lots of moms and dads, but now, he suddenly realized, he was the only guy there. There were a few moms, talking amongst themselves, and mostly foreign-looking babysitters.

Simon had thought Jeremy was wiped out and would play calmly the rest of the morning, but it turned out his calmness was a ruse and he was actually conserving his energy. When Simon told him it was time to get out of his stroller, fit number two promptly began. He refused to budge and started screaming at the top of his lungs for Margaret. Simon got sympathetic looks from moms and babysitters, but he knew they were all thinking, *Look at that pathetic guy, he has no idea what he's doing.*

The louder and wilder Jeremy got, the more self-conscious Simon got. Was he imagining it or were some of the babysitters laughing at him? One was smirking, texting, maybe telling a friend about the overwhelmed dad in the playground who couldn't control his son. When Jeremy ran away and grabbed two fistfuls of sand from the sandbox and threw them at Simon's face Simon had had enough. He grabbed Jeremy and somehow managed to strap him into the stroller and then they hightailed it out of the playground. Jeremy was still wailing so loudly that a couple of cars on Central Park West slowed down as the drivers wanted to see what the hell was going on. Simon decided he'd had it—he was going to push Jeremy around in his stroller until he calmed down or fell asleep, whichever came first.

About two hours later, Jeremy conked out. Sweaty and exhausted, Simon went into a Starbucks on Broadway. It was almost noon and Alison wouldn't be home till five thirty, six o'clock, or later. He knew every day wouldn't be this bad, but he still wasn't sure he could pull off being a stay-at-home dad without losing his mind.

He checked his e-mail, hoping for a miracle—Tom had reconsidered, Simon could have his job back. But nope, Tom hadn't responded yet. Was it possible he hadn't seen the e-mail yet? He probably had meetings all morning, and if he had a lunch he might not get back to the office until two or later. He'd probably at least read the message on his iPhone already, but sometimes Tom didn't respond to e-mails on his phone and waited until he was back at his Mac.

Jeremy woke up from his nap and Simon took him to a pizza place on Amsterdam for lunch. He wasn't screaming and yelling anymore, but he was still in a grouchy, difficult mood. He asked for a cup of sauce on the side to dip his pizza into, and then of course he promptly spilled the sauce all over himself and the floor.

Trying to go with the flow, not get too upset, Simon ignored the likely surge in his blood pressure and said, "It's okay, kiddo, everybody spills things," as he tried to mop up the sauce with wads of napkins.

Simon had cleaned up only about half the sauce when Jeremy said, "I have to go to the bathroom."

"Okay, we'll be home in a few minutes," Simon said. "Can you hold it in?"

"No." Jeremy was cringing, his face turning pink.

Simon and Alison had recently toilet-trained Jeremy, but he'd had a few accidents.

"Okay, you're going to have to wait," Simon said.

"It's coming out, Daddy."

"It's not coming out. Think about solid things. Think about bricks, cement . . ."

Simon picked up Jeremy and carried him to the bathroom in the back of the pizza place. A note was taped to the door: BROKE.

"Oh come on, you've gotta be kidding me," Simon said.

"I think I'm pooping," Jeremy said.

"You're not pooping," Simon said. "Steel, concrete, wrought iron . . ." Then to the guy behind the counter, he shouted, "Is there an employees' bathroom?"

The guy shook his head.

Simon carried Jeremy back toward the stroller, saying, "We're only a few blocks from a bathroom; can you hold it in for two minutes?" but it was too late. Jeremy's face had turned bright pink and he was making his scrunched-up "pooping face."

"No, not the pooping face," Simon said. "Not the pooping face." Then he could smell the suddenly overwhelming odor of feces. Other people smelled it too, and a woman winced as she moved to another table with her slice of pepperoni.

"More's coming," Jeremy said.

Simon could tell Jeremy was getting upset, so he reassured him, saying, "Okay, don't worry, everything's going to be okay, kiddo. It's okay."

The smell was getting worse.

A guy nearby said, "Can't you take him outside, bro?"

"Sorry," Simon said, and, carrying the stroller and pooping son, he went out to the street.

"I think I'm all done," Jeremy said.

The wet poop was leaking through Jeremy's clothes and over the back of his pants onto Simon's arm and chest.

"Okay," Simon said, "we have to get you in the stroller so we can get you home."

"Change me," Jeremy said.

"Change you into what? I didn't bring a change of clothes."

"Margaret always brings clothes."

"Well, I'm not Margaret." Simon immediately wished he could suck the words back in and swallow them. Reminding Jeremy that Margaret wasn't here was the worst thing he could've done, especially with Jeremy already in such a vulnerable state.

"Sorry," Simon said. "I didn't mean that. I just meant . . ."

But it was too late. Jeremy's lips quivered and another meltdown ensued.

Simon tried to calm him down, telling him everything would be okay, bribing him with promises of ice cream, candy bars, new games for his Leapster, but nothing worked. Jeremy was crying hysterically now, fighting as Simon tried to get him into the stroller. There was poop all over Simon's arms now, and Jeremy was shrieking at the top of his lungs. This day had officially become a nightmare.

Simon gave up trying to get Jeremy into the stroller and carried him home. In the apartment, he got him out of his poopy clothes and put him right in the tub and turned on the shower. The water was a little too hot at first, and Jeremy screamed and started crying again. It took Simon about half an hour to clean Jeremy up and get him into new clothes.

Simon needed a break; time for the electronic babysitter. He parked Jeremy in front of the TV, watching PBS Kids, while he went online on his laptop. Still no response from Tom, but he could still be at lunch or in a meeting or involved in something else. Although the long day made it hard to focus, Simon wanted to be as productive as possible. He sent a couple of e-mails to headhunters he knew, though he wasn't very optimistic about finding a job quickly. Browsing the latest wanted ads was pretty discouraging as well. He could see where this was heading already—he was going to be overqualified for the available jobs, and the jobs he wanted wouldn't exist. He had a troubling feeling that he was going to be unemployed for a very long time.

After sending out several more informal queries to headhunters and contacts he had at other agencies, he went to the New York State Department of Labor website to file for unemployment. As he filled out the online form, answering questions like *Did you look for work this week?* he had a surreal feeling of *I can't believe I'm actually doing this*. If someone had told him last week that he'd be filing for unemployment today, he'd have thought that person was insane. Last week he'd been flying high, zeroing in on the Deutsche Bank deal, anticipating a promotion. As he entered his social security number he felt thoroughly humiliated, like he was being fired all over again; he could hear Tom saying, *I'm sorry, but we're going to have to eliminate your position*, and he could feel the same sudden cramping in his gut.

At that moment an e-mail arrived. Maybe it was kismet; Tom was getting back to him, telling him he wanted to let bygones be bygones, or better yet, rehire him. Maybe the nightmare was over; he was about to wake up. They'd set up a time to have a drink and smooth things over and soon Simon would be able to resume his old life.

The message wasn't from Tom; it was from Joe in HR.

Dear Simon Burns,

Per the e-mail you sent to Mr. Harrison earlier today and per provisions in your pending severance agreement, please cease all communication between yourself and Mr. Harrison effective immediately.

If you have any further questions on this matter, you may contact me directly.

Sincerely,
Joe McElroy
Associate Director, Human Resources

Simon was stunned. He stared at the monitor blank-faced until the screen saver came on, and then he stared at the screen saver. Had Tom actually forwarded a personal e-mail to Joe? Simon felt betrayed, humiliated. After everything he'd done for Tom and the agency over the past seven years, all the extra time he'd put in, making him look good on so many campaigns? Making it worse, this was a guy Simon had considered a friend. Okay, not a *friend* friend, but how many times had they gone to lunch and after-work drinks, or to entertain clients at Knicks games and Broadway shows? A few years ago when Tom was going through a rough patch in his marriage, Simon had given him some advice to help him through it. Another time, Tom had a relative who was going for bypass surgery; Simon put him in touch with a friend who'd used a renowned surgeon for his heart surgery, and Tom's friend had wound up using the same surgeon. And after all that, Tom had not only fired him, but forwarded an e-mail to HR? Simon didn't get what he'd done to deserve this kind of treatment. He hadn't harassed anyone or committed a crime; he'd been fired and broken a picture frame.

Simon paced the apartment, trying to figure out what to do next. He wanted to call Tom—e-mail was sometimes such an ineffective way to communicate—and clear the air, but he knew that would only make things worse. Obviously Tom was trying to avoid contact with him, and if Simon started calling now, after the warning to "cease all communication," maybe the powers that be at S&O would try to screw with Simon's severance.

Simon couldn't remember the last time he'd been so angry. Worse, he had no way to express himself. Yeah, he could write back to Joe in HR. The fact that Joe had acted like such a prick at the office, and sent such a cold, formal note, was yet another humiliation because Simon had always been friendly with Joe. They said hi to each other in the elevator and whenever they passed each other in the hallways and had chatted in the concessions area a few times. Simon could write back to Joe, but say what? That he was upset? Simon still couldn't get over that Joe had called him "Mr. Burns."

Back on his laptop, Simon read the e-mail maybe a dozen more times, still amazed by the coldness of not only Tom, but the whole company. Although Simon had no idea what his colleagues thought about the situation, it wasn't exactly like his inbox was flooded with fond farewells and words of encouragement. Okay, maybe people were being overly PC, toeing the company line, but Simon couldn't help imagining that they were all coldly blowing him off, the way Tom and Joe had.

Simon did some more job hunting, but the more searching and researching he did, the more discouraged he got.

Alison came home at around six fifteen. After she opened the door, she paused and looked around the apartment. She was probably noticing the dirty dishes in the sink and on the countertop, the dishes from breakfast still on the dining room table, and Jeremy sitting on the rug watching *Dora the Explorer* with toys splayed out all around him.

"I guess I didn't see the weather forecast for today," she said.

"Weather forecast?" Simon, still absorbed in thoughts of how his agency had screwed him over, was lost.

"I didn't know a hurricane would come through the living room today," she said.

Simon didn't smile. In his current mood, he didn't think anything was funny.

"Oh, come on, I'm only joking, sweetie," she said.

Alison kissed Jeremy and gave him a big hug, and then she went over to Simon and kissed him and said, "So . . . how was it?"

"How was what?" Simon asked.

"Your first day as a stay-at-home dad."

His exasperated expression must've said it all.

"That good, huh?" Alison said. "I want to hear all about it later, I just have to do an important conference call in a few minutes. Oh, and guess what, I closed that big deal I've been working on."

"Deal?" Simon asked.

"With Dr. Wong. He placed a big order with us today."

"That's great," Simon said, trying his best to sound happy for her.

"It *is* great," Alison said. "I think it might turn into a lucrative con-tract, maybe over multiple product lines. Of course, it depends how many actual scripts he writes, but right now it looks very encouraging." She glanced at Jeremy, sitting Indian style on the rug in front of the TV. "How long has he been watching TV?"

"I don't know," Simon said. "A few hours."

"He should only be watching TV for a half hour or an hour a day tops." She flicked off the TV and said to Jeremy, "Dinnertime."

She looked over at the kitchen and said, "You didn't start making dinner yet? He has to eat at six and be in bed by eight." Alison's nostrils flared. "Why does the apartment smell like poop?"

"You're on duty now," Simon said, and took the laptop with him into the bedroom.

During dinner Simon was still in a grouchy mood and didn't feel like talking about his day.

Later, when Jeremy was in bed, Alison sat next to Simon in the living room and said, "So are you ready to talk now?"

Simon told her about the poop fiasco at the pizza place.

"Is that what this is all about?" Alison asked. "Because you got a little pooped on?"

"It wasn't a little poop, it was a lot of poop."

"You know what they say," Alison said. "Poop happens."

Almost smiling, Simon said, "Easy for you to say. You didn't have to walk five blocks covered in it."

"You could've taken a cab."

"We're trying to cut down on cabs, remember? And you should've seen Jeremy, he was hysterical. I swear it was like I was with Rosemary's Baby or something. He was shaking, drooling. I think he was crying louder than when he was born."

Alison laughed.

"You think it's funny?"

"No," she said, still laughing. "Okay, yes, I think it's funny."

Simon couldn't help laughing a little himself, but he said, "Trust me, if you were me today you wouldn't be laughing right now."

"If it isn't poop, it'll be something else," Alison said. "He'll fall off the slide one day and need stitches, or a bee will sting him, or he'll suddenly get a high fever. You have to just roll with the punches."

"That's not all that happened today," Simon said.

"Oh no, what else happened? Did a bird poop on you too?"

Alison laughed, but Simon was stone-faced.

"I'm sorry," she said. "I'm just joking. Okay, what happened?"

He told her about the e-mail to Tom and Joe's response.

"I know how frustrated you are," Alison said, "but the past is the past, and your responsibility is to Jeremy now, not to your old job. You have to just let go."

"I think I might've made a big mistake," Simon said.

"Oh stop, it's just one e-mail. It's not a big—"

"No, I mean firing Margaret. I thought I could handle this whole

being-a-stay-at-home-dad thing, but I just don't think I'm cut out
for it."

"That's ridiculous," Alison said. "You're a great dad, and you're great
with Jeremy. And it's only been one day. You have to give it a chance."

"But he keeps asking for her."

"He's three years old. It's going to take him time to adjust."

"Maybe we can pay Margaret out of our savings."

"We need that money for the mortgage and maintenance and
oh, how about food? Did you forget food? We've been through this,
crunched all the numbers, and there's no other way right now."

Simon knew she was right. "Well, I don't know if I can handle another day like today."

"I think what you need is a schedule," Alison said. "You have to
make child care regimented, like a job. At nine o'clock you do this, at
ten o'clock you do that, lunch at noon, et cetera, et cetera. And you
have to change your attitude too. You have to appreciate how lucky you
are. Most moms and dads would kill to get to spend more time with
their kids, and now you're getting that chance." She held his hand and
squeezed it. "You're a *dad*, you have the best job ever. You make your
own hours, you call all the shots, and think about the great job security
you have. After all"—she kissed him on the cheek—"nobody can ever
fire you from being a father."

THREE

Simon started the next day with a fresh, upbeat attitude. If he was going to be a full-time dad, he wanted to be a great full-time dad, and he definitely didn't want his situation with Tom to trickle down and affect his parenting. So he took Alison's advice and made up a schedule. He'd make Jeremy breakfast, then get him dressed and out the door by ten o'clock. They'd go to the Great Lawn and play ball and run around till noon, then have lunch at Subway, and then go to the library for a story hour at two, and then they'd have a snack—granola bars and chocolate milk—before trekking up to the playground near 101st Street in Riverside Park.

But the schedule got derailed from the get-go. Jeremy wouldn't eat the French toast Simon made—"It's too mushy, Daddy"—and he had to make him grilled cheese as a backup. After Jeremy finished breakfast, it was already past ten o'clock, and then it took much longer than Simon had anticipated to get him dressed, and then Jeremy spent maybe half an hour going to the bathroom; he said it was because his tummy hurt, but it was probably actually because he was afraid of having another accident.

Finally they got out of the apartment around eleven. When they got to the park it started raining, so that KO'd Wiffle ball and soccer. Though Simon had remembered to pack a jacket and an extra pair of clothes for Jeremy, he'd forgotten to bring the plastic covering for the stroller, so Jeremy got soaked. Instead of changing him out of his wet clothes in a public bathroom, Simon took him back home instead. Of course, right as they entered their apartment building the sun started shining brightly.

While Simon was changing Jeremy out of his wet clothes, Jeremy asked, "Why can't Margaret take care of me anymore?"

"Because I'm taking care of you," Simon said.

Simon took deep breaths, trying to stay in control.

After Subway for lunch, it was too late to make the library reading. Okay, so this day hadn't gone exactly as planned, but at least there hadn't been any major meltdowns or poop disasters so far. Baby steps.

At the playground in Riverside Park, coincidentally Jeremy's friend Matthew was there with, Simon thought, a new babysitter. Simon had seen Matthew with his mom in neighborhood playgrounds and a couple of times with a different, blond babysitter. This babysitter had long straight dark hair and seemed to be Mexican or Puerto Rican. She was young, maybe twenty-five, and was sitting alone on a bench.

As the kids played, Simon stood and nodded and smiled at her a few times, politely acknowledging her presence, and then he decided to sit down next to her.

"I'm Simon," he said.

She squinted, as if not understanding him right away, then in a thickly accented voice said, "Bianca."

"Nice to meet you," he said.

He made comments like "The weather has been so nice lately" and "The kids play so well together." Bianca smiled politely, didn't say much, but Simon got the sense she was being shy, not rude. She got a call on her cell and had an animated conversation in Spanish. Meanwhile, Simon, almost unconsciously, checked his e-mail. No messages from

Tom, Joe, or anyone else from work; just a note from a headhunter he'd contacted that began, *Thank you for your inquiry, but we currently have no avail* . . .

When Bianca ended her call, Simon asked her where she was from—Guadalajara—and how long she'd been in the country—two years. She said she was taking classes at night at Hunter College and wanted to work in the fashion industry. Simon continued trying to keep the small talk going. For a while she seemed shy and barely spoke, and there were awkward silences while Simon tried to think of new questions to ask. But gradually she opened up, became more talkative, and even asked *him* questions, including what he did for a living. Caught off guard—no one had asked him about his job since he'd gotten fired—he said, "I, um, work in advertising." Before she questioned him further, he said, "But I'm taking some time off now, doing some consulting from home." He felt silly lying, but at least for right now he felt too much shame to say out loud, *I'm unemployed.*

Though Simon had nothing in common with Bianca and it was hard to have a conversation in broken English, it was nice to talk to someone, to not feel completely alienated in a playground. Meanwhile, Jeremy and Matthew were laughing, taking turns going down the slide. It would be great, Simon thought, if he could set up play dates for Jeremy with Matthew one or two days a week. Then if he found a couple of regular story hours and went on trips to the museums once a week and found a few other activities, before long he and Jeremy would have a good daily routine.

So he said to Bianca, "Hey, I was thinking, it would be great if we could meet here again sometime."

She seemed confused, like she didn't understand what he was saying.

"Another time," Simon said. "Another *tiempo* . . . to meet again . . . we make a date."

Something suddenly clicked and she crossed her legs and shifted away a little.

"*Tengo novio,*" she said.

Simon had retained enough of his high school Spanish to know that this meant *I have a boyfriend*.

"Oh no, no," Simon said. "I didn't mean *that* kind of date. I meant a play date, for the kids. For the *niños*."

"Sorry," she said. "I'm not interested."

"Interested in what? No, really, you don't understand, *no comprendes*. I'm not asking you on a date. I'm married, see?" He held up his left hand to display his wedding band, then realized he wasn't wearing it; he'd taken it off this morning when he'd showered and must've forgotten to put it back on. "My wedding ring's home," he said, "at my apartment."

But Bianca had stood up already. She said, "Excuse me," and went to get Matthew. Then, without looking in Simon's direction, she put the child in the stroller and they left the playground.

Simon knew he hadn't done anything wrong and it had been a total misunderstanding, but he still felt like he'd blown an opportunity for a potential ongoing play date for Jeremy.

Jeremy came running over to Simon and said, "Why did Matthew have to go home?"

"I guess it was his nap time," Simon said.

Jeremy frowned.

Simon let Jeremy play for a little while longer, but he seemed sad. At least when it was time to leave, he got into the stroller without a fuss.

Over the weekend Simon had some time to himself as Alison did most of the parenting. He'd planned to take the time to work on his résumé, do some job hunting, but he wound up not doing much of anything. On Saturday, he slept late, then spent most of the rest of the day on the couch in boxers and a T-shirt watching movies and sitcom reruns on TV. He didn't get out of the apartment on Sunday except for a walk to Duane Reade to buy milk and toilet paper.

"You should go to the gym," Alison said, "or running in the park, or *something*. Sitting around all day like a lump won't make things any better."

Simon wasn't offended by the "lump" comment because he knew she was right. He was probably slightly depressed, which made sense given his situation, but he couldn't snap himself out of it.

On Monday morning, Simon and Alison had an eleven A.M. marriage counseling appointment. They'd arranged for Christina, a postgrad who'd moved back in with her parents down the hall, to babysit for a couple of hours, and then they met at Dr. Hagan's office on Park Avenue—Simon coming from home, Alison from work.

Alison was usually chatty before their sessions, but today she wasn't talking much. When he asked her if something was wrong she said, "No, why?"

He said, "I don't know, you just seem upset about something."

"I'm just tired, that's all," she said, not looking at him while thumbing through a random magazine.

In the office Simon and Alison took their usual seats on the couch and Dr. Hagan sat in the armchair facing them. Dr. Hagan was a wiry man with salt-and-pepper hair and a bushy mustache. He was a good therapist, but he had one odd quirk—he always dressed in single-color-coordinated outfits. Some days everything was red, other days green, yellow, blue, and so on. Today he was wearing purple shoes, purple pants, a purple turtleneck, and purple tinted glasses. Weird, yeah, but compared to the other psychotherapists they'd interviewed he'd seemed like the sanest one by far.

Alison's distant attitude carried over into the session, and Hagan picked up on it right away.

"Are you uncomfortable?" Hagan asked.

"No," she said, uncrossing her legs, then crossing them again. "I'm fine."

Hagan nodded, absorbing this, then asked, "So how are things going lately?"

Alison looked at Simon as if saying, *You take this*, so Simon said, "Actually a lot has happened this week."

Simon explained that he'd been fired and become a full-time stay-at-home dad.

"It sounds like you're both going through some major changes," Hagan said. "How is this affecting the marriage?"

Again Alison looked to Simon to take the lead.

"Honestly we haven't been spending enough time together," Simon said. "I'm with Jeremy during the day, and when Alison comes home she has him, then we go to sleep. So, yeah, it's been a lot of tag-team parenting."

"Has there been time for intimacy?"

Simon wasn't looking directly at Alison, but in his peripheral vision he saw that she was staring straight ahead at Hagan.

"No, not really," Simon said, "and I'm fully willing to take all the blame. I've been so exhausted, chasing a three-year-old around all day, that by ten o'clock I've been zonked. Now I know what moms mean when they say they're too tired to have sex."

"Periods of change are always challenging times for a marriage," Hagan said. "But going forward it's going to be even more important for you two to create time for each other. I'm not necessarily talking about sex either. Remember—intimacy starts outside the bedroom."

Simon reached across and held Alison's hand. "You're right," he said. "I'll definitely make more of an effort."

During the rest of the session they talked about strategies to increase intimacy in the marriage. Simon thought it was a good session, but Alison still seemed distracted.

Later, leaving the office, Simon tried to ease the tension, saying, "So it was a purple day today, huh?"

Alison barely smiled.

There was silence, and then Simon said, "So how about from now on we try to get Christina to babysit one set night a week so we can have a regular date night?"

Distracted, she said, "That sounds like a good idea." Then she glanced at her watch. "Oh shoot, I have to run to a meeting. Let's talk about this later, okay?"

She kissed him quickly on the lips and walked away down Park Avenue, going as fast as she could on her heels. Simon waited for her to turn around and wave good-bye the way she usually did, but she turned the corner onto Eighty-sixth Street without looking back.

FOUR

Later, at the apartment, Simon said to Jeremy in an upbeat tone, "Are you ready to have fun today?"

"Where are we going?" Jeremy already sounded bored.

"To the playground," Simon said, trying to make it sound exciting.

"Again?" Jeremy asked.

Simon couldn't blame him for being unenthused.

"Okay, I have a great idea," Simon said. "We'll do something different today."

Simon took Jeremy out in the jogging stroller, and instead of going to Central Park, Simon jogged downtown along the Hudson River bike path, pushing the stroller ahead of him. He started off strong, fueled by the excitement of getting out of the Upper West Side for a change. But after about a mile the cramping and fatigue set in, and he had to walk most of the rest of the way to Battery Park in lower Manhattan, to one of Jeremy's favorite playgrounds. Spending another day at a playground wasn't exactly a huge change of pace, but at least it was a different playground.

Jeremy was having a great time, and for the first time in days he hadn't asked for Margaret. He started playing with several kids who were kicking around a soccer ball. Normally Jeremy was shy around kids he didn't know, so Simon was glad to see him acting so outgoing.

Then Simon looked over and saw three guys sitting on a nearby bench. Simon could tell they were the kids' dads. The big blond guy looked almost exactly like his son, and the good-looking Latino guy was obviously the father of the good-looking Latino boy. The other boy, who was the tallest of the three, was definitely the son of the gray-haired guy with a smooth, youthful face who kind of looked like Richard Gere in *Pretty Woman*.

The gray-haired guy said something to the other guys, and then they all looked over toward Simon.

The blond guy smiled first, then the Latino guy, and finally the gray-haired guy.

Simon smiled back, then thought, *Might as well be social*, and he walked over to the guys.

"Hey," Simon said.

"Hey, how's it goin'?" the blond guy asked.

"Pretty good," Simon said. "Nice day today, huh?"

"Beautiful," the Latino guy said.

"Absolutely wonderful," the gray-haired guy said.

Simon noticed that the gray-haired guy had very dark eyes, or maybe they just seemed so dark in contrast with his gray hair. He was dressed in beige slacks and a black turtleneck, and although Simon was no fashion expert, it was obvious that the clothes were expensive and more likely purchased at Barneys than at H&M. The big blond guy was in jeans and work boots, and, although he was wearing a baggy gray T-shirt, he had broad muscular shoulders and was obviously in great shape. The Latino guy may have been the best-looking of all; what with his delicate features and longish black hair, he looked like a male model. Like the gray-haired guy, the Latino guy was very well dressed—in a pressed black sport jacket over a black T-shirt and neatly pressed black slacks—and hanging from his neck was a large gold cross.

One thing the guys had in common—they were all scruffy. Not grunge scruffy, *stylishly* scruffy, like the old Don Johnson look of the eighties. They all looked hip, relaxed, and very cool. If GQ were doing a story on New York dads, these guys could be featured.

"Your son is enjoying himself," the gray-haired guy said.

"Yeah," Simon said, watching Jeremy running and laughing. "He's having a blast."

"He's your only child," the gray-haired man said.

Simon detected a vague accent, maybe German or Austrian.

"Yes," Simon said. "Yes, he is."

"Same with us," the gray-haired guy said.

"Yep, we all have one boy," the blond guy said.

"One and done," the Latino guy said.

"That's cool," Simon said. "Yeah, boys are great, aren't they?"

There was a long pause as Simon and the guys watched their sons play. But it wasn't an awkward pause, like when Simon had strained conversations with the babysitters uptown. Simon didn't feel any pressure to think of something to say next. The silence seemed normal, relaxing.

Then the gray-haired man extended his hand and said, "I'm Michael."

"Simon," Simon said.

They shook hands. Although he didn't seem to be exerting any extra energy, Michael had a very firm handshake.

"Charlie," the blond guy said.

"Ramon," the Latino guy said.

The other guys had firm handshakes too, but not as firm as Michael's.

"So you live around here?" Ramon asked.

"No, actually I live uptown," Simon said.

"Me too," Charlie said. "Well, midtown. I'm in Turtle Bay."

"El Barrio," Ramon said.

"How about you?" Simon asked Michael.

"Tribeca," Michael said.

"Very cool," Simon said. "So how do you guys know each other?"

"We met right here at this playground," Ramon said.

"Nice," Simon said. "I mean that's great that you found each other."

"You're new at all this, huh?" Charlie asked.

"How can you tell?" Simon said.

Charlie laughed. "You just have the look."

"What look is that?"

Ramon laughed, then said, "That I-don't-know-how-the-hell-I-got-here look."

Charlie and Ramon laughed harder. Michael was smiling a little, but not actually laughing.

Simon joined in, laughing, saying, "Yep, that pretty much sums up my life lately."

It felt great to laugh, let loose a little. Until he started laughing, Simon hadn't realized how much stress he'd been under lately.

"We've all been there," Charlie said. "Don't worry, it gets easier."

"That's good to know," Simon said. "I have something to look forward to, then."

"You're with your son every day," Michael said.

He said this as a statement, not a question; again Simon detected a hint of an accent.

"Yeah," Simon said. "I got laid off from my job so I didn't really have any choice."

"Join the club," Ramon said. "I'm an actor so I pretty much live my whole life laid off."

They all laughed.

"So it happened suddenly, huh?" Charlie asked.

"Very suddenly," Simon said. "I was completely blindsided. No warning, no real explanation, but, hey, that's just the way it goes. Yeah, it's been a big change, you know, but there are a lot of positives too. It's great to spend more time with my son."

Simon was surprised how comfortable he felt talking about his job situation with the guys.

"We're all very fortunate to have time with our sons," Michael said.

"Yeah, I agree," Simon said. "*Very* fortunate."

Jeremy looked over toward Simon and waved, smiling widely, and Simon waved back. Simon hadn't seen Jeremy look so happy in a long time.

"Your kid's adorable," Charlie said.

"Thanks," Simon said.

"Yeah, I agree, man," Ramon said. "Well done."

"So," Simon said, "do you guys hang out here a lot?"

"Yes," Michael said.

"That's great," Simon said.

Looking at his BlackBerry, Ramon said, "Damn, I gotta get back uptown. My mother wants to take Diego out later."

"Yeah, I should get going myself," Charlie said.

The guys got their stuff together and told their kids it was time to leave. Simon was impressed with how well-behaved the kids were; they didn't protest at all and happily got right into their strollers.

"Do we have to go now too?" Jeremy asked.

"We can stay for another fifteen minutes, okay?" Simon said.

"Okay," Jeremy said, and, suddenly seeming a little sad, walked toward the slide alone.

"Well, it was nice meeting you, man," Charlie said. "Hopefully we'll see you here again sometime."

"Yeah, hopefully," Simon said.

The other guys said good-bye too and then left the playground, pushing their strollers ahead of them.

Simon felt a letdown, the way he did when a good party ended and the last guest left. It had been nice to hang out with some like-minded guys for a change.

Simon was checking his e-mail on his phone when he heard, "Hey, Simon."

Charlie had returned, without the stroller, and was standing in front of him.

Smiling, happy to see him, Simon said, "Hey."

"We were just talking," Charlie said. "You seem like a really cool guy and our kids love your kid, so if you want to come down and hang out with us again sometime, that would be great."

"Wow, thanks for the offer," Simon said. "That's really nice of you."

"We'll be here tomorrow at around noon if you want to come by."

"We don't have any plans so we might just do that," Simon said. "Thanks very much."

Charlie rejoined the other guys, who were waiting outside the gate of the playground. The gray-haired guy nodded in Simon's direction— maybe saying good-bye—and then Simon watched them walk away.

"So Jeremy and I had an interesting day today," Simon said. Alison had just gotten home from work and was looking through the mail, which Simon had left on the bureau near the front door.

"Oh really?" she asked.

Simon thought she sounded upset, or at least irritated.

"Yeah," Simon said. "I took Jeremy down to Battery Park, you know, to that playground he likes there."

"That's nice," she said, distracted, looking at the mail.

"He met a few friends there and had a great time and I hung out with their dads."

"We're a month behind on the cable bill."

"I can tell you're distracted, I'll tell you about it later."

"I'm sorry, I heard you, I heard you. You met some dads at the play-ground, that's great. Maybe you can hang out with them again sometime."

"Actually they asked us to hang out with them again tomorrow."

"So what's the problem?"

"I don't know," Simon said. "I mean it's all the way downtown in Battery Park, and I'm not sure they really want us to be there. I think they might've just invited us there to be polite."

Alison made eye contact with Simon for the first time since she'd come home and said, "I don't understand where all this insecurity is coming from. They wouldn't have invited you there if they didn't want you there. And you said Jeremy had a good time, right?"

"He had a blast," Simon said.

"Then I don't get what the problem is. He likes the kids, you like the dads. This sounds like a great situation for you."

"Yeah," Simon said. "I guess it does."

Alison said, "Remember to pay the cable bill later, okay?" and then went down the hallway toward the bedroom to change out of her work clothes. Simon was going to follow her, to ask her why she was acting so weird today, but he was tired from the long day and decided to just let it go.

FIVE

At M Bar at the Mansfield Hotel in Midtown, Olivia Becker, into her third Vodka Collins, said to her friend Diane Coles, "What happened to all the good, solid guys in this city? I mean, seriously, where are they hiding? I mean it's not like I'm asking for much. I just want somebody decent looking, somebody *employed*, who isn't going to tell me about his coke addiction on the second date. I don't know, I just never expected to be in this situation, you know? I never expected to be thirty-eight and alone. In my twenties, I always had boyfriends, usually older, in their thirties, and they were good, solid guys. What happened to those guys? Where did they disappear to? Now I own my own business, I have a fabulous apartment, the only thing I don't have is a guy. And I'm so sick of playing games with these jerks who just want to go out three times till you sleep with them, and then they stop calling. It was okay five years ago, but now it's pathetic. Men in this city act like the world's one big frat party." She sipped her drink miserably. Her lips were numb on the glass, so she knew she was already drunk.

"You can't meet somebody when you want to meet somebody,"

Diane said. "When it happens, it just happens. Like when I met Steve, okay? I'd totally given up, I just didn't care anymore. Then I was on line at Starbucks, on my way home from the gym, no makeup, looking like total crap, and this guy just starts talking to me. See? You can't plan to fall in love. It's all totally random."

"Yeah, right." Olivia downed the rest of her drink and signaled to the bartender for another. "I've tried the not-trying technique and, guess what, when I try not to meet anybody, I don't meet anybody. On Match it seems like I can't get anyone under fifty to write to me. I've gone to speed-dating parties, I even went on that JDate singles cruise. I hate the whole trying-to-meet-somebody game, I just hate it. How many days have I spent in Central Park, sitting on benches, reading books, acting like Miss Happy to Be Alone, and then I come home and sit on my couch and watch TV and paint my toenails all weekend feeling like crap? You tell yourself it's just because the right guy hasn't come along yet, like you're living in some freakin' fairy tale—Prince Charming will eventually show up and whisk you off into the sunset. Then reality sets in and you realize all the Prince Charmings rode their horses into the sunset ten years ago. Meanwhile, the men my age and older, they have it easy—no ticking clocks and their wrinkles are considered sexy. I mean I get it—why would any decent, sane guy in his late thirties or early forties want to date me when he can just date some wide-eyed, unjaded twenty-four-year-old? It's just a fact of nature. The only guys who are interested in me are the dorky commitment-phobes who still live with their parents or the fiftysomething potbellied divorced guys who've been in bad marriages for twenty-five years and just want to get laid."

The bartender brought Olivia's drink, and she immediately took a big gulp. Realizing that the bartender—he was in his late twenties, blond, cute—hadn't even made eye contact with her, she said, "See? Ten years ago that guy would've been all over me, trying to get in my pants. Now? *Bubkes.*"

"You should probably stop drinking," Diane said. "You're getting drunk."

"Oh stop it, I'm not drunk."

"Trust me. When you start complaining about guys in Yiddish . . . you're drunk."

"I am not drunk," Olivia insisted, though she did feel pretty tipsy. Her lips were numb, and was this her third or fourth drink? Eh, what difference did it make? She took another big swig, then put the glass down harder than she intended and said, "I'm sick, I'm just so sick of feeling so powerless, you know? In my twenties, *I* had the power. I'd go to a bar and ten guys would hit on me and I'd have my pick. It's not fair that men are in control now, calling all the shots." She steadied herself on the bar stool, then said, "That's it, from now on I'm not gonna wait for guys to come up to me. From now on *I'm* gonna be the man. Seriously, I can't remember the last time I asked a guy out. College? Next time I see a good-looking guy I'm just gonna go for it and see what happens. Because who the hell cares, right?"

She took another big gulp of her drink.

"Okay, how about that guy near the door?" Diane said.

Olivia turned to look, not exactly subtly. She jerked her head so quickly she could've gotten whiplash. She saw a guy on a couch in the lounge area looking—at least it seemed—right at her. He was mid to late forties, ruggedly handsome with wavy graying hair and wearing faded jeans and a white button-down shirt with the sleeves folded up to his elbows. The top few buttons of the shirt were undone, exposing some graying chest hair. The look could have been sleazy on another guy, but he pulled it off.

"Wow, he is kind of cute, isn't he?" Olivia said.

"Kind of?" Diane said. "He's a total hunk."

Olivia turned again and said, "He kind of looks like Richard Gere in *Pretty Woman*."

"Maybe he's as rich as Richard Gere in *Pretty Woman*," Diane said. "I think you should go for it."

The guy noticed Olivia and looked right at her and smiled. There was something about his eyes. They were so dark and intense; it was hard to look away from them.

"He just smiled at me," Olivia said.

"So," Diane said, "what are you waiting for?"

"He's probably waiting for somebody."

"You don't know that," Diane said. "Come on, if you're serious about this whole dating-like-a-man thing, get your butt over there."

Knowing Diane was right, Olivia had another sip of her drink for confidence, then went right up to the guy and said, "Can I join you?"

The line was so corny, it came off as cool and clever. Well, at least she thought it did, but maybe it was the alcohol encouraging her.

"I knew you'd come over here," the man said.

He was looking right at her with those wildly intense eyes.

"Oh, really?" Olivia said, trying to be flirty. "And how did you know that?"

"I always know when a woman wants me," the man said.

If some other guy had said this, Olivia would have thought he was a total jerk and walked away and maybe even dumped a drink on his lap. But there was something about this guy. He was oozing charm.

"You think I want you?" Olivia asked.

"Yes," the man said. He sniffed noticeably—she saw his nostrils move—then said, "You're wearing Safari."

Olivia was stunned. How had he guessed her perfume?

"Yes," she said. "How did you—"

"I like it," he said, "and I'm not just saying that to compliment the perfume. I'm not a big Ralph Lauren fan; I really prefer Dior, Givenchy, or Creed. It's because the perfume's on *you* that it smells nice. It's the combination of the perfume and your own scent that makes it so irresistible."

Even drunk, Olivia realized that this guy was, well, out there. Still, she liked him. He was different anyway, which was a nice break from the cookie-cutter lawyers she'd been dating lately. He was manly too, which was a relief. She was sick of all the metrosexual losers in this city.

"Well, that's probably the most interesting compliment I've ever gotten," she said.

"I'm Michael . . . Michael Hartman." He smiled and extended his hand and looked right in her eyes. She felt like she was staring back at two dark magnets.

"Olivia . . . Olivia Becker," she said, and they shook. He had a very strong grip that hurt a little, but she didn't mind. Holding his hand made her feel strangely secure, protected. She didn't want to let go and felt the disappointment when he did.

"I'll be direct with you," Michael said. "I know you're attracted to me—if you weren't you would've walked away by now. So, the way I see it, we have two choices. We can talk, get to know each other, then meet a few times before I ask you back to my place in Tribeca, or we can go back right now. . . . So you'll come home with me now."

Olivia was staring at Michael, thinking, *Is this guy for real?* Part of her didn't even know why she was having this conversation. She was normally reserved, even standoffish, and would never have put up with a guy hitting on her so crassly. Hadn't she just been complaining to Diane about how Manhattan was turning into a frat house? Still, there was something about this guy that was so refreshing. Maybe it was because she was sick of the game-playing too and knew where he was coming from. Or at least she knew where he was coming from with the alcohol content of four Vodka Collinses traveling through her bloodstream.

"Let's go," she said. She heard the words as if someone else had said them and she were just another listener in the room.

"Great," he said, and stood.

She knew this was insane, that she shouldn't be doing this, but noticing how sexy he looked, with his well-developed shoulders and muscular—but not too muscular—arms, she said, "Let me just tell my friend I'm going."

When she told Diane, Diane said, "Are you out of your mind?"

"What?" Olivia said. "It'll be an adventure."

"An adventure? Are you insane? You don't even know this guy. You were talking to him for what, two minutes? Not even two minutes. Come on, you're joking, right?"

"I'll text you later and let you know how it is."

Olivia started away, and Diane grabbed her wrist and said, "How *what* is?"

Olivia looked over at Michael, noticing his dark and dreamy eyes again, then said to Diane, "Please let go, you're embarrassing me."

Diane didn't let go and said, "You're drunk, okay? You're not making a good decision. Go tell this guy that it was great to meet him, maybe ask for his phone number, and let me take you home."

"I'm not a child," Olivia said seriously. "Now can you please let go of me?"

Diane let go reluctantly, then said, "Fine, but please . . . be careful."

"I will," Olivia said, and went over to Michael and said, "Okay, let's go."

They went outside, down a few steps to the street.

"It's right this way," Michael said.

Olivia didn't know what "it" was, but she didn't bother to ask. Michael held her hand again, with a strong, masculine grip, leading her along the sidewalk. Although it had to be before seven P.M., it was already dark, the days getting shorter in October. The cool air was sobering her up a bit and, though she was still excited about the unpredictability of all of this, she was starting to wonder if this might be a mistake.

Then Michael went up to a double-parked black Lexus SUV and opened the back door. There were two plush black leather seats facing a mini bar.

"You've gotta be kidding me," Olivia said.

"Please get in," Michael said.

Remembering what Diane had said, about how Michael might be as rich as Richard Gere in *Pretty Woman*, Olivia said, "What the hell?" and got in the car. Michael sat next to her, still holding her hand. The car pulled away toward Fifth Avenue.

"This is so insane," Olivia said. "I can't believe I'm doing this."

"You think you're insane," Michael said.

"Not literally," she said. "But going home with a guy I just met isn't what I normally do."

"It's not insane at all," he said. "It's actually very natural. You saw something you wanted and you're acting on it. If you just sat there and did nothing and let the chance to meet me disappear, I think that would have been insane."

This made sense to Olivia.

"I guess that's another way to look at it," she said. "So do you always get driven around the city and try to pick up women?"

"Sometimes, yes," he said.

She had to laugh. It seemed like the only appropriate response.

"Where are you tak— I mean, where are we going?"

"No, you were right the first time, I'm taking you," he said. "We're going to my place."

"Right, you said you live in Chelsea?"

"Tribeca."

"Right, Tribeca, of course." She was looking at the bottles of alcohol, wondering if she should have another drink; it probably wasn't a good idea. "Can I have a drink?" she asked.

"Of course," Michael said. "You're drinking Vodka Collinses."

Olivia let go of Michael's hand and crossed her arms in front of her chest and said, "Okay, how did you know that?"

"Let's just say I'm a very observant person," Michael said as he started making the drink, pouring the vodka.

"I don't know why you're not freaking me out," Olivia said.

"Because you're insanely attracted to me," Michael said.

"See? *Insane* might be the right word choice," she said.

"It's nothing to be ashamed of," he said. "You're open and honest with your feelings. You don't hide from your emotions. I think that's wonderful."

"Seriously," she said, "how did you know I was drinking Vodka Collinses?"

He was finishing making the drink, mixing it.

"I notice details that other people don't notice," he said. "I guess you can call it a natural gift."

She still thought it was weird. She wondered if he was stalking her or something. Then she wondered why she didn't care.

He put the glass in front of her and said, "Sorry, no sugar."

"How come you're not drinking?" she asked.

"My family's from Germany," he said. "We used to own a brewery."

She was going to ask him what kind of brewery and what this had to do with not drinking, but she was distracted by the sip of the drink she'd just taken.

"Well, you're a good bartender," she said.

After another sip she put the drink down. The car had cut over to the West Side and they were going down—it looked like—Broadway. She felt like she'd gotten her buzz back.

"So don't you want to know anything about me?" she asked.

"I know your name, that's more than enough."

"You don't even know what I do for a living, and I don't know anything about what you do."

"What I do doesn't matter."

"Well, I own my own graphic design comp—" Olivia said, but was silenced when Michael started kissing her.

Like any other thirty-eight-year-old single woman, Olivia had kissed many men. Every guy had his own unique style of kissing, but she couldn't remember ever being kissed with so much passion, so much genuine emotion. Michael's lips were strong and firm, and his tongue was magical. She felt like he wanted her, like he couldn't get enough of her, like he wanted to devour her.

She was so caught up, almost gasping, that she didn't realize the car had stopped until Michael pulled back for a moment and said, "This is it."

Her lips were still parted and her eyes were still closed.

"What is?" she asked, still lost in kiss-land.

"My place," he said.

They got out of the car. She wasn't sure what street they were on, but it was far west—West Street and the river were less than a block away. The street was poorly paved, exposing old cobblestones, and it was hard to balance on her heels.

Michael led her into a renovated industrial-type building that had one of those elevators you have to call for.

"Nice place," Olivia said. "What floor do you live on?"

"Every floor," he said. "I own the building."

Olivia thought, *A top-of-the-line SUV, a building owner, who is this guy, Donald Trump?* She squinted at him, wondering if he *was* Trump. Hey, she was drunk, so you never know. Nope, not Trump, but handsome as hell.

They rode the elevator up a few flights, and then they were in a tremendous loft. It was something out of a style magazine, in a spread of the most spectacular apartments in Manhattan. The ceilings were at least twenty feet high and dividers separated the place into rooms, and there was a spiral staircase leading upstairs.

"Oh my God, this place is incredible," Olivia said.

Michael picked her up and carried her through the loft into a large bedroom. Then he dropped her on the bed and started getting undressed in front of her. Okay, this was definitely one of the weirdest nights of her life, but she thought, *Just relax, go for it.*

His body was incredibly sexy, or at least she thought it was. He was big and muscular and hairy. Normally she was attracted to well-groomed guys, but on him the hairy look worked.

"Get naked," he said.

A guy had never talked to her this way before, but she liked it.

After she got undressed, he took off his clothes and climbed onto her, pinning her down hard and kissing her the way he had in the car, and she felt like she was on an adventure to some forbidden land far, far, far away, and she wanted to stay there forever.

Later, Olivia was curled up into Michael's sweaty body. He had a pungent, musky odor unlike anything she'd smelled on a man before, but she liked it . . . a lot.

She was still tingling all over, amazed by how great the sex had been. Usually she had had to be with a guy three or four times before she felt in synch, and some guys she never connected with. But with Michael she felt comfortable from the get-go, and she wanted to give everything to him, and lose herself.

She snuggled closer. She was sobering up but she was still pleasantly buzzed, from the remnants of alcohol in her system and from the aftermath of the powerful orgasms she'd had. She thought about the events leading up to tonight, how she'd acted impulsively at the bar, but how great it had worked out. Maybe she'd discovered the secret for meeting a man in Manhattan—get tanked and leave with the first good-looking guy you see. If this worked out, she could write a book about it and make millions.

She laughed at the thought, and Michael's eyes opened.

"I thought you were asleep," she said.

"I don't sleep," he said.

She chuckled, but when she saw he was serious, she said, "What do you mean, you don't sleep?"

"I mean I don't sleep," he said.

"Everybody sleeps," she said.

"Not me," he said.

"Okay, then what do you do?" She found this amusing.

"I rest," he said.

"That's what sleep is, isn't it? When you rest, when you're unconscious."

"But I'm not unconscious," he said. "I'm always aware, ready to react."

She'd known him for less than two hours, but she knew him well enough already to know that it would be impossible to get a straight answer out of him, or at least a logical one.

"Well, you're definitely one of the most unique guys I've ever met," she said, "and you're also one of the sexiest."

"I *am* the sexiest," Michael said, deadpan.

Olivia laughed. "God, you don't have a small ego, do you?"

She started kissing his neck, under his jaw.

"So tell me," she said. "How did you get so good in bed?"

"I've been with a lot of women."

"How many is a lot?" She stopped kissing him and shifted away. They'd used a condom, but still.

"I've satisfied all of them," he said.

She had to laugh. She kissed him again, then said, "You don't like to answer questions, do you?"

"I answered your question," he said.

"I guess in a way you did," she said. "Well, you don't have to tell me about your past tonight; it's more exciting if we prolong the mystery, don't you think?" Now she was on top, kissing his chest. "Mmm, you smell so good."

"You're glad you came," he said, as a statement.

"Yes," she said. "I'm very, very, very glad I came." She laughed at the double entendre.

"Your friend told you you're not making a good decision," he said seriously.

"If she had experienced what I just experienced, she wouldn't have said that." Olivia continued kissing him on his firm, sweaty, hairy tummy, and then something clicked and she sat up and said, "Wait a sec, how did you know that?"

"Know what?" he asked.

"She had her back to you at the bar, she had to be like twenty feet away. How did you know she said that to me?"

"I have excellent hearing."

"But the bar was so noisy, with music playing, people talking. How could you possibly have heard that?"

"The problem isn't that I don't answer questions," he said. "The problem is you ask too many."

He turned her over swiftly and was on top again, manhandling her.

She couldn't believe he was ready for another round already. What was it with this guy?

In the middle of the night, after they'd had sex four times, Olivia had to go to the bathroom. Michael was sleeping soundly—*He never sleeps; yeah, right*—so she got out of bed quietly and headed toward the bathroom off to the right. She was about to go in when she saw a big section of the loft she hadn't seen yet, so, out of curiosity, she went to check it out.

There was a sort of lounge area, with very expensive-looking furniture and an area that had tall bookshelves filled with very old books, which somehow seemed jarring in the otherwise ultramodern apartment. Further, there was a large pool table, a Ping-Pong table, and was that a tricycle?

"You're lost."

Michael's voice startled her. He was about ten feet away from her, buck naked.

With a hand over her chest, she said, "My God, you scared the hell out of me. I thought you were asl—" She caught herself and continued, "I just didn't expect you, that's all."

"You should go home now," he said. "My driver will take you where you need to go."

"Oh, okay," she said. "I live on the Upper East—"

"I'll tell him you're coming down," he said, and headed back toward his bedroom.

Normally she would have felt like she was being kicked out, but somehow she didn't mind. This night had been what it had been. She had no expectations.

While Michael made the call to his driver, Olivia got dressed. While she was slipping on her shoes, she glanced over toward his clothes on a chair and saw a holster. Okay, so the guy had a kid and carried a gun. Who wasn't walking around this city with a few secrets?

"Ready?" Michael said. "I'll walk you down."

He put on a red silk robe, like one Hugh Hefner would wear, and they rode the elevator to the ground floor. She was going to ask him about his kid—what was the big deal about having a kid?—but then she figured, what difference did it make? They'd had a one-night stand. She'd probably never see him again.

On the street, he opened the door of the Lexus for her. She was surprised; not even a kiss good night? Oh, well, what could you do?

She got in and he said, "See you tomorrow," not as a question, of course. He wasn't asking her out, he was *telling* her out.

Before she could answer, he slammed the door shut and the car pulled away.

SIX

The rain was lashing against the apartment's windows.

"Looks like an indoor day today," Alison said. "Why don't you take Jeremy to a movie or something? I think there's a new Pixar movie playing at the IMAX."

She was dressed for work in a black pantsuit and heels, in full makeup. Simon was in bed in boxers.

"Yeah," Simon said. "I guess the playground's out today."

Alison had her back to him, looking in the mirror.

"So I wanted to talk about the counseling session," Simon said.

"What about it?"

"I just wanted to know why you're—"

"Mommy!" Jeremy called from his room.

"Can you get him?" Alison asked. "I have to run, I'm already five minutes late."

"Can we talk about this later?" Simon called after her.

"Sure, later," she said, and left the apartment.

Simon got Jeremy dressed and gave him breakfast. Simon was get-

ting better at managing the morning routine. He knew in which drawers to find the jeans and the T-shirts and sweatshirts. He still couldn't
make the pancakes quite the way Margaret used to, but with a little
work he'd get there.

After breakfast Simon said to Jeremy, "So what do you feel like
doing today, kiddo? A movie? A museum?"

"I want to play with those kids again," Jeremy said.

"We can't today," Simon said. "It's raining."

"No, it isn't," Jeremy said.

Simon looked toward the window and saw that the rain had in
fact stopped and the clouds were breaking and some sun was peeking
through.

"I don't know," Simon said, "the playground'll be wet. I'm not sure
those kids'll even be there today."

"But I want to," Jeremy said.

"I'll tell you what," Simon said. "Let's see what the weather's like at
noon. If it's nice we'll go, okay?"

At noon the sky had clouded up again and it was drizzly out, but
Jeremy had been having a good day—maybe his best-behaved day yet
since Simon had become a full-time parent—and Simon didn't want to
risk a regression.

"Okay, we can go by there and see," Simon said.

"Yay," Jeremy said.

Simon's legs ached from yesterday's jog, so they took the subway
downtown. When they got out at South Ferry it was still drizzling, and
raw and chilly too, and Simon wished he'd insisted that they stay uptown today. Still, the playground wasn't far away, so he figured since they
were downtown anyway they might as well go by there.

As they walked along the Hudson, the drizzle became light rain.
Jeremy said his legs were tired—they hadn't brought the stroller—so
Simon had to pick him up and carry him. They didn't have an umbrella,
so they were both getting soaked and Jeremy was complaining that he

was cold. Simon was going to turn around and just bag it when up ahead he was surprised to see the three guys he'd met yesterday. They were playing soccer with their kids in the playground and seemed undeterred by the weather. Ramon spotted Simon first and waved to him, and then Michael and Charlie looked over.

Jeremy saw the kids and said excitedly, "They're here!" and wriggled out of Simon's arms and ran over there.

"Slow down, it's slippery," Simon called after him, but, of course, he didn't slow down and dashed into the playground at full speed.

When Simon entered, Charlie came over to greet him.

"Hey, man," Charlie said, smiling widely, and the other guys seemed genuinely happy and excited to see him. "It's great to see you."

"It's great to see you too," Simon said. "I wasn't sure you guys would be here today."

"Oh, a little rain doesn't bother us," Charlie said. "Come on."

Simon and Charlie went to the other end of the playground. Like yesterday, the guys were scruffy, well dressed, and very warm and friendly.

"Welcome back, my friend," Ramon said when he shook Simon's hand.

Then Michael shook Simon's hand very firmly, looked right into his eyes, and said, "We're very glad you came."

They sat on the bench and exchanged some small talk about how nice the playground was and how the kids seemed to be having a great time. As a fellow stay-at-home dad, Simon felt an unusual connection to the guys. It was as if he'd been lost in some remote foreign country and had suddenly stumbled upon a group of friendly Americans.

Then Simon saw Michael's nostrils flare, as if he were smelling something, and he went to one of the strollers and from a pouch took out a diaper, a small package of Huggies wipes, and A&D cream.

"Jonas!" he called, and his son immediately ran over to him.

Simon was impressed; Jeremy never would've acted so obediently.

He was also impressed that Michael had been able to tell that his son needed a diaper change from across the playground.

"Impressive," Simon said to Michael. "How'd you do that?"

"Father's instincts," Michael said, and then he led his son to an empty bench and started to change the poopy diaper.

Simon remained on the other bench with Charlie and Ramon.

"We're really happy you came back," Charlie said. "My son, Nicky, was saying how much he likes Jeremy."

"Diego was sayin' the same thing on the way home yesterday," Ramon said. "He was like, 'Is Jeremy coming back tomorrow?' And I was like, 'I hope so 'cause I think his dad's really cool too.'"

Ramon, wearing the same gold cross he'd worn yesterday, was smiling widely. It was a perfect, infectious smile, and it was almost impossible to not smile along with him.

"Jeremy likes your kids too," Simon said. "He was practically begging me to come down here today."

"So you have Jeremy every day now?" Charlie asked.

"Yeah," Simon said. "My wife works and we don't have a babysitter. . . . Are you guys married?"

"I'm divorced," Charlie said.

"Oh, sorry to hear that," Simon said.

"Only married people say that," Charlie said. "Divorced people always congratulate me." He laughed. "Seriously, it was rough at first, but it's the best thing that ever happened to me. And it's better for my ex and Nicky too. My ex and me, we're still good friends, we just couldn't live together, you know?"

"How about you?" Simon asked Ramon.

"Me, I'll never get married," Ramon said. "I love the ladies too much."

"That's Ramon," Charlie said. "Gotta love his logic."

Simon and Charlie laughed.

"Seriously," Ramon said. "I live for women. Women are the most beautiful things in the world. And I'm not just talking about the women in fashion magazines. You can point to any woman on the street and I'll show you something beautiful about her. It could be her eyes, her hair, her hands, or the tone of her voice, or the sound of her laugh, but every woman has something that makes her beautiful and special. And the way I see it, if God wanted us to be with one woman, he wouldn't have put so much beauty in the world."

"Okay, I guess that's one way to look at it," Simon said.

"Or more than one way," Charlie said.

They all laughed. Simon really liked these guys.

"Actually there's one woman I would've married," Ramon said, "but she took off on me so I had no choice." Ramon was suddenly teary eyed. "But I'm not mad at her for it. How could I be? She gave me the best gift ever. Diego's my life now. I can't imagine living without my son, and my mother, his *abuela*, helps me raise him, so it's all good."

Michael finished changing the diaper, and Jonas ran off to play with the other boys.

During the rest of the play date, Simon had a great time talking to Charlie and Ramon, but Michael wasn't quite as talkative. Occasionally Michael laughed or smiled or made a comment, but mostly he just sat there, listening and watching his son play.

When the play date ended and the guys were pushing their strollers toward the gate, Charlie said to Simon, "Hey, I think I'm heading your way. Want to ride the subway up together?"

"Yeah, that would be great," Simon said.

They walked along the Hudson toward the South Ferry station.

Simon made sure Michael wasn't nearby, then said, "So what's the deal with Michael anyway?"

"Deal?" Charlie asked.

"He doesn't talk much," Simon said.

"That's just the way he is at first."

"Oh, okay," Simon said. "Because I thought maybe he didn't like me or something."

"That's crazy, he thinks you're a great guy. Michael can just be, what's the word I'm thinking of? Reserved. Yeah, he can be reserved. But you'll see, he opens up once you get to know him."

"Is he married?" Simon asked.

"I don't think so," Charlie said. "Actually he doesn't talk about Jonas's mother. But, yeah, Michael's a great guy . . . He really changed our lives."

"In what way?" Simon asked, and then he saw Jeremy running ahead with Nicky and he said, "Hey, Jeremy, no running, you have to walk, okay?"

When Simon and Charlie caught up with their kids again, Charlie said, "I'm a fireman."

"Wow," Simon said. "I had no idea. That's very cool."

"See? That's what everybody kept telling me, how cool I am. You know how it is—a fireman post-9/11 in New York, you're an automatic hero. But what did I do? I was home sick that day, hundred and three fever. But afterward, people would cheer and congratulate me, tell me what a great job I was doing. Kids wanted my autograph, people called me 'sir' and held doors for me. I didn't think I deserved it, you know, so I walked around with a big chip on my shoulder. It took a toll on my marriage too. Nicole and me, we'd been having trouble for years anyway, but still, my life was falling apart . . . Then I met Michael and I can't really explain it. The guy's like one of those whatchamacallits . . . motivational speakers. He has a way of making you look at yourself differently, of *transforming* you. It sounds corny, I know, but it's true."

They continued to the subway and rode the 1 train uptown together. Charlie asked Simon about his old job, and Simon told him about the clients he'd had and the campaigns he'd worked on.

"Well, if there's anything I can do to help, you just let me know," Charlie said. "I mean if you need to go on interviews, need somebody to babysit Jeremy, whatever. I work two twenty-four-hour shifts a week and my ex works full-time, so I'm with Nicky a lot during the day."

"Thanks," Simon said. "That's really nice of you."

At Times Square, Charlie and Nicky got off and Simon and Jeremy waved good-bye to them through the window as the train pulled away.

"His problem is he doesn't have any passion," Alison said.
She was on the corner of Lexington Avenue and Seventy-seventh Street, near Lenox Hill Hospital, talking on her cell with her sister, Lauren, who lived in San Francisco.

Alison continued, "When I met him he was a go-getter, he was motivated. I remember how excited he used to be when he talked about the future, all our plans. We were going to have two kids, live in a bigger apartment, I wouldn't have to work because he'd be a big-time ad exec someday. Honestly I'm not surprised he got fired. He just doesn't have that fire under him anymore, he doesn't want to compete. You should've seen him this weekend, just sitting on the couch like a lump, doing nothing. I don't know who he is, but he isn't the man I married."

"Did you discuss any of this with him?" Lauren asked.

"I was going to say something during our last counseling session," Alison said, "but what's the point? He is who he is, he's not going to change. We've been living like roommates for months."

"You mean you're not having any sex at all?"

"No, we do it once in a while," Alison said, "but I feel like we're going through the motions. It always seems like something we just have to do to get it over with, like a chore. He would deny it, I'm sure, but I feel like he doesn't actually *want* me. I'm not just talking about sex—he hardly ever touches me anymore, and I don't feel connected to him. All our conversations are about Jeremy or other minutiae. I know it's a cliché, but he doesn't buy me flowers or do anything to show he actually appreciates me. That's what it is right there. Bottom line, he doesn't appreciate me."

"Look, I'm not defending him, but he's going through a lot right now," Lauren said. "You're both going through a lot. You have to give things time to settle in."

"I know but it's not only now, it's . . ."Alison had another call coming in, from a doctor she'd been trying to reach. She said, "I have to take this."

"Everything's going to be okay," Lauren said. "I promise."

"Thanks for saying that," Alison said. "I just wish I believed you."

Alison took the other call. Switching to her upbeat, professional work persona, she said, "Hello, Dr. Sadacca, how are you today?"

Dr. Sadacca was a prominent York Avenue gynecologist. Alison had taken him out to dinner a few weeks ago, as an introductory meeting, to discuss the new line of oral contraception she was repping, and Dr. Sadacca said he was available next Thursday afternoon for a follow-up meeting. Normally Alison would have been happy about the potential sale, but lately it was hard to get excited about anything.

She'd thought she'd be happier with the new situation, being the breadwinner, but it was hard not to feel resentful. Simon got to spend hours every day with Jeremy and she was running around the city, working her butt off? It just didn't seem fair.

When she ended the call with Sadacca she saw a man in a business suit dash across Lexington Avenue and hug the pretty red-haired woman who was waiting for him. He was so happy to see her that he picked her up and held her for several seconds before he put her back down. Alison watched them, wishing she had a man in her life who was that excited to see her, who hugged her tightly, like he didn't want to let go.

Later in the afternoon, when she was coming out of her next meeting, she got a text from Simon:

I'm thinking about you right now

During their last counseling session Dr. Hagan had suggested they text each other during the day with loving messages as a way to increase intimacy in their marriage. She knew that Simon was only texting her because he felt he had to do it, like a homework assignment; it wasn't heartfelt.

But it would be too antagonistic to *not* respond, so she texted back:

Thanks ☺

She immediately regretted sending the text, and especially adding the smiley face. Why was she playing this game, letting him think every-thing was okay, when things were clearly not okay?

After work, when she arrived at the apartment, as usual it was a total mess—dirty dishes on the table and the counter and toys strewn all over the living room floor. But unlike other nights, when she'd tried to be considerate of what Simon was going through, with all the changes in his life, this time she couldn't control herself.

"Isn't fair, just isn't fair," she muttered—maybe to herself, maybe to Simon, maybe to no one—as she started to rinse dishes and put them in the dishwasher.

Simon said something about how he was sorry and he'd been plan-ning to clean up before she got home, but she'd come home earlier than he'd expected.

She cut him off with, "I can't work all day and then come home and spend an hour cleaning up after you two. If you're going to be home all day, you have to do some housework too. I can't do everything."

"You're right, I'm sorry," Simon said. "We were downtown in Bat-tery Park again and I meant to clean up, but we didn't have a chance."

"These dishes are from breakfast. You could've cleaned up before you left."

"You're right," Simon said. "Next time I'll do all the dishes. I'm sorry."

Alison didn't say anything, knowing that their real problem had nothing to do with dishes.

She wanted to talk to him and express how she was feeling, but after she got Jeremy bathed and to sleep she wanted to have a little time to herself, so she watched part of *The Rachel Maddow Show*. When she got into bed Simon was asleep and she lay down next to him, turning in the opposite direction.

Simon had had his best night's sleep in days. He was in the kitchen, pouring coffee, when Alison came in, dressed for work, saying, "I left an apple and a banana on the counter; make sure Jeremy has them in his stroller today. He hasn't had enough fruit lately."

"Don't worry, I'll make sure he has a good eating day," Simon said.

Alison kissed Simon on the lips so lightly it was practically an air kiss, then hurried out of the apartment.

Simon had no idea why Alison was acting so distant the past couple of days, but he decided to not let it get to him. They'd gone through many periods during their marriage when they didn't get along, and things always somehow got resolved. Stressing or making a big issue about it would only make things worse.

Simon had a pleasant, relaxing morning with Jeremy. They played Candy Land and then Jeremy watched some TV while Simon did his e-mail. Jeremy didn't put up any fuss about getting dressed or having his teeth brushed, and when it was time to head downtown to Battery Park, he got right into his stroller. Jeremy was definitely getting used to Simon being his primary caretaker, and now that he'd met the three guys and their kids and had a semiregular routine, Simon was feeling much more comfortable as well.

Later, at the playground, they had another great afternoon. It was amazing how well the four boys played together. They shared well and didn't argue at all. Simon enjoyed hanging out with the guys. Charlie and Ramon were great as always, and though Michael still seemed very reserved, Simon was getting used to his idiosyncrasies, like how he spoke in statements, even when he seemed to be asking questions. Though he didn't get what Charlie had said, how Michael was "like a motivational speaker," there was definitely something intriguing about him and it was obvious that he was a great dad. He seemed in tune with his son, Jonas, watching him even when he didn't seem to be watching him, and almost instantly responding to his needs, including diaper changes and water and snack breaks.

The guys invited Simon to another play date, and Simon suggested meeting uptown for a change. Everyone loved this idea, so the next afternoon they met at Sheep Meadow in Central Park. It was a sunny, warmer day, and they all played soccer—dads against the kids. Simon thought he was in pretty good shape, but it was hard to keep up with the guys, who were all excellent athletes. While the kids were having their snacks, the guys played Frisbee. Charlie was able to toss the Frisbee incredibly far, maybe the length of a football field, and Michael could chase it down every time, no matter how out of reach it seemed. Michael was a stocky guy and didn't seem like he'd be so fast, which made the spectacle seem even more amazing. People stood around oohing and ahhing like they were watching a fireworks display.

When they took a break, Simon said to Charlie, "Wow, that's amazing. How do you do that?"

"Played a little ultimate when I was growing up," Charlie said. "And sometimes I toss a Frisbee around with the guys from the firehouse. On family picnics, you know?"

"And how can you run so fast?" Simon asked Michael, noticing that he didn't seem to be sweating at all even though he'd done about twenty consecutive hundred-yard sprints.

"I've always been a fast runner," Michael said.

"But you're *really* fast. You should be a track star or something."

"I don't like competitive sports," Michael said, "but I love running, especially at night. There's nothing quite like it."

As they left Sheep Meadow at around five o'clock, the four guys walking together behind their four boys, Simon said, "Well, this was a blast, and the kids seemed to have a blast too."

"You'll come out with us tomorrow night," Michael said.

"A play date at night?" Simon asked.

"No, just us four men," Michael said. "No kids, no women. You'll come to my family's old brewery in Brooklyn."

"Oh, that sounds cool," Simon said. He and Alison didn't have any plans, so he didn't see why it would be a problem.

"We hang out there once in a while," Charlie said. "Guys' night out kinda thing, you know?"

"Man, wait till you see the place," Ramon said. "You won't believe it."

It had been a long time since Simon had gone on a guys' night out. His other guy friends were all working full-time and they were married with kids and didn't see their kids often enough during the week, so getting together with Simon on weekends didn't work out because they wanted to spend time with their families. Simon had been in constant daddy mode now for over a week, and a night out with the guys was exactly what he needed.

"Tomorrow night sounds perfect," Simon said. "What time do you want me?"

SEVEN

"Have you ever felt in perfect unison with a guy? Like you weren't two people? Like your bodies were physically and spiritually merged? That's how it is with Michael and me. It's like whenever we're together I'm transported to some faraway land that's beautiful and dangerous and terrifying and exhilarating all at once."

Olivia and Diane were walking on the grass through the center of Bryant Park, holding their bags of take-out lunch—salads from Cosi. It was a bright sunny day, a nice break after all the rain lately, but they could have been in a monsoon and Olivia still would have been in a great mood.

"Wow," Diane said, "that's quite a review, especially for a guy you've known what, three and a half days?"

"I know it hasn't been a long time," Olivia said, "but, you know, maybe time is overrated. After all, some people spend a whole lifetime together and never really know each other. . . . And it's definitely the most amazing sex I've ever had."

"Really?" Diane was intrigued.

"Trust me," Olivia said. "You have no idea."

They sat at one of the green metal tables that were set up around the park. A lot of businesspeople and tourists were taking advantage of the nice weather, and most of the tables were occupied and the paths were crowded.

As she took her Shanghai chicken salad out of the bag, Diane said, "I think I have *some* idea. I mean, I've had good sex before."

"I've had good sex too," Olivia said. "But there's good sex and there's goooood sex. I've had good sex before, but this sex is goooooood."

"Why is it gooooood?" Diane laughed.

Olivia, not trying to be funny, said, "It's like nothing I've ever experienced. It's raw, it's visceral, it's violent, it's—"

"Whoa," Diane said. *"Violent?"*

"Violent in a good way." Olivia pulled up her blouse a little to show Diane part of a black-and-blue mark above her waistline.

"Oh my God," Diane said, "he did that to you?"

"You should see what my arms and legs look like," Olivia said. "His hands are so strong, it's almost like he can't help himself. He pins me down to the bed so hard, I can't move at all."

"And that's fun?"

"And his eyes," Olivia went on, "they're so intense. He looks right into my eyes while we're doing it and, I know this might be hard to understand, but it's like . . . well, it's like I can see right into his soul."

"Please tell me this isn't real," Diane said. "Please just tell me the guy turned out to be the typical jerk lawyer who stopped calling you and this is all some kind of joke."

"You know what he says to me when we get into his bedroom?" Olivia said. "'Get naked.' He doesn't say it like he's asking me to take off my clothes. He says it like an order."

"That sounds so romantic."

"I wouldn't use that word," Olivia said. "No, it's not romantic. It's not erotic either. It's passionate. It's just so amazingly passionate."

"Being roughed up and ordered around is passionate," Diane deadpanned.

"Yes," Olivia said. "I'm so sick of trying to figure out what guys are thinking. I think every guy I've ever dated has had trouble expressing himself. With this guy it's all out in the open. There's no silly misunderstandings, no walking around on eggshells. There are no walls."

"Okay, nothing you're saying right now is making any sense."

Frustrated that she and Diane were on such different wavelengths, Olivia said, "You know how usually the first time with a guy it's awkward? You don't know how to express yourself yet? Everything's unspoken?"

Diane nodded tentatively.

"Well, with Michael there's none of that. He takes control, in a good way, like an expert dancer. I feel confident when I'm with him. He makes me feel safe, protected, like nothing can ever hurt me. It's like I've been with boys my whole life and now I'm with a man. But it's not even like he's a man. He's so much more than a man."

Diane, holding a forkful of salad in front of her mouth melodramatically, stared at Olivia. Then said, "I think I know what the problem is. You're settling."

"How'm I—?"

"Just try to remove yourself from this fantasy land you're stuck in and look at it the way a ration— the way *I'm* seeing it. We went out the other night, you met a guy. I didn't think you were making the right decision, but okay, you went home with him. Everybody has their weak moments. You had some good sex—sorry, goooood sex—and it's blinded you. You think you have to settle for Mr. Violent Weirdo because you might not meet anybody else. But you will meet somebody else. Because you're an amazing woman."

"Thanks for the pep talk," Olivia said, "but I don't think you get it. . . . I really do like him. I think he's the most amazing man I've ever met. I'm in love with him."

"Oh my God, you didn't tell him that, did you?"

"I'm not an idiot," Olivia said. "I've fallen for enough guys to know that saying *I love you* too soon is an automatic relationship killer. But that doesn't change the way I feel."

"I don't know what to say," Diane said. "I mean, if being ordered around and getting bruised up is your idea of a great relationship, who am I to argue with you?"

"Did I tell you about the way he smells?"

"No," Diane said. "I think you left out that part."

"Oh, God, I just love the smell of his skin." For emphasis, Olivia took a deep breath and let it out slowly. "Seriously, I just can't get enough of it. You know how they say French men don't wear cologne and French women find it such a turn-on? I'd never really understood the allure. To me, it always seemed like having sex with a taxi driver or something. But now I get it. When we're doing it, Michael smells so musky and pungent . . . it's amazing. His scent is just so unique and intimate. I can't get enough of it." The memory of his scent made it feel like she was actually in bed, having sex with him. She closed her eyes and moaned, "Mmmmm," much louder than she'd intended. When she opened her eyes, two middle-aged guys in business suits at the table were looking over, smirking.

"Oh, sorry," Olivia said, forcing a smile.

When the guys looked away, Diane said, "Look. I get that you're excited because you met this new eccentric guy, and I get that you're really attracted to him, and I get that you've been having great sex. But take it from someone who's removed from the situation—it's weird, okay? It sounds like he's manipulating you or something. You're not acting the way you normally act."

"You mean I'm not as miserable as I normally am? You mean I'm not whining about how I can't meet anyone new, and how I'm sick of meeting the same jerks?"

"No," Diane said, "what I mean is you're not looking at the situation clearly. It's not normal to have bruises from sex."

"He's not *hurting* me—"

"And you know nothing about this guy. Did you even find out what he does for a living?"

"His family used to own a brewery. I think he comes from old money."

"You 'think'?"

"I don't want to probe, okay? It's like he told me the other night, 'Questions only complicate things.' When I thought about this, I realized how it's so true. I'm always questioning relationships, finding reasons not to like guys. He's too this, he's too that, he not enough this, he's too much that. Not knowing is so much simpler."

"It sounds like he's trying to hide something from you."

"No, it's the total opposite. Everything's out in the open. There're no secrets, no boundaries."

"You know nothing about him."

"I know he has a kid."

"He told you this?"

"No, I just saw his kid's stuff in the apartment."

Diane considered this for a few moments, then said, "Well, that makes me feel a little better, at least. I mean, if he has a kid how crazy can he be, right?"

They ate for a while without saying anything. While Diane was eating her salad, avoiding eye contact, and Olivia was picking at hers—she hadn't had much of an appetite lately, losing four pounds in the past few days—she was imagining Michael pinning her down on the bed while she ran her fingernails down his muscular back. He'd told her he couldn't get together tonight, that he was going out with some friends. It was going to be rough not being with him. She already felt like she was in Michael withdrawal.

After maybe thirty seconds had gone by, Olivia broke the silence with, "Well, enough about me and my crazy sex life. How have you been?" She was purposely trying to make light of the whole situation, to hopefully ease the tension. It worked—well, for a little while anyway. Diane started telling her how she and Steve were planning to take their first vacation together, to Turks and Caicos, and Olivia tried to focus, but her mind kept drifting. She managed to make appropriate comments like, "Wow, that sounds great" and "You're so lucky," but the conversation seemed forced, more like a business lunch than a lunch with a close friend.

Diane seemed aware of the awkwardness, rushing to finish her salad, like she couldn't wait to get away. When she looked at the time on her iPhone and said, "Oh, shoot, it's almost one, I have to get back to my office for a phone conference," Olivia knew it was just an excuse.

They left the park and didn't talk at all until they were on Sixth Avenue when Olivia said, "I'm really sorry if I sounded a little nutty before. You know how excited I always get when I meet someone. This time, for some reason, it's just so much more intense."

"No, it's my fault," Diane said. "I shouldn't've come on so strong. I was probably out of line."

"No, you were just looking out for me, and I appreciate it," Olivia said. "But don't worry about me. I'm a big girl."

They hugged good-bye.

"How about we do lunch again next week?" Olivia asked.

"I'm swamped and then I'll be in Turks and Caicos," Diane said.

"Oh, that's right. Then how about when you get back? Or, I know, how about the four of us go on a double date? I really think you have the wrong impression of Michael. If you just got to know him, you'd see why I think he's so special."

"Okay, I'd love that," Diane said, but Olivia could tell she wasn't into the idea at all.

On the way back to her office, Olivia wanted to call him just to hear his voice, but she remembered him telling her he didn't like to talk on his cell phone. When he'd called her the other day, what had he said? Oh yeah, "Don't call me." His directness was so damn sexy.

Suddenly she realized she was in her office, at her desk. Wow, how did that happen? It seemed like only a few seconds ago she was saying good-bye to Diane and somehow she'd walked across Sixth Avenue and along Fortieth Street, ridden the elevator to the seventh floor, and gone down the corridor to her corner office. This had been happening a lot lately—she was always so involved thinking about Michael that she seemed to skip from place to place and thought to thought in a delirious daze and it was hard to get anything accomplished. It was unlike her to get so distracted because normally she was extremely focused, especially at work. She routinely put in fourteen-hour days and micromanaged her company. She had nine employees plus two interns from the School of Design, and usually she was on top of everything that went on at her company.

Diane had been right—she definitely wasn't acting normal—but why was that such a bad thing? She'd finally found a guy she connected with, who raised her pulse. Spacing out was just a side effect of falling in love.

She answered work e-mails that had accumulated in her inbox, including one from her assistant, who had set up a meeting with Mr. Kyoto, a potential major client from Japan who was coming to town soon. Kyoto was the decision maker for a chain of high-end Japanese restaurants expanding in the city and was considering hiring Olivia's firm to do the signage, menus, and other graphic design. She tried to focus on her work, but it was hard to get Michael out of her head.

Later in the afternoon, at a staff meeting, Kathleen, a project manager, was giving a presentation.

"What do you think?" Kathleen asked.

Fantasizing about Michael's irresistible manly scent, Olivia said, "I'm sorry, what exactly are we discussing?"

EIGHT

Looking in the full-length mirror behind the bathroom door, Simon couldn't tell if the beige turtleneck and navy sport jacket made him look hip or uptight. He knew the guys would be well dressed tonight, and he wanted to be well dressed too. But he wanted to be casual, relaxed; he didn't want to look like some stuffy college professor.

"Like what you see?"

Simon hadn't heard Alison enter, and he jerked a little.

"Wow, and nervous too," Alison said. "Jeez, what is it with you today? It's like you're going on a date."

"Sorry, didn't expect you to sneak up on me like that," Simon said.

"Isn't that the third outfit you've tried on?" she asked.

Actually it was the fifth.

"Second," he said.

"I thought you were just going out to a bar tonight?"

Was he imagining it, or was there a slight accusatory tone in her voice? Yeah, probably. When you've been married for eleven years, the subtleties in your spouse's tone were hard to miss.

"It's not a bar," he said. "It's a brewery."

"How do I know you're not having a wild affair with some beautiful young nanny you met at the playground?"

He knew she was being sarcastic, but he detected bitterness in her tone. This time he decided not to let it go. "Did I do something wrong? Are you angry at me?"

"No." She turned away. "Why?"

"You've been acting distant the past few days," Simon said, "and you barely said a word during our last session with Hagan."

She turned back suddenly and said, "Okay, there *is* something wrong, okay? I want things to get better, and they're not getting any better."

"I don't know what you're talking about," Simon said. "What things?"

"You, us, our lives," she said. "I just thought everything would improve without you working. I thought you'd be under less stress and we'd . . . I don't know . . . be happier. But we still have the same problems."

"I know I've been a little distracted lately," Simon said, "but I think I have a pretty good reason for it, don't you?"

"This has nothing to do with you getting fired."

"Look," Simon said. "Like I said in counseling, I'll work on it, and I was serious about what I said about getting Christina to babysit. I think we should have a regular date night."

"It's not just a date night," Alison said. "Don't you get it?"

"Mommy." Jeremy was at the door.

"Yes, sweetie?"

"My neck feels funny."

Jeremy always said his neck hurt when he had a sore throat.

"Okay, sweetie, I'll be right there."

Jeremy left the room.

"I better take his temperature," Alison said. "I hope he's not getting sick."

"I think we need to discuss this," Simon said.

"I don't think there's anything to discuss," she said, and went to tend to Jeremy.

Simon hated when Alison did this—started a big drama or discus-

sion about something and left before he had a chance to express himself. He knew from experience that when she lashed out it usually had
nothing to do with him. She was probably just stressed out about work,
or her family situation—her parents had been killed in a car accident in
Florida three years ago and her sister in San Francisco was her only close
relative—and was taking it out on him the way she sometimes did. He
would talk to her about it another time, when she was ready to actually
have a conversation.

He tried on a few more outfits—including the turtleneck and sport
jacket again—and finally settled on a simple pair of jeans and a black
long-sleeved shirt. It was perfect—he looked casual, not too dressy, and
not like he was trying too hard to look good. He usually didn't blow-
dry his hair, but what the hell, he could use a little volume; after all, his
hair wasn't getting any thicker. Finally he added some gel, and his black
leather bomber jacket completed the look. He checked himself in the
mirror again, thinking he looked good . . . damn good. Yeah, he'd definitely fit in well with the guys tonight.

Then he went out to the living room and saw Jeremy on the couch
next to Alison. He looked noticeably pale and she was holding a moist-
ened washcloth against his forehead.

"He's one oh one point four and it's going up fast," Alison said. "It
was just a hundred point nine."

"Oh no." Simon felt Jeremy's head. "Yikes, he does feel hot. Did you
give him Tylenol?"

"Yes, I gave him Tylenol."

Alison sounded snippy, but Simon didn't take it personally. She always got anxious when Jeremy was sick.

"Did you hear about any viruses going around?" Alison asked.

"I think one of the babysitters mentioned something about a virus;
I'm not sure."

"My throat hurts really bad." Jeremy was making the sad, heart-
breaking face that all children mastered.

"I hope it's not strep," Alison said.

"Maybe I should cancel and stay home," Simon said.

"No, it's fine," Alison said. "Once the Tylenol kicks in he'll fall right asleep. In the morning I'll call Dr. Leibner."

"Are you sure?"

"Positive. Go out with your friends tonight. Have fun."

If she thought she was hiding the nastiness in her tone, she wasn't.

"My neck really hurts, Mommy." Jeremy started crying.

"It's gonna be okay, kiddo," Simon said.

"I don't want you to go, Daddy," Jeremy said.

"Just go," Alison said. "Before he has a total fit."

Simon kissed Alison good-bye and left the apartment quickly. In the hallway, as he locked the door, he heard Jeremy wailing.

Riding the elevator to the lobby, Simon felt awful. In the lobby he was about to call Alison to make sure everything was okay. But he stopped himself, realizing a phone call right now might upset her even more. After all, he didn't want her to think he was usurping her in some way. Besides, there was no real reason to stay home. Jeremy was just having one of his usual melodramatic crying fits and had probably settled down already.

As Simon headed toward the subway at Eighty-sixth and Central Park West, guilt kicked in—not about Jeremy, but about what Alison had told him, about how she wasn't happy. Maybe she wasn't dumping on him and had a legitimate gripe. It was true he hadn't been paying enough attention to her lately. He didn't kiss her enough or compliment her when he knew that was what she wanted from him. He loved her and wanted to make her feel special and do nice things for her, but life always seemed to get in the way.

Then, remembering Dr. Hagan's advice about one way to increase intimacy in their marriage, he texted her:

Just want you to know I love you very much and I'm thinking about you!

Knowing how much she'd appreciate the intimate text, he descended the steep stairs to the Eighty-sixth Street subway station.

* * *

Outside the Bedford Avenue subway station in Brooklyn, Simon checked the GPS on his phone, trying to orient himself. He'd always had a lousy sense of direction, and even with a map and his location and the location of the brewery indicated, he was still afraid he'd get lost.

Michael had said the brewery was "near DUMBO," but the hip, gentrified neighborhood was nowhere in sight. Following his GPS, he headed into a no-man's-land of old abandoned factories and empty trash-filled lots toward the old Brooklyn Navy Yard. It was near dusk, but the streetlights weren't on yet, so it was darker than it would be at midnight. According to his phone he was heading in the right direction and still had a few more blocks to go. He turned onto Assembly Road, a dingy, barren street, and walked toward the East River. Could this be right? It certainly didn't look like a block where there was a brewery, at least not an active brewery. He reached a building on the corner, and according to the GPS this was the address Michael had given him.

The entrance to the building was gated shut. Simon looked around but couldn't find a bell to ring. He tried rattling the gate, hoping it would get the attention of someone inside, but there was no response.

He'd just realized he didn't have the guys' cell numbers when he heard, "Hey, big guy."

He tensed, his city instincts kicking in, thinking he might be in danger. But he looked to his right and saw Ramon approaching, smiling widely.

"Hey." Simon was glad to see him too. He extended his hand to shake, but Ramon gave him a big tight hug instead.

"It's great you came," Ramon said. "It's so amazing to see you, bro."

Simon let go right away, but Ramon kept squeezing for a few seconds longer than necessary before finally letting go.

"Yeah, you too," Simon said. "Actually, I didn't know if this was the right place. There's no bell to ring or anything."

"You gotta be buzzed in."

"But how do you—"

"Michael!" Ramon's voice boomed so loud Simon actually had to cover his ears. "Charlieeeeeeeee!"

Several seconds went by, and then a buzzer sounded and Ramon opened the gate.

They entered into a big dilapidated lobby with peeling paint on the walls and piles of torn-up floorboards and other garbage strewn around. A large rusted chandelier hung from the ceiling, but only a few bulbs were functioning.

"Beautiful, right?"

Simon wasn't sure if Ramon was joking or not, but he didn't think he was.

"Yeah, I love comin' down here," Ramon said. "It's like an oasis in the middle of the city."

Oasis?

Simon thought this was a little weird, but so what, he'd have a fun night out, an adventure. What with all the parenting he'd been doing lately, and everything he'd gone through at work, he deserved to have some fun.

Ramon called for the old steel industrial-style elevator. The door opened halfway and got stuck.

"Don't worry, that's just the way it is," Ramon said. "Come on."

Simon got on with him and the doors shut and then, after a dramatic pause, the elevator began creeping upward. Simon, who suffered from mild claustrophobia, was suddenly glad he wasn't alone, though he didn't know what Ramon could do to help if the elevator stalled. This was the type of elevator you could die in if it got stuck and you couldn't get a signal on your cell phone.

"By the way, meant to say when I saw you, I love that jacket." Ramon reached toward Simon and rubbed the collar of the jacket between his fingers. "What brand is it?"

Simon felt a little weird, like Ramon was violating his space.

"Um, Guess," Simon said.

"Calvin Klein," Ramon said.

"No, I meant it's Guess," Simon said. "That's the brand."

Ramon laughed. It sounded especially boisterous, but maybe it was just because they were in the elevator. Then he said, "I love how the leather's so worn; that's what gives it its character. Clothes say a lot about a person. My grandmother, God rest her, was a clothing designer in Puerto Rico. She taught me all about clothes. Like she always told me, *'No es cómo se mire, es cómo se siente.'* It's not how you look, it's how you feel. But you pull it off, man. That's all I'm sayin'."

Finally Ramon stopped rubbing Simon's collar.

"Thank you," Simon said. It felt good to get the compliment, especially after stressing for so long about what to wear tonight. He was going to reciprocate, tell Ramon that he liked the black blazer he was wearing, but then the elevator suddenly stopped short again and after another very long pause the doors opened.

Simon was stunned. After seeing the lobby he was expecting the entire building to be in disrepair, but this floor was immaculate. Simon was no expert on architecture, but it looked to be from the period of the Empire State Building. Art deco, high ceilings, and an incredible view of Manhattan at dusk across the river.

"Wow." Simon couldn't think of anything else to say. That pretty much said it all.

"This way," Ramon said, and led Simon through a room that seemed to be a lavish office with floor-to-ceiling windows and a panoramic view of the Manhattan skyline. It was almost fully dark, and the moon loomed low, just above the highest buildings.

"Okay, so now I know what you meant by *beautiful*," Simon said.

Simon, following Ramon, was still admiring the stunning views as they went through the office, and then they went into a much darker, windowless room. It was so dim, Simon could barely see. Michael and Charlie were seated next to each other on a leather sofa but immediately sprang up when they saw Ramon and Simon enter.

Charlie was first over, saying "Hey, my man," and giving Ramon a bear hug that lasted at least ten seconds. Then Charlie hugged Simon, and Michael hugged Ramon. Lastly Michael hugged Simon, and his grip was noticeably tighter than the other guys'. Simon actually felt like his lungs were being squeezed and it was hard to get a breath. He was about to tell Michael to let go when he released him.

Simon's arms and rib cage ached, and he had to catch his breath. Then he said, "Thanks . . . thanks so much for having me here. This place is something else."

"Yes, I love it," Michael said.

"So, um, when did the brewery close?"

"It's been in my family for centuries."

"This brewery?"

"We had one in Germany too."

"Is it still active in Germany?"

"No, my family is no longer in the beer business, but, as they say, life goes on."

Simon was trying to think of another question when Michael said, "You'll have some steak now."

"Steak?" Simon wasn't sure he'd heard him correctly.

"Yeah," Ramon said. "You should see the way my boy Michael cooks 'em. Best damn T-bone in New York City."

"Yeah, Michael makes awesome steaks," Charlie said.

"Oh, wow, that's very nice of you," Simon said. "But I'm not really hungry. I already ate before I got here."

Michael seemed offended.

Then Ramon said, "Michael's a great cook."

"Thank you," Simon said to Michael. "I really appreciate it. But the thing is I rarely eat red meat anyway. I'm not a vegetarian, I just try to avoid it."

Everyone was looking at Simon, confused.

"You know, for health reasons," Simon continued. "High blood pressure, cholesterol. I have a family history, so I try to be careful."

Still no one seemed to understand what he was talking about.

"Sorry," Simon said. "I mean, I didn't mean to offend—"

"It's really good steak," Charlie said.

Wanting to put an end to all the tension, Simon said, "You know what, I think I have a little room left after all. I'd love to have some steak."

Ramon and Charlie smiled widely, but Michael remained deadpan as he went through a door toward the back of the room.

"I should give him a hand," Ramon said, and followed him.

Unlike at the playground and the park, when Simon had felt so comfortable with the guys, the steak discussion had caused some awkwardness.

"So," Simon said to Charlie. "How've you been?"

"Hanging in there, hanging in there," Charlie said. "So is everything cool?"

"What do you mean?"

"I don't know, you just seemed kind of, I don't know, put on the spot with the whole steak thing. If you're really not hungry or whatever, I could have a talk with Michael and—"

"No, no, I have some room," Simon said. "But thank you, I appreciate it."

Charlie looked toward the room Michael and Ramon had exited to, then moved closer to Simon and said in a hushed tone, "That's just how Michael gets with his quirks, you know? The steak is just a kind of tradition with him; every time we've been here he's cooked us steaks, but take it from me, a guy who cooks for a firehouse full of hungry firemen, the steaks are damn good."

"Well, it sounds great," Simon said. "I can't wait to try it."

"You sure? You still seem a little freaked out."

Simon laughed, then said, "No, I'm fine. There just seems to be new surprises all the time with you guys, but I'm getting used to it."

"Yeah, I know where you're coming from," Charlie said. "I remember when I came here the first time, I felt the same way. I was like, what is this place? It's run-down, in the middle of freakin' nowhere . . ."

"Exactly," Simon said.

"And the hugging. I was like, what's the deal with this? I mean, I'm not one of those homophobics, but I was like, whoa, man, take it easy. But then when I got to know the guys and found out what this was all about, my attitude changed. I got, what's the word I'm looking for? . . . unguarded. Yeah, I got unguarded. I mean, we're just a bunch of guys who like each other's company, so why hold back? Why not show it? I don't know about you, but I'd always had problems being emotional. My ex, man, she got on me about it all the time, saying I never talk, I keep my emotions to myself, you know? Even as a fireman I never felt that, you know, camaraderie with the guys you're supposed to feel. I never felt that bond, I never felt *part* of something. But here that's all changed. After I met Michael, and started hanging with him and Ramon a lot, it's like my whole life changed." Charlie was suddenly teary eyed. "See?" he said. "See? This is a whole new side of me. I never used to get like this."

Charlie looked away, as if he didn't want to cry in front of Simon. Simon was moved himself, seeing this big strong fireman get so vulnerable.

Then Ramon and Michael entered, Ramon grinning, saying, "Who's ready to eat some steak?"

Ramon and Michael placed four plates of T-bones on the table. There was nothing else on the plates—just the steaks. Ramon gave everyone a knife and fork except Michael, and then Ramon and Michael sat in the brown leather armchairs facing the coffee table and Simon and Charlie sat on the couch.

"*Bon appetit,*" Ramon said.

Simon watched Michael pick up his steak with his hands and hold it like a piece of corn. He started at one end and, chewing incredibly fast, knocked off the entire bottom of the steak. Then, like a typewriter, he shifted back to the other end of the steak and kept repeating, devouring half of the steak in about thirty seconds. Simon stared at Michael, amazed, but Charlie and Ramon seemed to think this was perfectly normal, barely noticing Michael as they began eating their own steaks. They used knives and forks, cutting pieces and chewing and swallowing.

Though they weren't eating nearly as fast as Michael, they were still eating extremely fast, almost if they were racing to finish. Meanwhile, there was no talking; they were totally focused on eating.

Michael was nearly done with his steak when he suddenly looked at Simon. It was only a momentary glance, but his dark, unflinching gaze gave Simon a jolt. Not wanting to offend his host again, Simon cut a piece of his steak and took his first bite. Wow, Ramon was right—it was amazing. Simon had eaten at Smith & Wollensky in Manhattan and at Musso and Frank in Hollywood, and this was as tender and flavorful as any steak he'd ever had.

"Wow, this is amazing," Simon said. "Seriously. Great job, Michael."

Michael, who had finished eating and was sucking on the bone, either didn't hear Simon or chose not to answer. A few minutes later, Charlie and Ramon finished and started sucking on the bones.

A couple of minutes later, Ramon rested his perfectly clean bone on the plate and said, "Damn, that was good."

Charlie put his bone down and said, "Awesome, as always."

The guys began a normal conversation that they could've had at the playground, trading stories about their kids. Ramon said his son had wet his bed a couple of nights ago, and Michael suggested a good book for him to read on the subject. Then Charlie said that his son wanted a tricycle, and Simon told him about a sale he'd heard about at a bicycle shop on Lexington Avenue. The guys were extremely friendly and outgoing, and compared to all of the awkwardness before, everything seemed very normal.

Simon ate most of his steak but was too full to finish. Thirsty, he asked Michael, "Do you have any water or something?"

Michael immediately stood, the way an old-fashioned gentleman gets up when a lady enters a room, and said, "You'll have beer."

"Cool," Simon said. "I'd love a beer."

Michael exited to the room from which he'd brought the steaks and returned a few minutes later with a tray of four pints of beer. Three beers were light and one was noticeably dark—not as dark as Guinness, but close.

"My man's getting the special brew," Ramon said, sharing a knowing glance with Charlie.

"Um, what's the special brew?" Simon asked cautiously.

"It's just a family recipe of Michael's," Charlie said.

"It's a special beer from the homeland in Germany," Michael said.

Michael's gaze was so intense, Simon had to look away.

"We had it the first time we were here," Ramon said. "Just get ready—it has a kick."

"Yeah, it's pretty strong," Charlie said.

Simon gripped the glass, hesitated, then brought the beer up to his nose. It didn't smell like dark beer, or *any* beer. It was pungent, vinegary.

"Strong in what way?" Simon asked.

"It's hard to describe," Charlie said.

Ramon closed his eyes and said, "Mmm, I love that smell." The reaction seemed odd because Ramon couldn't possibly smell the beer from the other side of the coffee table.

Simon's gaze met Michael's again. It looked like Michael might be offended. Wanting to avoid awkwardness, as before with the steak, Simon sipped the beer.

It was bitter, making him wince, but it was a good bitter, with the bitterness of horseradish or really black coffee. At the same time, it tasted very much like beer.

"Interesting," Simon said. "I don't think I've had anything quite like this before."

"Just wait, man," Ramon said. "It'll get you."

Simon took another, longer sip, getting used to the distinctive flavor. He didn't feel much of anything and didn't expect to. He'd had high-alcohol beers before and had always had a high tolerance. In college, his friends used to wonder how he could have six or seven beers and act pretty much normal while they were totally sloshed.

Charlie said to Ramon, "So tell us about that woman you met on the subway last week."

"Ah, Francesca," Ramon said, drawing out the name with a heavy

Spanish accent, as if trying to make it sound as sexy as possible. "Her voice, man, it's like music. I love listening to her speak. She could be talking about the weather, or something she heard on the news, or whatever, and it sounds like poetry. She's definitely the most beautiful woman I've ever been with."

"Yeah, like we haven't heard that before," Charlie said laughing.

As Ramon told the guys the story of his date—"I picked her up at her apartment at six P.M. Man, she looked stunning . . ."—Simon continued to sip his beer. Still, he had no unusual reaction. Yeah, okay, he felt a little buzzed maybe, but that was it. Meanwhile, the flavor was growing on him and he liked the texture too—it was heavy, yet smooth and dry, but not too dry. Though Michael's attention was fixed on Ramon—who was talking with increasing passion and exaggerated hand movements—Simon still had the feeling that Michael was watching him.

Then it hit. It came suddenly, out of nowhere. At one moment, he was sitting there, listening to Ramon, and everything was normal, and the next moment the room was blurred, distorted. His eyes weren't eyes anymore—they were kaleidoscopes. He could make out snippets of Ramon's dialogue—"her skin was so lovely" and "most beautiful hands I've ever seen"—but he couldn't follow what he was saying. But he didn't feel frightened or panicky; it was the complete opposite, actually. He felt relaxed, numb, like a visitor in someone else's body.

He heard himself say: "I . . . think . . . something's . . . not . . . right."

He didn't know if he was actually talking slowly, or if he wasn't talking at all and was just imagining he was. He hadn't smoked pot in years, but he couldn't remember ever feeling so out of it when he was high.

This was way beyond getting high. Something was definitely happening to him.

Then he looked straight ahead at Michael's infinitely dark eyes. He could've looked away if he'd wanted to, but he *didn't* want to. The darkness was soothing, calming. Then, gradually and peacefully, he drifted off and became a part of it.

NINE

Tom Harrison arrived at his home in Bernardsville, New Jersey, a little before nine o'clock (later than usual; his official explanation was that he'd gone out for "a drink with the guys at work") and had dinner (reheated chicken cutlets, a baked potato, and string beans) while watching some of the Knicks game on the sixty-two-inch LCD TV in the living room. His wife, JoAnne, was upstairs, reading or watching TV, and their sixteen-year-old daughter, Gail, was sleeping over at a friend's.

When Tom was through eating, he loaded the dishwasher, then went upstairs and popped his head into the bedroom where JoAnne was lying down watching TV and said, "Hey."

"Hi, honey, how was your day?" JoAnne asked.

Tom said, "Good, thanks," and continued to his office at the other end of the hallway.

The great thing about living in a large suburban home was that you could spread out and not be on top of each other. JoAnne could be at the other end of the house and he could escape to his office and have all the privacy he wanted.

He went online on his PC, his heart rate already accelerating. He opened Yahoo! Messenger, saw that Krenj22 was online, and IM'd:

i miss u so much baby

Actually he'd seen Karen less than an hour ago—they'd had a couple of hours of sex at the Hotel Chandler on Thirty-first Street, and taken the 8:02 train back from the city together—but he couldn't get enough of her.

They'd been having an affair now for, Jesus, six years. They'd met on a New Jersey Transit train. For months they both rode on the 7:18 train on the second car from the back and noticed each other and exchanged smiles and polite conversation before Tom finally sat next to her one morning and struck up an actual conversation. It turned out that Karen worked in marketing too—on the client side—so they had a lot to discuss, even knew some of the same people. They were the same age, had both grown up in central Jersey, near Princeton, and seemed to have everything else in common. Tom felt like he'd finally met his soul mate.

One day they met for a drink after work and then made out passionately on a dark side street near Penn Station. A full-blown affair quickly ensued—hotel rooms, late-night office hookups, and frequent e-mails, phone calls, and texts. They even concocted out-of-town conventions neither of them actually needed to attend so they could see each other on weekends. They kept the affair a total secret—they didn't even tell their closest friends. In the beginning, caught up in the insanity of their attraction to each other, they'd been reckless and had a few close calls. Her husband, Richard, had almost seen a couple of text messages, and JoAnne overheard a snippet of a phone conversation Tom was having in the garage and he had to scramble for a plausible excuse. Figuring they needed a way to potentially explain away all of the texts and phone calls, they introduced their spouses to each other. The two couples went out to dinner and movies, and gradually Karen and JoAnne became good friends, and Tom enjoyed hanging out and watching football games with

Richard, and playing golf together once in a while. Their kids became friendly too. Karen had two boys—Matt, who was Gail's age (they'd even dated for a while), and Ricky, who was two years older than Tom's oldest, James. Ricky and James were both away at college.

At times, Tom felt guilty. He'd even considered—not seriously—breaking off the affair. He rationalized that if he hadn't met Karen and found an outlet for the boredom and lack of passion in his marriage, he would have almost certainly gotten divorced, which would have created a whole new set of problems. The affair had probably saved not only his marriage, but Karen and Richard's as well, and avoided a lot of pain for both families.

Okay, Tom had enough self-awareness to realize that there were major flaws in this logic, but the deceit wouldn't go on for much longer. When Gail and Matt went off to college next year and the two nests were empty, Tom and Karen were going to announce that they wanted divorces. Then, after a year or two, when the divorces were finalized, they'd announce that they were a couple. He knew JoAnne would be devastated at first—being a fifty-two-year-old single woman in the suburbs would be rough—but it would be for the best. They didn't have a prenup, so she'd do well in the divorce. He'd give her a lump sum, set her up in an apartment somewhere. She'd be fine.

He honestly didn't know where things had gone so wrong in his marriage. He used to be crazy about JoAnne; they were practically inseparable. Then the kids came along, which was fine for a while, until she changed. She'd always complain to him that he was the one who'd changed, but that was ridiculous because she was the one who'd become completely different. She wasn't interested in his work anymore or anything else about him. When they'd met, she was working in advertising, and he'd encouraged her to go back to work, but she hadn't, and now he felt like they didn't have the same connection.

Tom typed:

Tomharr: you were so good tonight

Karen replied:

Krenj22: awww, thank you ☺ u weren't so bad yourself stud ☺
Tomharr: God, I'm so horny for you right now baby

And he *was* horny. It was amazing how just IM'ing with Karen made Tom feel like his hormones were raging.

Krenj22: I know, me 2. I can't wait to see you on Saturday

On Saturday Richard was going to be gone for the day and JoAnne and Gail were going shopping in the city. Karen was planning to come over to Tom's place for a few hours.

Tomharr: it's going to be so amaz

He heard footsteps approaching along the carpeted hallway and typed

Tomharr: J

J was their code for *JoAnne's coming*. He quickly shut the chat window and opened a blank e-mail document.

Then JoAnne entered and asked, "Coming to bed?"

"Yeah, one sec." He pretended to be absorbed in typing.

JoAnne, who couldn't see the monitor from where she was standing, asked, "Working late again?"

"Yeah, you know," he said, "I have to prepare for that big pitch meeting next week."

"What big pitch meeting?"

See? *She* was the one who didn't listen to *him*. *That* was the problem in their marriage. "Remember? I told you about it last week?"

"You always have some important meeting or conference." She sounded irritated. "How am I supposed to keep track?"

"I'll only be a few more minutes," he said.

"Okay, I'll try to wait up for you," she said, "but I don't know if I can. I'm really exhausted tonight."

When JoAnne left, Tom was relieved. She was exhausted—good, that meant if he delayed long enough she'd fall asleep and he wouldn't have to have sex with her. The hardest part about maintaining the affair for the past six years was also maintaining a normal sex life with JoAnne.

He checked to make sure JoAnne had gone back to the bedroom, and then he went online to Yahoo! Messenger again. Damn, Karen was offline, but she'd sent him a final IM:

Krenj22: have 2 go 2 good night can't wait to hear your voice tomorrow love you xoxo

Tom read the message a few times, not liking it at all. *Have 2 go 2?* Where did she "have 2 go" at eleven o'clock at night? She claimed she only slept with Richard occasionally—not because she wanted to, but because she had to in order not to raise suspicion—and he wondered if she was in bed with him right now. The thought of her naked with another man disgusted Tom and brought up the taste of acidic chicken cutlet. He couldn't help it; he wanted her all to himself.

Trying to not let the disturbing images seep too deeply into his brain, Tom checked his work e-mail—nothing very important, just an update on a couple of accounts from his assistant and a note from HR about Simon Burns's severance agreement. Tom was glad that Simon had stopped e-mailing him directly because the guy's behavior was starting to get pathetic. Slamming the door and breaking the picture frame was one thing, but begging for his job back and sending that e-mail was just unclassy. Simon's position had been eliminated because he'd deserved to have his position eliminated, end of story. Despite the Deutsche Bank deal, his accounts had been down for months and he wasn't as hungry as some of the younger guns at the agency, like Paul Kramer. Tom liked Simon personally, but someone had to go and Simon had brought this on himself.

At around eleven fifteen, Tom got into bed with JoAnne. She was on her back, snoring. He nudged her a little until she turned onto her side, away from him. He flicked on the light on his night table and read for a few minutes—*100 Simple Secrets of Successful People*—but tired quickly and shut the light off and let the book drop onto the floor beside the bed. He started to doze, and then JoAnne turned back onto her back and started snoring again. God, it was so annoying; why didn't she just get that deviated septum fixed already? Sometimes he felt like he was sleeping next to Seabiscuit.

Eh, it didn't matter though. Soon he'd be divorced, living with Karen. He always slept so well next to her. As he'd often told her—it was like they were two puzzle pieces that fit together perfectly.

He nudged JoAnne again, practically pushing her, but she was sleeping too deeply and didn't budge. He was afraid if he woke her up she'd go to the bathroom to pee and come back, fully awake, and want to have sex, so he let her go on snoring and turned the other way, one ear pressed against the mattress, the other with a pillow tightly over it to block the noise.

An animal noise jolted Tom awake, but it wasn't JoAnne with her horselike snoring. It was Duncan, their cocker spaniel. He was downstairs, barking like crazy.

"Oh, come on, give me a break," Tom said. He was always grouchy when he was woken up, especially if he hadn't been asleep for very long.

"Can you go see what's wrong?" JoAnne asked.

"It's probably just a deer or something. Let's just forget about it. He'll shut up eventually."

But the barking wasn't letting up; if anything, it was getting louder, more shrieking and persistent.

"Fine," JoAnne said with that instantly annoyed tone in her voice that always made Tom's stomach burn. "I'll go check."

"It's okay, I'll check, I'll check," Tom said, getting out of bed.

He put on his slippers and headed downstairs. Duncan was really barking like nuts.

"Cool it, Duncan! I said, cool it!"

Yeah, like that would work.

Duncan was in the kitchen, scratching against the back door.

"What? What is it?"

Tom peeked through the curtain on the door but couldn't see anything. He flicked on the light on the deck and checked again. Nothing, but Duncan didn't let up.

"There's nothing there," Tom said, holding up the curtain. "Look, look."

Duncan continued scratching and screeching—Tom had never seen him get like this. He considered locking him in the den for the night, but, knowing Duncan, that probably wouldn't do much. He'd continue barking, making a racket.

"Okay, you win."

Tom got the flashlight from the tool drawer and went onto the deck. There was probably a deer out there, spooking Duncan. He shined the flashlight at the woodsy area behind the house but didn't see anything. It had probably taken off already, but Duncan continued barking furiously.

"Fine, want me to look? I'll look. Then you promise to shut up?"

Shining the beam ahead of him, Tom went down the steps to the backyard lawn. He figured he'd take a lap around the house, Bambi would run away, Duncan would stop yapping, and everyone could sleep happily ever after.

As he went along the back of the house, away from the porch, it got darker, and he had only the beam from the flashlight to guide him. Then he hesitated for a moment, a thought suddenly troubling him. *What if it's a skunk?* He'd seen a skunk in the driveway, when was it? Yesterday? Well, that would be a perfect ending to this night, wouldn't it? Getting skunked and having to soak in V8.

He was heading around the side of the house, where it was even darker, when he was attacked. It happened so suddenly, he didn't even realize what was happening until he was already on the ground and the man was on top of him. By the time the idea of fighting back or screaming even occurred to him, he was too weak and dazed to react. He must've dropped the flashlight because he couldn't see anything—just swirling darkness—and all he could hear was the loud growling.

He scratched at the man's hairy face, and then he felt the pain in his neck. For a few seconds he didn't know what was happening, and then it set in that the man was biting him.

Growling? Biting him? Hairy face? What the hell?

He tried to free himself, but it was useless. He was too weak and the man was too strong and his mouth was like a clamp. This was it—he was going to die—but he couldn't die now. What about Karen? He had to see Karen tomorrow. His thoughts were becoming distorted, nonsensical, the way they did when he was starting to dream. He was in a lake, floating on his back, and the sun was so warm, and Karen was there. But why did she look so angry? Why was she walking away?

Karen, baby, come back to me! Karrrrrrrren!

TEN

My head's killing me.

That was Simon's first thought when he woke up. His next thought:

Where the hell am I?

He recognized moist rotted leaves, sticks, a large ant crawling by a few inches in front of his face.

He sat up quickly, his headache worsening, but this was the least of his concerns. Jesus Christ, he was in the woods.

He got up quickly, light-headed because his pulse was pounding. He tried to think, make sense of this, but his brain was stuck, his thoughts unable to connect in any logical way. He closed his eyes, took a couple of deep breaths, trying to get hold of himself. No luck there. When he opened his eyes, he was even more terrified and confused. He was freezing too, and then he realized why.

He was naked.

No, God, no, this wasn't happening. This *couldn't* be happening. He held his hands over his private parts, looking around frantically for his

clothes. If he could've cried or shown any emotion aside from sheer terror, he would have been wailing.

Where *was* he?

Okay, he had to focus. Panicking wasn't going to solve anything.
He had to stay calm, in control; if he could just find his underwear,
everything would be okay. Compartmentalizing his predicament made
it more manageable and—at least for the moment—less horrifying.
His underwear had to be here somewhere. He couldn't've just been
plopped into the middle of a forest naked, right? He had to search, but
he couldn't be frantic about it. He had to search *logically*. He decided to
walk, fifty steps in each direction, then go back to his original spot, and
then fifty steps in a slightly different direction, and repeat until he had
covered an area stretching fifty feet in every direction. If his underwear
was somewhere in this area, he'd find it.

This was good—he'd formulated a plan, he was taking charge. Soon
he'd find his underwear and the rest of his clothes and figure out some
way to get out of here—wherever the hell *here* was.

He was shivering, his teeth rattling. It wasn't freezing but it had to
be, what, upper forties? He looked up at the treetops, specks of light
shining through. It was hard to tell what time it was, but it seemed
like morning because he heard birds chirping, but did that really mean
anything? Didn't birds chirp all day long? Why the hell was he thinking
about birds when he needed his goddamn underwear?

How had this happened? *Michael, that bastard*. He knew that
crazy son of a bitch was somehow responsible for this; what other
explanation could there be? Simon's last memory was of being in
the apartment, feeling dazed from that beer. *"Family recipe" my ass.*
Michael was obviously insane, had drugged him and dumped him
out here in the middle of the woods. He was furious with himself
for not trusting his gut about those guys. Yeah, he meant *guys*, plural,
because Charlie and Ramon were just as responsible. Ramon saying,
"It has a kick," and Charlie was the craziest of the three, coming on
as Mr. Supportive and Down-to-Earth when he was just as bonkers.

What was this for them, some kind of practical joke? Were they sitting together now laughing?

Then he had a thought that truly terrified him. Drugged, naked, was it possible that . . . ?

He didn't want to go there, but was encouraged because he didn't feel any unusual pain or soreness. But he knew he wouldn't have taken off his clothes willingly, no matter how drugged they'd gotten him. The guys must've done it; crazy goddamn perverts.

Fueled by anger, Simon walked faster. He was stepping over sharp twigs and branches, but he barely noticed, maybe because his feet were so cold.

He counted, *Forty-nine, fifty*, then returned to his original location. He headed out in a slightly different direction, counting out another fifty steps. After doing this several times he realized he was probably wasting his time. Yeah, he'd cover a chunk of ground, but his clothes could be miles away for all he knew.

He did what he probably should've done right away—he screamed for help. He didn't know how many times he screamed "Help!" and "Help me!"—probably more than a hundred. He stopped when his voice got hoarse and his throat hurt too much to continue. Then it hit him that this could be it, he might actually die out here. He'd read an article online somewhere about how people could survive without water for something like forty-eight hours. There didn't seem to be any lakes or rivers or streams nearby. Maybe he'd find one eventually, but what if he didn't? He had no survival skills. He was a New Yorker, for God's sake. He knew how to hail cabs and order in takeout, and that was about it.

He was convinced this was the end. He'd starve or freeze to death— whichever came first. Jeremy would have to grow up without his dad and Alison would be a thirty-seven-year-old widow. Suddenly he felt responsible for all of their recent problems. Losing his job had been out of his control, but he could've been a better husband. He'd been distant and irritable, the past couple of years especially, and hadn't made as much of an effort to improve his marriage as he could've. He wished he had a chance, just one more chance, to tell Alison how much she meant to him. At least he'd made that payment two weeks ago on his $500,000 life insurance policy. She'd be able to reduce her hours, spend more time with Jeremy. In some ways, his family would be better off with him dead.

Then he noticed something. It was a tiny black object, far in the distance, maybe fifty yards away. It was so far away he didn't know if he was actually seeing it, or if he just thought he was seeing it, but he knew it was there. It was probably nothing, but he walked slowly toward it anyway and then, as he became more encouraged, he walked faster. Then he started jogging and finally running toward it. Maybe it was because he was so excited, or his adrenaline was pumping, but he seemed to be running extremely fast. But it was really there—he wasn't imagining it. An incredible sense of relief and joy overwhelmed him when he reached out and picked up one of his socks.

He was so happy he couldn't hold back and started to cry again. He quickly found the other sock about twenty yards away. Covering his privates with the socks, somehow he knew where the rest of his clothes were; it was almost like he could smell them. Could he smell them? Sure enough, soon he found his T-shirt, and then, thank God, his underwear. He shook some dirt off them and then pulled them on, muttering, "Thank you, thank you, thank you, thank you."

Suddenly, with some hope returning, his brain seemed to be functioning again. His headache had eased and, although he was half naked, he wasn't freezing or even cold anymore. His mouth felt funny though, slightly numb, the way it did a half hour after getting dental work. He continued along, searching for the rest of his clothes. Within a few minutes, he found his pants and leather jacket and one of his shoes. Even better, nothing important seemed to be missing. He had his wallet, keys, and cell phone. The money from the wallet—about sixty bucks—was gone, but that was the least of his concerns. Before he put on his pants, he checked the time—okay, it *was* morning, eight thirty-seven A.M. He figured he drank the beer at ten P.M. last night, which meant he'd "missed" over ten hours. Then he checked the GPS and found his location:

Mendham, New Jersey.

Mendham was in northern Jersey about, what, an hour out of the city? What the hell was he doing here of all places? He didn't have any family in Jersey. His old roommate Ivan from college at Cornell lived in Red Bank, on the Jersey shore, but that was on the opposite side of the state.

Figuring he'd try to unravel the mystery later, he quickly got fully dressed—well, sans one Rockport loafer—and then checked his phone again and saw that he had sixteen missed calls, seven new voice mails, and eight new text messages.

He called home and heard, "Where the hell are you?" Alison sounded angry but also extremely concerned.

"Thank God," Simon said. "You have no idea how good it feels to hear your voice."

"Are you okay?" she asked. "I called you so many times, I think I slept an hour last night. I was ready to start calling hospitals."

"I'm sorry," he said. "But I'm fine. You don't have to worry."

"How come you didn't call? Where *are* you?"

"I don't know," he said.

"You don't know? What do you mean you don't know?"

He was suddenly embarrassed and ashamed for allowing himself to get into this situation, and he didn't want to upset Alison more than he already had. He'd caused enough problems for her lately, what with losing his job and putting a financial strain on the family. He was supposed to be a provider, a father, and now he was unemployed and naked in the woods in God knew where.

No, this was his mess, and he was going to get out of it alone.

"I'm in Brooklyn still," he said. "I guess I had a little too much to drink."

"What do you mean, too much to drink? Where did you go?"

"Just to the brewery. I guess I passed out there."

"You guess?"

"I mean I did."

"Why didn't you call me?"

"I kind of lost track of time." He said this confidently. It was the truth, after all.

"You have no idea how scared I was." She sounded angrier now. "You weren't answering your phone, I was worried something awful happened to you, and Jeremy got really sick."

Simon's heart raced. "Is he okay?"

"I got his fever back down to one oh one, but he has a bad rash. I'm taking him to Dr. Leibner at . . . damn it, I'm running late."

Simon felt awful. "I promise," he said, "nothing like this will ever happen again."

"When are you coming home?"

Looking around, realizing he had no idea how he was going to get out of the woods, he said, "As soon as I can."

"Well, can you pick up milk and toilet paper? And I don't know if Jeremy's going to need any medicine—if he does, I'll text you and you can stop at the pharmacy."

"No problem," Simon said. "Whatever he needs, I'll get it, just let me know. . . . And I love both of you . . . so much." It was hard not to get a little choked up, especially on "so much," but he thought he'd done a good job of hiding it.

After a long pause—Simon imagined her biting on her lower lip and shaking her head, the way she did when she was very annoyed—she said flatly, "I love you too," and clicked off.

Okay, so Simon had his work cut out for him when he got home, but compared to his predicament of just a few minutes ago, when he was naked and thought his life was going to end, being in the doghouse with his wife for a couple of days wasn't exactly a huge concern.

He looked around for the other shoe, but he knew he wasn't going to find it; he just had a hunch it wasn't there. He looked around anyway for a while, then decided, *To hell with it*. He could live without a shoe and he just wanted to get home ASAP.

Without bothering to check the GPS, he started walking very fast.

Cognitively, he had no idea where he was going, but somehow he just knew, instinctively, that he was heading in the right direction, toward the nearest town. Just to make sure, he checked the phone and, sure enough, he was walking toward the town center of Mendham. He had no idea where this sudden great sense of direction was coming from. For years Alison had teased him for being "bad with the map." He was the type of guy who, during family trips, frequently stopped and asked for directions at gas stations and still wound up getting lost.

He wanted to save time and he had a lot of energy, so he ran through the woods. Even with one shoe he was able to run pretty fast, and he wasn't getting winded at all. Must have been adrenaline or stress release because the last time he was in the gym—when was it, last month?—after twenty minutes on one of the elliptical machines, he was gasping.

He saw a clearing in the woods up ahead, and then he reached a road. It was two lanes, occasional cars passing in each direction. He wanted to find some kind of landmark, a store or something, so he could call for a cab or car service. He had no idea which way the closest store was, but he smelled pizza to his right, so he headed in that direction. Whoa, *smelled* pizza? How was that possible? There was nothing along the road up to the nearest bend, maybe two hundred yards ahead. He couldn't possibly smell pizza from so far away. It had to be some kind of hallucination; the way people stranded in a desert imagine that they see lakes and streams, he was smelling pepperoni and anchovies.

He ran along the road and made the turn and then stopped short when he saw the strip mall and Sal's Pizzeria. Okay, this was weird, but then he decided that it had to have just been a lucky guess, or maybe the wind was blowing the pizza odor down the road. There didn't seem to be any wind—the leaves in the trees weren't moving at all—but whatever. He was just glad he was right and had taken another step closer to getting home.

He went into the pizzeria, and the teenage girl working at the cash register gave him the address of the restaurant and the phone number of a car service. He called for a car from his cell and was told it would be there.

The combined aroma of garlic, onions, green pepper, sausage, and of course pepperoni and anchovies was practically overwhelming, and he realized he was starving. At an ATM next door he withdrew two hundred dollars, and then he bought a plain slice, devoured it, and ordered another. He wolfed down the second slice and was still hungry, so he ordered a third with extra sausage and pepperoni. He normally never had pizza with so much meat—it was a cholesterol nightmare—but he had a craving and couldn't resist.

He could've eaten a fourth slice, no problem, but the car arrived. The driver—a young blond guy—explained that it would cost $140 to go to the city. Simon had a feeling he was getting ripped off by at least forty bucks, but what the hell, he wanted to get home.

The cab reeked of Old Spice. Simon didn't mind Old Spice—he used to use it himself actually—but how much had this guy put on? He opened the windows, but the exhaust from the truck ahead of them wasn't any more pleasant, so he closed the window, figuring he'd just have to put up with the Old Spice.

He got a text from Alison:

Leibner thinks it's a virus get more Tylenol

He replied:

Ok!!

The text from Alison was a little on the cold side; still, he was relieved that things at home seemed to be on the mend, but he didn't know exactly how to deal with the situation with Michael and the guys. He wanted to call them right now and chew them out, but he didn't have any contact info. He didn't even know Ramon's and Charlie's last names. He considered looking up Michael Hartman to see if he could get a number, but what exactly was the point? So he'd call Michael and yell at him, curse him out, then what? There was no real way to get revenge. He could call the police, claim he'd been drugged, but did he really want to get into a whole mess with the cops? He wasn't even sure he could prove anything had happened to him, and even if the police did believe him, so what? Michael would probably claim it had been a practical joke. Would the police really do anything to Michael, press any charges, or just let it go with some kind of warning?

Simon ruminated about it during most of the ride, and when the car headed over the George Washington Bridge, entering the city, he still didn't know what to do. He was leaning toward trying to forget about the whole thing. He'd never see Michael or the other guys again, and he'd pretend that they didn't exist and that last night had never happened. Despite his anger, there was no point in trying to get revenge when there was no real revenge to get.

He had the car drop him off in front of a Duane Reade on Broadway. After he bought the stuff Alison had asked for, he headed to his apartment. The odors of the Thai, Chinese, Japanese, Italian, Mexican, Cuban, and Indian restaurants he passed along the way reminded him that he was still starving and the pizza had barely made a dent.

He entered the apartment and announced, "I'm home!"

Coming quickly from the hallway, Alison whispered, "Shh, I just put him down for a nap."

"Oh, sorry," Simon said. "And I'm really sorry." The second sorry was for last night, not for the way he'd arrived.

He could tell she was still angry at him. He went over to her in the dining alcove and kissed her hello. She kissed him back reluctantly.

"You smell great," he said. He didn't mean to say it; he'd blurted it out. But she *did* smell great.

"I do?" She was surprised. "I didn't even have a chance to shower yet today."

Remembering how he'd thought he was going to die earlier and he'd just wanted a chance to see Alison again, he wrapped his arms around her waist and said, "It's so good to see you."

She still seemed pissed off. "Last night was so awful," she said. "You always call."

"I'm so sorry," he said. "I'll never put you through anything like that again, I promise."

"I really thought something happened to you."

"Nothing happened to me," Simon said. "I'm fine. Mmm, do I smell hamburgers?"

"I made Jeremy turkey burgers last night, but he barely ate anything."

"Are there leftovers in the fridge?" Simon had already opened the fridge, though. He took out the plate of turkey burgers and rice and removed the tin foil and started eating, standing up at the kitchen counter.

Alison was saying, "Leibner definitely thinks it's viral. He said if his fever continues, or the sore throat gets worse, to call him and bring him in, but he says it's been going around and he had a bunch of similar cases in his office last . . . What's that?"

She was squinting, looking downward slightly, toward his neck.

"What's what?" Simon said through a mouthful of food. He took another few quick bites, stuffing his mouth again, then went to the mirror in the living room and saw what looked like streaks of blood. "Huh, I don't know." Maybe he'd cut himself last night, when he was running around naked in the woods? Seemed plausible, except there weren't any cuts on his neck, just the red streaks. Then he said, "I know, it's pizza sauce."

"Pizza sauce?"

"Yeah, I had a couple of slices in Jer . . . I mean, downtown, before. I mean, in Brooklyn. I don't know how the sauce got on my neck, though."

He looked closer in the mirror. It didn't look like pizza sauce, it looked like blood. Eh. He'd probably scratched himself when he was running naked in the woods. He was lucky something worse hadn't happened.

"Where's your other shoe?" Alison asked.

"Oh. I, um, lost it."

"How do you lose a shoe?"

"I didn't *lose* it, lose it. I mean I left it at Michael's." He smiled, making it into a joke. "I mean I couldn't find it, but I'm sure it's there some-where, it'll turn up. Sorry, I have to pee like a racehorse."

After he peed, he showered quickly, feeling refreshed and energized. Funny, you'd think after everything he'd been through last night and this morning he'd need to crash, but nope, he was raring to go.

He went to the bedroom and came out, wearing the Ralph Lauren robe Alison had bought him for Valentine's Day a couple of years ago. He'd kidded with her that the robe made him feel like he was James Bond.

Alison was in the kitchen, rinsing some dishes, loading the dish-washer. He entered and said, "Hello, Moneypenny," putting on his best Daniel Craig, but he barely sounded British.

Alison almost smiled. Mmm, she did smell great. It wasn't perfume or even shampoo or conditioner; it was *her*.

"You smell wonderful today," he said, thinking out loud.

She looked at him, surprised, as if thinking, *Where's this coming from?* Then she said, "Thank you."

She continued with the dishes and he watched her, admiring the curve of her heart-shaped ass in the Gap bootleg jeans, the muscle tone in her forearms and biceps, the way a few short strands of her wavy brown hair fell over her forehead right above eye level, and, of course, her wonderful scent. What was up with him and his sense of smell today?

Maybe it was because this morning he'd thought he'd never see her again, but he suddenly appreciated Alison in a way he hadn't in a long time.

He came up behind her, grabbed her hips firmly, and pressed up against her. Then he closed his eyes and breathed in, savoring her unique essence, and said, "Mmmmm." Then, "Is Jeremy asleep?"

Alison turned off the water and said, "Yeah, he was exhausted, poor thing. But what're—"

"How're you feeling?" he asked.

Getting his meaning immediately, she asked, "Now?"

"What's wrong with now?"

He was kissing her neck, using his teeth a little.

"Wow," she said. "That feels so good."

He continued kissing and sucking on her neck. He couldn't get enough of her.

She said, "You don't have to do this just because you think I'm mad at you."

He kissed and sucked her neck harder, then moved higher, to her ear, nibbling on the lobe.

"Wow, that feels so good." She moaned softly, the way she did when she was starting to get turned on. "What's gotten into you?"

He didn't answer. He wanted her so badly.

He turned her around and backed her up against the fridge. While kissing her, he reached under her T-shirt, worked his hand up her already sticky back, and undid her bra. Then he shifted his hand back around, cupping one of her breasts. He felt her nipple harden against his palm.

She managed to get her mouth away from his just long enough to say, "We can't."

He massaged his pelvis against hers, wanting her to feel how ready he was for her. "Why not?" he asked.

He didn't let her answer, kissing her, biting on her lower lip a little while grinding up against her.

Then she pushed him back with her hands against his chest and said, "Jeremy could come out of his room."

He knew she was right, but he didn't stop.

Then she was able to get her mouth free again and said, "Let's go."

She took him by the hand and led him to their bedroom. Normally, she took control during sex. That was just the way it had always been. She was the initiator, and their favorite position was woman on top. So it was a little unusual when Simon pushed her onto the bed, onto her back, and mounted her. But she didn't seem to mind. As he pinned her down and continued kissing her neck and face, she wrapped her legs around his waist and let him take charge.

* * *

About half an hour later, he was on his back and she was curled into him, resting her head on his sweaty shoulder and chest.

"Wow, that was incredible," she said. Her eyes were closed and she was starting to doze, but she was still smiling.

Without a doubt, it had been the most passionate, most energetic sex they'd had in a long time, maybe ever. Alison would agree that they'd never been a very sexual couple, but in addition to not having enough sex lately, the quality of the sex had definitely declined over the years. It was usually rushed, a little awkward, and—though Simon would never go as far as to describe it as boring—it was certainly predictable. It was almost like they knew each other too well. They knew what positions they liked, what turned them on and what didn't, and there was no variation. Simon admitted that the problem was mostly his. Alison often made suggestions of new things to try, and had even brought home sex toys and provocative lingerie, but Simon just couldn't get into it. He usually blamed it on job stress, but sometimes he wondered if she was right and he did have a libido problem, or some kind of hormone imbalance, because he just didn't have the interest in improving their sex life that he probably should've.

Until today.

Today it had been completely different. He was suddenly incredibly horny and passionate and virile. But the biggest change was how he'd behaved mentally. He was usually passive in bed; when something didn't feel good he would just wait for her to decide to do something else. Today he'd told her exactly where to put her hands and how he liked to be kissed and touched. He'd taken control in a way he'd never taken control before, and he had to admit it had felt great.

"Why don't we do this more often?" Alison asked, shifting a little to kiss his shoulder, right above his armpit.

"I don't know," he said, squishing against her closer, hugging her a little tighter.

"Well, we should," she said. "Especially on weekends. We're both home and Jeremy usually takes a nap. It's a perfect time to be together."

"Deal," he said.

They were silent for a while. It was nice being together like this in the middle of the day, and she was right, they *should* do this more often. He could tell, by the sounds of her breathing, that she was starting to doze, but, despite everything he'd been through last night and this morning and a round of energetic sex, he was alert and awake, as if he'd just had a strong cup of coffee.

"Promise me," she said. She was almost asleep. Her voice was soft, barely audible.

"Promise you what?"

"What?" She was disoriented.

"You wanted me to promise you something."

"I did?" She opened her eyes. "Oh . . . Promise me . . . Promise me you'll never do that to me again."

"Do what again?" He was confused; had he done something during sex that she hadn't liked? He was much more aggressive than normal, but she'd seemed into it. He said, "I thought you thought it was wonderful."

"What?" she said, confused. She'd closed her eyes again. Then she added, "No, I meant about last night. I was so worried about you, you have no idea. Promise me . . . Promise me, you'll never . . ." Her voice was fading. ". . . scare me like that . . . again."

"Promise," he said.

She was asleep. He held her, gently twirling pieces of her hair, and then he felt something and could hardly believe it. Having great sex and taking charge was one thing, but what was happening now was almost unprecedented. After all, they'd only finished having sex, what, five minutes ago? He shifted and pulled up the covers; nope, it wasn't a false alarm. He was ready for another round.

ELEVEN

Simon was so horny he considered waking up Alison, but she was sleeping so soundly he decided against it. He distracted himself by thinking about the usual—basketball. Didn't work. If anything, thoughts of all that physicality and aggression got him *more* aroused. He thought about last night with the guys at the brewery, waking up in the woods naked, and how angry he'd been. Then he started thinking about Tom Harrison and the work situation; that got him soft in a hurry, but he knew it wouldn't last for long. He felt such a strong attraction to Alison that it seemed impossible to be near her without getting turned on.

Then Simon heard Jeremy stirring in his room, so he got out of bed quietly, put on boxer briefs and a T-shirt, and went down the hallway.

Jeremy was just starting to wake up, and Simon wondered how he'd heard him stir. The master bedroom was down the hallway from Jeremy's room, and Simon and Alison usually never heard him when both doors were closed unless he screamed at the top of his lungs. When he was younger they'd had to use a baby monitor to hear him.

Simon sat on the bed and felt Jeremy's forehead.

"Cool as a cucumber," Simon said, smiling.

Jeremy sat up immediately and asked, "Where's Mommy?"

"Sleeping," Simon said, "so how're you feeling, kiddo?"

"I don't know," he said.

"You have to know. Are you feeling tired? Do you want to go back to sleep?"

"Let's play basketball," Jeremy said, getting out of bed and grabbing the Nerf ball from atop the dresser.

"I guess that means no," Simon said.

They took turns shooting baskets. Despite being sick, or recovering from being sick, Jeremy had his usual unbridled three-year-old energy. He was dashing around the room, chasing after the ball. Usually Simon sat on the bed and took a couple of shots, then watched Jeremy play, but today he had more energy than his three-year-old son, and he was chasing after the ball too, moving practically nonstop.

Finally Jeremy, clearly exhausted, asked, "Do we have to keep playing, Daddy?"

Simon realized that running his son around while his body was still fighting off a virus probably hadn't been such a great idea.

"I know, how about a food break?" Simon asked. "Hungry?"

"I don't know," Jeremy said.

"*I don't know* means yes," Simon said. "Come on."

Talk of food reminded Simon that he was still famished. Jeremy's leftover dinner from last night was still on the kitchen counter, and Simon gobbled it up in several poorly chewed bites.

"How about peanut butter and jelly?" Simon asked.

"I don't know," Jeremy said.

"I'll make you a sandwich. You can watch TV meanwhile. I TiVo'd *The Wiggles*."

"Yay."

Simon wondered what was up with him and his appetite today. He felt like he could keep eating nonstop and still wouldn't get full. While he made Jeremy's sandwich, he made one for himself, globbing on the peanut butter until it was about an inch thick. Simon ate his sandwich standing up and then served Jeremy his with a glass of milk.

After a bite or two Jeremy announced that he was full. Then he said, "I want to go outside and play."

"You can't," Simon said, "not when you had a fever last night. You have to be fever-free for twenty-four hours before you can go out."

Jeremy made a sad face.

Simon had to admit—he was pretty bummed too. Lately he'd been a homebody, especially on weekends, content to hang out and watch TV or goof off on the Internet. But now he felt extremely antsy and cooped up. He was in a good-sized two-bedroom apartment in Manhattan, but he might as well have been trapped in a cage.

They stayed in watching more *Wiggles* and then playing Candy Land, but Simon found it hard to keep still and kept getting up between turns to stretch and sometimes do push-ups and jumping jacks.

Very late in the afternoon, Alison came into the living room, went right over to Jeremy, and said to Simon, "How is he?"

"Much better," Simon said. "His fever's way down."

Alison felt Jeremy's forehead with her lips and said, "You're right, it is down." She pulled up his shirt and checked his stomach. "The rash is going away too. Thank God."

"I'm gonna go for a run in the park," Simon said.

Alison narrowed her eyes, surprised. "Now?"

"Yeah, I just need to get out of the apartment, get some air. I won't be gone long."

Simon kissed Alison, then jogged into the bedroom. He came out a few minutes later in sweatpants and a hooded sweatshirt, and with his sneakers on. Alison was sitting at the table with Jeremy, playing picture dominoes.

Simon said, "I think I'll stop at Whole Foods on the way back and pick up some stuff."

"I just went shopping a few days ago," Alison said. "I think we're good till tomorrow."

"It's okay, I'll just swing by there after my run," Simon said.

"What is it with you and your energy today?" She gave him a flirty, knowing look. "Not that I'm complaining."

He kissed her good-bye, noticing that she smelled like sex, and then he left the apartment quickly, before he got too turned on.

On the elevator, he jogged in place, and then he ran out of the building. He wondered if he was making a mistake not stretching. He'd had some lower back problems in the past and had injured his right knee playing tennis and it had never completely healed. He didn't feel like stopping, though, and besides he felt extremely loose and pain-free.

He ran uptown, then along the path around the reservoir. Although it was dusk, the path was still very active with joggers going at varying speeds. Simon was barely aware that he was running, as he was preoccupied with how wonderful it felt to be outside, breathing in the relatively fresh air of Central Park. Although he could still detect some city pollution, the crisp autumn air was dominated by the scents of fallen leaves and manure from the bridle path nearby. He was also extremely attuned to the other sounds around him—crunching footsteps on the gravelly path, the wind in the trees, snippets of conversation from other joggers.

He realized he was running very fast. He hadn't gone jogging outside in ages, but on the treadmill at the gym he ran at level 5.0, which was basically fast walking. Now he ran without much effort, weaving in and out of other joggers, and didn't feel any of the usual tightness in his back or soreness in his knee. When he went into an all-out sprint, he felt a little winded, so he slowed to a pace that was still about twice as fast as he'd ever been able to maintain before. He'd never gone more than one lap around the reservoir—one lap was almost a mile and a half—but after one lap he didn't feel tired at all, so he did another lap, and then decided, *What the hell?* and did a third lap. He could have done a fourth but it was pitch-black and he didn't want Alison to worry about him, especially after he'd been out all last night.

He exited the park at West Ninety-sixth. Jogging in place at the intersection of Central Park West, he texted Alison—*be home in 15*—and then ran a couple more blocks to the Whole Foods on Columbus.

As when he was outside in the park, in the store he was very aware of the rich scents around him. The cheeses in particular stood out. There were so many varieties, and each had its own unique aroma. It was overwhelming, like walking into a greenhouse at a botanical garden and breathing in the scents of all the flowers and plants at once. He'd been in this store so many times and hadn't appreciated any of this, probably because he'd been so preoccupied with job stress, marital stress, and whatever other problems were gnawing on his subconscious. Now he felt like he'd been freed and could pay more attention to details he usually overlooked.

After he picked out a couple of cheeses—the Stilton and Maytag Blue were irresistibly pungent—he went right to the meats section, as if a force were pulling him there. He didn't know where this sudden craving for meat was coming from; it was especially unusual for a guy who normally ate meat so infrequently he was practically a vegetarian. Then he remembered Michael serving the steak last night and how great it had tasted. The memory increased his craving, making his desire for meat almost unbearable. He didn't just want to have meat; he *had* to have it.

He added several packages of beef sirloin flap steak and flat iron steak to his cart, and a few packages of chop meat. The lamb chops looked enticing, so he added them too. He couldn't resist the link sausages either—he could smell the meat and spices through the packaging.

When he got home, before he put the groceries away, he opened two packages of flap steak. He had no idea how to cook steak, so he just put two of them in a large frying pan and turned on the heat.

Alison, who'd been playing with Jeremy in his room, came into the kitchen and said, "What's going on out here?"

"Just cooking up some dinner."

"Steak?" Alison, who was an actual vegetarian, sounded almost appalled.

"Just had a craving, that's all."

Looking in the pan, she said, "You're going to eat all of that?"

"I built up an appetite from running."

She checked to make sure that Jeremy wasn't within earshot, then said, "Speaking of building up an appetite, you were amazing before. But where is this coming from?"

Simon, noticing that she still smelled deliciously like sex, said, "It's coming from me."

"But you've barely touched me lately, and suddenly you're all over me. You have to admit it's a big change."

"Maybe I'm just finally appreciating what a wonderful wife I have." He kissed her.

She pulled back and said, "We better not start anything we can't finish."

"Who says we can't finish?"

"You don't want your steak to burn."

Jeremy entered and said, "Hi."

Alison let go of Simon and said to Jeremy, "Let's get those hands washed." Then she whispered to Simon, "To be continued." She moved away quickly and opened the cupboard to take out plates and announced, "Dinnertime's in five minutes."

Five minutes later the family sat for dinner at the dining room table. Jeremy had macaroni and cheese, Alison had salad and reheated lentil soup from the other night, and Simon had the two pieces of steak on his plate and nothing else.

"Don't you want anything with it?" Alison asked.

"This is how we had it last night," Simon said. "It wasn't bad."

"You're having steak two nights in a row?"

"Come on," Simon said. "It's steak. It's not like I'm developing a cocaine habit."

"What's cocaine?" Jeremy asked.

"I said Coca-Cola," Simon said. "It's a soft drink."

"Why is it soft?"

"Where did you have steak?" Alison asked.

"Michael made steaks last night."

"Wow, that was nice of him."

"Why is it soft?" Jeremy asked again.

"Soda," Simon said. "It's another name for soda."

Simon suddenly remembered the beer Michael had served him, and how he'd probably drugged him as well and dumped him in the woods. Funny, Simon had almost managed to block out the whole experience already.

"Yeah," Simon said through gritted teeth. "Very nice."

"Maybe serving steak alone is trendy or something," Alison said. "Maybe Michael saw somebody do it on Food TV."

"Is Michael the man with the gray hair?" Jeremy asked.

"Yes," Simon said.

"When am I gonna see my friends again?"

"I'm sorry, we're not going to see them anymore."

Jeremy looked sad and shocked.

"Why not?" Alison asked.

"No reason," Simon said.

"But why—"

"I really don't want to discuss it right now." He was purposely curt, trying to end the conversation.

"Oh, I'm just surprised, that's all," Alison said. "I mean it sounds like you had a good time with them. You slept over at that guy Michael's place, for God's sake."

"It wasn't Michael's place . . . it was his brewery."

"Whatever, it sounds like it was fun . . . and Jeremy loves his new friends."

"I want to see them," Jeremy said, frowning.

"I just don't want to discuss it right now," Simon said, implying that he didn't want to have this conversation in front of Jeremy.

Alison got the hint and let it go. But later, after they'd put Jeremy to sleep and Simon was in the bathroom brushing his teeth, she came in and said, "So I don't get it, why don't you want to see your friends anymore?"

Through a mouthful of toothpaste, Simon said, "They're not my friends."

"They're acquaintances, at least," Alison said. "Did you have some kind of falling-out?"

Simon, continuing to brush his teeth, didn't answer.

"I can tell you don't want to talk about it," Alison said. "It's just too bad for Jeremy, because he likes those boys and it's not like you've been taking him on a lot of play dates with his other friends."

Simon rinsed, spit, and said, "You mean Matthew? I tried, but he has a new babysitter and she seemed a little . . . well, she didn't seem into having any more play dates."

"What about William? His mom takes him to that playground in Riverside sometimes."

"I'm not going to hang out with a bunch of moms all day," Simon said. "Besides, William hits Jeremy."

"He hit him once."

"I'm not going on play dates with William." He realized that had sounded a bit harsh, so he rephrased it. "I mean, I really don't want to, okay? But we'll find some new friends, I'm sure. Just leave it to me."

"Okay, that's fine," Alison said. "I'm just saying, Jeremy needs to be around kids his age during the day. I saw some dads hanging out in the kids section at Barnes and Noble the other day. Maybe you should hang out there."

"That's a good idea," Simon said. "Maybe I'll do that."

He just wanted to end the conversation, and it worked, as Alison went into the bedroom. He still felt bad for being so curt with her, but he felt like she was pressuring him to get together with Michael and those guys again, and there was no way in hell he was doing that.

After he washed his face, he looked in the mirror and stuck out his tongue. Was he imagining it or did his tongue look redder than usual? It also felt rough and numb, kind of like he'd scalded it by drinking hot liquid, but he hadn't had any hot liquid. His gums were still a little numb and his mouth was sore, maybe from chewing so hard on the steak. He'd polished off both steaks, yet he was still hungry.

Alison was in bed, reading *Allure*. Simon breathed in deeply, enjoying the scent of her skin, slightly annoyed that it was mingling with the scents of all the perfume samples in the magazine. He wanted to smell just her and nothing else.

"You smell so amazing," Simon said. "I can smell you forever and never get tired of it."

"Why, thank you," she said, blushing.

He wanted her. Badly.

She looked up from the magazine and recognized his lustful gaze immediately. How could she miss it? He probably looked like he wanted to devour her.

"Again?" she asked. She smelled unbearably good.

He didn't answer, just got in bed and started making love to her.

Simon woke up squinting because some horizontal bars of sunlight were seeping through the blinds, shining right on him. Although he didn't feel like he'd slept well—he felt like he'd been hovering above sleep all night, like when he was overcaffeinated—he felt fully rested.

"Time is it?" Alison asked groggily as Simon got out of bed.

"Six fifteen," Simon said.

"On *Sunday*? What're you doing up?"

"I'm not tired; go back to sleep."

Starving, he went to the kitchen and cooked the entire package of sausages—eight thick links. He was so hungry that he ate a couple of the links standing up in front of the stove, before they were fully cooked. He put the rest on a plate and was eating them at the dining room table when Alison came out of the bedroom in panties and a long T-shirt and said, "Check out the carnivore. What is it with you and meat this weekend?"

"I don't know," Simon said, and it was the truth—he had no idea what was happening.

Jeremy slept late—for him—waking up after nine o'clock. But after the good night's sleep his fever was still gone, and he seemed one hundred percent recovered. Simon suggested they have a family day, and Alison thought that was a great idea.

Later, they were riding down in the elevator when the woman with the brown Labrador retriever got in on the fifth floor. The dog was usually friendly and liked to be petted, but for some reason today when Simon said, "Hey there," the dog cowered away and hid behind its owner.

"I guess everybody has their shy days, huh?" Simon said.

"Not Maxie," the woman said. "What's wrong with you today, Maxie?"

In the lobby, the woman had to practically drag the whimpering dog out of the building.

It was a drizzly, chilly morning, but Simon didn't mind the weather at all. He walked, pushing the stroller, with his jacket open, enjoying the cool breeze against his chest. They had put the plastic covering over the stroller. Alison, holding the umbrella, asked Simon if he wanted to get under with her, but he refused. He liked the cold wetness against his face. It was refreshing, invigorating.

They went to the Museum of Natural History because Jeremy wanted to dig for dinosaur bones in the Discovery Room. Instead of watching the kids play as he normally did, Simon got in there with Jeremy and dug with him. Jeremy used a little stick and brush but Simon used both hands, digging very fast, removing dirt that would've taken the kids forever with their tools. Simon was lost for a while in the joy of playing with his son, and then looked over and saw Alison and the other parents watching him with ambiguous expressions; he couldn't tell if they were perplexed or amused.

After the museum they went to lunch at an Indian restaurant on Columbus. It was buffet style and Simon gravitated to the protein-heavy chicken and lamb dishes. He must've made six or seven trips to refill his plate and he was still hungry.

The skies cleared and it had turned into a sunny, mild afternoon, so they went to the park. Full of energy, Simon chased Jeremy on the paths and on any grassy areas they passed and carried him on his shoulders. They went on the carousel and then Jeremy wanted to climb the rocks near Wollman Rink.

"Okay, let's go," Simon said.

"You sure?" Alison asked.

He understood why she was surprised. *He* was the one who was usually paranoid about letting Jeremy take risks in the park and playground, and it was Alison who often told him that he was being overly cautious.

Holding hands, Simon and Jeremy climbed the rocks. At one point Jeremy hesitated, obviously scared to stretch across the space between rocks even though Simon was holding his outstretched hand.

"It's okay," Simon said. "Daddy has you."

Jeremy leaned forward, then leaped to the other rock and landed safely. He looked exhilarated.

"Careful, you two," Alison called out from below.

They went higher, to the top of the highest rock, where they had a great view of Wollman Rink below and the Plaza Hotel and the midtown skyscrapers.

Simon crouched down on all fours at the precipice of the rock and said to Jeremy, "Do you want to see me jump?"

"Yeah, jump, jump!"

"What're you doing?" Alison said from below.

He must've been twenty feet off the ground. He knew jumping was a bad idea, that he could easily break something.

"Jump, Daddy."

"Simon," Alison said.

Simon remained crouched, looking at the ground. At first he hesitated—it was too far, he could kill himself—but then he was convinced he could make it. Without thinking about it any further, he leaped off the rock. He landed hard on his feet, and even though he tried to cushion the fall by bending his knees on impact, he was expecting the pain to set in, especially in his lower back and bum knee. But, surprisingly, he felt fine. Like a kid who'd just gone on an exciting ride at an amusement park, he wanted to do it again, but as he ran to the other side of the rock he noticed that Alison wasn't there.

"Ally?"

No answer. Then he saw her heading down the rocks, holding Jeremy's hand. She looked furious.

Simon was confused. "What? What did I do?"

"I'm so angry at you right now."

"Why? I have no idea what—"

"You left him up there alone. What if he fell off? He could've broken his neck."

He realized she was probably right. He couldn't believe he'd been so thoughtless.

When Alison reached the bottom, still holding Jeremy's hand, she didn't even make eye contact with Simon. She just walked right by him as if he weren't there.

Simon hurried to catch up and said, "Look, I'm sorry, okay? I'll never do anything like that again."

The rest of the way home they talked to Jeremy but not to each other. Simon felt awful, but he knew that trying to talk to Alison when she was upset wouldn't get him anywhere and would only make things worse.

He waited until they were back at the apartment, in the living room, and Jeremy was in the bathroom. "I'm sorry," he said. "I don't know what else you want me to say."

"I don't understand," she said. "Why did you do it?"

"I don't know," he said.

"I've never seen you do anything like that before. You're always ultra careful on the rocks and now you're leaving Jeremy up there alone and *jumping* off them?"

"Look," he said, "I acknowledge that leaving Jeremy up there while I jumped was a mistake, okay? I screwed up and, believe me, I really do feel awful about it. But let's not overexaggerate this. I mean, I jumped from a rock, not an airplane."

"Still, it was weird. It's like you're suddenly acting so hyper. Where's all this energy coming from?"

"You didn't seem to be complaining last night."

He smiled, trying to ease the tension. It worked, as she couldn't help almost smiling herself.

"No, I have no complaints about *that*."

He seized the moment, hugging her tightly. Then, seeing her cringe, he realized he was holding her too tightly and loosened his grip. With his face maybe an inch away from hers—he could smell the rosemary and curry and cardamom on her breath even though her mouth was closed—he said, "Don't worry, I promise I'll never jump from high rocks again, especially when Jeremy's up there. I can't believe I did that. I feel awful."

After a spicy, openmouthed kiss, she said, "It's probably just stress related. Maybe you need a break from full-time parenting."

"A break? But I've only been doing it for what, a couple of weeks?"

"Maybe I can take a week's vacation next month."

"But you've been trying to accrue vacation days so we can go to Maine next August."

"How are we supposed to afford Maine? Have you seen the checking account lately?"

"It sounds like *you're* the one who's stressed."

She breathed deeply. "You're right. I guess having a money conversation on a Sunday afternoon isn't the best idea, is it?"

"Do you think Jeremy wants to take a nap?" Simon asked suggestively, wrapping his arms around her waist.

"I'm afraid I'm out of commission in that department," she said. "My body's just not used to all this activity."

"I guess being stressed does have some perks," he said, and they both smiled.

"I think we missed the window for a nap today anyway," she said. "If he naps this late he'll never get to sleep tonight."

Later, Alison and Jeremy were on the couch, watching some G-rated movie about a dog who was also a detective. Simon wasn't sure, but he thought he'd seen it.

Feeling pent-up again, Simon announced that he was going to the gym. Alison shot him a surprised look, but Simon ignored it and left the apartment.

Simon was a member of New York Sports Club and usually went to the one on Ninety-fourth and Broadway. Well, *usually* probably wasn't the best word to describe his exercising habits, because his gym schedule was erratic at best. When he was working, he'd tried to get to the gym four days a week but was lucky if he made it one or two. Lately, since he'd become a stay-at-home dad, he'd been so exhausted in the evenings that he hadn't gone at all.

As before he went running yesterday, he felt loose and didn't bother stretching. He went to a bench press machine. Normally he did three sets of 70 pounds and went on to another machine. Today, though, 70 pounds felt like he hadn't even put the pin in. He moved it to 90, then 110, then 120, then 130. At 140 he felt it, but he was still able to do ten reps. What the hell was going on? Was the machine broken? Didn't seem like it. When he was through, another guy—about twenty-five, in noticeably great shape, with cut arms and shoulders—used the machine and was struggling with the pin at 90.

Simon used several more machines and also seemed to be able to handle an unusually high amount of weight.

A bulging bodybuilder-type guy standing nearby saw and said, impressed, "Way to go, bro."

Simon walked away, his heart racing, not because he was tired—because he was panicking. Alison was right—something odd was happening and he had no idea what it was. It was true he'd been under a lot of stress lately, but stress didn't increase your energy and make you stronger. Besides, he'd been under stress for days—hell, weeks—and these strange changes had been happening only over the past couple of days, since the night at the brewery.

Suddenly he couldn't get a deep breath. He was standing still, but his heart was pounding as if he were in a full sprint. He felt tightness in his chest—maybe muscle strain from using the bench press machine, but how did he know it wasn't something much worse? The words *heart attack* were somewhere in his consciousness, but he was trying to ignore them. Although it felt as if he were dying, he knew that wasn't possible. He was young—well, young*ish*—and in good shape.

Or was he?

Maybe all the exercise he'd been getting was too much for his body to handle. Didn't young basketball players, in the best shape of their lives, sometimes collapse on the court? He could *hear* his heart pounding and he could barely breathe. He rushed into the men's bathroom and splashed cold water onto his face, trying to get hold of himself. Even if this wasn't a heart attack, he knew something awful was happening. Maybe he was having a stroke or had a brain tumor. Wasn't a warning sign of brain cancer a change in appetite? Well, he definitely had that symptom. And what about his increased sense of hearing and smell? Weren't those symptoms too?

"You feeling okay, bro?"

He looked in the mirror and saw the muscle head behind him.

Simon tried to say, *Help me,* but couldn't get enough air in his lungs. He needed air—fresh air. Not this stale, health club bathroom air that reeked of urine and sweat.

Suddenly he was out on the sidewalk, in front of the health club, but he had no idea how he'd gotten there. Oh God, was he suffering from memory loss now? Everything was white, distorted. He had to get to a hospital.

He hailed a cab, opened the door, and said, "St. Luke's Hospital," to the driver, then rethought it and said, "Never mind," and got out.

He realized he was having a panic attack. He'd had them before— like that time six years ago when he and Alison were visiting friends in Seattle and Simon was convinced he'd eaten tainted salmon and he insisted on going to the ER at two in the morning. But he'd worked on the problem and hadn't had a panic attack in years.

He stood in front of the health club, leaning against the building in case he lost his balance or passed out or both. A few passersby asked him if he was okay or needed help, but he waved them away.

Eventually, after about ten minutes, he felt a little better. At least the whiteness was gone and he could get a full breath. He knew he was okay, that he wasn't going to die, but just in case he was going to make an appointment to see his doctor as soon as possible, hopefully tomorrow morning.

"How was your workout?" Alison asked when he entered the apartment.

"Great," he said, and went directly into the bathroom, into the shower.

The massage feature helped knead out some of the stress from his neck and shoulders. Funny—he didn't feel worn-out the way he did after past panic attacks. He actually felt pretty good.

From the bathroom Simon smelled dinner cooking—a stir-fry of onions, peppers, tofu, and was that mushrooms? When he went out to the kitchen, Alison was cooking at the stove. He saw that he'd nailed the ingredients, including the mushrooms.

At dinnertime, although he was craving meat again, he stuck to the stir-fry, determined to get over this phase, or whatever it was. His improved sense of smell was truly amazing, though. From across the table he could tell that Alison had washed Jeremy's hair earlier with Johnson & Johnson baby shampoo. He also could tell that Alison had used that new moisturizing cream with aloe and some other coconut-based cream, probably on her hands. But nothing she had put on could disguise the smell of sex. It was getting him excited again, and he had to keep his legs crossed tightly during the entire meal to avoid getting an erection.

Jeremy went to bed at his usual time, seven forty-five, and Alison watched TV on the couch for a while, then announced she was exhausted and going to bed before ten. Tomorrow was the beginning of a workweek for her, and she had to get up early.

Simon wasn't tired at all, though. It was just the opposite; he was raring to go. He did multiple sets of sit-ups, but couldn't exhaust himself, and then easily did fifty push-ups, when his usual limit was about twelve.

He'd been physically active for the past thirty-six or so hours, and he hadn't gone online or checked the Internet at all. With the hope that staring at a computer screen for a while might tire him out and get him sleeping, he sat on the couch in the living room and booted up his laptop.

After he mindlessly skimmed a few of the top news stories, he checked his e-mail. He scanned a message from his cousin Craig—a forwarded joke that wasn't very funny—and a coupon offer from Redbox, then scrolled to a message from marosen76@yahoo.com with the subject *Did you hear?* He didn't recognize the address and thought it might be spam. He was going to just delete it but then decided to open it, just to see what it was:

Hi Simon,

Writing from my home e-mail. Don't know if you heard the awful news about Tom. I'm still in shock. Haven't heard anything about funeral arrangements yet, but when I do I'll let you know. Anyway, just wanted to let you know in case you hadn't heard yet.

Mark

Simon reread the e-mail from his ex-assistant about a dozen times, but it still didn't seem real. Awful news about Tom? Funeral arrangements? Agonizingly, the note had no details. Tom was actually *dead*? How did it happen? Was it a car accident? A heart attack or stroke? Jesus, Tom's family. Simon had met his wife, JoAnne, several times, at the annual Christmas party one year and a few other times, and she'd seemed like a great woman. Oh, God, and his poor kids. The guy had the perfect suburban family and then, boom, it had all been destroyed.

Suddenly Simon's recent problems seemed so petty in comparison. Their differences aside, Tom was a good guy and didn't deserve to die. Yeah, life was unfair, but this was beyond unfair. This was downright cruel.

Simon went into Jeremy's bedroom, kissed him on the forehead, and whispered, "I love you so much." Then he went into his own bedroom, where Alison was sleeping facing him, snoring gently, and he kissed her and said, "I love you, honey." She mumbled, "I love you too," and fell back asleep.

He returned to the PC. He wanted more details about what had happened. He was going to e-mail Mark or call him but figured he'd look online first and see if there was any news about it.

There was more coverage than he'd expected—an entire page of results from online versions of papers including the *New York Daily News*, the *New York Post*, and the *Newark Star-Ledger*. If Simon hadn't been in such a manic state he probably would have heard about Tom's death yesterday.

He read a few of the short articles, which contained pretty much the same information: Tom Harrison, executive VP of the ad agency Smythe & O'Greeley, had been mauled to death by an animal, perhaps a large dog, outside his home in Bernardsville, New Jersey. According to the articles, Tom and his wife were awakened by their dog's barking at around midnight on Saturday morning, and Tom went out to investigate when he was attacked. His wife discovered the body and called 911, but Tom was pronounced dead at the scene. There wasn't much more information about the attack except that the police and the New Jersey Division of Fish, Game and Wildlife were investigating the incident. All of the articles were dated Saturday, and there didn't seem to be any follow-up stories on Sunday.

Reading about the incident, Simon was shocked and horrified and realized his mouth was actually sagging open. Jesus, mauled to death by a dog—what a horrible way to go. Then, all of a sudden, he was overwhelmed by guilt. He'd always believed in karma, and he felt awful about all of the anger he'd had toward Tom lately about the firing. If he hadn't put all that negative energy out there, maybe that dog wouldn't have attacked Tom. Though, rationally, Simon realized that this logic was ridiculous, on some deep, primal level it seemed to make perfect sense.

He was rereading the article from the *Star-Ledger* to see if he had missed any details when he came across part of a line that made his whole body tense up: "Harrison left his house in Bernardsvile in northern New Jersey . . ." All the articles mentioned that Tom lived in Bernardsville, but Simon had been reading quickly and was so overwhelmed by the news of Tom's death that he hadn't paid much attention to the details or made the obvious connection:

Tom had been killed in northern New Jersey, early Saturday morning, and Simon had woken up in the woods in northern New Jersey early Saturday morning.

Simon wasn't sure what to make of this weird coincidence, but just out of curiosity he went to Google Maps and typed in "Bernardsville, New Jersey." He'd heard of Bernardsville but wasn't exactly sure where it was. He expected to find that it was in a completely different part of northern New Jersey from where he'd been that night, maybe a hundred miles away. What was the name of the town where he'd called for the car service? Men-something. Mendham, yeah, that was it.

A map of Bernardsville appeared. Then he zoomed out and suddenly felt like he was back in the gym, having another panic attack.

Bernardsville was the next town over from Mendham.

TWELVE

Simon stared at the map on the screen for maybe five minutes, trying to make sense of what he was seeing. He saw Mendham, New Jersey, where he had called for the car service, and the next town was Bernardsville. Maybe there were two Mendhams or different ways to spell it and he was making some mistake. He knew he was just kidding himself, though—there was one Mendham and he had been there. But how was it possible that he'd been so close to Tom's house? If Michael and the guys had taken him into the woods as some kind of incredibly unfunny practical joke, how had they randomly chosen a spot to dump him so close to where his ex-boss lived?

The whole situation, from being dumped naked in the woods to Tom's being killed by some rabid animal, seemed so surreal, so totally out there, that Simon wondered whether any of this was actually happening. Maybe hallucinations were another symptom of whatever had been going on with him lately. Maybe he was imagining sitting in front of the PC now, or dreaming it. Maybe he was actually still in the woods or in Michael's brewery.

He closed his eyes and counted to ten, telling himself that if this was all a construct of his mind, when he reached ten and opened his eyes he'd return to wherever he actually was. He knew he was acting childishly, but he did it anyway and when he reached ten there was actual suspense as he expected to open his eyes and see Michael, Charlie, and Ramon. But, alas, he was still in front of the PC, staring at the *Star-Ledger* story.

Counting had calmed him, though, and he was able to think more logically. Yes, it was a bizarre coincidence that he'd been in the area where Tom had been killed, but coincidences happened. A friend of his once went on a trip to China and ran into an old girlfriend. If you could run into an old girlfriend in China, you could wake up naked in the woods near where your ex-boss was mauled to death. If anything, Simon realized, he should feel lucky. After all, a rabid dog had been in the woods near where Simon had passed out. Simon was fortunate that *he* hadn't been killed.

One positive thing about this news—the stress was wearing Simon out and he was finally feeling drowsy. Tomorrow he'd call Mark, get some more details. If Simon had still been working at S&O, he definitely would have attended the funeral. But, given what had transpired between him and Tom, Simon wasn't sure what was the appropriate thing to do, and he figured he'd deal with it in the morning.

He got into bed with Alison but couldn't get comfortable. He loved being next to her, but her scent was arousing him too much and he knew he'd never be able to fall asleep. So he took his pillow with him into the living room and crashed on the couch.

As during the night before, he didn't sleep soundly, but he slept well. He felt fully rested when Alison came into the living room in the morning and said, "You slept here all night?"

He knew it would seem weird if he told her he was too turned on to sleep next to her, so he said, "Yeah, just a little insomnia, that's all. I fell asleep in front of the TV."

"Oh, I'm sorry," Alison said. "You should've woken me up. I would've given you one of my Ambiens."

"Thanks," Simon said, "but you know how I hate taking that stuff."

Alison went into the kitchen to put on a pot of coffee. When she returned, Simon was sitting up on the couch. It was amazing how wide awake he was already. Normally he needed two cups of strong coffee just to build up enough energy to get out of the house. But now he felt like he could run a marathon.

"So I got some bad news last night," Simon said.

He told her about how Tom had been killed outside his house in New Jersey. She was understandably horrified. He explained how he'd heard about it from Mark and had read "a little bit about it online." Of course he didn't tell her the weirdest part, that he'd been in the same exact area where the attack had taken place, because as far as she knew he'd crashed at the brewery on Friday night. Simon hated keeping secrets from her and wished he'd been honest from the get-go, but at this point telling her the truth seemed more complicated than continuing to lie. Or maybe *lie* was too strong a word. Continuing to *omit*.

"Are you going to the funeral?"

"I'm not sure," he said. "It's kind of awkward, you know? I think I'll probably just send flowers and a note to his wife."

"He had kids, didn't he?"

"Two," Simon said.

Alison shook her head. "It's so terrible. Can you imagine?"

The coffeemaker beeped, and she went back to the kitchen.

"Want a cup?" she called out.

"No, thanks," he replied.

The odor of the coffee was so strong it was making him nauseated. He opened the window to let in some air, but it didn't really help.

"You really don't want any coffee?" Alison had returned with a mugful.

"Yeah, positive," he said.

"Okay." She sounded skeptical. "I'm just surprised, that's all. I can't remember you ever turning down coffee in the morning. It's not because of what I said yesterday, is it? I mean about how you've been so hyper?"

"No," he said, "I'm just trying to cut back on the caffeine. I think it's been stressing me out."

The odor was so bitter, he felt like it was burning his nasal membranes. He couldn't believe he'd ever actually liked that stuff.

"I'm sorry I got so angry at you at the park yesterday," she said. "I feel like I acted like a big baby."

"No, I was the baby," Simon said. "I shouldn't've left Jeremy up on those rocks. I'll never do anything like that again. No more stupid risks."

"What happened to your boss does put things in perspective, doesn't it?"

"What do you mean?"

"Just how your whole life can change in an instant. One second, everything's perfect. The next moment, your whole life's ruined." She finished a sip of coffee, then said, "I don't know what I'm saying, I think my brain's still asleep." She added, "You sure you're okay?"

"Why?"

"It's just the way you're acting. You do seem stressed out."

He realized he was rotating his shoulders and shifting his neck from side to side, and he stopped and tried to stand perfectly still. "Sorry, it's just the whole Tom thing, I guess. I just feel bad about the way things had been between us, you know? I mean, I'd been so angry at him and now he's dead."

"You can't feel guilty about stuff like that."

"It's not guilt. It's just a feeling I have of . . . I can't really explain it. *Responsibility.* I feel this weird sense of responsibility."

"Feel sorry for his family, not yourself." Alison glanced toward the cable box below the TV. "Ugh, look at the time. I can't believe it's another workweek already. I feel like the whole weekend just flew by."

Simon heard Jeremy stirring in bed. "I'll get Jeremy," he said.

"Maybe you should let him sleep today," Alison said. "He's still getting over being sick."

"He's already up."

"How do you know?"

Simon didn't know how to answer this. How could he have possibly heard Jeremy shifting in bed from the opposite end of the apartment?

"Mommy!" Jeremy called from his room.

"See?" Simon said.

Simon got Jeremy dressed and made breakfast—French toast and sausage. Simon made the whole package of sausage, as he couldn't resist another meat fix. He was at the table eating with Jeremy when Alison came out of the bedroom, dressed for work, wearing Juicy Couture perfume. The perfume, combined with the other scents of her shampoo, conditioner, and moisturizing cream, made him feel like he was in the cosmetics department at Bloomingdales.

She must have seen him wincing because she asked, "Is something wrong?"

"No," he said. "The food just, um, went down the wrong pipe." He sipped from the glass of whole milk.

"Another low-fat meal, huh?" Alison asked.

"I'll go for a run later to work it off." Simon looked at Jeremy. "It looks like a nice day; maybe we'll play some soccer."

"I want to see my friends again." Jeremy had that tone he got when he was about to have a fit.

"We can't see them," Simon said.

"Why not?"

"I'll let you handle this," Alison said to Simon. "Have a great day, you two."

Simon called the office of Dr. Segal, his general practitioner, and tried to get an appointment for that morning, figuring he could get Christina to babysit.

"Is it an emergency?" the receptionist asked.

"Um, not really," Simon said. "I just had some strange symptoms I wanted to describe to him."

"What kind of symptoms?"

"I've had a lot of energy and I can hear and smell really well."

The line was silent. He realized how ridiculous this probably sounded.

"If he could just fit me in, I'd appreciate it," Simon said. "I think I might be having some kind of reaction to something."

"The soonest appointment is in two weeks," the receptionist said.

"He can't squeeze me in today?"

"I'm sorry, do you want to make an appointment in two weeks?" She sounded a little irritated.

Simon made the appointment, but just talking to the receptionist, describing his symptoms out loud, convinced him that he'd been overreacting and there was probably nothing seriously wrong with him. Serious diseases made you feel worse, not better, and the idea that the symptoms of a brain tumor had happened to emerge on the same day that he woke up in the woods in New Jersey was just ridiculous. The symptoms he was experiencing were obviously side effects of whatever drug the guys had given him that had caused him to pass out that night. That was the simplest explanation and the most logical.

Simon took Jeremy to Central Park's Great Lawn and kicked a soccer ball around. The physical activity helped Simon's mood a lot. He could've kept playing all day, but after about an hour Jeremy said he was hungry and they took a break for a snack, yogurt and a banana Simon had taken along.

Sitting next to Simon on a park bench, Jeremy said, "You're the best, most funnest dad in the whole world." Then he added, "Don't ever change."

Simon wasn't sure what Jeremy meant by that, but he thought the precocious comment was adorable and made a mental note to tell Alison about it later.

"Promise," Simon said. "I'll never change."

Simon felt as if he and Jeremy were bonding, getting so much closer than they'd ever been, which was amazing. Suddenly his decision to become a stay-at-home dad seemed like a great one. As Alison had pointed out, life was precarious and there were no guarantees. He had to savor what was most important, and nothing was more important than spend-ing time with his son.

"What are we going to do now, Daddy?"

It was only about ten o'clock. They could go back to the apartment, have lunch, but then what? He would've loved to go back to the park to run around some more, but he didn't think Jeremy would want to. They could do a playground, but the thought of hanging around with the babysitters all day seemed depressing. They'd just gone to the Museum of Natural History, and besides, it was Monday so the museums were closed.

"How about a movie?" Simon asked.

"I don't wanna go to a movie."

Simon didn't want to go to a movie either. What he wanted to do was see the guys at the playground downtown. Strangely, he didn't feel the same anger toward them that he had yesterday and the day before. Or at least a strong need to see them again, to get some answers, over-rode the other emotions.

"I have an idea," Simon said. "Let's go on a mystery ride."

"What's that?"

"If I tell you, it won't be a mystery."

Beaming, Jeremy shouted, "Yay! Mystery ride!"

Simon had never realized how hellish the New York City subways were. The air was dank and stale and the mingled odors of urine, must, and everyone's body odors were so obviously vile; how could anyone stand it? And the noise was out of control. Every time the train came to a screeching halt, Simon thought his brain was going to explode.

He was relieved when they arrived at South Ferry, and when they went up the stairs to the sidewalk, Simon, carrying the folded jogging stroller with one hand and holding Jeremy's hand with the other, felt as if he'd been working in a coal mine all day and was breathing in his first fresh air in hours. Not that the downtown Manhattan air was par-ticularly fresh, but compared to the subway, it was like being in the Alps.

Simon put Jeremy in the stroller, and they entered Battery Park at State Street. Jeremy had caught on that he was going to see his friends, and he was very excited.

"Are we there yet?" he asked impatiently as Simon pushed him along.

"Almost," Simon said.

"I wanna get out," Jeremy said, fidgeting.

"I have a better idea," Simon said, and he ran, pushing the stroller ahead of him. They veered onto the promenade alongside the river. He didn't realize how fast he was going until he saw that he was passing bikers. He slowed down and peeked in the stroller to see if he'd scared Jeremy, but Jeremy was grinning, having a blast.

The playground was up ahead. Simon didn't see the guys there, and he wondered if they'd changed their plans for some reason. Maybe one of them had a conflict and they were meeting up later today, or not at all. Well, Jeremy could still play, but Simon felt let down. He'd really psyched himself up about getting some answers.

But, wait, they *were* there. Simon didn't see them, but he heard Ramon talking, even though he had to be, what, a hundred yards away? There was a lot of other noise too—kids screaming, adults' conversations, birds chirping, waves on the river crashing against the docks. It was amazing how noisy even a trafficless part of the city was when you were paying attention, and somehow Simon was attuned to even the most subtle sounds without consciously trying.

They got closer and Simon still didn't see the guys—though he could swear he heard Ramon laughing—and then Jeremy, pointing straight ahead, shouted, "There's Diego! And there's Nicky."

Sure enough, the guys' kids were there, playing in the sandbox, and in front of the sandbox—not toward the back of the playground where they usually hung out—were Michael, Charlie, and Ramon. They didn't see Simon and Jeremy yet, though; or, if they did, they were playing it incredibly cool, continuing their conversation, talking about—shock and awe—steak. Ramon was describing how he'd made sirloin steaks the other night when he had a date over to his apartment for dinner. The steak talk did give Simon a serious craving, but he tried to ignore it.

Jeremy, wiggling excitedly in the stroller, said, "I want to get out, I want to get out."

Inside the playground, Simon unfastened the straps, and Jeremy darted to the sandbox and started playing with his friends. Then Simon looked at the guys, and they noticed him for the first time. Simon, holding his ground, tried not to show any fear. He didn't want to give the guys the satisfaction of feeling like they'd succeeded in humiliating him. He expected them to be surprised to see him, or to ignore him, or to have some sort of strong reaction. The last thing he expected was for them to be *happy* to see him.

"Hey, there's the man," Ramon said, grinning. He jogged over and gave him a big warm hug.

Then Charlie came over and said, "Brother, how's it goin'?" and hugged him too.

Finally it was Michael's turn. He looked directly at Simon's eyes, holding his gaze for several seconds, then said, "Welcome back to us," and hugged him extremely tightly for maybe ten seconds before letting go.

Simon wondered, was this part of the game? Were they trying to act normal, like nothing had happened Friday night, just for more kicks, for another round of the Humiliate Simon Burns game?

"Come on, sit down," Charlie said, acting like Mr. Nice Guy.

"Yeah, chill with us," Ramon said. His big gold cross was hanging over his chest, over his tight black long-sleeved V-neck shirt.

It was clear to Simon that these guys were seriously disturbed, maybe even insane, but he wasn't going to give them the satisfaction of leaving. That was exactly what they wanted—for him to run—so why give them what they wanted? So, instead he did the opposite of what they actually wanted and joined them on the bench. Yeah, that was the way to stay in control.

"So how was your weekend, man?" Charlie asked.

Simon looked at him, searching for a hint of sarcasm, but Charlie wasn't cracking. Okay, if this was the way they wanted to play it, then this was the way they'd play it.

"Pretty good," he said. "How was yours?"

"Eh, not bad," Charlie said. "My ex had Nicky, so I was on my own. I watched a movie with my girlfriend on Saturday night. Yesterday we just stayed in all day too."

"Makin' love, right?" Ramon said smiling, egging Charlie on.

"Yeah, a little of that too," Charlie said. "You know how it is."

Charlie and Ramon high-fived.

"How about you, Michael?" Simon asked, looking right at him, wanting him to see how fearless he was.

"I had a lot of sex too," Michael said.

"Yeah, Michael has a new lady, but he didn't show her off to us yet. He didn't even tell us her name."

"Maybe she's the one," Charlie said.

"Yeah, watch out, soon he'll stop hanging out with us," Ramon said. "He'll be like, 'I'm too busy for you guys, have fun on your own.'"

Ramon and Charlie laughed, but Michael stayed serious.

"You know I'll never leave you," Michael said. "We'll be together forever."

"Aw, man, you know I'm just playin' with you," Ramon said, putting an arm around Michael.

"What about you?" Charlie asked Simon.

"What about me what?" Simon asked.

"You do anything exciting this weekend?"

Simon thought, *Is he serious?*

"No, not really," Simon said. "Spent a lot of time with my family."

"That's cool," Ramon said.

"Yeah," Simon said, "it *was* cool. We went to the museum yesterday, the park, walked around. I spent time with them Saturday too, I mean after I came back from New Jersey."

He thought this would definitely get a reaction—one of them would flinch at least. But nope, they were all acting perfectly normal.

There was a long pause, and then Ramon asked, "So what were you doing out in Jersey?"

Was it possible he really didn't know?

"Nothing much," Simon said. "Just hanging out . . . at a friend's."

"Cool," Ramon said. Then he shouted toward the sandbox, "Hey, Diego, you gotta share the shovel with him. Let him have his turn. That's right." Then he looked back at Simon and said, "A friend's, huh? Yeah, I was seeing a woman in Princeton for a while. Stunningly beautiful. Long dark hair, like Cleopatra."

Ramon went on, praising his ex-lover, and then Charlie changed the subject and said something about how well the kids played together, and Michael chimed in, commenting about how it was "like they're brothers."

Then Simon interrupted whatever Ramon was saying and asked, "Can I ask you a question?"

The guys looked at Simon, waiting for him to continue.

Finally Simon asked, "Aren't you guys surprised to see me here today?"

"Why would we be surprised?" Charlie said. "It's Monday and you said you'd come on Monday."

"When did I say that?"

"When you left the brewery Friday night?"

Ramon and Charlie seemed confused. Michael was looking away, smiling at something his son was doing.

"What's the matter, man?" Ramon asked. "What's going on?"

"Okay, look," Simon said. "That's enough. I know what happened, okay?"

Now Michael was looking over, but it was so hard to read him. Was he surprised? Angry? Intrigued? All of the above? Simon had never met anyone quite like this guy.

"What happened with what?" Charlie asked.

Either these guys were the greatest actors in the world or they were total lying psychopaths. There was no middle ground.

"The other night," Simon said. "There was something in that beer.

Or maybe it was the steak, I don't know, but you did something to me. You drugged me and you dumped me in the woods in New Jersey, and I just want to know why you did it. I mean, was it a big joke for you guys? Is this what you do to get off? Meet some guy at the playground, invite him out, and then try to totally humiliate him?"

Simon was so emotional as he was speaking that he wasn't aware of the guys' reactions. Now he noticed that they didn't seem to have any reaction at all. They were staring at him, blank-faced. Even Michael seemed believably baffled.

Then Charlie said, "*You're* the one who's joking, right?"

Frustrated, Simon said, "Look, I just want to know what you did to me because I think the drug is giving me strange side effects."

"This is crazy, man," Ramon said, shaking his head.

"I know it's crazy!" Simon didn't intend to raise his voice. A few nearby moms and/or babysitters looked over.

"You really think we *drugged* you?" Charlie actually looked hurt.

"I didn't say *you*." Simon glared at Michael. "He was the one who brought the trays out."

"I didn't drug you," Michael said. "I gave you my family beer."

"Oh, give me a break, all right?" Simon said. "It wasn't just beer. I've had beer before, I have beer all the time, and it doesn't make me pass out and wake up in goddamn New Jersey. You put something in the beer. What did you do, slip me a roofie?"

Again women were looking over.

"Seriously," Charlie said, "you're gonna have to keep it down, man."

"Why do you think *we* brought you to Jersey?" Ramon asked.

"How else did I get there?" Simon asked.

"Wait, none of this makes sense," Charlie said. "You say you were drugged, but when were you drugged? You got a little drunk, that's all."

"I warned you about the beer," Ramon said, "but you seemed to handle it okay. I was impressed."

"How did I seem to handle it?" Simon said. "I blacked out at the brewery."

The guys exchanged confused looks.

"The last thing I remember," Simon said, "is sitting on the couch, so *something* happened to me."

"You got a little drunk," Ramon said, "but not *drunk* drunk. You were acting pretty normal, actually."

"You don't remember playing pool?" Charlie asked.

"Pool?" Simon had no idea what he was talking about.

"Yeah, we shot some pool. Spanked me in that last game. I still don't know how you made that combo shot. That was crazy."

No one was flinching.

"What happened after pool?" Simon asked, wondering, *Was it possible that they were telling the truth?*

"We went up to the roof," Charlie said. "Just to get some fresh air. You really don't remember any of this?"

"Did I have anything else to drink?" Simon asked.

Ramon shook his head. "Nope, no one did. We just mellowed out, talking about our kids and, oh yeah, you told us how you got fired from your job."

Simon felt a hollow, sinking sensation in his gut, as if a doctor had just diagnosed him with a terminal illness. Trying not to show any reaction, he asked, "What did I say?"

"Just how your boss totally blindsided you, how it wasn't fair, how he wasn't returning some e-mails, how pissed off you were at him. . . . You okay?"

Simon, dazed, couldn't focus. Then he realized he was sucking on something—a straw. Charlie had given him one of his kid's juice boxes.

"Drink," Charlie said.

Simon sipped some apple juice and felt a little better. Well, at least he didn't feel like he was about to pass out.

"You okay?" Charlie asked.

"Yeah," Simon said. "I'm fine." He couldn't have been telling a bigger lie.

"What happened to you is perfectly normal," Michael said. "Some people have strong reactions. It's impossible to predict."

"Yeah, and we told you it's strong," Ramon said, "but you wanted to give it a try anyway. You were like, 'Strong beer, so what? I can handle it, no problem.'"

This was all true, Simon realized. They hadn't forced him to drink the beer. He'd made that choice.

"Did you really wake up in Jersey?" Charlie asked.

Simon sucked in the rest of the juice, then stood and said, "I should probably get going now."

"But you just got here," Ramon said.

"Sorry," Simon said. "I—I have to leave."

Simon went to the sandbox, grabbed Jeremy's hand, and said, "Come on, we're going home."

Knowing the key to avoiding an all-out fit was to move quickly, Simon picked Jeremy up in one arm and lifted the stroller with the other and walked quickly out of the playground, without looking in the guys' direction, but he could sense that they were watching him and talking about him. He couldn't make out what they were saying—they were whispering—but he heard his name in the conversation.

Outside the playground, Simon put Jeremy in the stroller and strapped him in, ignoring his protests. He walked away, heading uptown. He was angry and humiliated and frightened and he wanted to get away as fast as he could. What had he been thinking, coming down here? He'd wanted answers, but all he'd gotten was more questions. It had been such a perfect morning and now everything was a mess again.

Jeremy was crying, saying, "I don't want to go! I don't want to go!"

Not only had coming down here been a mistake, it had been unfair to Jeremy—letting him play with his friends for a few minutes and then dragging him away.

"It's going to be okay," Simon said. "I promise."

But Jeremy continued writhing and wailing. To distract him, Simon ran, pushing the stroller ahead of him. As before, he was going very fast and after a few minutes Jeremy calmed down, enjoying the ride. Simon made it uptown, over five miles, in about half an hour. That meant he'd been running, what, six-minute miles, pushing a kid in a stroller? He didn't think he'd ever run faster than a ten-minute mile and, amazingly, he was barely winded. He still had no idea where all this energy and endurance was coming from, but now he had other things on his mind.

Jeremy said he was hungry, which made sense—it was after one o'clock and Simon had forgotten to give him lunch. They went to a Chinese restaurant on Broadway—Jeremy had moo shu chicken and Simon had pepper steak with a double order of barbecue spare ribs. With food in his system, Jeremy was suddenly in a good mood, talking and laughing, and seemed to have forgotten all about being taken away from his friends. Ah, to be three years old, when problems are so fleeting.

After lunch they returned to the apartment. Jeremy had fallen asleep in his stroller, so Simon carefully transferred him into his bed to continue his nap. Simon was restless and easily did a hundred push-ups, but it didn't help to relax him. As he did crunches, in his head he kept repeating parts of the conversation with the guys. He wanted to talk himself into believing they were lying, that they were all in collusion on some elaborate hoax, but he couldn't make a compelling argument. They all seemed too convincing, and there was no way they could've made up the part about Simon trashing Tom. The night had probably gone exactly the way they claimed it had—Simon had had a strong reaction to the beer, then blacked out and went to New Jersey on his own. But why had he gone there? To talk to Tom? To confront him? Was it possible he'd even talked to Tom before he was killed? And how the hell had he gotten to New Jersey anyway? He remembered that about sixty dollars had been missing from his wallet. That wasn't enough to cover cab fare over an hour out of the city. Was it possible he'd used the money for the cab fare, or at least part of the cab fare? Maybe he didn't have enough money to pay for the fare, and the driver caught on and dropped him on the side of the road near the woods. Okay, that was possible, but Simon had no idea why he'd run into the woods and taken off all of his clothes. That part made no sense at all, and it was so terrifying and humiliating he didn't even want to think about it anymore.

When Jeremy woke up from his nap, Simon, anxious and stir-crazy, suggested going back outside to fly a kite or play more soccer, but Jeremy said he was tired so Simon parked him in front of the TV for the rest of the afternoon until Alison came home from work. Alison hadn't seen Jeremy all day and Simon wanted to give them some time alone together, so he announced he was going for a run. He ran around the reservoir five times. He didn't know how fast he was going, but he was practically sprinting and no other joggers passed him. He wanted to go around a few more times, but it had gotten dark and he had to get back for dinner.

Before he got in the shower he caught a glimpse of himself in the mirror. Why was he so scruffy? He'd just shaved this morning, and he could usually go two or three days without growing anything resembling a beard. As he shaved, he noticed the muscle tone in his arms and shoulders. Was it new tone or was it just because he was looking at himself more closely, the way you notice details in a painting when you stare at it? Whatever. He looked great and he felt great, that was all that mattered.

When he was through shaving, he flexed for a while, admiring his physique, then weighed himself: 182. Last time he weighed himself— when was it, last week?—he'd weighed 175. He checked again, to see if it was a mistake, but 182 came up again. Funny, he didn't look like he'd gained weight. He looked trimmer, more fit. Muscle weighed more than fat, but how could he have put on seven pounds of muscle in a week? If eating steak and sausage could pack on muscle so quickly, why would athletes waste their time with steroids?

After he showered and changed into sweatpants and a T-shirt, he went out to the dining room, where Alison was setting the table for dinner, and asked, "Is something wrong with the scale?"

"No," she said. "Why?"

"Nothing, I just gained a little weight." Figured he'd minimize it, but was there really anything to minimize? What was the big deal about seven pounds anyway? It wasn't like he hadn't gained weight suddenly before. Hell, he'd put on four pounds after he put too much soy sauce on his sashimi.

Alison smiled seductively and said, "You look great to me."

If Jeremy hadn't been awake, playing with his Leapster in the living room, Simon would've seduced her right then. He imagined pulling down her pants and panties, then swiping away the dishes from the table, letting them shatter on the floor, and then bending her over the table, grabbing her ass hard as he . . .

"Oh my God," she said.

She was gazing downward slightly, covering her mouth with her hands in mock surprise as she noticed the tent in his sweatpants.

Simon was surprised too. He knew he was excited, but not *that* excited. He must've gotten hard almost instantly. When was the last time that had happened? When he was sixteen?

"I guess I should cancel the order on that Viagra," Alison said. She checked to make sure Jeremy wasn't coming and then came to Simon and rubbed up against him. She whispered flirtatiously, "I wish I could take care of that for you."

"Oh God, you smell so amazing right now." Simon breathed deeply.

"Well, I'm feeling better tonight," Alison said. "I think I'm ready for another date."

"You're on," Simon said, and he kissed her softly, enjoying her scent for a while longer, and then she went into the kitchen to finish preparing dinner.

Alison had made chicken salad with a side of steamed carrots and broccoli. Simon was dying for that last steak in the fridge, but he resisted, wanting to do the right thing for his cholesterol. Still, his appetite was ravenous and he was eating much faster than he normally did, barely chewing some bites.

"Wow, Daddy eats fast," Jeremy said, impressed.

"Don't you imitate him," Alison said. Then to Simon, "You should really slow down, sweetie; you'll give yourself reflux."

Simon nodded. He chewed the next few bites slowly, then couldn't hold back and started shoveling the food down again.

Alison spent most of the evening playing with Jeremy. Simon was incredibly horny and couldn't wait for Jeremy to go to sleep so he could make love to his wife. Like a pent-up schoolchild who couldn't wait for the final bell to ring so he could charge out of the school, Simon kept checking the time. He checked at seven o'clock, and when he checked again at 7:05 he couldn't believe only five minutes had passed because it had to be eight o'clock, seven forty-five at the earliest. Maybe like a watched pot didn't boil, a horny man didn't get laid. Every time he thought about sex or imagined Alison naked, he got a hard-on, so he had to pace around the apartment and occasionally did push-ups, crunches, and jumping jacks. Though it was nearly impossible to think about anything but sex, it was a nice distraction; at least he wasn't thinking about that other stuff.

Finally it was Jeremy's bedtime. As per the nightly routine, Simon went in to read him a bedtime story. Wanting Jeremy to fall asleep as fast as possible, Simon read *Where the Wild Things Are* so quickly it was barely comprehensible.

"Daddy, you do everything too fast," Jeremy said, smiling.

Almost as if unconsciously trying to prolong Simon's sexual frustration, Jeremy wouldn't go to sleep. He kept calling for Alison and Simon, asking for water, saying he had to pee, claiming there were monsters in his bedroom—anything to stay awake. Finally, a little before ten o'clock he fell asleep. Alison was in the bathroom, bent over the sink, washing her face, but Simon couldn't wait. He grabbed her from behind and started kissing and biting and sucking on her neck, loving how she smelled and tasted. He ran his hands through her hair and kissed her. Her face was still wet and sudsy and the water was still running, but who cared?

"I'm not done washing up," she said.

He ignored that and carried her into bed. Within a few seconds her clothes were off and they were going at it. Kissing her, smelling her, biting her; it was unrestrained and intense on so many levels. Between moans Alison said she was concerned about the noise, so Simon stuck her iPod into its docking station and then resumed making love to her with Nickelback drowning out their sex noises.

Maybe half an hour later, Simon lay in bed, Alison's warm body nestled into him. Simon breathed deeply. God, this was amazing; how come he'd never appreciated the scent of his wife before? He'd had this amazing sex goddess in bed with him for years, and he'd taken her for granted. After a few minutes of talking and cuddling, he climbed on her again.

"But I have work tomorrow," she said.

"What's more important, work or sex?"

She grabbed his shoulders and pulled him onto her.

Later, around three A.M., after they'd made love for the fourth time, she passed out, but he wasn't tired at all. If anything, he was more turned on. It almost seemed ridiculous now that over the weekend he'd thought something could be wrong with him. He felt better than he had in years; he had limitless energy and a raging sex drive.

So, he asked himself as he lay on his back next to his amazing, sexy, irresistible wife, *what exactly is the problem?*

THIRTEEN

Alison had no idea what was going on with her husband lately, but she was liking it—a lot. Before—when was it? Saturday? Just three days ago?—it seemed like she'd be in a distant, troubled marriage forever, but now, suddenly, it was like she had a brand-new husband.

She'd been complaining for years about the lack of intimacy in their marriage, but now suddenly he was all over her? Naturally she was skeptical. Was this really Simon? *Her* Simon? The same guy who sometimes went days without touching her suddenly couldn't get enough of her?

At first she figured it was only because he felt guilty for pulling the all-nighter. Maybe instead of showing up with flowers or jewelry, his way of apologizing was transforming into a Don Juan. But it was hard to fake that kind of passion. It didn't seem like he was just trying to make up for bad behavior; for the first time in months she felt that Simon was genuinely making an effort to save the marriage.

And the changes went way beyond sex. The way he looked at her and treated her was completely different, and she felt like he wanted her in a way he never had before. When he looked at her in the kitchen or across the dinner table, she could see the lust in his eyes. Sometimes it was almost too much, as if he were a character in a corny romance novel, but compared to the way things had been lately, any change was welcome.

Did the sudden changes have something to do with all of the protein he was eating? It was strange to see Simon eat so much meat. Maybe she'd been right and the problems weren't just in their relationship— maybe there was some chemical component as well. Maybe it wasn't testosterone; maybe he'd had some kind of amino acid deficiency that screwed up his sex drive. But it seemed weird that some steaks and burgers had had such a drastic effect, and besides, how had a burst of protein changed his personality, made him more interested in her? He'd been complimenting her maybe fifty times a day, telling her how beautiful she looked or how great she smelled. He was really into smells lately—in the park, in the Indian restaurant, in the bedroom—especially in the bedroom. In bed he was sniffing her everywhere, and how many times had he asked her about her perfume? She'd worn Juicy Couture for the past few years and it had never even garnered a comment. But now he seemed very fixated on her scent and she loved how, when he smelled her, his nostrils flared a little, as if he were savoring the odor, as if he were tasting wine or something.

But, all the weirdness aside, she was enjoying the new Simon. After all, a husband who wanted to have sex all the time and couldn't seem to get enough of her—what wasn't to like? In between sex, he snuggled with her and actually *talked* to her. Was this the same guy who used to roll over and turn away and fall asleep after doing it? In a matter of a few days, she hadn't only gotten her lover back, she'd gotten her friend back as well.

She was enjoying the sudden change so much that she didn't want to overanalyze what was going on. She was just hoping it wasn't just a phase, that they could build on this and put the difficult period in their marriage behind them forever.

On Monday night, she was washing her face, getting ready for bed, when Simon started kissing the back of her neck, the way he'd been kissing her lately—using his tongue and teeth—and then he actually carried her into bed. She loved how he took control during sex; it was so different from how the sex used to be. In the past they'd do the usual positions and there would always be a rush to finish, but now he seemed to really enjoy making love to her—looking into her eyes, acting like he actually wanted her.

Simon's behavior in bed had changed too—he was suddenly doing things he hadn't been into in the past, like going down on her. He used to do it, grudgingly, but in recent years he'd stopped completely. When she'd brought it up during a counseling session, he'd gotten very uncomfortable and changed the subject. There was something different about his tongue too; it was firmer or seemed bigger and hit the right places.

Alison just couldn't get enough of her sexy husband. She loved the muscle tone in his back and shoulders—was he getting in better shape or had she just not paid attention lately? His chest hair seemed sexier somehow too.

In the morning, she was running her fingers through his sweaty chest hair, saying, "You're so sexy."

"Don't stop," he said. "That feels so good."

She continued caressing his chest with her fingertips, just enjoying being with her husband in bed, when Simon suddenly sat up.

"What's wrong?" she asked.

"Jeremy's up," he said.

"He is?" She listened. "I don't hear him."

"Daddy!"

Simon's look said, *I told you so*.

"And check that out," Alison said, "he's calling for *you* now in the morning."

"Don't be insulted."

"I'm not. Actually I think it's wonderful."

Simon went to Jeremy's room, and Alison stretched out in the bed, thinking that this *was* wonderful. Now that she felt that Simon was making the extra effort to save the marriage, her resentment about not being home with Jeremy during the day was fading. Jeremy seemed happier too the past few days and was clearly starting to bond with Simon, the way he used to be so close with Margaret. There was something special about a father and son having so much alone time together; maybe the decision for Simon to be a stay-at-home dad was working out after all. With the concessions they were making, they were getting by financially, and for the first time in ages, they were all happy.

Alison dozed again. She woke up to Simon kissing her.

"Mmm," she said. "That was nice."

"It's past eight," Simon said.

"Thanks, I better get up." She kissed him again. "But I don't want to. I just want to stay in bed with you all day."

"I'd love that too," he said. "I made you coffee."

She saw that he was holding a mug. "That's so nice of you, wow." She took the mug and sipped a little, then said, "I can't believe you're not exhausted. We did it what, three times last night?"

"Four," Simon said. "But who's counting?"

"I must've fallen asleep during the fourth."

"You did, but you were still incredible."

They kissed again. She had to remind herself that this was the same man about whom she'd complained, "He doesn't kiss me enough," during a recent marriage counseling appointment.

"I wish I could stay in bed with you all day," she said.

"Why can't we?" he asked.

She wasn't sure if he was joking. "Well, I think it would be a little hard to explain to Jeremy. Besides, I have so much work to do today."

"In that case," Simon said, "to be continued."

He kissed her again, longer this time, running his hands through her hair. She had flashes of the sex they'd had last night. If she hadn't had so much work to do, she would've seriously considered staying home today and taking him up on his offer.

She should have been exhausted, but after the shower she felt invigorated. Maybe the marriage issues had been wearing her down more than she'd thought. Now that she had a new outlook and all this great sex, a few hours' sleep was more than enough to get her going.

Simon was in the kitchen. He'd unloaded the dishwasher and put all the dishes away and now he was—shock and awe—scrubbing the stove. He had officially turned into the world's most perfect husband.

"Get over here," Simon said when he spotted Alison watching him.

She went over to him, and he kissed her hard and passionately, with his arms around her waist, pulling himself in close.

On the crosstown bus she tried to read the *Times* on her iPad, but flashes from last night kept intruding on her concentration. She had a morning staff meeting with two other Manhattan sales reps at the Starbucks on Eighty-first and Second. Chandra, a young blond rep, noticed a change in Alison and asked, "Did you lose weight?"

"No," Alison said. "I don't think so."

"Well, you look amazing," Chandra said.

"It's true," Rachel, another rep, said. "You're like totally glowing."

After the meeting, she texted Simon:

you were amazing last night!

This wasn't an obligatory text to follow through on a suggestion from their marriage counselor; she'd texted Simon because she'd *wanted* to text him.

About a minute later she got:

I can't wait to make love to you again

Was this really happening? Was she really exchanging nonfake, intimate, sexy texts with her husband?

She had a break, so at the Starbucks she got a table upstairs in the corner where there was no one around, and Skyped with her sister in San Francisco.

"Long time no see," Lauren said.

Alison realized she'd gone several days without being in touch with her sister, and hadn't returned a couple of phone messages and a text over the weekend.

"Sorry," Alison said. "A lot's happened lately."

Alison told her about the sudden shift in Simon's personality, and about all the sex they'd been having.

"It's almost like he knew he had to do something drastic to save the marriage," Alison said, "and for the first time I get the sense that he really cares, that he wants to fix things."

Lauren was staring, blank-faced. "You're gaslighting me, right?"

Alison held up her hands in front of the camera. "See? No fingers crossed."

"So let me get this straight," Lauren said. "The guy who you were complaining has no passion, who doesn't touch you anymore or seem to want you, is now *too* into you?"

"I'm not complaining," Alison said, "but, yeah, it's like all of a sudden he's a completely different person. I literally can't get him off me."

Lauren had become distracted by something. "One sec," she said, and got up. About a minute later she returned holding Isabella, her three-month-old.

"Oh my God, she's beautiful," Alison said. "I wish I could hold her."

When Isabella was born, Alison was thrilled, of course, but she couldn't help feeling occasional pangs of jealousy and regret. Lauren had two beautiful kids, but for Alison, it was one and done. For financial reasons, and because things had been so difficult on her marriage, having a second child was out of the question. For a long time it had upset Alison that Jeremy would never have a sibling and she'd never have a chance to have a daughter. But now that things had gotten so much better with Simon, she suddenly had a new perspective on her life. The regret was gone, and in the scheme of things, was having one amazing child really the worst thing in the world?

They talked about the baby for a while, and then Lauren said, "So you really think he changed?"

"Well, let's see if he keeps this up," Alison said. "To be honest, though, I don't see how he possibly can." She looked around to make sure no one was within earshot, then leaned close to the mike and said in a hushed tone, "I mean, it's crazy how much stamina he has, and I don't know how I can keep going like this either . . . I can barely walk today."

Lauren was suddenly glaring seriously. "And you say this happened after he stayed out all night?"

"Yes." Alison knew her sister so well, she could see the machinations in her brain. "Why? What's wrong?"

"I'm not saying this to scare you," Lauren said, "but I think you have a serious problem."

"Problem? What do you—?"

"I don't know how to say this," Lauren said. "I mean, I'm three thousand miles away and I'm just hearing what you're telling me and I don't have anything else to go on. I mean, maybe there's more to this situation, and I don't want to say anything to frighten you if there's no reason to."

"Can you just tell me already?" Alison asked.

Lauren waited several seconds, glaring for melodramatic effect, then said, "I think he's cheating on you."

Alison laughed. "Simon? Please."

Lauren was still glaring.

"I'm telling you," Alison said, "it's ridiculous. First of all, he's just not the kind of guy, he'd never do that. And he's a horrible liar, he'd never be able to pull it off."

"That's what I used to say about Alex," Lauren said.

Alex was Lauren's first husband. They had been married for four years when Lauren discovered he was still secretly seeing his old girlfriend. And it was true—Lauren used to say that Alex would never cheat on her, even when the signs were obvious to Alison.

"Simon is not like Alex," Alison said.

"Remember, Alex suddenly got interested in sex too," Lauren said. "I was like, where is this coming from? And he didn't come home some nights, or came home at three in the morning, always with excuses, and like an idiot I believed him. Not that I'm saying you're an idiot, but you know what they say—the woman is always the last to know."

"I thought it's the woman always knows?"

"That too."

Alison thought about it for a few seconds, but it just didn't make sense to her. She and Simon had had their problems, but he wasn't a cheater.

Alison changed the subject back to Isabella and, as if on cue, Isabella spit up on Lauren. Lauren had to go clean up the mess, so they signed off.

Alison had back-to-back meetings the rest of the day, and at some point the lack of sleep last night caught up with her. When she came home at the usual time, sixish, she was zonked, but Simon was like the Energizer Bunny. He'd already given Jeremy his bath and gotten him ready for bed and dinner was ready—steak and potatoes for himself, but he'd thoughtfully made a Greek salad for her.

The focus at the dinner table was on Jeremy, but every once in a while Simon gave her the same seductive looks he'd been giving her lately. It was like he wanted to jump across the table to rip off her clothes and was doing everything he possibly could to restrain himself. Alison couldn't help remembering what her sister had told her. It was true that Simon's behavior, especially his sexual behavior, had changed drastically. Was it possible that this was all just his way of covering up an affair, or even a one-night stand? She remembered how on Friday night, before his guys' night out, he'd been stressing about what outfit to wear. When had Simon ever stressed about how he looked? She'd read an article in *New York Magazine* about some Upper East Side mother whose husband left her for a nanny he'd met at the playground. Maybe Alison was being incredibly naïve about all of this. Maybe Simon was the typical cheating husband and she was too deep in denial to realize it. She didn't think she was in denial, but wasn't that the definition of denial?

"Did I tell you you look beautiful tonight?" Simon asked.

Alison knew she looked awful, with bags under her eyes. Still, it was nice of him to lie.

"No," she said, "you didn't."

"Well, I'm telling you now. You look beautiful."

He was gazing at her so lovingly. It was hard to imagine that he was cheating on her and none of this was real, but she'd have to keep an eye on him just in case.

FOURTEEN

Waiting in front of her East Sixty-fifth Street brownstone, Olivia was experiencing the usual buzz she had before a date with Michael. This relationship was so different from anything she'd experienced with past boyfriends. There was always an addictive freshness about a new relationship, but with other guys the intensity started to wear off after the first few dates, after they got to know each other. But after each date with Michael, her attraction was getting more and more intoxicating.

As usual, Eddie, his driver, picked her up in the black Lexus SUV. Eddie was a young black guy, maybe twenty-five years old. Olivia had tried to strike up conversations with him, but he barely spoke, probably on instructions from Michael. Olivia would have loved to pick Eddie's brain and find out more about Michael. The enigma was sexy as hell, but it was frustrating sometimes when Michael answered her questions with questions or was just flat-out evasive. She was determined to get some answers. Some real answers.

They wove through rush-hour traffic, eventually making it all the way downtown to Tribeca. The car pulled up in front of Michael's building.

"Thanks, Eddie," Olivia said.

Eddie didn't say anything; he just drove off.

After Olivia buzzed Michael's apartment, he sent the elevator down for her. She got on, and then just before the doors closed, they reopened and a very old man got on with her.

She'd never seen him before. Going by his extremely wrinkled face, he had to be ninety-something years old, but he seemed in remarkable shape for his age. He walked very well and there was no curvature in his back. Weirdly, Olivia thought he was extremely attractive. She wasn't usually into older guys. She'd had friends who dated guys in their sixties and seventies—well, when the guys were rich enough—but she didn't get the allure. She once went out with a retired surgeon—he was seventy-four, but in good shape, swam seven days a week, and colored his hair. He looked ageless in a longtime-game-show-host kind of way, but she still felt like she was having sex with her grandfather.

This guy did it for her, though. He had thick gray hair, was in a black turtleneck, and had an aging rock star quality. If it weren't for his severely wrinkled face he could've passed for sixty, easy.

He didn't seem to notice Olivia at all, acting as if she were invisible. In Manhattan, this wouldn't have been unusual in a crowded elevator, or an elevator in a heavily populated building. But in a building that Michael had implied that he lived in alone, that had a private elevator, the old man's total obliviousness seemed odd.

Figuring just because he was being rude didn't mean she had to, she gave him her most cheery smile and said, "Good evening."

Still no reaction. She said it again, much louder, but he still didn't look over. Well, she gave it her best shot, what could you do? Then, suddenly, he turned toward her, glaring sharply. It wasn't the evil eye; it was the evil eye on steroids. He was sizing her up, judging her, and hating her all at once. Now she realized why he'd looked so familiar. She'd seen those eyes before; they were just like Michael's—so dark brown they were practically black. He had to be a relative or something.

"Hi, I'm Olivia."

If anything, this just made his glare colder and emptier. Olivia might have even been afraid that the guy would try to attack her or something, if he weren't so old and if she didn't think he was a relative of Michael's. Still, he was spooky as hell and she had her hand near her purse, where she kept her pepper spray, just in case.

The elevator reached the top floor, where Michael lived, and the doors opened. She got off quickly, and he stayed on. As the doors closed she looked back and saw that he was still glaring at her as if he were Hannibal the Cannibal and she were his next meal.

"You're here."

Michael's voice actually almost made her jump.

"Jesus, you scared the—"

Then she did a double take, shocked all over again. Michael was several feet away, buck naked with a full erection.

"Oh my God." Olivia was covering her mouth with her hand, now more turned on than shocked.

"You look beautiful tonight," Michael said, acting as if greeting a woman at the door with a hard-on were perfectly normal.

"Thank you," she said, trying not to stare, but it was impossible not to. "So do you."

He came over to her and closed his eyes and breathed deeply, as if he were savoring the aroma. The thing was, there was no real aroma to savor. She wasn't wearing perfume because he'd told her he preferred her natural scent.

"You smell lovely this evening," he said.

He walked behind her and took a few more deep breaths. He'd done this on their other dates as well—sniffing her when she arrived, as if he were pretending he was a dog. With any other guy, all of this would have seemed completely bizarre, but Michael could pull off practically anything. She'd never met a guy with a perspiration fetish before, but if that was what it took to turn him on, who was she to complain? Besides, she'd dated guys who wouldn't get up from the couch or put down the

PlayStation joystick when she entered a room, so in comparison being sniffed didn't seem so horrible.

"Well, I can see you're pretty excited to see me," Olivia said.

Michael either didn't get it or refused to smile, it was impossible to tell. Without another word, he took her by the hand and led her through the loft to the bedroom. Then he said, "Get naked."

She happily obeyed.

Olivia's wrists still hurt and her hands were practically numb from being pinned down so hard for so long. She said, "This probably isn't exactly a news flash, but this is the best sex I've ever had. I know a lot of women say that and, I'll be honest, I've said it to practically every man I've been with, but I was lying all those times. This time I'm not. This is honestly the best sex I've ever had."

"You're in love with me," Michael said.

Olivia sat up, startled. Was it possible she'd blurted out the L-word during the sex? She didn't think she'd said it, but she'd been so caught up she could've said practically anything.

"What do you mean?" she asked. "Did . . . did I say something while we were—"

"Love is the easiest emotion to spot," Michael said. "People can disguise fear and hate, but they can't disguise love."

"Is this a bad thing?" Olivia asked.

"Yes," Michael said. "Love is weakness. Only humans love. Other animals never love."

"I don't know about that," Olivia said. "I had a friend who had two Chihuahuas, and they seemed to be pretty tight."

"You must stop loving me immediately," Michael said, his German accent suddenly coming through.

Olivia had to laugh—his total seriousness made the conversation seem even more absurd. Then she said, "Look, I'm not saying I'm in love with you. But I have loved other guys before, and I know from experience that love isn't something you can turn on and off like a faucet."

Michael, staring at her with his dark blank eyes, didn't say anything.

Olivia said, "Look, I get that you probably have commitment issues, okay? I mean, you're an older guy, you've never been married, or at least I don't think you've ever been married, and I know it's way too early to even be having this conversation. I get it, okay? But I just want you to know that I'm not *that* woman. What I mean is, I'm not out to sink my claws into you. So how about we shelve the whole love conversation and pretend it never came up?"

Michael was still staring.

His eyes were so captivating that she lost her train of thought for a few seconds, and then she continued, "What, you think I'm kidding? I'm telling you, I won't put any pressure on you. I gave up looking for a husband a long time ago. And I'm not into having kids, if that's what you're worried about."

He remained silent. Was he absorbing what she was saying, or had he been completely ignoring her?

After maybe ten seconds he said, "Leave now."

Olivia was used to the abruptness. He'd asked her to leave by saying "Leave now" on all of their dates; it was part of his crazy charm. Or *was* part of it. Suddenly his attitude seemed more rude than sexy, and her paranoia was setting in. Although he'd never invited her to stay overnight, he'd never wanted her to leave so early before—it wasn't even eight o'clock.

"Are you trying to break up with me?" she asked. "Because if that's what's going on here, I'd appreciate it if you'd just do it. I hate slow-motion breakups."

"If I wanted to break up with you, I'd break up with you."

"Then what do you want?"

He didn't answer.

"Of course, Mr. Strong Silent Type doesn't say anything. You have this act down cold, don't you?"

Olivia dressed quickly while Michael remained in bed, lying on his back, his eyes wide open.

"Okay, you like to be honest; well, I'm going to be honest," Olivia said. "I can't keep doing this forever. I think you're a great guy and the sex is amazing, but eventually there has to be some better communication if we're going to continue this relationship, or whatever we want to call it. Eventually you're going to have to start opening up."

"My driver will pick you up tomorrow at seven," Michael said.

Olivia breathed deeply, venting frustration, then said, "Fine, whatever," and left the room. She was halfway toward the elevator when she marched back and said, "You know what, it's not fine. If you want me to stick around, you better start letting me in."

"You're angry at me," Michael said.

"You're damn right I'm angry at you."

"Anger is good. Anger is much healthier than love."

"See? That's what I'm talking about. You won't *talk* to me."

"I'm talking right now."

"You're talking, but you won't *say* anything. I want to know what's going on inside your head. I want to know the real Michael Hartman."

"You don't want that."

"Yes, I do want that. Isn't that what a relationship is all about?"

He was still facing the ceiling.

"You don't want to know me," he said.

"Of course I want to know you," she said. "I want to know everything about you."

"You say that, but there are things about me you won't understand, things you're better off not knowing."

"I'm telling you, you don't have to be worried about saying the wrong thing to me. Nothing you can say is going to scare me away."

He stared at her for a long time, but in a different way, as if he were trying to solve some complicated problem.

Then he said, "You know about my family."

"Well, I saw a tricycle the first night I was here. . . . I was going to say something, but I thought maybe you were sensitive, thought I'd get turned off or something because you have a kid."

"His name's Jonas," Michael said.

"Does he live with you all the time?"

"Yes."

"Oh," Olivia said. "So who's—?"

"His mother's dead."

"I'm sorry."

He didn't say anything.

She asked, "And what about the elderly man I saw on the elevator? There seemed to be a family resemblance."

"You met my father."

"Well, I didn't really *meet* him, I just—"

"Volker was born in Germany."

"Does he live here?"

"Yes."

"How come you didn't tell me about your family before? I mean, why does it have to be this big secret?"

"I've chosen you as my sex partner."

She waited to see if he'd expand on this. He didn't. So she said, "What does that have to do with anything?"

"He doesn't want me to have sex partners. He doesn't want me to have friends either. He wants me to be alone."

"I don't see why it's any of his business what you do," she said. "I mean, you're a grown man and you can date whoever you want to date. And not having friends? That's just ridiculous."

"I told you there are things you wouldn't understand."

She had no idea what he was talking about, but at least she felt like she was having her first seminormal conversation with him. She was making progress, albeit very slow progress.

"Well, thank you for telling me all this," Olivia said. "I really appreciate it. And see? I'm still here. You didn't scare me off."

She kissed him on his lips, his muskiness turning her on again.

"Leave now," he said.

"What's the big rush to get rid of me tonight? Are you angry at me?"

"Yes."

She almost laughed, then realized it wasn't funny. She asked, "Why? What did I do?"

"You ask too many questions."

"If you answered them, I wouldn't have to ask them. Why do you want me to leave so early?"

Looking away again, he said, "I have a job to do."

"What kind of job?"

"That's why I don't like questions. Because questions lead to more questions."

"Normally questions lead to answers."

"You won't understand my work."

"Does it have to do with the brewery business?"

"No."

"I don't get why it has to be such a big mystery. It's just work. What are you, a male prostitute or something?"

He had no reaction. Maybe he was ignoring her or maybe she'd nailed it—it explained why he was so focused on sex and so emotionally distant. He'd certainly felt comfortable picking her up at the bar that night, and he knew what he was doing in bed.

She was about to ask him if he was a gigolo when he said, "I'm going to kill somebody tonight."

"Excuse me?" She wasn't sure she'd heard him correctly.

"I'm going to kill somebody tonight," he said again.

Was *kill* some kind of hip gigolo lingo for *screw*?

"Who do you have to kill?" she asked.

"I don't know," he said.

"So you're just going to kill some random person?"

Oh no, he wasn't one of those freaks who had sex with strangers in bathrooms, was he? Was she going to have to go get tested for God knows what diseases?

"No," he said.

"You don't put your dick in glory holes, do you?"

"I don't understand," he said.

"I don't understand either," she said.

"I told you you wouldn't," he said.

Then she had another flashback—the holster he was wearing that night. "Wait," she said, "you don't mean you're going to kill somebody tonight literally, do you?"

"Yes," he said.

"Why are you going to kill somebody?"

"It's my job."

"People hire you to—"

"Yes."

"But who—"

"I don't know."

"You don't know—?"

"Yes."

Why did she suddenly feel like she was in a David Mamet play?

"So let me get this straight," she said. "Someone you don't know hires you to kill people. You mean like a hit man?"

"I am a hit man," he said.

"Wow," she said. "So who do you work for? The Mafia?" She laughed.

"You're not afraid," he said.

"Why would I be afraid? You're not going to kill me, are you?" She was trying to make it into a joke, flirt with him, but he wouldn't go there.

He said, "You're not like other women. Other women would run, but you stay." He waited several seconds, then added, "You say you want to know my secrets, but you won't understand my secrets." He got up—of course he had a hard-on—and said, "You must leave now."

She wanted to know more, but she felt like she'd pushed her luck, getting him to open up as much as he had, and it was time to call it a night.

In the car back to the Upper East Side, she was still buzzed from another exhilarating night with Michael. He was right—the idea of him as a killer didn't frighten her at all; it actually kind of turned her on. Besides, it was easy to accept anything Michael told her because she knew none of it was real. Everything—his odd communication style, the melodrama, the wild sex—was so over the top, how could she possibly be frightened, or even mildly concerned? Telling her "I'm going to kill somebody tonight," in that serious, foreboding tone? Come on. Obviously, since the night they'd met, she'd been a participant in an elaborate role play. If he wanted to pretend he was a psychotic hit man, that was fine with her. As far as she was concerned, this whole relationship, or whatever they wanted to call it, was just a wild roller coaster ride, a welcome break from the mundane cookie-cutter guys she'd been dating for years.

The car braked in front of her building, and she said to Eddie, "See you tomorrow, same bat time."

Walking up the stairs of her brownstone, Olivia, giggling, said out loud, "I'm a hit man."

In bed she was still laughing over it, and she could barely wait for the next big twist. Seriously, he wanted her to believe he killed people for a living. What could possibly top that?

FIFTEEN

"So how did the weekend go?"

Simon and Alison had just arrived for their marriage counseling session and were sitting next to each other on the black leather couch, facing Dr. Hagan, who was wearing dark green shoes, green pants, a green turtleneck, and green tinted glasses.

Simultaneously Simon and Alison said, "It was amazing."

They all laughed, overenthusiastically, and then Hagan said, "Well, it's nice to see that you're both in agreement for a change."

Simon held Alison's hand and said, "Want to begin, sweetie?"

"Well, there's been a really dramatic . . . well . . . change," Alison said.

"Change?" Hagan was intrigued.

"Yes," Alison said. "For the last several days . . . well, since Saturday, there's been a sudden change in our whole marriage, actually."

As she went on explaining, Simon was distracted by the strong odor of cigar smoke. He'd smelled the odor before in Hagan's office, but it had never been so intense. Although there was no visible smoke in the room, the room smelled like a cigar bar.

"Excuse me," Dr. Hagan said to Alison. Then to Simon, "Is something making you uncomfortable?"

"It's just the odor," Simon said.

"Odor?" Hagan was confused.

Alison sniffed, then shrugged, as if she didn't detect anything unusual. Simon was amazed they couldn't smell it; it was so strong.

Then Hagan caught on and said, "I apologize, I didn't think it was noticeable. I usually smoke outside, but the other day I smoked one cigar in the office."

Hagan got room freshener from his desk drawer and sprayed it around the room, but, oh God, that was worse. The fake citrus scent was so strong Simon felt like he was choking.

Hagan noticed Simon's discomfort and said, "I didn't realize you were so sensitive. Is it really that bad?"

Between coughs, Simon said, "Maybe you could just open the window."

Hagan opened the window in the below-street-level office and it helped a little but not much.

"Thanks," Simon said hoarsely. "I'll be okay."

"This has been another big change lately," Alison said. "Simon has been very, well, sensitive to smells lately."

"It's true, I have been," Simon said.

"Mmm-hmm," Dr. Hagan said, as if he weren't sure what to make of it.

"His hearing's better too," Alison added.

"Oh?" Hagan said to Simon, "Did you have a hearing problem?"

"No," Simon said. "She means I just hear better, that's all."

"Oh, and he has a lot more energy," Alison said. "Not just sexually, physically too. He goes on long runs to the park. And his diet has changed too."

"Changed how?" Hagan asked.

"I've been having these cravings for meat," Simon said.

"And he's never been a meat eater," Alison said. "I mean, when I met him he was practically a vegetarian. That's one of the things I initially—"

She stopped herself, but Simon knew she'd been about to say *liked about him*. Instead she said, "It's just been a big surprise, that's all."

"I see, I see," Hagan said. "Well, I really don't think this is so unusual. This is probably something that should be addressed in individual therapy, but dietary changes are often a control issue. Simon has gone through some big life changes lately, and he's said he initially found single parenting to be overwhelming, so I'm not surprised to see him taking control with a new exercise and dietary regimen. What I'm saying is, I don't think it's any cause for concern unless there's dangerous weight loss or it's causing a problem in the marriage."

"Oh, trust me, I'm not complaining," Alison said, putting her arm around Simon's back and shifting closer to him on the couch.

"But there does seem to be quite a dramatic emotional turnaround," Hagan said. "How do you account for it?"

Simon and Alison looked at each other. Simon could tell Alison wanted him to take the lead, so he said, "I'm not really sure. I guess I realized what a wonderful, sexy woman I'm married to. I guess I got into a rut and I wasn't appreciating her the way I should've been."

Suddenly Alison's eyes got glassy as if she were on the verge of tears, and then she kissed Simon. He kissed her back, and they actually started making out on the couch in front of Dr. Hagan. They were so caught up in it that they didn't realize what they were doing until Hagan cleared his throat loudly.

After the session, they returned home and relieved Christina from babysitting. Simon took a long evening run in the park, and when he returned, Jeremy was already asleep, so Simon and Alison made love for a few hours.

"I never thought it could be like this," Alison said.

"Like what?" Simon asked.

She was running her fingers through his sweaty, very thick chest hair.

"So perfect," she said.

*   *   *

Thursday was sunny and mild—a great playground day. Jeremy wanted to see his friends downtown, and with everything going so well lately, Simon didn't see any reason to keep avoiding the guys. After all, play dates were about the kids, not the parents, and denying Jeremy the chance to play with his friends seemed like the wrong thing to do.

Despite how Simon had left the other day, so suddenly and melo-dramatically, when he and Jeremy arrived the guys acted as if it were any other afternoon, and they didn't even seem surprised to see them. They gave Simon the usual warm hugs and then sat on the bench talking about the usual subjects—food, sex, and their kids. Simon still thought there was something very off about the guys, especially Michael; he was starting to get what Charlie had meant about Michael being like a motivational speaker. Although he couldn't place exactly why, there was no doubt that spending time with the guys made Simon feel confident and secure, and it had definitely been having a positive effect on his marriage.

That night, Mark e-mailed him the information about Tom's fu-neral, to be held the next day, Friday, at a funeral parlor in Bernardsville, New Jersey. Everyone from the office had been invited, and Mark wrote that he was "just passing the info along." Although, for the most part, Simon had managed to do a good job of putting that night behind him, he was still upset with himself for going to New Jersey, possibly to con-front Tom, and he was on the fence about going to the funeral.

Later Simon and Alison were in bed, their naked, clammy bodies intertwined, and Simon said, "Part of me thinks I should go, because I worked with the guy for seven years. On the other hand, he fired me, and wasn't even returning my e-mails."

Alison said, "Funerals are for the family, not for the deceased. If you go, you'd be going for his wife and kids, not for him."

This made a lot of sense, and as Simon had met Tom's wife, JoAnne, a few times, he decided that going was the right thing to do.

In the morning Simon took the 8:18 train from Penn Station to Bernardsville and then a taxi to the funeral parlor. The quaint upscale town looked totally unfamiliar, and it still amazed him that he'd been in this area last Friday night, almost a week ago. He was tempted to have the cabdriver take him past Tom's house, just to see if it sparked a memory, but he didn't want to miss the beginning of the service.

He made it at around ten fifteen, just as people had started filing into the chapel. It was less crowded than he'd expected. He'd assumed there would be a huge turnout—after all, Tom had been fairly young—but there seemed to be about seventy-five people, tops. Aside from Tom's wife, who was sitting in the first row with two teenagers, probably her kids, the only people Simon recognized were several people from work, including Mark, who was sitting with Jennifer—Tom's old assistant—toward the back. He also noticed a couple of senior VPs with, oh Jesus Christ, Paul Kramer, the ass-kisser who'd gotten the promotion Simon had been supposed to get. Simon didn't want to get into an awkward conversation with Paul, and suddenly coming to the funeral seemed like a big mistake; what had he been thinking? He'd assumed that dozens of people from the office would attend, but with only the people Tom had been close to here, Simon felt extremely out of place. He was even considering leaving—no one had noticed him yet and no one would miss him. Then Mark spotted Simon and waved for him to come over, so there went that idea.

"Hey," Mark said, "I saved a seat for you."

Simon sat and said, "Thanks."

Andy Wallace, one of the senior VPs, looked over at Simon, and they acknowledged each other's presence with half smiles and head nods. Then Simon noticed that Paul was looking in his direction, but they didn't smile at each other; Simon just stared at the jerk until he looked away.

The mood in the chapel was appropriately somber, with light classical, maybe Tchaikovsky, playing. Although people were quiet, Simon could make out whispered conversations. There was so much "whisper noise" it was hard to decipher any individual conversations, but then Simon was able to focus on Paul and could make out him saying to Andy: "I know. What is he even *doing* here?" Then a few seconds later, Paul added, "I hope he doesn't think he's getting a job now. It's so pathetic. The guy's such a freakin' loser."

All the whispering stopped, but the crying and sniffling continued as the funeral began. It was clear that the funeral director, an older
bearded man who could have competed in an Abe Lincoln look-alike
contest, had never met Tom and was speaking from information he'd
been given. He did a good job of making it seem like he actually knew
Tom and comforting the family, even if the whole eulogy had a de-
pressingly detached vibe. The immediate family, especially the kids, were
visibly upset, crying loudly throughout. Simon was teary eyed too. The
poor kids had lost their father, and Simon couldn't help imagining his
own funeral someday with Jeremy sitting there crying. He couldn't wait
to go home and give Jeremy a big tight hug.

Then Simon noticed a woman seated toward the back of the chapel
who seemed particularly upset, sobbing and even wailing once or twice.
She was attractive, in her midforties, with short blond hair, and it struck
Simon as odd that she was acting as emotionally as the family. Then it
all clicked: maybe six months ago, in the men's room at S&O, Simon
washing his hands, overhearing Tom telling Greg in accounting about
a woman he'd been "fooling around with lately." Simon assumed the
distraught woman in the back had been Tom's lover.

The funeral director invited Tom's wife up to the podium, but she
was too distraught to speak. When his daughter spoke and said, "My
daddy didn't deserve this. No one deserves this," practically everyone in
the audience was crying.

Finally the funeral director invited everyone to come to the cemetery for the burial. Simon planned to slip away, but in case anyone
asked he had a built-in excuse—he had to get back to the city to take
over child care duties.

As everyone was exiting the chapel, Mark said to Simon, "Brutal, huh?"

"Yeah," Simon said. "Very."

Mark looked around, then whispered, "I hear his wife has been taking
it really hard. She even had to be hospitalized. Has a congenital heart mur-
mur, or some kind of heart condition, and they were worried she might
have a heart attack or something. At least she made it here, but man."

Simon shook his head sympathetically.

Mark continued, whispering, "It's one thing to lose someone you love, but all the mystery has to make it worse. I mean, they haven't even found the wolf yet."

"Wolf?" Simon asked.

"You didn't hear?" Mark said. "Yeah, now they're saying a wolf did it. There's a preserve or something nearby, and the cops or wildlife commission or whatever have been searching, but apparently they haven't found anything yet. . . . Oh, and they found a carcass of a deer. They think the wolf killed the deer too. Are you okay, man?"

Simon was going for an appropriately baffled, sympathetic reaction, but apparently he wasn't pulling it off. He said, "Fine, yeah. It's just all so . . . shocking."

"Yeah, I know it is, isn't it?" Mark said. "Every time I think about it, I'm like, the guy was killed by a wolf in his own backyard? I'm like, you've gotta be kidding me. You sure you're okay?" Mark said. "You seem, I don't know, kind of, like, pale?"

"I'm probably just thirsty, I haven't had lunch and I was up early." Simon realized he was babbling. "Excuse me a sec."

He slipped away and went to the bathroom and splashed his face with cold water, trying to settle down. Coming here had been a horrible idea; what had he been thinking? If he really wanted to forget about what had happened to him that night, he had to put it all behind him, instead of continuing to confront it.

After a few minutes he felt a little better. He just wanted to get home—eat some steak, go for a long run, play with his son, make love to his wife. Life was good now, and he wanted to appreciate every second of it.

When he left the bathroom Tom's wife was right there, a few feet away, being consoled by a couple. She looked distraught and weak, with noticeable dark circles under her eyes. Simon felt he should say something, so he said, "Excuse me. JoAnne?"

Tom's wife looked at him as if he were a stranger.

"Simon Burns . . . from S&O. I worked . . . well, used to work with your husband."

She continued to appear baffled, then said, "Oh, thank you, and thank you so much for coming."

Simon suspected she still didn't know who he was—they'd met only a few times and she probably didn't recognize him out of context. He said, "I just want you to know how sorry I am. Your husband was a great, great man."

Okay, so he was exaggerating . . . a lot . . . but the whole point of being here was to comfort the family, wasn't it? And it was obvious that JoAnne appreciated his thoughts. She hugged him tightly, as if she didn't want to let go, and said, "Thank you . . . thank you so much."

As he was hugging her, he made eye contact for the first time with the guy who'd been giving her his condolences before he came over. The guy was middle-aged and overweight, and he had an air of arrogance that rich, entitled people have. He was looking at Simon inquisitively.

"How do I know you?" the guy asked.

Simon and JoAnne ended their long embrace, and another couple came over to offer condolences to her.

Simon had never seen the guy before in his life. He said, "I'm a colleague of Tom's."

"You live in the area?" the guy asked.

"No," Simon said.

"Oh, I thought I might know you from the country club or something. You look really familiar, I don't know why." He stuck out his hand. "I'm Alan. Alan Freedman."

Simon shook his hand. "Simon Burns."

The guy was still staring at him, and it was starting to make Simon uncomfortable.

"Simon Burns," Alan said, squinting. "Nope, that doesn't ring a bell. But you really do look familiar. I know I've seen you somewhere."

"I guess it's just one of those things," Simon said. "Well, it was nice to meet you."

Simon walked away. When he got to the front of the room, he looked back and saw Alan was still watching him. Simon forced a smile and then noticed that Mark and Jennifer were distracted, in midconversation, so he slipped outside. He'd gotten a business card from the cabdriver who'd brought him here, and he was punching the numbers into his cell when he heard, "Not going to the cemetery?"

Still on edge after the weird interaction with Alan Freedman, Simon felt a jolt in his chest, and then he looked back and saw Paul Kramer. Paul was oozing cockiness and half-smiling, which seemed especially inappropriate considering the setting and circumstances. Come to think of it, he didn't seem nearly as upset as he should've been during the funeral itself. Simon couldn't help wondering if it was because with Tom out of the way, Paul suddenly had his eyes on another promotion. Simon wouldn't put it past Paul, who had proved himself many times over to be a slimy opportunist.

"Yeah, I have to take care of my son this afternoon," Simon said.

"Oh, okay, that makes sense," Paul said, still half-smiling. "Just thought if you came all the way out here you'd go for the full monty, but if you have to get back to the city I'm sure the family understands. By the way, do you even *know* the family?"

"Excuse me?"

"I'm just surprised you're here at all. I didn't know you and Tom were close. Actually, I thought you hated him . . . I mean after what transpired and all."

His smirk had morphed into a full smile.

"Hated him?" Simon realized he was talking too loud and said in a lower voice, "Why would I hate him?"

"Well, *numero uno* because he canned you."

If they'd had this conversation last month, in the office, Simon might've been intimidated. After all, in office conflicts Simon hadn't exactly been an aggressive go-getter. His lack of a cutthroat demeanor had definitely hampered his climb up the corporate ladder and had probably ultimately cost him his job. Guys like Paul, who were willing to bully and backstab their way to the top, fared much better in the business world than guys like Simon, who shied away from aggression.

But now Simon noticed something strange. He wasn't backing down from Paul at all. Instead, he was holding his ground. Beyond holding his ground. He was the aggressor, taking control.

He took a couple of steps toward Paul, his chest slightly expanded, and said, "I came because I worked with the guy for seven years, and because I wanted to pay my respects to the family."

It was obvious that Paul sensed that this was a different Simon Burns, a Simon Burns he couldn't push around the way he used to. The smile was gone. Did he even look a little fearful?

"Oh, okay," Paul said. "I was just surprised, that's all."

"I'm not surprised," Simon said, taking another step toward Paul, enjoying the way he was suddenly able to intimidate him. "It makes sense that you're here, especially since Andy Wallace is here."

"What . . . what do you mean?" Paul asked.

"Come on, it's so obvious," Simon said. "You want Tom's job now. You couldn't even wait for his body to get cold before you started campaigning, could you?"

"That's ridiculous."

"I bet you've been dropping hints to Andy every day. Maybe I should have a talk with him myself. Tell him that you told me you want Tom's job."

Simon started toward the chapel, but Paul cut in front of him and said, "Just chill, okay? Just chill."

Simon glared at Paul menacingly, like a bully on a playground. Paul was clearly frightened; it almost seemed as if he were on the verge of tears. Finally Paul said, "I should go," and headed back inside.

Simon called after him, "Oh, and by the way . . ."

Paul stopped and looked back. He was practically trembling.

"I think *you're* a freakin' loser too," Simon said.

Paul's stunned expression was priceless.

SIXTEEN

Alison was enjoying her day off work with Jeremy. In the morning they went to a story hour at the New York Public Library on Eighty-first and Amsterdam, and then Jeremy wanted to go play with his new friends downtown.

"Pleeeeeeaaase," he begged, frowning adorably.

The cuteness was almost unbearable, but Alison said, "No, that's what you and Daddy do together. We'll do something else today."

So they went to the playground in Central Park, near Ninety-sixth. There happened to be a kid, Miguel, he knew from a gymnastics class he'd taken last year. Miguel's mother wasn't there—his nanny had taken him to the playground—so Alison sat on a bench, playing Sudoku on her iPhone for a while, and then her sister called.

Alison explained that she'd taken a day off work so Simon could attend his ex-boss's funeral, and then Lauren asked how things were going with Simon.

"I have to say," Alison said, "amazingly well."

She described how Simon seemed to be making "a serious effort to change," and how it was like she had "a brand-new husband."

When Alison was through raving, there was silence on the line. Thinking the call had been dropped, she asked, "Are you still there?"

"I'm here, I'm here," Lauren said.

"Uh-oh, what's wrong?" Alison said, but she knew her sister was going to get on her case about Simon again.

"You tell me," Lauren said.

"Okay, let's not get into *that* again."

"I'm sorry, I'm just very dubious. In a marriage, when something seems too good to be true, it usually is."

If anyone else had told her this, Alison probably would have blown off the advice. But it wasn't like Lauren to butt into someone else's personal business. She'd always been the logical, levelheaded one in the family. Alison was the one who tended to make emotional decisions, and if Lauren felt that something wasn't right, Alison couldn't ignore the possibility that she could be on to something.

"I totally get what you're saying," Alison said, "but the idea of him actually cheating on me seems so remote."

"Okay, I'm going to ask you a question," Lauren said, "and I want your honest answer. Don't even think about it, just answer from your gut. Ready?"

"Ready."

After a dramatic pause, Lauren asked, "Do you think Simon's hiding something from you?"

"Yes," Alison said, with no hesitation.

"'Nuff said," Lauren said.

Alison let out the deep breath she'd taken. "So what am I supposed to do, confront him about it?"

"No, I wouldn't do that," Lauren said. "You don't want to cause drama if you don't have to. Maybe you could, I don't know, find some evidence?"

"Evidence? You want me to hire a detective?"

"It doesn't have to be that drastic, but you can do a little snooping yourself. Can you check his cell phone?"

"He always has it with him."

"Always?"

"Usually."

"What you have to ask yourself," Lauren said, "is do you want to find out sooner or later? Take it from somebody who lived with a cheating husband for four years—sooner beats the hell out of later."

Alison knew her sister was right. Something strange was definitely going on, and she knew that if she let this drag on and then found out about an affair a month from now, or a year from now, she'd kick herself for not acting sooner.

Back at the apartment, when Jeremy went down for his nap, she went online with Internet Explorer and checked the cache of sites Simon had visited lately. As she scrolled through his recent Google searches, she tried to brace herself for the worst—searches for hotels, sex toys, lingerie, or some other evidence of an affair. At the same time she knew that there was no way to actually prepare for the humiliation she'd feel if her suspicions were confirmed.

She didn't find anything unusual, though. He'd been to eBay, The Street.com, and the New Jersey Transit website, and he'd done several searches for news stories about his ex-boss's death. Suddenly she felt extremely guilty for checking up on him. If a marriage was about trust, then in a way she felt like *she* was the betrayer.

She logged off and busied herself with housework—dusting and vacuuming. She was trying to forget about the whole situation, but she kept hearing her sister's voice: *If something in your marriage seems too good to be true, it probably is.* Though she still felt bad about distrusting Simon, she reminded herself that she wasn't the one who'd brought this on. She wasn't naturally paranoid. Until very recently, the idea of Simon cheating on her wouldn't have even occurred to her. *He* was the one who'd caused all this with his weird behavior, and she had good reason to be suspicious.

Alison shut off the vacuum and went back online and did a search: "signs husband cheating." As she scanned the results, she became even more convinced that her paranoia was justified. Many of the sites warned that one of the most telltale signs that your husband is cheating is when his behavior changes. Lately Simon's behavior hadn't changed—it had changed drastically. Another major sign of trouble was if he suddenly becomes overly concerned about his appearance. She remembered that night he'd gone out with his friends when this had all started, when he was stressing about what to wear, trying on multiple outfits. She'd even made that quip about him having a date. At the time, she didn't seriously think he was going out to meet a woman, but what if he was? Maybe he'd been at some woman's apartment, some babysitter he'd met at the playground, and she'd been stupid enough to believe that he'd gotten drunk and crashed at his friend's brewery.

She heard a key turning in the lock, and then the front door opened. She X'd the browsing window as Simon entered.

"Hey," he said enthusiastically.

"Hi," she said, purposely subdued. "I didn't expect you home so soon. I thought you were going to be home closer to dinnertime."

"Yeah, I thought so too," Simon said. "I went to the service, but I decided not to go out to the cemetery."

"Really? How come?"

"I paid my respects to his wife, and I thought that was enough. Besides, I missed you guys."

She was still sitting at the computer. He hugged her from behind and kissed the back of her neck. What was up with the way he was biting her so much lately? Kissing her hello at all was unusual behavior too—well, unusual before last Saturday. She tensed while he kissed her, but he didn't seem to notice.

"Missed us?" she asked. "You were only gone a few hours."

"Yeah, I know," he said, "but the funeral was so sad, seeing the family so upset. It made me appreciate what I have. . . . Mmmm, you smell so amazing. Is Jeremy napping?"

"Yeah, but he should be up in a few minutes." Actually she expected his nap to last for at least another half hour, but she knew what he was hinting at.

Sure enough, he asked, "How about a quickie?"

She wondered, *Did he really go to the funeral?* Maybe he'd been screwing his girlfriend all afternoon and this was just more of his lies.

He kissed her again and she got up very suddenly, as if the chair had given her an electric shock, and said, "No, not now."

Picking up on her abruptness, he asked, "What's wrong?"

"I have to finish cleaning," she said, and resumed vacuuming.

Simon didn't push it.

When Jeremy woke up from his nap, Simon took him to the park to play soccer. Why did Simon want to run around the park so much lately? Who was he getting in shape for?

After soccer, Jeremy looked exhausted, as if he'd been running around nonstop, but Simon, with his unbridled energy, announced he was going out for a run in the park and to start eating without him. Alison couldn't help imagining that he was planning to go to his lover's place for a booty call. Maybe she lived in the neighborhood, around the corner. Maybe every time he came back sweaty from his runs, he'd really been with her. If he couldn't get some from his wife, he went out to get it elsewhere. Suddenly it seemed so obvious that he was cheating on her; she couldn't believe she'd been so oblivious.

"Who . . ." She almost added *is she?* but managed to restrain herself. She knew she was reacting emotionally right now, and without solid evidence. For Jeremy's sake, she didn't want to create unnecessary drama.

"Who what?" Simon asked.

"Never mind," Alison said.

When he returned from the run, he went right into the shower. Was it to get her smell off him? He also took his cell phone with him into the bathroom. Was he texting her?

She couldn't wait to get her hands on that phone.

Later in the evening she had her opportunity. After Simon read a bedtime story to Jeremy, he came into the bedroom, where Alison was lying in bed, watching *The Rachel Maddow Show* DVR'd. He stripped to just his boxer briefs and Alison noticed his chest, which looked even hairier than it had last night.

"Have sex with me now," he said.

"Excuse me?"

They'd been having a lot of sex lately, but was he seriously *demanding* intercourse?

"Sorry," Simon said, seeming almost embarrassed. "I don't know why I said it that way. I meant, Jeremy's asleep, so do you want to make love now?"

She glanced toward his crotch and saw that he had a hard-on. She saw a flash of him and his lover.

"No," she said.

"Is something wrong?" he asked.

"No," she said, looking at Rachel Maddow. She wished Simon would just leave, because she couldn't bear to see his lying, cheating face right now.

"It seems like you're angry at me for some reason," he said.

"I'm not," she said.

"Oh," he said. "Then how come you don't want to—"

"We don't have to have sex multiple times every single day."

"We don't have to," he said. "I thought you wanted to have more sex. I thought you liked it."

"I did . . . I mean do . . . but I feel like you want to break records or something. And I don't understand why you . . . Never mind. I'm just tired and want to go to sleep early tonight, that's all."

She saw that he still had a hard-on, and she shook her head in frustration.

"Okay," he said. "I can tell you're in a bad mood. I'll leave you alone."

He went into the bathroom. She didn't hear water running or him lifting the toilet seat cover. She wondered if he was masturbating, and if so, who was he thinking about?

Then she spotted his phone on the dresser. She opened it and checked his recent received and dialed calls. Besides calls to and from home and to her cell, there was a call to Mark, his ex-assistant. How did she know it was really Mark? Maybe he'd purposely mislabeled his lover's number, thinking it would prevent him from getting caught. She opened her purse and took out a pen and a business card and jotted down the digits. Then she checked his texts. There were no messages in his sent messages or inbox. This was strange because Alison had texted with him several times recently. Had he deleted all of his messages for a reason?

"What're you doing?"

She looked over and saw Simon standing there near the bathroom door.

She put down the phone quickly and said, "It started beeping. I thought the alarm was going off."

It was a lame excuse, but the best she could come up with at the spur of the moment.

"It's okay," he said. "If you want to use my phone, you can."

His gaze was aimed downward, toward the business card she was holding. Instinctively she made a fist, crushing the card.

"It was just the alarm," she said.

When he returned to the bathroom, she put the business card back in her purse and got back in bed. She felt awful about the whole situation. Just this morning everything had been going so well and now she was in a troubled marriage again.

She was determined not to let this drag on. She was going to get answers and put this all behind her one way or another.

On Saturday morning, after Simon returned from yet another long run, she went out to do some grocery shopping. On her way, she stopped at a phone booth on Columbus. She hadn't made a call from a phone booth in ages, but she wanted to check the number she'd written down and didn't want Caller ID to pop up from her cell phone.

Mark's number was actually Mark—his voice mail picked up. She was more frustrated than relieved. If Simon was having an affair, she wanted to find out about it already, and her instincts told her that something was going on, that what had been going on lately definitely wasn't normal.

The rest of the weekend Alison didn't actively check up on Simon, but she was attentive and didn't notice anything. He was his usual self—well, usual as of late: exercising, eating meat, and wanting to have sex with her, well, pretty much constantly. He was talking in this weird, demanding tone too. When he asked questions he'd leave out the question mark. Like during dinner one night he poured himself a glass of apple juice and then said to her, "You want apple juice," but not as a question, as a statement. He'd done it maybe a dozen times, and it was getting very annoying.

On Saturday night she told him she was tired again. He seemed disappointed but didn't question her about it. But when she turned him down again on Sunday, he said, "Can you please tell me what's going on? I'm not a mind reader. If you're angry at me about something, tell me what it is."

Alison knew that a discussion would erode into an argument, so she said, "What's the point?" and watched a DVR'd *Rachel Maddow Show* until she fell asleep.

Alison didn't sleep for long. After about an hour, she woke up, ruminating about Simon's strange behavior and whether it really meant he was cheating on her. Maybe he was just acting weird for no reason, as part of some kind of midlife crisis. After all, he'd lost his job and had become a stay-at-home dad—these were major life changes. She had no evidence that he was cheating on her, so maybe she was jumping to incorrect conclusions. Maybe all of the crazy exercise and interest in sex was just his way of making an extra effort at saving the marriage. Hadn't she been asking him to make more of an effort for months? Maybe she was being extremely unfair. Now that he was actually making an effort, she was freaking out.

On Monday morning she had a sales appointment with Dr. Greenberg at his office on Eighty-fourth Street between Park and Madison. The receptionist had her wait in the waiting room until Greenberg was available, close to noon, and Alison actually had started to doze when the nurse said she could see the doctor now. Alison didn't know Greenberg particularly well, and her pitch was uncharacteristically rushed and scattered. He took her samples and told her to call for a follow-up meeting, but she could tell it wouldn't lead to anything. She felt bad because Greenberg was an influential, prestigious gynecologist who could be elusive, and she felt that she'd blown a major opportunity.

Alison walked down Madison Avenue, pulling her suitcase with samples behind her, trying not to be too hard on herself; she'd been going through a lot lately, and everyone was entitled to an off day every now and then. It had turned into a beautiful sunny afternoon—shoppers were out in abundance and the outdoor tables at the side street cafés were filled. She texted Simon:

Hope you're enjoying the beautiful day!

He didn't write back right away the way he usually did lately. She kept checking as she continued downtown, but there was still no response. She imagined him angry at her, deleting the message without even bothering to read it. If she was wrong about this and he wasn't having an illicit relationship, all she was accomplishing with her suspicion was pushing him further away. Maybe her sister and the websites were wrong, and Simon's behavioral changes were just his weird way of making an extra effort to work on the marriage.

It seemed weird, waiting for him to write back, so she called him.

He picked up after the fourth ring and said, "Hey."

"Hey, just saying hi," Alison said. "And I wanted to apologize for the way I've been acting this weekend. I've just been stressed out, but I've been taking it out on you and I'm sorry."

"It's okay," Simon said. "I miss you."

She couldn't remember the last time he'd told her he missed her—when they were dating? He sounded sincere, which made her feel even guiltier for the assumptions she'd made.

"I miss you too," she said. "So where are you guys? Battery Park?"

"No, the guys came uptown today. We're hanging out in Sheep Meadow."

"Oh, that sounds great. Well, you two have a great day. And give Jeremy a big kiss for me."

"I will. I love you."

"Love you too."

Alison ended the call, feeling awful. Not for saying "Love you," to her husband—that felt great and normal; she felt awful because of the way she'd been treating him lately. All of her reasons for doubting him and acting so distant toward him over the weekend seemed ridiculous. She missed him and couldn't wait to see him later.

She tapped out a text: *I miss you!* but didn't hit send, as it occurred to her that she was about a ten-minute walk from Sheep Meadow and she didn't have another appointment until after lunch. Wouldn't it be nice to surprise Simon and Jeremy?

Without giving it any more thought, she headed toward the park.

She went up the hill, and gradually Sheep Meadow came into view. She spotted Simon and his friends right away—they were impossible to miss. In the middle of the field, people were cheering, watching Simon and the other men playing Frisbee with their shirts off. Alison was surprised to see Simon with his off—he never went shirtless in the park, even on the hottest summer days—and she was also surprised to see how hairy his chest was. She'd seen it in the bedroom, of course, but the lights were usually dimmed. Out in the open his hairiness somehow seemed more startling. The other guys seemed noticeably hairy too. She stopped and watched as the man with thick gray hair—she assumed this was Michael—flung the Frisbee extremely far and a Latino-looking guy chased it down and sprinted back to him like a happy dog. After the stocky muscular guy retrieved the Frisbee, it was Simon's turn. Alison watched in awe as Simon ran at blazing speed and snared the disk, then ran back to Michael, grinning, and not appearing to be out of breath at all. Jeremy and the three other boys were cheering with the other onlookers.

Alison watched the scene, thinking, *Is this really happening?* Why was Simon acting this way, and how was he able to run so fast? He'd never been a particularly fast runner, but all of a sudden he was like a track star. He couldn't have gotten in such great shape during the past week, just from going running in the park and playing soccer with Jeremy.

Now the guys were taking turns hugging one another. Simon hugged the gray-haired guy for a long time, maybe a minute, and then the guys shouted at each other stuff like "Woo-hoo" and "Yeah, baby." Then the guys high-fived some more, still acting like overgrown frat boys on speed. Alison had seen guys with lots of machismo in the park before. On weekends in the spring and summer, the park was filled with testosterone-fueled soccer and touch football games. But this didn't seem like usual male bonding. They were emitting a weird energy that seemed practically euphoric.

Alison had no idea what to make of any of this, but her gut told her that it had to be related to Simon's other odd behavior lately. It was too coincidental that he'd met these guys and changed right around the same time. There had to be some connection; she just had no idea what it could possibly be.

She decided not to say hi after all and walked away quickly before Simon and Jeremy noticed her.

Between afternoon appointments, Alison stopped at the Starbucks on First and Seventy-fifth and went online and did searches for "husband suddenly fast" and "husband suddenly hairy" and "husband suddenly eats meat." The results didn't give her any insight into Simon's situation, though one site suggested that the hairiness could be related to a hormone imbalance. Were there too many hormones in the meat he was eating? Alison did a search for "meat hormones hairy husband," but it didn't solve the mystery.

The rest of the workday, Alison couldn't get the images out of her head of Simon shirtless, high-fiving and hugging the guys. Where was all that machismo coming from? Simon had never been so outwardly touchy-feely with guys before. Come to think of it, he didn't even have a lot of male friends. Once in a while he met his friends, Stu or Kenny, for beers, but he wasn't exactly a guy's guy. That was one of the things Alison had liked about him when they first met. Most of her previous boyfriends were sports fanatics, and it was refreshing to be with a guy who'd rather go to a wine tasting or a gallery opening than sit slumped on the couch watching a hockey game.

Recalling Simon and Michael's ultralong hug, Alison said, "He's not gay, is he?"

Alison didn't intend to say this out loud. Cheryl, a barista with whom Alison sometimes chatted, was mopping the floor nearby and asked in a gossipy tone, "Who's not gay?"

Covering, Alison said, "Oh, just, uh, some actor I saw on TV last night."

"Actors?" Cheryl laughed. "Trust me, girl . . . they're *all* gay."

Alison had never gotten any gaydar from Simon before, and he'd seemed very straight—especially lately. That said, although he wasn't exactly a metro style freak, he dressed better than most guys and was usually well groomed. She remembered teasing him when they first met because he used an apricot facial scrub and a "skin-firming" body moisturizer. Maybe he and that gray-haired guy Michael were having an affair. Maybe that explained the all-nighter, and why he was going running and going to the gym all the time—to get in shape for his boyfriend. And maybe all the interest in heterosexual sex was just some kind of overcompensation so he could stay in the closet. Maybe Alison wasn't his wife; she was his beard.

Though she wasn't convinced that any of this was true, it seemed as logical as any of the other theories she'd come up with lately. If he wasn't gay, he had some big secret, and maybe it had something to do with his new friends.

That evening when she came home from work, she didn't talk to Simon much. He asked her how her day was, and she said, "Fine," and then played with Jeremy for a while. She felt so uncomfortable around Simon, she actually found it hard to look at him.

After dinner, Jeremy was watching *The Wiggles* and Simon was washing dishes. Figuring there was no reason to put it off any longer, Alison came into the kitchen, asking, "Did you have fun with your friends today?"

"Fun" was loaded, but Simon didn't pick up on it.

"Yeah, we did actually. Jeremy had a blast too."

"I thought you were going to stop hanging out with them."

"I changed my mind," Simon said. "I think they're cool guys. I really like them."

Getting that vision again, of Simon hugging Michael, Alison asked, "What do you like about them?"

"What do you mean?" Simon asked.

"I'm just curious," she said. "I mean, what's so special about them?"

"I don't know," Simon said. "I guess I just fit in with them. I mean, we're all stay-at-home dads, or part-time stay-at-home dads, we each have one son. . . ."

"Do they exercise a lot too?"

"I'm not sure, but they're all really athletic. What's going on? What's wrong?"

"You don't have to do this anymore," Alison said.

Simon, scrubbing the frying pan in which he'd cooked the pork chops he'd had for dinner, asked, "Do what anymore?"

"All of this," Alison said, letting loose with her frustration. "If you have some secret, or if something's going on, you can talk about it with me. Or we can talk about it with Dr. Hagan. But all of this acting out, or whatever you want to call it, isn't accomplishing anything."

Simon shut off the faucet and said, "I'm sorry, but I'm really confused right now. You're the one who's been acting weird, not me."

"Me?" Alison said. "How've I—"

"Maybe I was in Dr. Hagan's office with a different wife who was talking about how great things have been lately and how much our marriage has improved."

"It's true I like some of the changes," Alison said. "I mean, I like that we've been more intimate, and it's nice to be having sex again, but all of it's just too much. Your exercising, your meat-eating, the way you suddenly have this great hearing and you have more hair on your body than you've ever had before." Alison realized how crazy all of this sounded, but she continued, "I know there's something going on, something you're not telling me, and don't say it's all my imagination because it isn't. I know it isn't."

Simon dried his hands with the dish towel and then tried to put his arms around Alison, but she backed away.

"Look, I know I've been acting different lately," he said. "I was concerned myself at first, but I called Dr. Segal's office and described my symptoms and they pooh-poohed the whole thing. Then I thought, why was I concerned about this when our lives were getting better? We weren't fighting as much, we were having great sex, and Jeremy was happier. That was what we wanted, right? We wanted to figure out a way to be happy, to improve our lives, and it was happening, so why fight it?"

Alison didn't answer right away, at first finding it hard to poke any holes in this logic. Then she said, "But what about the physical changes? The crazy meat-eating and your hairy chest?"

"I don't know how to explain it," Simon said. "All I know is I feel amazing."

For emphasis Simon smiled widely, but to Alison the smile seemed exaggerated, kind of maniacal, the way he'd looked earlier when he was high-fiving with his friends in the park. She had no idea who this man was, but he wasn't her husband.

"I feel like I'm losing you," she said.

"How are you losing me?" he said. "I'm right here."

But he wasn't there. This hairy meat-eating man who chased Frisbees in the park and bear-hugged his friends was a total stranger.

"I just want to go back to the way things were," she said. "I'll take all of our old problems over this. I just want my husband back."

The rest of the evening she didn't say a word to him. She was hoping that giving him the silent treatment would send him the message that she was seriously upset, and hopefully he'd come to her and let her in on what was going on. But he didn't seem to get the hint at all. When Jeremy was asleep he came into the bedroom and said, "I want to have sex with you."

Alison lost it and shouted, "Why do you keep talking to me in that weird way?! Can you just stop it, for God's sake?!"

Simon, seeming shocked and offended, didn't answer and went into the bathroom, probably to masturbate. In frustration, Alison flung her pillow against the headboard and then pounded it a few times with her fist. She couldn't believe they were having marital problems again.

Exhausted from the long, stressful day, she shut off the light and fell asleep. She woke up to Simon's loud screaming. Disoriented at first, she wasn't sure what was going on, then realized she must have been asleep for a while because Simon was in bed, tossing and turning violently, yelling, "No! No! God, no! Noooooooo!"

"Wake up." Alison shook him. "It's just a dream. Wake up."

Then he screamed louder than she'd ever heard him scream before. It was a scream of total terror.

"Simon, can you hear me? *Simon*."

He was still screaming, wailing, "No, no! Please, nooo!" and now Jeremy, in his room, was screaming, "Daddy! Daddy!"

Alison shook Simon, pleading with him, but nothing helped.

Jeremy was crying hysterically. "Daddy! Daddy!"

Alison shouted, "I can't take this anymore! I just can't!" as she rushed out of the bedroom.

SEVENTEEN

Simon's dream:

He was hungry, in the dark, and couldn't see anything, but he could smell everything. He smelled trees and cold, fresh country air, but most of all he could smell his next meal.

His meal was coming toward him. He waited silently, for the right moment, and then he was moving extremely fast, practically flying. He leaped toward his meal, biting into the delicious flesh, feasting on it. Mmm, it was the best meal he'd ever had. He wanted to keep eating forever. He couldn't get enough of it.

Then he was running again in total darkness. Although he couldn't see a thing, he could see everything. He was already hungry again. He heard something far away and he stopped and listened more closely. Was it an enemy? No, it was a meal, but he knew he had to be quiet or the meal would escape. He was quiet for a long time, watching his meal in the dark. Then he wasn't there anymore. He was removed, watching himself, but he wasn't himself, not the self he knew anyway. He had the body of a human, but he was also a ferocious animal with sharp teeth and claws. He was devouring his meal, warm blood splattering everywhere.

He woke up screaming, relieved to be in his bedroom and not in that pitch-black forest. Alison was holding Jeremy in her arms. Jeremy was extremely upset, sobbing.

"What's going on?" Simon asked. "Is he okay?"

"You scared the hell out of him," Alison said.

Simon said, "How did I—" Then he remembered being in the forest, seeing himself as a vicious animal. "Sorry," he said. "I was just having a nightmare, that's all."

Jeremy was still crying. Simon got out of bed and said, "Let me hold him."

Alison backed away and said, "It's okay, I can take care of it." She turned to leave, adding, "Maybe you want to sleep on the couch tonight."

Simon didn't understand why Alison was so angry with him. Just a couple of days ago, everything seemed so great, and suddenly she was unhappy again, complaining, turning him down for sex. He wanted to talk to her about it but knew he wouldn't be able to resolve anything now, in the middle of the night, while she was so cranky, so he took his pillow and went out to the couch.

He couldn't sleep, though; the nightmare was too fresh in his mind. The first part, when he was hungry, searching for a meal, felt exhilarating; but the next part, when he felt removed from the scene, watching the animal-like version of himself, was terrifying. He didn't know why it seemed so scary—it was just a dream, for God's sake.

Then, with a sudden revelation, he thought—*I was the wolf.* The first attack in the dream had been the wolf attacking Tom, and the second attack had been the killing of the deer in the woods. Simon wasn't exactly an expert in dream analysis, but it seemed logical that the dream had to do with repressed guilt. He felt guilty about all the anger he'd had toward Tom, and the dream was some kind of perverse fantasy. This was the only explanation that made any sense.

But understanding the dream didn't make it seem any less terrifying. It had seemed so real that he'd actually felt like he was there, biting into the salty flesh, and he was afraid to fall back asleep, fearing that the nightmare would resume. This wasn't the only reason he couldn't sleep, though; he also had an annoying erection. It had been two days since he and Alison had last had sex, but it seemed like eons ago. He had no desire to masturbate, though. He wanted to make love to his wife, not a fantasy version of her.

Eventually he fell asleep, but the nightmare repeated. It was even more vivid now. It was clearly an attack on Tom. He could even see Tom's face and hear his screams. The attack on the deer was more vivid as well. The deer flesh was tougher than Tom's; Tom had been a fattier, more satisfying meal.

In the morning Alison was still in a bitter mood and barely spoke to him. He felt bad about the distance between them lately, but he had no idea how to make things better. He'd tried to talk to her last night, but he couldn't understand her anymore. If men were from Mars, she was from a different universe. He knew that trying to discuss it would be pointless and only widen the rift, so he decided he wouldn't mention anything until their next marriage counseling appointment.

Simon took Jeremy downtown for a play date with the guys in Battery Park. In sharp contrast to how awkward he'd felt around Alison lately, when he saw the guys he felt instantly calmer, at peace. The guys just seemed to get him in a way that Alison didn't.

While Simon was hugging Charlie, Ramon said, "Everybody wants a piece of the hero today."

"What do you mean?" Simon asked.

"You didn't see the papers today yet?" Ramon went to the bench and grabbed a copy of the *Daily News* and held it up so Simon could see the picture on the front page of Charlie, grinning, with his arm around an attractive blonde. The headline was simply:

MY HERO

"Charlie pulled a woman out of a fire yesterday," Ramon said.

"Eh, you know how the papers are," Charlie said modestly. "They blow everything out of proportion."

"Out of proportion? You went into *fire*, man." Then Ramon continued to Simon, "Paper says if he didn't go in, in like a minute, the lady would've died. He had to break down the front door to get her, and it had like three locks on it. He busted the door down by himself."

"It was no big deal," Charlie said. "Any guy on my team would've done it."

"Yeah, but they didn't do it," Ramon said. "That's what makes *you* a hero."

"We're very proud of Charlie," Michael said. Then he said to Simon, "You're proud of Charlie."

The silence seemed to drag on as they all looked at Simon, waiting for him to respond.

"Of course I'm proud of him," Simon finally said.

Michael seemed pleased.

"Thanks," Charlie said to Simon. "That means a lot to me, man."

"And you saved a beautiful woman's life; I'm sure she's gonna be very thankful," Ramon said. "You got her number, I hope."

"Of course," Charlie said, smiling.

Ramon put an arm around him, pulling him close, and said, "That's my boy, that's my boy."

After the playground the guys took the kids to a nearby McDonald's. The kids had Happy Meals and the dads had Angus burgers. Simon had planned to get two burgers, but the smell of fried meat whetted his appetite even further, so he ordered four burgers and a bottle of water. Ramon and Charlie also had ordered several burgers each, but Michael bought eight.

They sat in the middle of the restaurant with their overflowing trays. Simon was aware of people watching them, but he was too focused on the food to really care. Michael removed the burgers from the sandwiches and stacked them up into a large pile of meat. Charlie and

Ramon did the same, and Simon, realizing that it would be much more pleasurable to eat the meat on its own, also stacked his burgers.

He couldn't chew the meat fast enough—he just wanted to get it all into his body as fast as possible. The other guys were downing their burgers. Simon was aware of people from other tables looking over at them, but he didn't care. All he could think about was how hungry he was and the meal in front of him, and nothing else mattered. It reminded him of a feeling he'd had recently, during the nightmare, when he saw Tom—his meal—in front of him. As Simon swallowed a large chunk of burger, he saw a flash of himself as the man-wolf, sinking its teeth into Tom's neck, and he gagged as the meat got caught in his windpipe.

Charlie was up first and seemed to be instantly behind Simon's chair, ready to give him the Heimlich maneuver, but Simon was able to cough up the meat on his own.

"I'm okay," Simon said between coughs. "I'm . . . I'm fine."

"Don't worry, Charlie's trained in CPR," Ramon said. "You ain't gonna die from no Angus burger when we got a hero fireman around."

At the next table, Simon saw that Jeremy was looking over, frightened.

"It's okay, don't worry," Simon said. "Daddy's going to be fine, I promise."

Placated, Jeremy went right back to talking and laughing with his friends.

Simon coughed a few times, continuing to recover, then said, "I guess I was eating too fast."

Michael seemed confused, as if he didn't hear him, maybe didn't understand him.

After a swig of water, Simon resumed eating, more slowly. He was okay at first, but then he was back there, digging his teeth into Tom's neck. It was even clearer before and so real, more like a memory than a dream. He gagged again, but not as bad as before.

"You sure you're okay?" Charlie asked.

"Yeah," Simon said. "Fine."

Simon managed to finish the rest of the burgers without further incident, but he was still shaken up. The other guys had finished eating as well.

"You're afraid," Michael said to Simon.

Simon, who'd become used to Michael's abrupt and direct style of communication, said, "Yeah, actually I am. How could you tell?"

"Fear is weakness, like love."

Simon squinted, trying to figure out what Michael was talking about. When it was clear Michael wasn't going to elaborate, Simon said, "I had this weird dream last night."

Three sets of eyes were suddenly fixated on him, waiting for him to continue.

"I dreamed that I was, well, a wolf," he said. "Or not really a wolf. I had wolf features—the teeth and claws and, I guess, fur, but otherwise I was myself. Anyway, I dreamed I attacked a man and killed him, and then I attacked and killed a deer."

Simon had purposely left out any mention of how the dream was related to what had happened to Tom. The guys were looking at him blank-faced, as if waiting for the punch line of a joke.

"That was it," Simon said. "I woke up screaming."

"It was a happy dream," Michael said.

"No," Simon said, "it was terrifying. Well, that isn't really true. Part of it was terrifying, at the end. At the beginning I wasn't happy or scared."

"You were strong in the dream," Michael said.

Simon had felt powerful in the dream.

"Maybe," he said. "But not strong in a good way. Strong in a scary way."

It felt weird, being psychoanalyzed by a dad from the playground in a crowded McDonald's. Simon didn't know why he'd brought any of this up.

"Oh wow, look at the time," Simon said, checking his cell. "We should be heading back uptown."

In front of McDonald's the guys hugged good-bye, and then Simon jogged toward the Upper West Side, pushing Jeremy in the jogging stroller. As usual, the exertion calmed Simon, and the nightmare about

Tom wasn't upsetting him as much. The great thing about nightmares was that they didn't haunt you forever; they were eventually replaced by new nightmares. He just had to live his life and let go.

A balding middle-aged man in a dark sport jacket was standing near the doorman's desk, watching Simon as he entered the lobby. The way the man was looking at him, Simon wondered if he knew the man from somewhere, although he didn't look at all familiar. Simon smiled instinctively, but the man didn't smile back. Instead the man glanced to his left toward James, the doorman, and must have gotten some sort of signal or acknowledgment from James because then he said to Simon, "Excuse me, Mr. Burns?"

Simon stopped and eyed the man more closely. He still couldn't place him. "Sorry, do I know you?"

The man flashed a badge and said, "Dan Dorsey, Bernardsville Police Department. Can I have a word with you, please?"

EIGHTEEN

Unable to process what was happening, Simon first thought that this had to be some kind of misunderstanding.

"I'm sorry," he said, "I think you have the wrong address."

"Are you Simon Burns?"

"Yes, but—"

"Can we sit down for a moment?" Dorsey gestured with his jaw toward the leather sofa and matching chair at the other end of the lobby.

"I think you have the wrong Simon Burns," Simon said.

"Unless there are two Simon Burnses at this address, I don't have the wrong Simon Burns."

Realizing a misunderstanding was out of the question, Simon asked lamely, "What's this about?" as he saw a flash of himself biting off a chunk of Tom's face. Then his knees buckled and he almost lost his balance.

Dorsey reached out quickly and grabbed Simon's arm and asked, "Are you okay, Mr. Burns?"

"Yeah, fine," Simon said. "I just think I might be coming down with something. I've been feeling kind of queasy today."

"Come sit down for a few secs," Dorsey said. "This shouldn't take long."

"I'm here with my son," Simon said, tilting up the stroller.

Dorsey glanced at James, and James said, "Yeah, I can watch him, that's fine."

Reluctantly Simon left Jeremy with James and joined Dorsey at the end of the lobby. Simon's brain was churning, trying to figure out why the police could possibly want to talk to him. They must have somehow figured out that he was in Bernardsville the night Tom was killed. Had they found his shoe in the woods? If they had, Simon had no idea what explanation he would give for why he was there other than the truth. And why not tell the truth? What did he have to hide?

Dorsey sat in the chair, so Simon sat across from him on the couch, saying, "I still don't get what this is about." Then he realized he probably shouldn't sound *so* naïve, so he added, "I mean you said you're from Bernardsville. This doesn't have to do with my old boss, Tom Harrison, does it?"

"Yes, as a matter of fact it does," Dorsey said.

"I'm confused," Simon said, thinking, *He has the shoe. He must have the shoe.*

Suddenly he had that taste of blood in his mouth again. He felt dizzy for a second or two, but it passed.

"Do you own a wolf?" Dorsey asked.

"Excuse me?" The question sounded so odd he wasn't sure he'd heard it correctly.

"A wolf," Dorsey repeated. "Do you own one?"

"No," Simon said. "Of course I don't own a wolf. Why would I own a wolf?"

"Some people own them as pets illegally," Dorsey said. "But you say you don't own one, so—"

"I absolutely don't own one," Simon said, knowing that Dorsey must have had a very good reason to come all the way to Manhattan to question him, and the only reason that made any sense was that he'd found the shoe. Simon was considering whether he should bring up the shoe on his own, just be honest and straightforward. Was there a reason *not* to be honest and straightforward?

"I assume you don't have access to a wolf?" Dorsey said. "Maybe a friend's wolf?"

"No," Simon said. "Of course I don't have access to a wolf. What kind of ques—"

"Were you in New Jersey the night Tom Harrison was killed?"

Simon hesitated. He was going to tell the truth, just blurt it out, but then he heard himself say, "No, I wasn't."

"Then can I ask where you were that night?"

"That was last Friday night, right? I was in New York, staying at a friend's."

Dorsey nodded slowly—knowingly, or was he just thinking? Simon had no idea what he'd do now if Dorsey said he had the shoe. He wanted to tell the truth, admit he was there, but at the same time he couldn't shake his memories of the nightmare he'd had and his over-riding feeling of guilt. Maybe he had something to hide after all. He'd blacked out that night, so how did he know that he wasn't there in New Jersey? He'd been angry at Tom and had motive for wanting to kill him, so maybe he'd gotten hold of a wolf and brought it with him to Tom's house that night? It was absurd, of course, but not any more absurd than waking up in the woods naked. How could he rule anything out?

"The reason I'm asking," Dorsey said, "is someone thought they saw you near the house."

"Saw me?" Simon saw a glimpse of the nightmare—his animal self biting into the delicious flesh. "That's crazy."

Simon was actually terrified, but his reaction must have come off as anger or frustration because Dorsey said, "Take it easy, Mr. Burns. I understand you're upset, but you're gonna have to calm down. I'm just doing my job, following up leads, trying to close this case."

Simon collected himself the best he could and said, "I'm sorry. I was just surprised, that's all. You said someone saw me?"

"Yeah, neighbor on the block," Dorsey said. "He said he saw you at the funeral home and thought you looked familiar."

Simon remembered that guy—what was his name?—who'd spoken to him while he was giving his condolences to Tom's wife. Feldman? No, Freedman—Alan Freedman. If Freedman claimed he'd seen Simon that night at the house, he probably had seen him. But Simon was relieved that they didn't have the shoe. He could deny that he'd been seen—it was his word against Freedman's—but he couldn't argue with a shoe.

With confidence Simon said, "Well, I wasn't there. That's absolutely ridiculous. And what's this all about? Are you trying to accuse me of something?"

"Like I said before, sometimes people keep pets illegally. So we're just checking out if someone might have had a wolf and brought it there."

"Wait, so let me get this straight. You think I brought my illegal wolf all the way out to Bernardsville and my wolf mauled my old boss to death?"

"I'm just doing my job, Mr. Burns. We have a witness who claims he saw you in the area, so I have to follow up the lead. But if you say you weren't there, then I apologize for inconveniencing you."

"I wasn't there," Simon said, maintaining eye contact, trying to come off as earnest as possible.

"Were you in the city that night?"

"Yes," Simon said. "I spent the night at a friend's place."

"In that case, I'm sorry," Dorsey said. "Trust me, there are things I'd rather be doing today than wasting your time. But look at it from our point of view. First we thought a rabid dog or something attacked him, and then the ME determined it was a wolf. Trust me, if this had happened in Newark instead of Bernardsville they wouldn't've even bothered with DNA or *any* investigation. But it's an affluent neighborhood and people are concerned that there could be a wild wolf running around, so . . ."

"Isn't that the most likely explanation?"

"Yes and no," Dorsey said. "There's a wolf preserve all the way out in Knowlton Township, about fifty miles from Bernardsville. Even if a wolf somehow escaped the preserve, it seems highly unlikely that the wolf traveled all the way to Bernardsville. So then we started looking into the domestic pet angle. Believe it or not, we found a guy with a pet half-wolf about a ten-minute drive from Harrison's house. We confirmed that that wolf didn't escape that night. We were getting ready to drop the case, or at least put it way back on the back burner, when we had this witness come to us, saying he'd seen you at the house. So, yes, I agree it does seem bizarre, but you can see why we had to check it out."

Simon stood and said, "If that's all, I have to take my son upstairs now."

"Just one more thing," Dorsey said, standing as well. "You said you were at a friend's that night. Do you happen to have the friend's phone number?"

Simon had all the guys' numbers on his cell phone. He said, "Sorry, I don't."

Dorsey seemed confused.

"He's just an acquaintance really," Simon explained, "the father of one of my son's friends. Maybe I can get it for you, or—"

"It's no big deal right now," Dorsey said. "I'll tell you what, if I need it, I'll call you. Thanks for all your help, and sorry for the inconvenience, but, hey, at least you didn't have to drive two hours and sit in traffic on the GW Bridge to get here."

Dorsey smiled, as if trying to make light of the situation, then thanked Simon for his time and said to Jeremy, "You can have your father back now," as he left the building.

The rest of the afternoon, Simon and Jeremy hung out in the apartment. Simon tried to get Jeremy to nap, but it wasn't happening so Simon parked him in front of the TV. Meanwhile, Simon couldn't stop replaying the questioning from Dorsey. It seemed like Dorsey wasn't incredibly suspicious, but maybe he knew more and was just playing cool at this point, trying to get Simon to slip up. But slip up about what? That was the craziest part of all of this. Simon hadn't *done* anything. Though he couldn't rule out that he'd gotten hold of a wolf that night, the idea seemed so remote, so totally out there, that he couldn't take it seriously. He'd just been at the scene of a crime, or near the scene of a crime, but he hadn't done anything wrong.

Then Simon had that feeling again of biting into Tom's neck, tasting his flesh, and he suddenly shouted, "Stop it!"

Jeremy looked over, startled. Simon reassured him, told him everything was okay, but everything was far from okay. If he was really innocent and had nothing to hide, why did he feel like he had everything to hide?

Suddenly ill, Simon rushed into the bathroom, bent over the toilet, and started throwing up. The recent food he'd consumed—steak, sausage, and Angus burgers—didn't exactly come up easy. As he was gagging, the back of his throat burning, he saw a glimpse of the nightmare again, himself as the wolf swallowing the deer's flesh, and he gagged even harder. He felt as if he were going insane, and maybe he was. After all, insanity ran in his family. On his father's side, his uncle Ken in Ireland was in an institution, and on his mother's side, his cousin Roger in Michigan suffered from schizophrenia.

Simon needed to run. Lately running was the only time he felt truly happy and in control of his life, but he couldn't go running and leave Jeremy unsupervised. He asked Jeremy if he wanted to go to the park to play soccer, figuring that would at least be some physical activity, but Jeremy was cranky and didn't want to go out again. Instead, Simon did a hundred push-ups and a few hundred jumping jacks, but it didn't help. A fourteen-hundred-square-foot apartment had never seemed so small. He might as well have been spending the afternoon in a coffin.

When Alison came home she looked at the kitchen, at the dirty dishes in the sink, and at the toys strewn in the living room, and she immediately shook her head a few times; then, exposing her lower teeth, the way she did when she was really angry about something, she said, "This isn't fair. I shouldn't have to come home to this."

"I'm sorry," Simon said, rushing to pick up some toys from the floor. "I was planning to straighten up before you got home, but I got kind of sidetracked."

"Isn't fair, just isn't fair," Alison said, maybe to herself as she started to angrily load the dishwasher, clanging the dishes. "I have to work all day, giving up everything, and then I have to come home to *this*? You have to help out more. You can't do this to me."

Simon, holding a Nerf football, the Leapster, a bunch of stuffed animals, and several other toys, said, "You're right. I'll clean more from now on and make more of an effort. I promise."

Alison didn't accept his apology, or not accept it. She went into the bedroom, muttering, "Isn't fair . . . Just isn't fair." Even though Simon was in the living room and shouldn't have been able to, he heard her clearly.

Dinner for the grown-ups was ordered-in Japanese. Simon had the sashimi deluxe, and though the salmon and tuna and yellowtail gave him a nice jolt, it wasn't nearly as satisfying as a good piece of steak.

The focus at the table was on Jeremy. Simon tried to engage Alison in conversation a few times, but she replied each time in a clipped way and mainly seemed to be ignoring him, avoiding eye contact.

Until Jeremy blurted out, "The police came to see Daddy today."

"The police?" Alison looked at Simon for the first time during the meal.

"Yeah," Jeremy said. "A detective."

Alison asked Simon, "Is this true?"

"Yeah," Simon said. "It just had to do with what happened to Tom." Since Jeremy was listening, Simon purposely didn't mention anything specific about the mauling.

"Why did they want to talk to you?" Alison said.

"They're talking to everyone Tom worked with, and his friends and neighbors too. They're looking for the—" He spelled, "W-O-L-F."

"I don't get it," Alison said.

"W-O—"

"No, I mean, I didn't get why they'd talk to *you*."

Wishing he hadn't gotten into this, that he'd thought up a good lie instead, he said, "They just want to know if anyone knew about any friend of Tom's who'd had one as a pet, that's all. I guess they think somebody's pet attacked him."

"A pet attacked somebody?" Jeremy asked.

"How's that ravioli?" Simon asked, trying to nip the curiosity in the bud.

Alison still seemed confused, but she let it go, probably because she still seemed angry at him in general and didn't feel like having a conversation.

Simon bit into a piece of yellowtail and imagined biting into Tom. He gagged a couple of times, but he wasn't choking.

"You okay?" Alison asked.

"Fine," Simon said. "It's nothing."

She didn't seem convinced.

He couldn't eat anymore—partly because he was afraid he was going to choke to death, and partly because he was worrying about Dorsey's questioning. Although Dorsey hadn't seemed overly suspicious—actually, he seemed like he was just going through the motions—it was possible that his lackadaisical attitude was just a ploy. Maybe he actually had information, or at least a lead about where Simon had gotten the wolf, and he was waiting for Simon to slip up. Maybe Dorsey had said he didn't need Michael's contact info because he was planning to contact Michael on his own, before Simon had a chance to contact him.

Simon excused himself and went into the bathroom with his cell phone. He texted Michael:

I need to talk to you right away. can i come see you?

Simon wanted to talk to Michael in person in case the cops had tapped the phone line.

Okay, he knew he was probably being totally paranoid, but he couldn't help it.

A few seconds went by, then Simon got:

come to the brewery

They continued their text conversation:

ok great what time??

come to the brewery

now?

come to the brewery

great!

Alison was giving Jeremy a bath.

Poking his head into the bathroom, Simon said, "I'm meeting my friends for a drink."

"Now?" Alison sounded pissed off.

"Yeah," Simon said. "They just called and they're at a bar in midtown and they want me to swing by. I won't be out late, I promise. Is it a problem?"

"Is this with your playground friends?" Alison asked, in an accusatory tone, as if he were on his way out to meet a group of pedophiles.

"Yeah," Simon said. "What's wrong?"

"I don't want to discuss it now," Alison said, handing Jeremy his rubber ducky.

"I don't under—"

"I said I don't want to discuss it."

"Okay, that's cool," Simon said, actually relieved, because he didn't want to discuss it anymore either; he just wanted to get to Michael's ASAP. "Talk to you later." He leaned over the tub and kissed Jeremy's wet head and said, "Daddy will see you later, okay?"

"Okay," Jeremy said.

But Alison followed him out of the bathroom to the hallway and asked, "Are you gay?"

"What?" Simon asked.

"Just tell me the truth and I'll understand," she said. "There'll be a lot less humiliation if you're just up front about it."

"Is that what this is about lately? You really think I'm gay?"

"Are you?"

He couldn't believe this. "I'm not gay, okay? Hasn't that been evident lately?"

"I saw you hugging him."

"Hugging who?"

"Michael," she spewed.

"When did you—"

"At the park yesterday. I was in the area so I thought I'd surprise you guys, and I saw you hugging him for a long time."

Simon laughed; Alison didn't.

Simon said, "I know it probably looked weird to you—it was weird for me at first—but that's just the way the guys are."

"Mommy, the water's too cold!" Jeremy called out.

"Coming," Alison said. Then to Simon, "I know something's going on with you. You suddenly have all these secrets. You have these secret friends, you somehow learned to run really fast. What other secrets are you hiding from me?"

Tasting Tom's blood, Simon gagged. But he recovered quickly, saying, "I'm not hiding anything. I'm just going through something, a midlife crisis or whatever. I don't know what it is, but I promise I'll work through it."

"Mommy!" Jeremy called.

"You'd better work through it," Alison said, "if you're serious about saving this marriage."

She marched back to the bathroom and Simon went the other way, toward the front door.

Simon knew this wasn't just melodrama—Alison was seriously upset. He was pushing her away and he knew if he pushed her too far he'd lose her. Alison was patient in some ways, but when she made a decision she stuck to it and didn't look back. She'd hinted at divorce during past marriage counseling sessions and during arguments, never actually mentioning the word, but making statements like "I'm not sure I can continue like this" or "It might be time for a change." Their past arguments were usually based on misunderstandings, but now it was particularly frustrating because he knew exactly what was upsetting her, but he didn't know what to do about it. Though he was aware of his changed behavior, he didn't know how to change it back, and—more troubling—he didn't necessarily want to change it back. He felt like he wasn't in control of the decisions he was making, like he was a visitor in his own body.

Oh, God, maybe he really was going crazy.

He left the building and was walking toward the subway on Eighty-sixth and Central Park West, but he had so much energy, he sprinted the rest of the way, darting through traffic. The sprint felt great, but it wasn't enough. He wanted to run for hours, for miles, forever.

Waiting on the platform, he was annoyed by the young blond guy next to him whose iPod was blasting Lady Gaga. Simon had nothing against Lady Gaga, but did the guy have to play it so freaking loud? Simon was going to say something, then realized that no one else on the platform was reacting and that it must be his ultrasensitive hearing acting up again. To get away from the guy, Simon went to the other end of the platform and stopped next to a short bald guy in a business suit reading the *Wall Street Journal*. The guy glanced at Simon in a weird, knowing way—or at least Simon thought it was weird and knowing. Simon tried to ignore him, but when he looked over, the guy was still looking at him and, paranoia taking over, Simon wondered if the guy was an undercover cop, someone Dorsey worked with. Maybe that was why Dorsey had been so nonchalant at the end of the questioning, because he'd put a tail on Simon.

A train was approaching—Jesus, the noise was deafening; Simon had to cover his ears. After it screeched to a halt, Simon purposely didn't get on the same car as the bald guy. But he couldn't relax, as he could hear the combined noise of music leaking from maybe a dozen iPods. He put his hands over his ears and felt like everyone was staring at him— probably because they *were* staring at him. But were they staring at him because he was acting strangely or because one of them was a cop? One Asian woman wasn't staring at him, and he feared her most of all.

During the trip to Brooklyn, he switched cars several times but couldn't shake the feeling that someone was watching him. His paranoia only intensified when he arrived at Bedford Avenue in Brooklyn and ran along the dark, emptyish streets toward the old brewery. He must have looked back over his shoulder dozens of times, and he felt unnervingly out of control, as if some force beyond himself were guiding his behavior and he were merely a witness to it all.

At the brewery, he called, "Michael! Michael!" and the door buzzed.

A rat darted between him and the old elevator. Like the first time he'd visited the brewery, the ride up was excruciatingly slow. When he got out, once again he was startled by how upscale and immaculate everything was compared to the ground floor.

"Hello?" he said.

He waited. No answer.

He headed toward the windows with the panoramic view of Manhattan.

"You'll have steak."

Simon stopped, absorbing the jolt Michael's voice had given him. Although he was here to meet Michael and the voice wasn't particularly loud, the sudden noise was still startling, maybe because the room was otherwise so silent.

Simon turned his head and saw Michael standing near the entrance to the kitchen holding two plates, each with a T-bone steak.

Dying for a protein fix, he was about to say yes. Then he remembered the last time he was here, and how he'd had the steak and drunk the beer, and he decided that consuming nothing was probably the smartest way to go.

"I just ate," Simon said. "But thanks."

Michael didn't seem at all offended.

"Sit down," Michael said.

Simon sat on one of the sofas, and Michael sat across from him. Then Simon watched as Michael began eating one of the steaks, picking it up and eating it like corn on the cob. Simon knew not to interrupt his eating with conversation, as Michael wouldn't have responded anyway. So Simon just sat there while Michael ate both steaks. After ten or fifteen minutes he finished eating and then, acting as if all of this were perfectly normal, he said to Simon, "You still have fear."

"Yes," Simon said. "It has to do with what I was telling you guys at McDonald's today."

"Your dream," Michael said.

"Yeah," Simon said. "Except I don't think it was a dream. I think . . . I think I did something terrible."

Simon explained about how he had woken up in New Jersey near where Tom had been killed and how he was questioned by Dorsey.

"I thought it was just a coincidence that I was in the area that night," Simon said. "I mean, what could I possibly have had to do with an animal attack? But now there's a witness, this guy Alan Freedman who told the police he saw me there that night, and I can't rationalize anymore and keep telling myself it was coincidence when I know it wasn't. I was angry at Tom—even you guys said I was complaining about him that night. So I must've taken a cab there or something—and then got a wolf from somewhere and . . . Look, I know how crazy this all sounds. I *feel* crazy just talking about it. But what other explanation can there be?"

Michael remained silent for a while, then said, "You didn't tell anyone else about this."

"No," Simon said. "I mean, I would tell my wife, but we haven't been getting along lately. I don't think telling her I think I may have killed my boss would go over very well right now."

"You must not tell her," Michael said. "She won't understand."

"Oh there's, um, something else," Simon said. "The night I woke up naked in the woods . . . I couldn't find one of my shoes. If the police find the shoe they'll want to know why I was at Tom's that night and why I lied about being there. And now that there's a witness . . . Now you can see why I'm so afraid. I told the police I was here that night, and they might try to verify this with you. I didn't know what else to tell them. I've never been so afraid. . . . I think I killed him, I really think I killed him." Simon's lips were trembling; he was trying not to cry.

"I'll tell them you slept here all night," Michael said.

"Wow," Simon said. "You'd really do that for me?"

"I'd do anything for a member of my pack," Michael said.

Simon didn't exactly get what he meant by that, but he said, "Wow, that's so nice of you. I mean, I really appreciate it, but you don't *have to* do it. You can tell them it's possible I was here, but you didn't see me here. I mean, if you want to say something like that to cover for yourself, I'd totally—"

"I'll tell them you were here," Michael said, "and I saw you here all night. . . . And someday you will do something for me."

Simon had no idea what Michael was implying, but he was so happy and relieved he said, "Thank you. You have no idea what a burden this lifts for me. I mean, maybe the police won't talk to you, maybe the whole thing will just blow over. But knowing you'd do this for me, in a worst-case scenario, is probably the nicest thing anyone has ever done for me."

Michael didn't say anything. After a long period of silence, Simon got the sense that as far as Michael was concerned the conversation was over. Simon thanked Michael several more times and then said, "Well, I'll see you at the playground on Thursday, right?" and Michael said, "Yes," and then Simon left. On the subway back to Manhattan, Simon kept replaying Michael's words: *Someday you will do something for me.* He had a vague feeling that he might regret getting in deeper with Michael, but at the moment he was so relieved to have a solid alibi for Tom's murder that nothing else mattered.

NINETEEN

When Alison picked up Jeremy to take him out of the bath, he screamed and said, "No, no, I don't want to!" and Alison said, "You have to," and he screamed again, louder, and then Alison slipped on the wet floor and almost lost her balance.

Frightened, upset, and angry, Alison snapped, "See what happens when you don't cooperate! You could've killed us!"

She'd yelled much louder than she'd intended. Jeremy, frightened by the outburst, was crying hysterically.

"Go ahead, cry," Alison said, still fuming. "Cry all night if you want to. See if I care."

As Alison toweled Jeremy dry and put him in his PJs, she let his fit continue, and then she calmed down and suddenly realized what she'd done—taken her anger and frustration toward Simon out on her son.

She picked him up and said, "I'm so sorry, sweetie, Mommy's so sorry. Mommy didn't mean to raise her voice. Mommy's going through a tough time right now, but it has nothing to do with you, okay? Okay?"

"Okay," Jeremy said, sniffling.

Although he recovered quickly, Alison still felt guilty for snapping at him. The stress of the day and her marriage problems were getting to her. She didn't believe that Simon was serious about dealing with his problems, and even if he did deal with them she wasn't convinced that things would ever get back to normal.

She finished getting Jeremy into his PJs and ready for bed, then took care of some chores around the apartment. When they'd decided that Simon would be a stay-at-home dad, he'd agreed to do the bulk of the shopping and cleaning and take care of the general odds and ends around the house, but he hadn't kept his word. Simon had been so into his obsessive physical activity lately that he'd been slacking on house-work, and when she came home there seemed to be a sink full of dishes or toys strewn all over the living room floor or other messes to clean up around the apartment. He hadn't been doing the laundry either; it didn't seem like he'd done any laundry in about a week. Jeremy was out of clean clothes to wear and the hamper was overflowing.

"Not fair," Alison said as she prepared a few loads of laundry. "Just isn't fair."

A few seconds later she stopped for a moment, holding a pair of Simon's jeans that had been buried at the bottom of the hamper, no-ticing some dark stains. She was about to toss them into the darks pile when she stopped again, remembering that they were the jeans Simon had worn the night he'd pulled the all-nighter at the brewery and all the weird behavioral changes started. Examining the stains more closely, the color kind of reminded her of the way period-stained panties looked. Then she had another memory—the morning after the all-nighter, Simon had those streaks of blood on his neck.

In the bathroom sink she ran some water over the pants, and sure enough the water ran off pink. Alison's heart was racing, as if finding the blood on his jeans were some kind of revelation, that it proved something, but proved what? What did some blood have to do with her husband pos-sibly having an affair? It was just as confusing as everything else that had happened lately, like pieces of a puzzle that agonizingly didn't fit.

Alison was convinced that something was going on; there was just too much weirdness for it to not add up to something, and she was determined to find the answer. Maybe she should hire a detective? Or at least she should start thinking like a detective. Okay, what would a detective do? Follow him. That would be hard, without being spotted. Okay, what else? Follow the money. If he was cheating, there had to be suspicious charges.

After Alison put Jeremy to bed, she went online and checked the Mastercard, Visa, and Amex accounts. She went back for the past two months, well beyond the time all the craziness started, but she didn't see anything unusual. She was frustrated by the dead end but felt she was getting closer. There had to be *something*.

She logged on to the Chase online banking website and checked the recent account activity. There were many more ATM transactions than credit card transactions, but she went through the list slowly. Both his and her withdrawals were listed, but there were no unusual amounts or payments. It was mostly just cash withdrawals of two hundred dollars—their usual withdrawal amount—and various payments at drugstores and grocery stores. Alison was giving up hope that she'd find a transaction that would shed light on the situation. Though Simon wasn't normally sneaky, he was smart, and if he was cheating on her and didn't want to get caught he was probably paying for the hotel rooms and restaurant bills in cash.

She checked the next page of transactions and she saw one on October 11—for two hundred dollars in Mendham, New Jersey—and she had an adrenaline surge. That was the morning Simon had called her, saying he was at Michael's. The son of a bitch. He'd lied to her after all.

Everything was spinning; it was hard to focus and catch her breath. She couldn't believe this was actually happening. She was rocking slowly back and forth with her eyes closed, half furious, half in shock, waiting for it to set in, for it to seem real. Yeah, like reality would make it any better. She couldn't believe he'd done this to her, that he'd done this to his family. How could he be so goddamn selfish?

Finally she got up, her instincts telling her to leave, distance herself from this situation as soon as possible. She'd wake up Jeremy and they'd go away—to anywhere that wasn't here.

She went into Jeremy's room. He was sleeping contentedly, the blanket up over his chin, snuggling with Sam, the name he'd given to his favorite stuffed bear. She was about to nudge him awake, and then she hesitated, thinking, was this really the best thing for her son? Did she really want to subject him to all of this drama? Waking him up, telling him he had to leave his father? She was emotional now and probably wasn't making logical decisions. She had to take a step back, think this through.

She was back in the living room. God, she couldn't believe she was in this situation. As difficult as things had been in the past, and as awful as things had been lately, she'd never expected to be *here*. She'd assumed that they'd eventually hit rock bottom and Simon would make an effort, a real effort, to work out whatever had been troubling him lately and stop all his strange behavior—his acting out, or whatever the psychological term du jour was for it—and they'd go on with their lives. Meanwhile, he'd been cheating on her, actually *cheating*. He was probably with his little bitch girlfriend right now. Alison wondered what she looked like, if she was prettier than her, or younger. She was probably one of those girls Alison saw in the gym sometimes—with a perfect little body. She was probably encouraging Simon to exercise like a maniac and to change his diet. It disgusted Alison that she'd had all that sex with Simon recently. *Unprotected* sex.

Suddenly queasy, Alison rushed into the bathroom and bent over the toilet. She gagged a few times but didn't throw up.

She pulled herself together, deciding that she wasn't going to be weak anymore. If she was weak, it would be like *he* won. She thought about Skyping or calling Lauren but didn't want to use her big sister as a crutch. She wanted to handle this on her own: rationally and pragmatically.

She went online and got the names and numbers of several divorce attorneys. Tomorrow she had a couple of breaks in her schedule, and she'd interview each of them. Then, maybe the day after tomorrow, she'd go out with real estate agents and look at rentals—find an apartment she could afford. A one-bedroom in a decent building would be out of the question, but maybe a studio with an alcove. She could put up a wall, create a small room for Jeremy. She'd look on the Upper East Side. She didn't want to be too close to Simon, but Jeremy needed to see his father, so being on the opposite side of Central Park would be the best she could do.

It was past ten o'clock. Simon had been gone for over two hours. Alison was beginning to wonder whether he was planning to come back at all, or if he'd have some other ridiculous explanation. *Drinks with his friends, my ass.* She didn't care if he came home, though. He could stay out every night for the rest of his life for all she cared.

Maybe half an hour later she heard his keys turning in the lock. As he was hanging up his coat in the closet, she appeared in the hallway, saying, "I want a separation."

During all of their marriage trouble over the years, neither of them had uttered the word *divorce* or *separation*, knowing this would cross a major line that neither of them wanted to cross. So now Simon immediately recognized that Alison was serious.

"Come on, honey." He went and tried to hug her.

She swatted his hands away and said, "Get your claws off me."

"I don't understand," Simon said. "Why are you so angry?"

"I never thought you'd lie to me," she said. "I never thought you were capable of it."

"Capable of what? I don't—"

"Is it Juliet?"

Juliet was an old co-worker of Simon's whom Alison had met last year at the office holiday party. Alison had thought that Juliet had seemed a little too flirty with him, and although she didn't actually think he and Juliet were having an affair and didn't intend to mention her, at the moment it was the only possibility she could think of, and she was so upset she'd just blurted the name out.

"Juliet?" he said. "Is that what you really think?"

He seemed believably surprised, but at this point how could she believe anything?

"Then who is it?" she said. "Somebody you met at a playground? Or are you gay after all? Do you have a boyfriend in New Jersey?"

"New Jersey? Why New Jersey?"

"You made a bank withdrawal there the day after your all-nighter at the brewery."

She'd said *brewery* leaking sarcasm, and the way Simon's face flushed she knew she'd hit on something.

After a few seconds he took a step toward her and said, "I can explain."

"Get the hell away from me!" she screamed.

As an adult, she'd never hit anyone, but if he came another step toward her she was going to slap him across the face.

"Sweetie . . ."

He took another step and she slapped him as hard as she could, catching his cheek and nose. Apparently she got the worst of it, though. He didn't seem to have any reaction, but her hand killed.

"It's where Tom lived," he said. "I was not having an affair. I swear to God."

Her hand hurt too much to really process any of this. "I don't care," she said. "Just get the hell away from me."

"It's the truth," he continued. "I went there the night he was killed. I was embarrassed so I didn't want to tell you. I got drunk that night. Well, not drunk, but I had a reaction to this *family beer* Michael gave me. Anyway, I was angry at Tom, so I must've taken a cab out there or something. But obviously I had nothing to do with what happened to him or anything like that. It was a big coincidence, that's all."

Now she got enough of what he was saying to realize it sounded completely absurd.

"What?" she said. "What're you talking about?"

"That's why I was in New Jersey," he said. "I was there to see Tom, not a woman. But I had nothing to do with what happened to Tom;

it was a complete coincidence that I was there the night he was killed by the wolf. But that's why the police wanted to talk to me, because a neighbor saw me there."

Alison was amazed by how sincere he looked, how he could spin these tales effortlessly, as if he actually believed them himself.

"What has happened to you?" she asked.

"I know it all sounds crazy," he said. "It sounds crazy to me too, but I love you, okay, and I want things to get better between us. I think we should move up our next appointment with Hagan, see him tomorrow if possible."

"I've had it with Hagan," she said, "and I've had it with you."

She went down the hallway and tried to get into the bathroom, but he stuck out his hand and stopped the door from closing.

"I don't understand why you're so upset," he said. "I didn't do anything wrong."

"Will you let go of the door, please?"

"What did I do? Tell me what I did."

"You lied to me."

"I'm sorry, okay? I was embarrassed. I'd never blacked out like that before. I was going through a rough time too—losing my job, adjusting to being a stay-at-home dad. How about cutting me a little slack?"

She hated that she was starting to feel guilty. Then a thought hit her and she said, "What about the blood?"

She watched his face flush.

"Blood?" he asked. "What blood?"

He seemed genuinely frightened. She felt as if she'd hit on something.

"I found blood on the jeans you were wearing that night," she said.

"What do you mean?" he asked, stiff-lipped, but it was obvious she'd hit on something.

"I ran them in the water and it ran out pink," she said. "It was definitely blood."

"Oh," he said. "I, uh, I must've cut myself somewhere that night. I was really trashed and I woke up in the woods. I was just so embarrassed about the whole thing; that's why I didn't tell you."

The explanation sounded so bizarre, she didn't know what to make of it.

"I really don't care anymore," she said. "Now will you please let me use the bathroom?"

He moved out of the way, and she closed and locked the door. She sat on the toilet, realized she didn't have to pee, and cried instead. She was thinking about how things used to be between her and Simon—when they were dating and were best friends, joined at the hip, and how different everything was now. She had no idea how they had gotten from point A to point B. She believed him that he was at Tom's house in New Jersey that night, but it seemed weird that he just happened to be there.

She sobbed harder. She wished he were having an affair. An affair would have been manageable; an affair would have been resolvable.

Simon was banging on the door. "Can you open up? Can you just open the door and discuss this, please?"

She didn't answer. He continued to bang on the door, and she ignored him until he finally went away.

TWENTY

On Wednesday afternoon, Olivia was at her office, preparing for her meeting tomorrow with Mr. Kyoto from Japan, when her assistant, Stephanie, poked her head into her office and said, "You have a call on line one."

"I saw," Olivia said, "Can you just take a message? I'm swamped here."

"It's Diane. She said it's urgent."

Diane? She was in Turks and Caicos this week with Steve. What could be so urgent?

"Okay, thanks," Olivia said.

Stephanie left, and Olivia took the call on speakerphone.

"How's it going, sweetie?" she asked.

There was silence at first, and then Diane said, "This is so messed up."

"Are you in Turks and Caicos?" Olivia asked.

"No, I'm in my living room," Diane said.

"Why? What happened?"

"I was all packed and ready to go when I got a text from Steve saying, 'Sorry, it's not working for me, good luck with everything.' I couldn't believe it. I thought it had to be some kind of joke. You know how Steve is, how his sense of humor misfires sometimes. It *could've* been a joke. So I called him back and got his voice mail and left a message. He didn't call back and I was like, what the hell? So I texted him a couple of times, and then he calls me and tells me it's over. That's it, no explanation, just good-bye, have a good life."

"Ugh, I'm so sorry."

"I have the flight, the hotel booked on *my* credit card. I can try to cancel part of it, but it's still gonna cost me money. Can you believe him? I mean, what a prick."

"There's nothing you can—"

"You should've heard him, telling me all this crap, just *two days* ago. He was like 'I'm so into you,' 'I can see spending the rest of my life with you,' 'You're perfect for me.' I mean, he was shoveling it on. And I'm usually so cautious about falling for that crap because I've been burned so many times before, but I finally gave in and opened up to him because I believed that one time, just one time, I'd met an honest, sincere, normal guy in Manhattan. And then this text message arrives."

"I'm so sorry, honey," Olivia said.

She gave Diane all the usual clichés like "He's just one guy" and "You have to get back on the horse," but Diane seemed to be taking it hard. Then Olivia had a brainstorm and asked, "What're you doing tonight?"

"Posting crap on Steve's Facebook page."

"Meet me at XR Bar on Houston and Sullivan," Olivia said.

"Are you kidding?" Diane said. "I look like hell right now."

"You have two hours to de-hell yourself."

"I really don't—"

"See you there."

Olivia ended the call and connected to Michael.

He said, "You're calling me."

"I missed you," Olivia said. "Did you miss me?"

"No," he said.

Expected, but it was crazy how his coldness turned her on every time.

"I was just wondering what you thought about going out tonight with a friend of mine. Just drinks and maybe a quick dinner and then—"

"I want to have sex with you tonight," he said.

"We will have sex, but my friend Diane needs some company."

Olivia explained the situation and where she was meeting up with Diane. Then Michael said, "Your friend needs sex tonight too."

Thinking he was suggesting a threesome, Olivia said, "She's not that type of—"

Michael cut her off with, "I have a friend who'll have sex with her. I'll bring him with me."

"Oh," Olivia said. "That would be amazing. But I don't think she's the type to—"

Michael ended the call.

Olivia was going to call him back, but before the call connected she clicked off. Diane needed company, and Olivia wanted to see if she and Michael could do something together that didn't involve getting naked. Since meeting at the restaurant that night she hadn't even seen him outside his apartment or, for that matter, in the light of day. She was beginning to wonder if he was some kind of vampire or something.

Olivia cut out from work early and got dressed, casual/sexy—a short black skirt, a low-cut top, and the Anne Klein black patent leather tall boots she'd bought last month but hadn't worn yet. She always had high self-esteem, but she modeled in front of the full-length mirror and thought she looked damn sexy. She even said out loud, "I am damn sexy."

Olivia exited the cab in front of the bar on Houston Street at the same time Diane was arriving. The place didn't get active until much later on, and it was nearly empty. They ordered Vodka Collinses. Then Olivia checked the time on her cell phone and said, "I wonder where the guys are."

"Guys?"

Olivia hadn't told Diane about the double date.

Diane, suddenly catching on, suddenly angry, got up, saying, "I can't believe you did this. This is the last thing I need right now."

"I just wanted you to meet Michael, and his friend's single. How do you know he's not a great guy?"

"There *are* no great guys, don't you get it?"

Diane headed toward the door and Olivia went after her; they stopped at the same time as they saw Michael and an extremely attractive Latino enter. They were both in black—Michael in a black turtleneck and black chinos, and the Latino guy in very tight black jeans and a black blazer. The blazer was open and underneath he had a black shirt with embroidered stitching and the top four or five buttons open, exposing most of his hairy chest and a gold chain. On practically any other guy in the world, the look would have shouted *sleazeball*, but somehow this guy was able to pull it off. Well, at least Olivia thought so. Diane seemed somewhat horrified.

"Say hello to Ramon," Michael said.

Ramon locked gazes with Olivia and said, "You are simply stunning."

"Thank you," Olivia said, getting a vibe similar to when she'd met Michael for the first time. He had a raw, unrestrained masculinity that was so damn refreshing.

Ramon took her hand and kissed it, still gazing at her eyes.

"She's *my* lover," Michael said.

Wow, was Michael actually jealous? Olivia couldn't help feeling flattered.

"Oh, I apologize," Ramon said to Olivia. Then he turned to Diane and with the same enraptured look said, "You look simply stunning this evening."

Again, with any other guy, this routine would have come off as laughable, even pathetic, but somehow he made it seem sincere.

"I am Ramon," he said, of course rolling the *R* with his tongue.

Diane—maybe mesmerized, maybe horrified—said hesitantly, "I'm Diane."

"Come with me," Ramon, who hadn't let go of Diane's hand, said, and then he led her toward the back of the bar.

Diane looked back, and though she didn't say a word, Olivia could tell she was thinking, *I'm going to kill you for this.*

Michael sat next to Olivia at the bar, and when the bartender came over he said, "Bring me a glass of water, no ice."

"Yes, sir," the bartender, a short tattooed woman, said sarcastically, but Michael didn't seem to pick up on it—or if he did, he didn't seem to care.

Olivia looked toward the back, where Ramon was seated on a sunk-in sofa, sitting very close to Diane, still holding her hand. He seemed to be doing all the talking.

"She's not a happy camper," Olivia said.

"You like Ramon," Michael said.

"Oh, I think he's sexy as hell," Olivia said. "Not as sexy as you, of course, sweetie." She kissed him, then noticed the very noticeable bulge in his jeans. "Umm, you might want to do something about that."

"I want to have sex," he said. "I don't hide my emotions."

"So do I, sweetie, but we're in a public place right now."

"Only humans hide their emotions."

"And what? You're not human?"

He didn't answer.

Olivia said, "Seriously. Do we have to do this all the time?"

"We've never been to this bar before," Michael said.

"No, I mean *this*," Olivia said. "This role playing or whatever you want to call it."

"You want me to lie."

"No, I want you to *stop* lying. Can't we take a break from the game for one night? Or at least while we're here?"

"I don't play games," Michael said.

"Fine, whatever," Olivia said. "I mean, if this is what it takes to get you going, I'm game. I mean, I'll keep playing the game."

They sat silently, sipping their drinks. Olivia was waiting for Michael to initiate conversation, but staring at maybe himself in the mirror behind the bar, he didn't say a word. He just sat there, sipping his water, and he still had a hard-on. Five, then ten minutes went by, and he didn't break character, as if it were perfectly normal to go out with a woman to a bar and say absolutely nothing. She was amazed how much discipline he had. Was he some kind of method actor or something? If he wasn't, he was missing out on a great career.

Ramon was leading Diane by the hand back toward the front of the bar. Diane motioned with her eyes for Olivia to come over to her.

"Uh-oh, here we go," Olivia said.

Olivia went over to Diane while Ramon waited near the door.

Beating her to the punch, Olivia said, "Okay, I'm sorry, I owe you one, okay?"

"I'm going home with him," Diane said.

Olivia noticed something different about Diane; she was practically glowing. It was hard to believe this was the same heartbroken woman who'd arrived at the bar less than half an hour ago.

"Are you serious?" Olivia said. "I thought you were—"

"What can I say?" Diane said. "You were right and I was wrong. Some guys are charming and you see right through it, but this guy is so genuinely charming. It's like he jumped out of a romance novel. All that's missing is the white horse."

"I agree with you . . . obviously," Olivia said. "But as your friend I have to remind you, you're vulnerable right now. I mean, you and Steve just—"

"Oh, who cares about stupid Steve," Diane said. "I mean, I should've blown him off when he showed me a picture of his Porsche on the first date." She looked toward Ramon and smiled, then said to Olivia, "He wants me to go home with him and see his roof deck."

Diane returned to Ramon, who said, "I'm sorry if I was staring at you. But your beauty, it's simply mesmerizing."

The way Ramon was admiring Diane—longingly, with restrained passion—even made Olivia breathless.

Ramon and Diane linked arms and left the bar and went off into the night.

"Wow, I think I've officially seen everything," Olivia said. Then, suddenly horny herself, she said to Michael, "So should we head back to your place?"

"I have work to do tonight," Michael said.

"Tonight?" Olivia couldn't hide her disappointment. "You're getting me jealous. What are you going to do, go kill somebody?"

"Yes," Michael said.

It was amazing the way he never broke character.

"Really?" she said flirtatiously. "Can I come along?"

"You won't understand."

"Oh, will you stop with that already? Don't you get it yet? I'm not like other women in this city."

"You only want to share experiences with me because you don't know what I am. Once you see what I am, you'll hate me."

Wondering why he kept saying *what* instead of *who*, she asked, "Why won't you just let me in?"

"If I let you in, you won't be able to ever go back," he said. "You understand that." Not asking; *telling* her.

"Yes, I understand that," she said.

After a long icy glare—how did he do that without breaking character?—he walked away. She thought he was leaving, ditching her, and then he turned back and said, "Come with me."

She caught up and said, "Where are we going?"

He didn't answer, and she thought, *What the hell?* She was along for the ride, so she might as well enjoy it.

He turned onto Sullivan Street and went past Bleecker, all the way to Washington Square Park, then went back downtown on Thompson to Houston, and then went back uptown on another street. He didn't look at her the whole time and maintained a serious, determined, intensely focused expression. They continued zigzagging along the streets of the West Village for maybe another twenty minutes when he finally stopped in front of a parked car, an old Honda, and started fiddling with the lock. Was that what he was doing all this time, looking for his car? Then she realized he wasn't opening the lock, he was *picking* it, or appeared to be anyway. She reminded herself that none of this was real, that it was all part of a game—a game that was getting weirder and weirder.

He finally got the door open. Then he opened the passenger door and said, "Get in."

So now he was pretending what, he was a car thief? *Whatever,* she thought as she sat down.

The way they were heading, she thought they were going back to his place in Tribeca, but then he turned onto Canal and entered the Holland Tunnel.

"Where are we going?" she asked.

"We'll be there soon," he said.

She was quiet till they exited in New Jersey and got on I-78. Then she decided she didn't see why she couldn't ask the questions, even if he refused to answer them.

"So," she said, "someone hired you to do this job?"

"No, this one's a favor for a friend."

"Well, that's nice of you," Olivia said. "I can't get my friends to water my plants when I go on vacation, but you'll kill for yours. Wow, what a mensch."

Michael didn't smile, of course, but Olivia was cracking herself up.

"So my dangerous, scary, car-thieving hit man," Olivia continued. "Why did you decide to go into a life of crime?"

"Because I enjoy killing people," he said. "I would kill for free and I have killed for free. But if people will pay me to kill, it's even better."

"Aren't you worried about going to jail? I mean, I don't know if you're aware of this, but mass murder is against the law." Olivia was having fun egging him on.

"My father wanted me to run the brewery," he said. "But I didn't want to work for Hartman Beer, and I didn't want to work for my father."

"Wait, Hartman Beer," Olivia said. "That sounds familiar. I think we used to drink that when I was in college in Syracuse. . . . But we used to have a nickname for it."

"Fartman."

"Ha, that's right." She laughed. "But I didn't think it was *that* bad. I actually thought it was pretty good."

"You're lying."

"You're right, I'm lying."

Olivia was enjoying the banter; for once she and Michael were interacting like a normal couple.

The feeling didn't last for long.

A ten-minute period of silence reminded her that she was still just a participant in some weird game and she had no idea what the rules were.

"So," Olivia asked. "Why didn't you want to be in the beer business?"

"I have anger," Michael said. He was silent for a while, and she thought he was through. Then he said, "Anger is beautiful. Many people reject anger; they hide from it, they punish people for it. But why punish people for something that's natural? Do we punish people for eating? For breathing? Then why for killing? All animals kill. But do animals regret killing? Do they mourn their victims? No, animals accept their anger, they accept their rage. Humans can experience this bliss too if they merely accept their natural animal state. For me, being a hit man is the perfect way to express my natural anger."

Olivia absorbed all of this, trying to maintain a serious, interested expression, as if she were on a date with a normal guy—say a lawyer—and he was telling her about his job, but meanwhile she was thinking, *Wow, this guy's train has officially left the station.* A voice coming from somewhere inside her was telling her to get out now, while she still had a chance, but as usual the voice was faint and she was barely paying attention to it.

He continued through a part of New Jersey Olivia had never been to before. For all she knew Michael was going to drive across the entire country. It concerned her that she wasn't at all concerned about any of this.

But he wasn't going across the country, at least not without making a pit stop in Bernardsville, New Jersey, first.

He pulled over and took a piece of paper from out of his pocket—

presumably directions. The light was dim in the car; she couldn't understand how he could possibly read the paper. After examining it for several seconds, he continued to drive. She didn't bother to ask where they were going because she knew he wouldn't tell her.

They made a few turns and wound up on an upscale suburban block. Then he cut the headlights and they were suddenly in pitch-darkness.

Her heart rate accelerated. She asked, "What the hell are you doing?"

He continued at the same speed, then made a sharp turn. Olivia couldn't see a thing, and she reached out in front of her, grabbing the dashboard, bracing herself for an imminent crash.

"Are you out of your mind?!" she screamed. "Stop the car! Pull over right now!"

"Stop yelling or I'll have to kill you," Michael said.

There was steel in his voice, and if she hadn't known that none of this was real she would have been terrified. Instead, she was just pissed off.

She said, "Oh, can you stop with your ridiculousness already and talk to me like a normal person? And will you turn the headlights back on, for God's sake?"

He didn't stop, making another sharp turn. Olivia's eyes were adjusting to the darkness—there was some light from inside houses, but not much. She could make out the road, at least part of it, so although the headlightless drive was still scary, it wasn't totally terrifying.

Then he slowed, pulled up to the curb, and cut the engine. There were no houses in the immediate area, so now Olivia couldn't see at all. But she heard Michael fiddling with something; she didn't know what it was. It sounded like it was something hard, maybe metallic. Then she remembered the holster, how he'd claimed he was a hit man.

Her pulse pounding again, she asked, "What are you doing?"

More fiddling. She thought, what if she was wrong? What if this wasn't a game? What if all of this was real?

"Wait here," he said.

He got out of the car and walked away—it seemed like he was

crossing the street, but he disappeared in the darkness and it was impossible to tell where exactly he was heading.

Okay, this was getting more and more bizarre, and she had to admit, though she was terrified and was actually fearing for her life, on another level this was turning her on. Maybe that was the whole point—fear as an aphrodisiac.

"Move over, oysters," she said out loud, laughing, not because she was in the mood to laugh; it was purely for tension relief.

He was gone for a few minutes—she was even starting to wonder if he'd ditched her here—and then the sudden noise of the car door opening gave her a jolt.

He got in.

"So," she asked. "Did you kill whoever you wanted to kill?"

"Yes," he said.

He placed the object on the seat between them and, without turning on the headlights, made a U-turn and drove about a half block in total darkness.

"Come on, not again," Olivia said. "What're you doing?"

He went about another half block and turned on the headlights. Enough light made it into the car so that she could see that the object between them was a gun with what looked like a very long barrel. It looked like one of those, whatchamacallits . . . sound suppressors.

She wasn't concerned, though, knowing the gun was part of the game. He was just trying to get her to believe he was an erratic, dangerous hit man who was even willing to drive with no headlights.

In the dark he said, "You won't tell anyone what you saw tonight. If you tell anyone or even think about telling anyone, I will have to kill you, and I don't want to kill you. I like you."

"Thank you, that's probably the nicest thing a guy ever said to me," she said, leaking sarcasm, and why not? She knew he wouldn't pick up on it because he was so goddamn serious.

She looked away, toward the pitch-darkness outside the passenger-side window, and rolled her eyes.

Then he pulled over again.

"Why are we stopping?"

"Get out," he said.

She glanced briefly at the gun between them. She couldn't stop her heart rate from accelerating again. "Why?"

"Get out," he said.

She got out—the combination of fear and exhilaration was addicting. She could see faintly, as the moon was casting some bluish-white light. They seemed to be in some woodsy area. She couldn't see any houses.

Then he got out too. She noticed he left the gun, which kind of surprised her. She expected he was going to pretend to whack her or something.

"Follow me," he said.

"How can I follow you? I can't see anything."

He ignored this; why was she surprised?

Grabbing on to the back of his long leather jacket, she followed him in the dark. Although she couldn't see, she knew they were definitely in a woodsy area. She could smell the rotting leaves and feel the leaves and fallen tree branches crunching beneath her boots. Jesus, why did she have to wear her new Anne Kleins on tonight of all nights?

"You're ruining my new Anne Kleins," she said, realizing how spoiled and whiny she sounded. His only response was to walk even faster, at what seemed like a jogging pace. She gripped his jacket tighter, terrified to let go. There had to be trees all around them that they could potentially bang into faces first, but as when they were driving without headlights, he somehow knew where to go. Had he been here before? Did he hang out in the forest out in Nowheresville, New Jersey?

They continued walking at the same pace, zigzagging through the woods for maybe five minutes until they reached a small clearing. She knew there were no trees around because she could see the star-filled sky.

Looking up she said, "Wow," with the wonderment all native New Yorkers have for starry skies.

"Get naked," Michael said.

"Here?" Olivia asked, acting surprised, though she was kind of turned on by the idea. So this had been his idea of foreplay after all. Despite the cold it had been ages since she'd had sex outdoors—since that camping trip to Vermont like five years ago with her ex-boyfriend Todd.

"Why not?" she said. "I mean, 'when in Jersey,' right?"

She took off her boots and pulled down her skirt. Shivering, saying, "It's so cold, can't you put your arms around me or something?" she undid her bra and stepped out of her panties.

Her eyes were adjusting a little, and thanks to the moon giving off very dim light she could make out the outline of his body. He had taken off his clothes and was buck naked with his usual erection.

Then he was on her. It happened in an instant. One second she was standing, the next he was practically tackling her to the ground. She shrieked from being caught off guard, but she was into it. This was the crazy, unpredictable Michael she loved, the Michael she couldn't get enough of.

"Turn around," he demanded.

In the woods, under the moonlight, with only the noise of Michael's deeper-than-usual grunting, the sex was raw, unrestrained, and animalistic.

"Oh God, don't stop. Please don't stop."

She reached back to touch Michael's arm—why was it so hairy? He always had hairy arms, but this felt different. His arm was *covered* with hair.

She didn't give this too much thought because she was so close to coming and it was difficult to think, *really* think, about anything else. As always when she was about to orgasm, she consciously shut out the world, so focused on the intense feelings.

"Oh, God," she said. "Oh God, baby, you have me so close . . . I'm so, so close . . . Just like that, yeah, just like that."

About to climax, she looked back over her shoulder, but not at Michael, at someone else, or some*thing* else. He was part human, part animal. His face was covered with thick gray hair; his nose was thick and dark, like a dog's nose; his nostrils were flared; and he had huge sharp teeth. Only his eyes were recognizable. They were definitely Michael's eyes.

Had Michael put on some kind of mask? But how could a mask look so real?

If this had happened at any other time she would have screamed in sheer terror, but she was also so overwhelmed and caught up in the moment that her orgasming brain couldn't really process anything other than the intense pleasure she was experiencing. As she came, she relaxed her legs and spread out on the cold ground onto her stomach and then she felt his weight on top of her, and she wanted to see his face again. It had probably just been her imagination. They were having sex outside, like animals, so she'd imagined he was an animal; it seemed to make sense at the moment anyway. She wanted to look back at him again, expecting that he would appear perfectly normal now, when she felt his hairy face on the back of her neck and, because his face was so close to hers, his grunting, or panting really, seemed much louder.

This wasn't her imagination; this was actually happening.

She tried to turn her head but couldn't, and then she felt him biting into the left side of her neck. She knew she should be screaming, but she didn't want to scream and, besides, she couldn't move her mouth or her body. She wasn't paralyzed, though; she felt as if her inability to move was by her choice entirely. At the same time, she knew this wasn't normal, something was definitely happening to her, and yet she didn't care. It was the most pleasurable pain she'd ever experienced and she didn't want it to stop, ever. Her thoughts were fading and the black night was turning white. The thought *I'm dying* was somewhere in her consciousness, but she'd never experienced such sheer joy. If this was death, she wanted to die.

Her last thought before the darkness set in:

Bring . . . it . . . on.

TWENTY-ONE

Simon was up early with Jeremy. Alison, dressed for work and pulling her little suitcase filled with medical samples behind her, came into the dining room, where Jeremy was having his Cheerios, and kissed him good morning but didn't say anything to Simon or acknowledge his presence in any way. That was fine with Simon. He knew that when Alison was angry at him the best thing was to stay out of her way, give her a cooling-off period, because trying to talk about it would only make things worse.

Without looking at Simon, Alison said to Jeremy, "See you around seven o'clock, sweetie," and rushed out of the apartment.

Simon couldn't help feeling hurt, but he tried to focus on the bright side. Okay, so she was acting like he didn't exist, but at least she wasn't screaming at him about a separation. Baby steps.

Simon had a good day alone with Jeremy. The guys weren't meeting up today because Charlie had to work a twenty-four-hour shift, so Simon took Jeremy downtown to the Children's Museum of the Arts on Lafayette Street and they had a blast, playing with the big foam cubes. Afterward, they went to Simon's favorite pizza place, Ben's on Spring

Street. Jeremy had a plain slice and Simon had a slice packed with sausage and pepperoni piled on. It was nice to spend a nice, normal afternoon with his son.

When Alison came home from work she was acting the way she had earlier—very warm and loving with Jeremy and cold and distant with Simon. Figuring that getting into it again with her wouldn't accomplish anything and would probably make things worse, Simon went for a long run in the park instead. The flashes of attacking Tom had been subsiding—he'd had them only intermittently today—but he still hadn't been able to shake an underlying feeling of guilt. He did a couple of laps around the reservoir and then did the big loop around the entire park. Running was the only time he felt truly free, when the problems of his life seemed inconsequential.

When he came home, Alison was already in bed asleep. Simon was horny and wished they were on better terms, but for now he would just have to deal with it. He showered, then joined her in bed, eventually falling into a light sleep.

He awoke to the doorbell ringing.

Alison was up too. In the dark, she asked, "Who could that be?"

Simon glanced at the time—past four A.M.

The bell rang again. This was unusual in itself because when they had visitors the doorman always announced them.

"It's probably some drunk college kids," Simon said, although he knew this explanation didn't hack it, since it was a family-oriented building and there weren't a lot of drunk college kids carousing in the hallways in the middle of the night.

"Jeremy's going to wake up any second," Alison said, flicking on the light.

As if on cue, Jeremy called out, "Daddy!"

Alison seemed very annoyed, and Jeremy asking for Simon definitely wasn't helping.

"Okay, relax," Simon said. "You take care of Jeremy and I'll take care of whoever's ringing the doorbell."

Approaching the door, Simon heard a woman in the hallway saying, "He has to be home, ring again."

"Okay, coming, I'm coming," Simon said.

He expected it to be some couple, maybe friends of people in the building, or subletters accidentally ringing the bell to the wrong apartment. When they saw Simon they'd apologize embarrassedly and that would be the end of it. So Simon was naturally surprised when he opened the door and saw two cops there.

One was a short, attractive, maybe Puerto Rican woman; the other was a much taller, larger black guy waiting in the foyer, near the front door. Although the guy was in a plain black long-sleeved shirt and the woman was in plain black pants and a black sweater, their whole attitude shouted *cops*.

Sure enough the Latina said, "Mr. Burns?" He said, "Yes," and then she flashed a badge and said, "I'm Detective Geri Rodriguez, NYPD, you're going to have to come with us."

NYPD?

Panicking but trying not to show it, Simon said, "I think there's a mistake. I already spoke to somebody from the New Jersey police the other day."

"There's no mistake," Rodriguez said.

She sounded serious; this seemed very different from the "routine" visit from Dorsey. But what could the New York police possibly want to talk to him about?

"This is ridiculous," Simon said. "It's four in the morning and you woke my whole family up. I want to know what's going on."

"We're not arresting you, Mr. Burns," Rodriguez said, "we're just taking you in for questioning. Do you understand that?"

"Questioning about what? There's no reason to—"

"Did you hear what she's saying to you?" the black guy said. Although his tone was polite and he was even smiling slightly, his no-BS attitude told Simon that arguing would be futile.

"Why don't you put on some shoes?" Rodriguez asked.

Had she said "shoes" in a loaded way? Was she looking for some kind of reaction? Had they found his missing shoe in the woods? He felt a pang of fear and saw himself as the wolf, tearing into Tom's flesh.

As Simon put on his sneakers, he glanced toward the hallway, where Alison was standing with her arms crossed in front of her chest. Although she was looking right at him, Simon felt like he wasn't even there.

Frustrated, knowing that his being taken away by the police was the last thing their marriage needed right now, Simon said, "Don't worry, everything's going to be okay, I promise. This is just some kind of misunderstanding. I'll take care of it and be home as soon as I can."

Alison's expression didn't change.

On the street, Simon said to the cops, "I don't get this. If it's just questioning, why can't you question me at home?"

He rode in the back of an unmarked police car to a precinct uptown. As they entered, he saw on the building: MANHATTAN NORTH HOMICIDE.

"Come on, this is insane," Simon said. "I already spoke to Detective Dorsey from the police department in Bernardsville. Did you speak to Dorsey yet or not?"

Leading Simon down a hallway, Rodriguez's and the other detective's gazes were fixed straight ahead.

Then Rodriguez said, "Why don't you let me ask the questions? Put your taxpayer dollars to work."

They led him to an interrogation room. Gray walls, a rectangular table with one chair on one long side, two on the other. One wall was glass, a two-way mirror, no doubt. Even if they'd found his shoe, Simon didn't get what was going on; why were they treating him like an actual murder suspect? Getting paranoid again, Simon wondered if the police had found some new piece of evidence, or maybe another witness had come forward. What if someone had seen him with a wolf that night? What if he actually had sicced a wolf on Tom?

Stop it, he told himself. He knew he was being ridiculous. They were going to ask him some routine questions and that would be the end of it.

After they instructed him to sit on the side of the table with one chair, Simon tried again. "This is absolutely ridiculous; I don't understand what's going on." Again they ignored him and left him in the room alone.

About half an hour later, Rodriguez returned alone, taking the seat across from him.

"Where's the wolf?" she asked.

"The wolf?" Simon said.

"That's right, the wolf," she said.

"I've been trying to tell you guys, but you won't listen," Simon said. "I have nothing to do with any wolves, and I've been through all this with Dorsey. Did you even speak with—"

"Where is it," she asked, "at a friend's house? If you don't tell me, it's just going to make things worse for you."

"For the last time," Simon said. "I don't have a wolf. Why would I have a wolf?"

"Where were you earlier tonight between eight P.M. and ten P.M.?"

Now Simon had absolutely no idea what this was about. "I was home."

"All night?"

"Yes, all night, but . . . Wait, not all night. I went running in the park."

"For how long?"

"A couple of hours. Why? What happened?"

"A couple of hours is a long time for a run."

"I like to take long runs, I don't understand why—"

"When did you leave for the run?"

"I don't know, around nine," he said. "But what's going on? At my apartment, you made it sound like this would be routine questioning, but now—"

"What time did you get back from Jersey tonight?"

"Jersey?" Simon was clueless. "I wasn't in New Jersey."

She was studying his expression, as if trying to catch him in a lie.

Simultaneously Simon said, "Look, if you don't—" and Rodriguez said, "You shot and killed Alan Freedman and his wife, didn't you?"

"What?" Simon said, shocked. "I don't even—" Wait, Alan Freedman; why was that name so familiar? Then it came to him. Simon was suddenly dizzy, as if he were on the verge of passing out. "Wait, Alan Freedman. You mean Tom Harrison's neighbor?"

"You were afraid he was going to ID you, so you drove out there and killed him. His wife was there, so you killed her too."

"Wait," Simon said. "Alan Freedman is *dead*? And his wife is dead too? I—I don't understand. How is that possible?"

Simon suddenly remembered Michael telling him, *I'll do anything for a member of my pack.* But would Michael actually kill two innocent people?

"What's the matter?" Rodriguez asked. "Uncomfortable? You're gonna be real uncomfortable in the cell you'll be spending the rest of your life in."

"I was home tonight," Simon said. "I had nothing to do with any of this. I didn't drive to Alan Freedman's house in New Jersey. I barely even know Alan Freedman, and I have no idea who his wife is."

"Lemme ask you another question." Rodriguez stared at Simon. "How'd you know the Freedmans were killed in their house?"

"You told me they were," Simon said.

"No, actually I didn't."

Did she tell him? Everything was so jumbled he couldn't think straight.

"Then I—I—I just assumed they were." Weirdly, Simon felt guilty, like he had to cover for himself.

"How 'bout we cut to the chase," Rodriguez said, "and you tell me where you really were this evening."

"I was home," Simon said. "I was in New York. You can talk to my doorman. He saw me leave and he saw me return. Talk to James, and talk to my wife—they'll both tell you. I swear to God I had nothing to do with any of this."

"You a religious man, Mr. Burns?"

"No," Simon said. "I mean not really."

"Then why the hell do you think I care whether you swear to God or not?"

As calmly as possible—which wasn't very calmly at all—Simon said, "Look, I didn't kill two people last night, okay? That's just flat-out ludicrous. I'm not a killer, okay? I'm a father. I'm a husband."

Rodriguez seemed to be studying his reaction. Simon had a feeling he was getting through to her.

"Look at it from my point of view," she said. "On Tuesday you were questioned by the Jersey police because a man thought he saw you near Tom Harrison's house on the night he was killed. Then tonight the man and his wife are killed. You're going to tell me that's a coincidence?"

Or maybe he wasn't getting through.

"Yes," Simon said. "It has to be."

"So you want me to believe you're telling the truth and you didn't go to Jersey tonight."

"I *am* telling the truth."

"But maybe you hired somebody to go to New Jersey for you."

"What do you mean, hired somebody?"

"Like a hit man," Rodriguez said.

"Oh come on, give me—"

"What about the night Tom Harrison was killed? You're going to deny you were there that night too, even though Alan Freedman said he saw you there."

"Alan Freedman made a mistake," Simon said.

"Or maybe he didn't. Maybe you got a wolf to kill your old boss, thinking it was the perfect way to get away with murder, but you didn't count on somebody seeing you there."

"That's not true," Simon said. "I'm telling you, I wasn't in New Jersey."

Rodriguez was looking at him differently now; could she tell he was lying? Did she have the shoe? Was she just holding back this information to try to get a confession?

"I understand you were with a friend the night Tom Harrison was killed," she said.

"So you did talk to Dorsey," Simon said.

"Is there anybody else who can vouch for your whereabouts that night besides your friend?"

"No," Simon said. "It's just my friend."

"So you have your friend as your alibi for one murder and your wife for another murder. Is that right, Mr. Burns?"

"I want a lawyer," Simon said.

"Lawyer or not, it'll make it a lot easier if you give yourself up," Rodriguez said. "Look at it this way, you're going down no matter what, so why not save us all some time and confess?"

Simon felt like the room was getting smaller. Everything was closing in. It was hard to breathe.

"I want a lawyer," he said again.

Rodriguez got up, made it to the door, then turned back.

"Oh, one more thing, Mr. Burns."

This was it—they had found his shoe. If they had his shoe, he was through. There was no way he'd be able to deny he was at Tom's house the night he was killed, and they'd wind up somehow pinning the other murders on him as well.

"Do you know a man named Dave Doherty?"

Simon let out the breath he'd been holding and said, "No." It was true—he had no idea who Dave Doherty was.

"You sure?" Rodriguez asked.

Simon racked his brain—was Dave Doherty the father of one of Jeremy's friends? Was he the husband of one of Alison's friends? Somebody he went to college with?

"I honestly have no idea who he is," Simon said. "Wait, don't tell me he was killed too."

Simon was being completely facetious.

"Last year his body was found in Howard Beach, Brooklyn."

"Jesus Christ, I was kidding," Simon said.

"You think murder is funny, Mr. Burns?"

"Not kidding like that, I just . . ." Simon suddenly realized he was being accused of another murder. "Wait a second. If you're trying to say—"

"Doherty lived in Manhattan. Actually not too far from you. Hell's Kitchen. He was married, had a son. How old is your son, Mr. Burns?"

"What diff does—"

"How old is he?"

"Three," Simon said reluctantly.

Rodriguez smiled out of the corner of her mouth.

"Funny," she said. "Doherty had a two-year-old son. He would be three now. Same age as your son."

Simon was going to ask her if she thought murder was funny but had a feeling it wouldn't go over very well. Instead he said, "I told you, I've never heard of Dave Doherty. Why do you think that has anything to do with me?"

"Maybe it has something to do with the wolf bites on his body."

After glaring at Simon one last time, Rodriguez left the room.

Simon was left alone in the white, brightly lit room, thinking, *Did this just happen?* The whole situation—being questioned for three murders, two of which he definitely hadn't committed—had been completely bizarre, but Dave Doherty was the topper. Who the hell was Dave Doherty? Was Rodriguez seriously implying that Simon might have had something to do with a fourth murder, or was it just some kind of interrogation strategy to try to screw with his mind?

Simon was dizzy and claustrophobic. He started pacing the room, feeling like a wild animal in a tiny cage. Then he realized they were probably watching him in the two-way glass and that appearing nervous and agitated probably wasn't the best idea. So he returned to his chair and tried to stay as patient as possible, acting like he had nothing to hide, but the reality was he had something huge to hide. He'd been in denial about it for days, but he couldn't hide from the truth any longer—he'd definitely killed Tom. It wasn't a coincidence that he'd been in New

Jersey that night, and Alan Freedman hadn't made a mistake. The blood on his jeans was Tom's blood, and it was probably like the police said—when he blacked out he'd somehow gotten a wolf and brought it to Tom's house. But what had happened to the wolf? And had Michael actually killed Freedman and his wife? It was hard to imagine that Michael would actually kill two innocent people. Then Simon shuddered, realizing that his only alibi for Tom's murder might be a total psychopath.

It was hard to judge how much time had gone by, but Simon felt like he'd been sitting, waiting, for at least an hour when Rodriguez finally returned and said, "You can go."

"Thank you," Simon said. "I didn't know how much longer I could hold it in."

"No, I meant you can leave," she said.

"Are you serious?" Simon was in shock; he couldn't believe he was actually going to walk out of here. A few seconds ago he'd been convinced he'd never be free again.

"Yeah, but don't worry," she said ominously, "we're not through with you yet."

On his way out of the precinct Simon saw Dorsey, the detective from New Jersey. Instinctively Simon smiled and waved, but this wasn't the friendly, laid-back Dorsey who'd visited him the other day. This was an angry, all-business Dorsey whose icy glare was clearly meant to send Simon a message.

Simon needed to clear his head and relax in a big way, so he jogged back home to the Upper West Side. It was almost dawn, the first light of the day turning the sky a very dark blue. The effect of physical activity on his psyche was amazing as hope quickly returned. He managed to re-convince himself that maybe it was a bizarre coincidence that he had been at Tom's house that night, and that maybe the blood on his jeans wasn't Tom's blood, and the murders of Alan Freedman and his wife had also been a bizarre coincidence that had nothing to do with him or Michael.

It was great to be back at his building, to be walking past James again as a free man. But when he entered his apartment he immediately knew something was wrong. In the vestibule he inhaled deeply. Yeah, something had definitely changed.

In the dining room he smelled ink, maybe from a Sharpie. Then he saw the note on the table in Alison's handwriting:

This isn't what I want. I'm sorry.

Frantically he checked the bedrooms, shouting their names, but he knew it was hopeless.

His family was gone.

TWENTY-TWO

Olivia opened her eyes expecting to be in Cuba. She'd been dreaming that she was having sex on a beach—not the drink, actual sex on a beach—with some ripped Cuban guy, but instead she saw Michael looking down at her.

Then she realized she was in Michael's Tribeca apartment. She was too tired, and too in Cuba, to fully process any of this.

"I thought I'd have to bury you in the woods," Michael said.

She tried to sit up. Jesus, her head felt like there was a bowling ball attached to it. "Oh, God, I don't think I've ever felt like this. What happened to me?" She closed her eyes for a few seconds, then opened them suddenly and said, "What day is this?"

"You must rest," Michael said.

"Is today Thursday? Is it? Is it?"

"You can't go anywhere. You're not ready."

"What time is it?" She looked around for her pocketbook, managing to lift her head more than she had the first time. "Where's my bag? Where's my iPhone?"

"You have everything you need," Michael said.

"Oh no, it's Thursday, isn't it? Is it morning? Is it still morning?"

Olivia managed to wake up, realizing she was fully dressed in the same clothes, including the boots, that she'd worn last night. Oh God, it *was* Thursday.

"You won't leave," Michael said.

"You don't understand," Olivia said. "I have work to do. A major client's coming in from Japan to meet with me today. Where's my pocketbook?"

Olivia spotted her pocketbook on the dresser across the room. As she stood Michael grabbed her shoulders, trying to push her back down, and she pushed him back, much harder than she intended, and he fell backward, actually leaving his feet, and slammed against the brick wall.

"Oh my God," she said, "I'm sorry." She had no idea how that had happened. Michael probably weighed two hundred pounds; yeah, she was in a hurry, but how did she have the strength to push him so far?

"See?" Michael said; he seemed fine. "I told you you aren't ready. You don't know how to control it yet."

Olivia went to her pocketbook, fished around for her phone.

"Okay, it's eight fifty . . . I still have ten minutes to get to my office."

"You can't leave my sight," Michael said, now standing between her and the exit in a slightly crouched, ready position, as if he were expecting her to charge and he'd have to defend himself.

"Please get out of my way," Olivia said. "I can't be late for this meeting."

"You don't want to go to a meeting," Michael said.

"Yes, I do want to go to a meeting, so can you stop all this ridiculousness, I really don't have time for this right now." She realized her clothes were disheveled and dirty. "Oh my God, what happened to me?"

"I had to dress you," Michael said.

Suddenly it came back—the double date, the bizarre trip to New Jersey, having sex with Michael in the woods, the way his face had appeared as the face of an animal.

"You look normal now," Olivia said. "You look . . ." She was confused. Her head felt extremely heavy again, and she was aware of other strange pains in her gums and hands and feet especially. "God, what the hell happened to me? I must've blacked out, and I *never* black out. Did you slip me something at the bar? I mean, I don't see why you'd . . . or when you'd . . ." She had another memory—him giving her that massive hickey, biting into her neck. She felt the area, and it felt sticky and stung a little. There was definitely a wound there, which was a relief because it at least seemed to confirm that she wasn't going completely insane.

"The site will heal completely within a day," Michael said. "From now on all of your injuries will heal faster. It's one of the many gifts I have given you."

"Did you actually bite me?" Olivia said.

"Yes," Michael said.

Touching the wound again, wincing, Olivia asked, "Why did you bite me?"

"Sometimes during sex I lose control and I can't help it. But it should have killed you. Everyone I've ever bitten has died, including my son's mother. There is only one explanation for why you survived. . . . You are my soul mate."

"Wait, let me get this straight," Olivia said. "Last night you were threatening to kill me if I revealed your secrets, and now you think we're soul mates?"

"Yes," Michael said.

"Are you out of your—" Olivia cut herself off, thinking about her meeting again. "An iron. Do you have an iron?"

Blank stare.

"Of course you don't answer, why would I expect anything else?"

"I told you, you're not ready—"

"Will you please —"

"You feel the change."

"I feel like I have a bad hangover because you must've slipped me a roofie or something."

"You're just not aware of what is happening yet. You're not human anymore. You have wolves' blood now like me."

"Wolves' blood?" She had to laugh, then said, "First you're a hit man and now you're a wolf. You have some imagination, don't you? Well, I have to get to work."

Olivia shoved Michael out of the way, knocking him hard to the floor.

"Oh my God, sorry," she said. "I didn't mean to do that."

From the floor Michael said, "See? You don't know how to control it yet. I must teach you everything."

She realized *something* strange was going on, but she didn't have time to give it much thought or discuss it. She left the room and headed through the loft toward the exit.

Michael came running behind her, saying, "Your body is altered for eternity. You're not human anymore."

He caught up with her and grabbed her from behind. She was about to shove him away again when she saw Michael's father—several feet ahead of her, in front of the elevator. He was with a boy, maybe three years old, and they were holding hands.

Olivia and Michael stopped, and his father seemed extremely angry at him for some reason, but that was just his natural expression. The boy looked like a mini version of Michael, minus the gray hair. They had similar-shaped faces and practically identical eyes.

"Hi, I'm Olivia," she said to the boy. He didn't answer, and then, the bizarre awkwardness of the situation setting in, she added, "and I should be going."

She got on the elevator. She expected Michael to try to stop her, but he remained there, as if mesmerized by his father, and let her go. She recalled Michael telling her about how his father didn't want him to have lovers and wondered whether it had something to do with that.

Whatever, she thought.

Outside, Eddie wasn't waiting with the Lexus.

"Damn it," she muttered, and stepped out onto the cobblestone street, hoping to hail a cab. People's stares reminded her that she looked like hell. One woman on the sidewalk whispered to the guy she was with: "Someone's taking the walk of shame this morning." Olivia didn't care, but as she walked on she wondered how she'd heard what the woman had said. After all, she'd been a good twenty feet away and the woman had clearly been whispering.

Olivia's attention was diverted when she spotted an empty cab stopped at a red light on Warren Street.

"Taxi!" Olivia shouted, and sprinted to the cab. She was surprised how fast she'd gotten there—almost instantly, and in boots with three-inch heels no less.

"Fortieth and Sixth," she said.

Luckily there wasn't much traffic on West Street, and they were making good time. Olivia couldn't help noticing how many sexy men there were in Manhattan. Bike messengers, UPS delivery guys, drunks on street corners; she really used to complain that it was hard to meet guys in this city? Attractive men were everywhere, but, okay, what was up with her hormones? She couldn't remember ever being this horny. Even the thin, bearded, sweaty cabdriver didn't look so bad. Or smell so bad. He smelled pretty good, actually—raw and pungent, with no deodorant getting in the way of his natural scent. She could smell other guys in the cab as well, probably previous passengers. Their scents were lingering in the air and had seeped into the material of the backseat.

They hit traffic crossing east, so Olivia had the driver drop her at Thirty-seventh and Seventh. She walked quickly and then started running toward her office, weaving in and out of pedestrians. It felt great to run, as if she'd been caged for years, and she was hyper-aware of her surroundings. Every odor, honking horn, voice, car engine, cough, and sneeze seemed clear and amplified. When she focused she could hear individual conversations—a woman across the street complaining to her friend about the bad service at a restaurant they'd eaten at last night, a guy in a suit talking on his cell phone about a woman—"Tellin' you, bro, she's so into you." Was she really hearing all this? How was it possible? And what was up with her sense of smell? Pollution from the traffic was the most dominating odor, but despite this she could detect urine, dog feces, and cigarette smoke. She could also smell people's unique scents and the scents of many perfumes and colognes, and when she ran past a deli the odors of bacon and sausage were especially prominent and caused a surge of hunger. Although she was already very late for her meeting, she couldn't resist going into the deli and ordering bacon and eggs to go. As she watched the bacon sizzle on the skillet, it looked so enticing that she said, "Can you make that a double order of bacon, please?" Then it seemed like it was taking forever for the bacon to cook, so she said, "It's okay, I'll take it like that."

"But it's not done yet," the guy said.

"I don't care," she said.

She took the order of eggs and half-cooked bacon and scarfed it up, standing on the sidewalk outside the deli. As she was finishing off the last couple of strips, she thought, *I'm seriously eating bacon?* She usually avoided fatty, salty meat, but the taste was so satisfying and the food seemed to give her a jolt of energy and make her stronger and more alert. She wanted more—the ten or so strips she'd eaten had barely satisfied her—but she had to get to her meeting, so she rushed around the corner to her building.

Forty minutes late and impatient that the elevator wasn't coming, she took the stairs to the seventh floor. She climbed them two at a time, but wasn't winded at all when she went past reception, asking Denise, "Is Mr. Kyoto still here?" and even though she was already halfway down the hallway, she heard Denise say clearly, "In the conference room waiting for you."

Olivia entered and saw the middle-aged Japanese man in a business suit at the conference table with Kathleen, the project manager.

"So sorry I'm late," Olivia said. "The traffic was insane."

Mr. Kyoto stood and bowed.

"It's okay, no problem," he said. "It's a great pleasure to meet you, Ms. Becker." His English was thickly accented.

"Likewise," Olivia said, noticing his very masculine scent. It was intense—perhaps because he was nervous about the meeting—and it was the only male scent in the room, which somehow made it even more appealing. When she focused she could detect other odors in the room as well—Kathleen's Obsession by Calvin Klein, a citrusy scent of maybe Mr. Kyoto's shampoo or body wash, a strong coffee aroma, her own bacon breath.

"Is everything okay?" Kathleen asked.

Olivia realized she'd probably been flaring her nostrils or making some odd expression while detecting the different scents. She hoped the client hadn't noticed.

"Oh, yeah, fine," Olivia said. "It's just, um, allergies." She sniffled for emphasis.

"Mr. Kyoto was telling me this is his first time visiting New York," Kathleen said.

"Oh, is that right?" Olivia said, noticing how good-looking Kyoto was. She liked his slim body and the graying hair at the temples. Even his dorky Woody Allen–style glasses looked sexy. It was strange, because Asian men didn't normally do it for her. Usually she found their features too delicate; she'd dated a Thai guy for a while and broke up with him because she'd felt like she was kissing a woman. But this Kyoto was having a very different effect on her. She couldn't remember the last time she'd gotten so turned on by a guy she'd just met. But—she reminded herself—this wasn't just a guy; he was a potential client, a very important potential client. His line of restaurants was a huge account, and she couldn't lose this deal. She'd already made a horrible first impression by showing up late. Now she had to pull herself together, bring out her A game.

Then she noticed that he was looking back at her expectantly.

"Is something wrong?" Olivia asked, sensing that she'd done something inappropriate.

"Um, the card," Kathleen said nervously.

Olivia saw that Mr. Kyoto was holding out a business card for her.

"Oh, I'm sorry," Olivia said. "I honestly don't know where my brain is this morning."

According to Japanese business etiquette, Olivia was supposed to take the card with her right hand and place it on the table, but she was suddenly distracted again by the scent of Kyoto's body. She was staring at him and couldn't help imagining kissing his delicious neck, and she took the card with the wrong hand and put it on the table facedown. Kathleen realized the mistake immediately and turned the card over.

"Oh, I'm so sorry," Olivia said.

Smiling, Kyoto said, "It's okay, no problem." Then he added, "I brought gift for you from Japan," and held out a small wrapped package.

Olivia noticed that Kyoto had minty breath, probably from the toothpaste he'd used this morning, but she didn't know how she could smell his breath so well from several feet away. Then she imagined unbuttoning his jacket and shirt, running her hands over his smooth chest, and then kissing him, running her tongue gently along his skin.

"Thank you," she said. "This is, um, very kind of you."

Wondering how his skin would smell from up close, if it would smell even more appealing, she opened the gift—a digital camera—and said, "Thank you so much. I love it."

Kyoto seemed uncomfortable, and Olivia remembered that according to etiquette she wasn't supposed to unwrap a visitor's gift until the visitor had left.

"I'm so sorry, I know I wasn't supposed to do that," she said. "Is it hot in here?"

"No," Kathleen said. "I mean, I don't think so. Perhaps we should start the presentation now."

Mr. Kyoto sat at the conference table next to Kathleen.

Olivia began her sales pitch, saying, "First off, thank you for considering Becker Design. We're a full-service graphic design firm that will satisfy all of your needs, from layout and design to . . ." Then she caught a whiff of Kyoto's scent and it ignited a fantasy of their naked bodies intertwined and she said, "I'm sorry, what was I saying?" and had to restart her pitch. She stumbled more than once in her presentation. She could tell that Mr. Kyoto was getting frustrated, and Kathleen seemed extremely uncomfortable as well. Olivia knew she was blowing it big-time. But as badly as she wanted to rein in her erotic thoughts, she couldn't. She remembered Michael warning her, *You don't know how to control it yet*, and telling her that she wasn't human anymore and had wolves' blood now. Then she had a flashback to last night, Michael appearing like an animal right before he'd bitten her neck.

The crazy son of a bitch. What had he done to her?

Olivia heard herself saying, "We're a full-service design company that will satisfy all your needs," and then, overwhelmed by Kyoto's scent, she said, "I can't take it anymore. I'm sorry, Mr. Kyoto is just too . . . distracting."

Kathleen glared at Olivia—maybe confused, maybe horrified—and said, "Um, I think we should take a break for a moment."

Kyoto stood and said, "So sorry, I go back to my hotel now. Sorry."

"Please," Olivia said. "Give me another chance. I told you, I—I'm just not myself this morning."

"It's okay," he said. "Sorry. Good-bye."

He tried to get by her, to leave the room.

"No, you don't understand, this isn't me," Olivia said. "I'm not normally like this."

She reached out and grabbed Kyoto's hand, but feeling the warmth of skin against hers, and breathing his scent from up close, was unbearable.

"What are you *doing*?" Kathleen asked.

Olivia snapped out of it, realizing she was hugging Mr. Kyoto in a full embrace.

She let go of him. His knees buckled and he nearly fell.

"I—I didn't meant to do that," Olivia said. "I—I don't know what's happening. Are you okay?"

She tried to help him, but he managed to get to his feet on his own. Then he grabbed his briefcase, shouted something at her in Japanese, and left the office.

Kathleen went after him, pleading for him to come back.

Olivia was about to go after him as well, but then she recognized his strong scent lingering in the room and all over her body, and suddenly she didn't care about losing a major client or anything else.

The scent, and finding more of it, was all that mattered.

TWENTY-THREE

Simon spent the morning calling, e-mailing, and texting Alison dozens of times, but she wasn't responding to anything. He also contacted everyone he could think of—Alison's sister, her close friends, people she worked with, neighborhood moms—and they all claimed they had no idea where she was. Alison's boss, Kevin, her company's regional sales manager, said that Alison had e-mailed him early this morning, saying she was taking a personal day off from work, but he didn't know anything else.

Simon had never felt so helpless. All he could do was wait and hope she decided to come back or at least call or e-mail to let him know where she was. But for all he knew they'd left New York, or even the country. What if she'd decided to move to San Francisco, to be closer to her sister? Or Alison's old roommate from college, Michelle, lived in Adelaide, Australia. For all Simon knew, Alison could have taken Jeremy to Adelaide, and she could be planning to get a job there. Didn't she always say she wanted to live in Australia someday?

Suddenly convinced that Alison had run off with Jeremy to Australia, Simon went online to search for contact information for Michelle, what was her last name? Mason, Michelle Mason. Of course, there were a gazillion Michelle Masons, but as he was searching he realized he was jumping to a lot of conclusions. Alison wouldn't just pack up and leave her job to go to San Francisco or Australia or anywhere outside the New York area. She wasn't that unstable or flighty; she wouldn't just run away from her entire life. Several years ago, before Jeremy was born, Simon had brought up the idea of relocating to the West Coast, but Alison was against it because she didn't want to switch jobs or give up living in Manhattan.

This made Simon feel a little better, but not much.

Simon was so absorbed in trying to track down Alison that he'd nearly forgotten that he was a murder suspect. Finding the blood on his pants had probably been the last straw for Alison, and could he really blame her? Maybe she had done the right thing leaving him. If he'd actually been crazy enough to sic a wolf on Tom, maybe protecting Jeremy and getting as far away from him as possible was the smartest decision she could've made.

Then he remembered that the guys were meeting today in Battery Park at noon. All his troubles had started when he'd met them, and though he still didn't know what, if anything, they had to do with the chaos in his life lately, it was time to finally get some answers.

Without giving it any more thought, he left the apartment and headed toward the subway. Walking along West Eighty-ninth, toward Columbus, Simon kept checking over his shoulder to see if someone was following him. About a third of a block behind him there was a thin woman in her twenties in beige capris and a short dungaree jacket. When Simon turned onto Amsterdam and jaywalked diagonally across the street, he checked again and sure enough the woman had turned the corner, also going south on Amsterdam. Coincidence? Simon didn't think so, and when the woman continued behind him after he turned onto Eighty-sixth, heading toward Broadway, Simon was convinced the woman was a cop.

Simon had been planning to take the subway, but he didn't want to be confined, especially with someone following him. Then he had a much better idea.

He turned onto Broadway and broke into a full sprint—first zigzagging by pedestrians, then veering onto Broadway. He ran in the bike lane, keeping up with a bike messenger who was so amazed that he almost lost control of his bike and crashed into a laundry truck, braking just in time. When Simon was passing Zabar's on Eightieth, he looked back and the woman was nowhere in sight. Cop or not, Simon had left her in the dust.

When Simon arrived at the playground—sweaty but not tired—it was like any other afternoon. Michael, Charlie, and Ramon were seated on their usual bench as their kids ran around playing. They looked like normal dads—even Michael looked harmless, holding a big blue water gun. Despite everything that had happened lately, and everything he suspected had happened, Simon couldn't deny how being back with the guys—or with "the pack," as Michael would say—gave him a warm, familiar feeling.

Ramon spotted Simon first—his grin quickly morphing into a perplexed expression.

"Where's your little man at?" Ramon asked.

"With his mom," Simon said.

"So you came down here just to hang out with us?" Charlie asked.

"Yeah," Simon said. "I guess I did." He looked at Michael. "I mean, I'm part of the pack, right?"

Michael didn't have a reaction—just his usual blank, distant expression.

"Wow," Charlie said. "That's really nice of you."

Nicky, Charlie's son, came over and complained that Ramon's son was pushing him.

"I was not," Diego said.

"Was," Nicky said.

"Was not."

"Was."

Charlie and Ramon instructed their kids to play nicely and then the kids ran off, resuming their game of tag.

"So, yeah," Charlie said. "Ramon was in the middle of telling us about his latest girlfriend."

"Hey, man, I tol' you, this one's different."

"They're always different," Charlie said.

"That's true," Ramon said. "Women are like trees—no two are the same. But this woman was the most beautiful tree in the forest."

"Michael set him up," Charlie said to Simon, filling him in.

"Really?" Simon said.

"Friends do favors for friends," Michael said, looking right at Simon.

Simon didn't know if Michael was alluding to the alibi he had given him for the night of Tom's murder, or if he was implying that he'd killed Alan Freedman and his wife.

"Her name's Diane," Ramon said. "She was amazing. Definitely the most sensual woman I've ever met. I could make love to her every night for the rest of my life and never get bored."

Ramon went on, raving about his latest conquest. When he was through, he said to Simon, "So what's up with you, man? Still having those nightmares?"

Charlie and Ramon smiled.

"Actually, my whole life's been a nightmare lately."

Their smiles were suddenly replaced with serious, concerned expressions.

"What happened, man?" Ramon asked.

"Yeah, what's going on?" Charlie said. "Does it have to do with that thing in Jersey?"

"No, it has to do with another thing in Jersey."

Michael still didn't show any hint of emotion.

"What is it?" Charlie asked, concerned.

"Well, I already mentioned this to Michael," Simon said, "but that night my boss was mauled to death in New Jersey, this other guy—"

"You mean Alan Freedman?" Charlie asked.

Simon glared at Michael.

"There are no secrets in the pack," Michael said.

"I don't get it," Simon said. "You mean you told them—"

"Don't worry, man," Ramon said, smiling. "We got your back."

Simon paused, absorbing all of this. It had probably been a good thing that Michael had told the guys; it was a better alibi if three guys could vouch for the story, and Simon trusted Charlie and Ramon more than he trusted Michael. Still, Simon couldn't help feeling betrayed.

"So what about Freedman?" Charlie asked. "Did the cops ask you about him again?"

"Different cops, but yeah," Simon said.

"I don't get it," Ramon said.

"Freedman and his wife," Simon said, "they were shot and killed last night."

"No way, man," Ramon said.

"You're kiddin' me," Charlie said.

As usual Michael remained expressionless. If he played poker he could've made a fortune.

"Yeah," Simon said. "It's horrible. And pretty coincidental too, huh?"

"Wow," Charlie said. "That is a pretty big coincidence, isn't it?"

Charlie's and Ramon's surprise seemed genuine, but Michael was impossible to read.

"Look, I know this is probably all just a weird coincidence," Simon said, "but I have to ask anyway. . . . Did any of you have anything to do with this?"

Ramon did a double take, then said, "You serious? You really think I'd go kill two people?"

Charlie seemed just as hurt, saying, "Yeah, I mean, we're friends and I'd lie to the police to help you out of a tough spot. But killing people? You seriously think I'd do something like that?"

"I'm sorry," Simon said. "I just had to ask, that's all."

Simon glanced at Michael, waiting for his response, but he was silent. "What about you? Did you have anything to do with it?"

Short pause, then Michael said, "You're accusing me."

"No," Simon said, "I'm just asking you."

Long blank stare, then Michael said, "I was with a woman last night."

"Oh, okay," Simon said, realizing Michael hadn't answered the question. "I was just asking because the police don't think it's a coincidence that a guy who just reported seeing me near Tom's house wound up dead, and I don't think it's a coincidence either."

"He said he didn't do it," Charlie said.

"No," Simon said, "actually he didn't say that."

"You should remember who your friends are," Michael said.

Michael didn't elaborate, but he didn't have to because the implication was loud and clear. Accusing Michael of murdering two people was probably a bad idea when he was relying on him as an alibi for another murder

"Well, I guess last night was just a crazy coincidence," Simon said, backing off, trying to defuse the tension. "*Everything's* been crazy lately." Then, thinking about how he'd lost his family, maybe forever, he suddenly got emotional. He looked away, not wanting to cry in front of the guys.

"It's gonna be okay, bro," Charlie said.

"Yeah, it's gonna all blow over," Ramon said.

"My wife found blood on the jeans I was wearing the night my boss was killed. I don't know if it was my boss's blood, but who else's blood could it've been? Then the police took me in for questioning and when I came home . . . my wife and Jeremy were gone."

"Gone?" Charlie said. "You mean like they left you?"

Simon, still managing to hold back his tears, nodded.

"Ah, jeez, I'm sorry," Charlie said sincerely.

"Yeah," Ramon said. "I'm really sorry, man."

"There are many women," Michael said.

Simon took a few moments to absorb this, then asked, "What do you mean?"

"He's just sayin' there're a lot of fish in the sea," Ramon said. "And he's right, you can trust me on that one." Then Ramon's attention was suddenly diverted, and he called out to his son, "Hey, Diego, I said no pushing! You don't want me to have to put you in a time-out, do you?"

There was a long period of silence as the guys watched their sons play, and Simon had a feeling no one wanted to continue talking about the murders.

Simon got up and said, "Well, thanks, but I should get going."

They gave him the customary big tight hugs. As always, Michael's hug was the tightest and lasted the longest.

"Thanks for coming out," Charlie said. "And I'm sorry about your wife. From a guy who's been through a divorce, I know how rough it can be. I hope you guys can work it out."

"Yeah," Simon said. "Me too."

"We'll see you tonight at midnight," Michael said.

"Tonight at midnight?" Simon was confused. "What's tonight at midnight?"

"We're meeting at the brewery," Ramon said. "Just to hang out, eat some steaks. Don't worry, won't be any family beer or anything like that."

"You should come," Charlie said. "It'll be a blast."

"Why midnight?" Simon asked.

"That's what time we're meeting," Michael said.

"Thanks," Simon said, "but I have to see what happens with my family."

"You must join us tonight," Michael said.

Again Simon felt like he was being threatened.

"I have to go," he said.

As he walked away he focused his hearing, trying to eavesdrop on the guys' conversation, to see if they mentioned anything about the murders last night. But Charlie was just telling the guys about how tonight was a fellow firefighter's birthday and how he intended to go to a party at the firehouse before heading to the brewery in Brooklyn.

Simon started walking uptown along the Hudson, frustrated because none of his questions had been answered. As he walked uptown along the promenade, he checked his phone, but there were no messages from Alison. Though he was angry at her for putting him through this, could he really blame her? After all, what he'd put her through lately had been so much worse. He just hoped she'd contact him soon, from wherever she was, just to let him know that she and Jeremy were okay. If she did call, he'd beg her for another chance and do everything he could to save his marriage. His life would be empty and meaningless without his family.

Still paranoid about being followed by the cops, Simon looked over his shoulder every thirty seconds or so. He didn't see anyone suspicious, but when he looked again he noticed an old man trailing about twenty yards behind him. The man was extremely old, so Simon didn't think he was a cop, but there was something about him—maybe the way his dark eyes were so fixated—that made Simon uncomfortable.

When Simon checked again, the man was closer, maybe ten yards away, and his gaze seemed even more piercing. Simon walked faster and didn't think the old man could possibly keep up, but when he looked again the old man was the same distance behind him, walking remarkably fast.

Now Simon knew this wasn't his imagination—he was definitely being followed. He stopped, waiting for the old man to catch up with him, then asked, "Can I help you?"

Some of the wrinkles on the man's face seemed to be a half inch deep, and yet his gray hair was as thick as a teenager's.

"Come with me," the man said with a heavy German accent.

"Excuse me?" Simon asked.

"Come with me," the man said again.

The man left the path and went to an area partially concealed by trees.

Simon was going to ignore him, the way he'd ignore any crazy person in New York City, until the man said, "It has to do with Michael and his pack. You must come with me now."

TWENTY-FOUR

Olivia wanted sex. She considered texting Michael, but what did she need him for? Suddenly the city was filled with sexy men, and any one of them would do. Besides, she didn't know if she should love Michael or hate him. She still had no idea what he'd done to her last night, or why she felt the way she did; all she knew was she couldn't get enough of it.

Walking down Fifth Avenue, she hit on practically every guy she passed—smiling at them, saying "Hi" and "How are you?" to some, turning her head to check them out when they walked by. Passing a construction site on Fifth and Thirty-eighth was a total man-feast. There must've been twenty sweaty guys sitting on the sidewalk in front of the site, eating deli sandwiches and burgers. It was like the meat was oozing out of their pores, mingling with their perspiration. Ah, heaven.

The guys saw Olivia drooling over them, and one big sweaty guy shouted, "Yeah, baby, swing that ass for me!" and another, "Fries go with that shake?" Most women would have felt angry and violated and walked past without saying a word, so the guys were naturally surprised when Olivia confidently strutted up to the big guy and said, "If you want my ass, it's all yours, honey."

The guy was completely thrown off; he'd probably never had a woman come up to him that way. He actually seemed stunned.

"Come on, let's go to a hotel right now, it's on me," Olivia said. "But I'm warning you, you better bring your A game."

Olivia found that she wanted the guy's roast beef sandwich almost as badly as she wanted his body. She grabbed the sandwich from him, took a huge bite, said, "I don't have patience for limp dicks today," and continued on her way, taking the rest of the sandwich with her. The guy just let her walk away, probably too shocked and humiliated to do anything. His buddies stayed out of her way, as if they didn't know how to react.

She turned onto Thirty-fifth Street and went to the Playwright, a sports bar that she'd been to a few times and where she remembered there was a good pickup scene. She'd met a couple of guys there before—they'd both turned out to be total losers, but today a total loser would do just fine.

A group of boisterous Irish guys were gathered around the bar watching a soccer match on a big-screen TV. The other TVs were showing horse racing. There was so much testosterone in the bar that Olivia felt like a chocolate lover thrown into a vat of the best-tasting chocolate in the world.

Most of the guys in the bar checked her out because she was checking them out so blatantly. It wasn't every day a woman came into the bar and started undressing them with her eyes. Like the construction workers, they were intimidated by her attitude, but Olivia was loving it. She'd never felt so powerful, so in control.

Oddly, she was least attracted to the best-looking guy—the clean-cut Wall Street guy standing with a friend toward the end of the bar. He'd probably showered this morning—yuck. And he was wearing an overwhelming cologne—double yuck. She much preferred the guy behind him in jeans and a T-shirt who had sweat stains on his Belmont Stakes T-shirt and was reading a racing program.

Olivia winked at him. "Hey, how about it?"

The guy looked at her like she was insane and walked away.

Unfazed, like a thick-skinned telemarketer, she moved on to other guys, but got similar blow-offs. She didn't get it. Weren't heterosexual guys supposed to want to have sex with any woman with a pulse? This should have been like a male fantasy for them, but her directness seemed to be backfiring. For Olivia, it was just frustrating as hell. She wanted to have sex and didn't understand why it had to be so complicated.

"What does a girl have to do to get laid around here?"

All that got her were a few laughs and a judgmental look from the blond barmaid.

Olivia was about to give up and try another bar when she heard a guy's voice boom, "All right, gorgeous, let's get a room."

At the bar behind her was a heavyset guy with a pudgy face and thin hair slicked back, in a wrinkled suit. His eyes were glazed and bloodshot; he'd probably been drinking all day. She could smell whiskey, and was that beer? She remembered fleetingly how Michael had known exactly what she was drinking the night he'd met her. The alcohol odor was coming from the guy's mouth and through his pores, but she also detected his very musky BO.

In short, he was perfect.

She couldn't resist reaching out and squeezing one of his meaty butt cheeks. "Nice ass. The rest better be as good as that."

She couldn't believe the way she was acting, but it was so liberating to be able to say whatever was on her mind, to be filterless.

The guy didn't react, though, probably because he was so wasted. Was he *too* wasted? Impatient, wanting this guy's meaty body so badly, she was practically panting. She asked, "Do you want to do it in the bathroom?"

"Do what in the bathroom?"

"Me," she said.

"Wait." He slapped the bar with his open hand as if having a revelation. "How much is this going to cost?"

"Cost?" Olivia said.

"You're a hooker, aren't you?" The guy was a loud talker and this got people's attention, including the barmaid's.

"No, I'm not a hooker, I just want a little loving, and I want it now."

The guy had a dumb look, then said, "You mean you want me just because you want me?" He looked at his near-empty glass of whiskey and said, "I knew this stuff was good, but I didn't know it was that good."

"Excuse me," the barmaid said to Olivia, "you're going to have to leave now or I'll have to call the police."

That was all Olivia needed—to be arrested for prostitution. She'd be thrown in jail and she'd have no chance of having sex tonight. Well, sex with a man anyway.

Olivia grabbed the big guy's hand. "Come on, let's just get out of here."

On the sidewalk, she asked, "How far is your apartment from here?"

"Apartment?"

Now it was clear how drunk the guy actually was; he could barely stand up straight.

"Yes, apartment," Olivia said. "You know, where you *live*."

"Oh, I don't live in New York," he said. "I'm from Kansas City. I'm here for an insurance conference." He started digging into an inner pocket of his suit jacket.

He wasn't going to give her his card, was he?

Yes he was.

"Name's Jim, Jim Anderson, but my friends call me Jimmy."

Olivia pulled him toward the curb. She wanted his body so badly, she was thinking of tearing off his clothes in the backseat of a cab.

But then he said, "My hotel's right across the street."

Thank God, finally something was going her way.

Olivia put her arm through his and walked very fast, practically dragging him. He had to weigh over two hundred fifty pounds, but, maybe because she was excited about her imminent conquest, she felt like she was pulling a child.

They went up to his room in the Comfort Inn. She immediately began undressing, pulling off her top. As she was taking off her skirt she said, "Get naked."

"You mean right—?"

"Get naked," she said firmly.

Seeming panicked, even terrified, Jim said, "Oh, okay," and slowly took off his suit jacket.

"Faster," Olivia said.

Jim stripped quickly down to his baggy pinstriped boxers. Olivia liked being in control, telling him what to do. Who would've thought she had so much dominatrix in her?

"Panties too," she said, even putting on a *Deliverance*-style drawl for effect.

Jim was about to take off his underwear when he blinked hard and asked, "Is that for real?"

Olivia was confused. "Is what for real?"

He was cringing, looking toward her armpits. Then she lifted her left arm and saw the big clump of hair. It looked like a man's armpit, and she was sure she'd shaved in the shower before going out last night.

Was this part of whatever Michael had done to her?

"And your legs," Jim said.

Olivia looked down at her legs, surprised that it looked like she hadn't shaved in weeks.

"Hey, sorry," he said. "I'm drunk, but I'm not drunk enough for this." He started putting his pants back on.

There was no way Olivia was letting him leave. She'd finally found a man who was willing to service her, and she wasn't going to let this chance slip away.

"Oh no you don't," she said, trying to grab the pants.

"Please, I'm a married man." He held up a hand, displaying a thick gold wedding band. "You shouldn't even be here."

He turned, trying to get away from her, and elbowed her in the jaw.

"Hey," she said.

She was about to grab him when there was intense pressure in her face, especially her mouth, and then she was in agony, as if her body were exploding. But the pain was quickly replaced by something like an adrenaline surge. But it was more than adrenaline—it was a tremendous rush of energy and confidence and empowerment all at once. She was facing the full-length mirror next to the bathroom and saw thick dark hair actually *growing* on her face, and when she opened her mouth she saw her long sharp teeth.

She probably should've been scared, but it felt too incredible. It was as if she'd been dead her whole life and was finally alive. She looked in the mirror and bared her teeth and stared at her claws in awe. Then she flared her wide dark nostrils and touched her face with one of her paws. God, she loved how she looked. She could've stared at herself forever.

She tried to say, "This is awesome," but the sound came out as a loud growl.

"Sorry about that," Jim said. "I didn't mean to hit you. It was just a—"

Then she turned toward him and enjoyed his look of total shock and horror. It was such a blast, watching this big, strong man cower at the sight of her. No man would ever intimidate her again.

"Oh m-m-m-my . . ." Suddenly breathless, he couldn't finish the sentence.

She had the urge to push him, to test her strength, so, what the hell, she pushed him, and easily knocked him to the floor. She stood over him and growled, loving how much power and control she suddenly had. He got to his feet and backed away from her, obviously terrified, wondering what was coming next, knowing that he was defenseless, at her total mercy. He knew that this woman, this animal, could kill him anytime she wanted to—crush him with her bare hands, literally chew him up and spit him out.

Then she smelled urine, and she realized that Jim had peed his pants. Panicked, he turned and ran out of the room in his boxers, screaming for help.

Olivia thought about chasing him, having some more fun scaring the hell out of him, but then she suddenly felt weaker and less confident, and when she looked in the mirror she saw that she was starting to look like her normal self again. Her hair and teeth were receding and her other facial features that had been altered were changing back. Amazed, she felt her face with her human hands. Could she be making this all up, having some kind of wild hallucination? No, it had actually happened. She still had pains all over, probably some kind of residual effect from the transformation, and the pains were definitely real.

But how the hell was this happening? How was it possible?

Eh, there would be time to figure out all the details later, and it was so damn enjoyable she didn't really care. Even hornier than she'd been before, she left the hotel and roamed the midtown streets, resuming her evening on the prowl.

Simon examined the old man closely. His face was so wrinkled, he had to be a hundred years old, yet he didn't act like he was a hundred. His body was toned; he was sharp mentally. Simon examined the man's eyes again and saw an obvious family resemblance to Michael.

"Who are you?" Simon asked.

"Come with me," the man said.

Now Simon realized that the way the man spoke was just like Michael—well, like Michael with a thick German accent.

Simon followed him several feet off the path to the area near the trees.

Then the man said, "I must be quiet or Michael will hear me."

"How could he hear you?" Simon asked. "He's back at the playground, isn't he?" Simon figured they were about half a mile from the playground.

"He's close enough," the old man whispered. Then he added, "I am Volker Hartman, Michael's father. You are one of Michael's friends . . . the new one."

"What do you want?" Simon asked.

"You must stay away from my son," Volker said. "You must tell the others in the pack to stay away as well."

The old man's eyes were like black marbles, and as he stared at Simon he didn't blink at all. Simon assumed the man was insane or at least extremely senile, but he still wanted to hear what he had to say.

"What do you mean by *pack*?" Simon asked.

"What do you think I mean?"

"I don't know, that's why I'm asking you."

"You know," Volker said. "You must know. You must feel the changes. You must know you're different now."

Now Simon's heart was pounding so hard he could feel his pulse in his face. "No, I don't know. Tell me what the hell's going on."

"You have the blood of the *wolfe* now," Volker said. He pronounced *wolfe* "vulf."

"Of the what?" Simon was finding it hard to focus. He wanted to believe this was just the ramblings of a madman, that Volker's doctors from Bellevue would rush over at any moment and take him away in a giant net, but he couldn't deny feeling as if a gigantic burden had been lifted, like when a secret you've been keeping is suddenly revealed.

"The *wolfe*," Volker said.

Simon said, "Th-that's . . ." He was finding it hard to speak. He had to compose himself, then said, "That's insane." But he knew it wasn't. He knew it made perfect sense.

"It's not insane," the man said. "Now you are like Michael and me, you share our blood."

"B-but how—?"

"The beer he gave you," Volker said. "I warned him against it, but he refused to listen."

"So the beer made me . . ." Simon had trouble getting the words out. "The beer turned me into a wolf?"

"Yes," Volker said. "It was an old way, from the homeland. People outside our family can't handle the wolves' blood and, except for rare exceptions, a bite is always fatal. So Michael brewed a beer with his serum in it to prepare your body for the bite."

"Bite?" Simon said. "What bite?"

"You still must be bitten to become a permanent *wolfe*. Right now you and the other men are *temporarer wolfe*. You won't be permanent *wolfe* until you are bitten. But you must not let this happen, to you or the others. Do you understand me?"

Simon was dazed. He realized he'd probably been in some sort of state of shock all this time, and now reality was suddenly setting in. "So you're saying," he said, "he's going to try to *bite* us?"

"Yes," Volker said. "Tonight."

"Tonight?" Simon said. "You mean at the brewery?"

"Yes," Volker said. "You understand that this must not happen."

"I don't get it," Simon said. "Why does he want to bite us?"

"He has his reasons."

"What reasons? I—I don't understand."

"He says he's lonely, he says he wants a pack. He tried to bite others, before he made the beer, and they all died. He doesn't understand that we're meant to be alone. That's the way it has always been, since before our family came from Freiburg."

Simon thought briefly about Dave Doherty, the murder victim Detective Rodriguez had mentioned. Perhaps Doherty had been one of Michael's failed inductees, but Simon's mind was overloaded; it was hard to process all of this at once.

"I'm telling you all this so you can stop it from happening," Volker said. "If you aren't bitten you will no longer be a *temporarer wolfe*. Perhaps in a month, two months, the effects of the beer will wear off and you'll be fully human again. But if he bites you tonight there will be no turning back; you will be *wolfe* for eternity."

Again Simon noticed Volker's dark, penetrating gaze, and he had a flashback to the night he'd drunk the beer at the brewery, how he'd felt like he was being sucked into the darkness in Michael's eyes.

"B-but how—how am I supposed to stop them?" Simon asked. "I—I can't control what they do."

"It will be difficult because they have felt the power of the *wolfe*, which can be very seductive," Volker said. "But they can still be convinced. There is still time."

"But why are you asking me? Why not tell them yourself?"

"They won't listen to me, but they like you. You are their friend. You can convince them."

"What about Michael? He's your son, right? Can't you just tell him not to bite us?"

"He refuses to listen to me. He's too stubborn and I'm too old. I don't have the power to stop him. *He* has the power in our family now. He is the leader. He has enormous strength and can kill anyone he pleases."

"Great, then how am I supposed to stop him? What am I supposed to do, shoot him?"

Simon was being sarcastic, but Volker said seriously, "A gunshot wound probably won't kill him—not one shot, anyway. *Werewolfe* are difficult to kill, especially a powerful *wolfe* like Michael. The only sure way to kill a *werewolfe* is to rip apart the jaw and split its head open. You must do this to Michael if you are to have a chance, if we are all to have a chance."

Deadpan, Simon said, "You want me to rip your son's jaw apart and split his head open."

"You must, yes. It's the only certain way to save us."

"Come on, you're kidding, right?"

"I wish I were."

"But why—"

"There is no time for questions," he said. "You understand why I am warning you. If you become permanent *wolfe*, then you can make others *wolfe*. The *wolfe* blood is meant for our family only; it's not meant to be shared with others."

"What if I can't stop him?" Simon asked desperately.

"You must stop him," Volker said. "If our blood spreads, it will be the end of all of us." He glared melodramatically, added, "Good luck to you and to your friends," and then hurried away.

Simon was so flustered, so overwhelmed, that he didn't react right away. A few seconds later, when his brain jump-started and he realized that he still had more questions, it was too late—Volker was already gone.

TWENTY-FIVE

Alison and Jeremy had spent most of the day inside a small room in the Radisson Hotel on Forty-eighth and Lex. They went on a short walk to a pizza place to get Jeremy a slice for lunch, but afterward Alison wasn't feeling well—she was worn-out, nauseated, and a little dizzy—so they returned to the hotel and stayed in bed, Jeremy watching the afternoon lineup on Nick Jr.

Though Alison felt awful, she knew her symptoms were entirely emotional. Her decision to leave Simon had been impulsive—no plan about where she would go, or how she would actually live on her own. When the cops took Simon away, she was convinced he was lying to her about something; for all she knew he really had gotten a wolf to attack and kill Tom. She didn't think Simon was a psychopath, but the way he'd been acting, how could she rule anything out? He'd been angry about the firing, so how did she know he hadn't snapped and done something absolutely insane?

Angry, humiliated, and fed up with all the lying, she'd packed a suit-case for her and Jeremy—just randomly grabbing clothes from dresser drawers and the closet and stuffing them inside. She just needed to leave, get away, and wasn't really thinking about plans for the future or anything else. She scribbled a note and then woke Jeremy up. He was cranky and crying as she forced him to get dressed. Then she carried him out of the apartment, pulling the overstuffed suitcase behind her, hailed a cab on Columbus, and said, "Radisson Hotel" only because that was the hotel where her sister had stayed the last time she was in the city and it was the first hotel that popped into her mind. In the cab, Jeremy fell asleep and she didn't want to wake him up again, knowing he'd start crying again. So she carried him out of the cab—when he was asleep he always seemed to weigh twice as much as when he was awake—and then she was so focused on getting him settled and to bed that it didn't really set in that this was it, she was all alone.

Terror set in. She hadn't lived alone since she was twenty-three years old, and then her parents were alive. Now she had no one. She still had a few good friends in the city, but they were married and had their own responsibilities. Lauren was three thousand miles away, and the emotional support she got from her sister only went so far. She needed someone here, in person, not a Skype friend.

Simon wasn't only her husband, but for years he'd also been her only real support system in New York. Suddenly she was terrified and insecure and had no idea how she was going to get through this. Her complete lack of self-confidence was so foreign to her. She'd always been a solid, steady, middle-of-the-road person; she wasn't used to things veering off course. Assuming Simon wasn't arrested, what was she going to do, call a divorce lawyer? There was no way she'd settle for anything less than joint custody, and what with Simon's odd behavior lately she would have preferred full custody. But there was no way Simon would give up custody and—if he felt threatened—he might try to get custody himself. She'd have to argue that he wasn't fit to parent full-time, which would basically be a declaration of war. They'd both lawyer up and things would quickly get nasty. She knew couples who had spent over $100,000 each on their divorces. And even if she managed to get custody, how would she manage her life? She wouldn't be able to pay for child care and expenses on the apartment, which was why Simon had become a stay-at-home dad to begin with. They would have to sell the apartment, but then where would she go? Real estate in Manhattan was out of control and she'd need at least a large one-bedroom, but even if she could come up with a down payment, how would she afford the mortgage payments and maintenance? She'd also have to find child care. She could try to rehire Margaret—if she hadn't found another job yet or didn't have hard feelings about being fired. If Margaret wasn't available, she'd have to go through the process of finding a new sitter, which, right now, seemed completely overwhelming.

Simon had been calling and texting her all day, but she'd muted her phone and had glanced at the first few texts—*Where are you? I'm sorry, I miss you, I want to see you*, et cetera—but hadn't even bothered to open the others. Meanwhile, Jeremy had been asking about Simon all day, saying, "Where's Daddy?" and "How come I can't see Daddy?"

Around four in the afternoon, she got another call from Simon that she screened, but then she listened to the voice mail. Sounding distraught, he said he was "extremely worried" and begged her to please call him back.

Figuring that ignoring him at this point would border on just plain cruel, she gave in and sent a text:

All is well

It seemed like ten seconds later she got:

THANK GOD!!!!!

Then a couple of seconds afterward, he wrote her:

Where r u????????

Crying, she didn't respond.

Then he wrote:

Please see me. I can explain EVERYTHING. I PROMISE!!!

She couldn't deny that she missed him. Maybe it was because she had the old Simon—who was reasonable, whom she could get through to—stuck in her head.

After about a minute he wrote:

Hello??? R u there????

Looking at Jeremy, sitting on the bed, innocent and blissful, she decided she couldn't keep him away from his father forever. So she texted back the address of the hotel. About half an hour later, she and Jeremy were in the loud, active lobby when Simon showed up.

"Daddy!" Jeremy called out, and ran toward Simon, who was crouching down and smiling widely with his arms extended.

Alison had to admit—initially it was nice to see Simon too. She had to remind herself of everything he'd put her through lately and recharge her pissed-off persona.

Simon lifted Jeremy in the air, then hugged him tightly and said, "That's my boy," and kissed him on top of his head.

"I'll let you two spend some time together," Alison said.

"Wait," Simon said, "I have to talk to you."

"This isn't the time."

"It's important."

Alison detected a different tone in his voice—well, different for lately. Maybe her leaving had scared him as much as it had scared her, and he was willing to seriously work on their problems. It couldn't hurt her to hear what he had to say.

With her arms crossed tightly in front of her chest, she said, "Fine. What is it?"

From his messenger bag, Simon removed a couple of coloring books and a sixty-four-pack of Crayola crayons. He said to Jeremy, "Look what Daddy brought for you."

Jeremy was very excited, but he loved his dad so much he would have been excited about any present he'd brought for him.

Jeremy sat on the couch and was immediately absorbed, coloring.

"So . . ." Alison said.

"So . . ." Simon suddenly seemed very nervous. "So how have you been?"

"You said you have something important to tell me. What is it?"

"First off, I'm sorry," he said. "You were right and I was wrong. I admit something's been going on with me lately. Something that I didn't want to acknowledge because . . . well, because it was too terrifying. . . . But I understand what's going on now, and I'm not going to be in denial anymore."

Simon was getting choked up, and Alison was getting concerned; was he going to announce that he had been diagnosed with a terminal disease?

"What's wrong?" she asked. "Did you find out you have something?"

"Yes," he said.

"What is it?"

He looked away, in the opposite direction from where Jeremy was sitting, and when he looked at Alison again his eyes were so watery the pupils looked out of focus.

"I really don't know how to say this," he said.

"Tell me already." She was terrified. Was he really going to die? She didn't know how she was going to handle this. She still loved him very much and couldn't fathom actually *losing* him. And how would she explain it to Jeremy?

Now a couple of big tears were dripping down his cheek.

"Please just tell me," she said.

He glanced at Jeremy, who was still coloring, then turned back to her and said in a low voice, practically whispering, "Well, I found out that I'm . . . well, that I'm a werewolf."

He had spoken so quietly she couldn't hear him clearly.

"I'm sorry," she said, "what did you say?"

"I'm a werewolf," he said, just as quietly as before.

Maybe because she was still in shock about the prospect of his being diagnosed with a fatal illness, she still couldn't process what he was saying. It sounded like he'd said "wah waf."

"What the hell is *wah waf*?" she asked. "Is that some kind of virus?"

"Not *wah waf*," Simon said. "Werewolf. I'm a werewolf."

This time she'd heard him loud and clear. Her concern about his health was suddenly replaced by anger.

"Why are you doing this to me?"

"I didn't mean to do it," he said. "It just happened to me that night when—"

"Coming here," she said, "acting like you've had this big shift, you're ready to seriously work on our problems, then playing these emotional games with me all over again? How much of this do you think I can stand?"

"Please," Simon said. "Just listen—"

"No, you listen," she said. "I left you because I was tired of all the lies, tired of you acting like nothing was wrong when obviously something very big was wrong. But if you're going to show up here and act like this is all some big joke—"

"I understand," he said, "okay? I get it."

"Have fun with Jeremy." She went over to Jeremy and said, "Mommy's going to do some shopping now, and you're going to spend some time with Daddy, okay?"

"Okay."

Alison walked past Simon, but she didn't get far before he came up behind her and grabbed her arm.

"I know it sounds crazy," he said, "but think about it. Just think about it, okay?"

"Can you let go of me, please?"

He didn't let go, saying, "The changes all started that night I went to Michael's for the beer."

"I want you to let go of my arm."

"You don't understand." Simon let go, but now he was in front of her, preventing her from leaving. "I think I killed Tom," he said, obviously much louder than he'd intended. His eyes darted back and forth as if he were afraid someone had overheard him. Jeremy, on the couch, had looked over, and Simon asked him, "How's that drawing going?"

"Okay," Jeremy said.

"Good," Simon said. "Keep drawing, kiddo, okay?" When Jeremy returned his attention to the coloring book, Simon continued to Alison in a quieter voice, "I think I killed Tom . . . Not *me* me, but me in another state. I don't mean another state like New Jersey. I mean, it *was* Jersey, but I mean another state like in another nonhuman state. When I was—well, when I was a wolf. Look, I know how crazy it sounds, but if you think about it, if you just think about it. I had the blood on my jeans, but a wolf killed him. It didn't make any sense until I spoke to Michael's father, and now it makes perfect sense. I didn't bring a wolf to kill Tom. I *was* the wolf."

Alison was looking at Simon as if she'd never seen him before. He was a total stranger—worse, a maniacal total stranger. It amazed her how he actually seemed to believe all of this; it wasn't some put-on. The situation was worse than she'd ever imagined. He had completely lost touch with reality.

"You need help," Alison said, trying to remain as calm as possible. "Serious professional help."

"Alison, please, if you'd just—"

"Call Dr. Hagan's office," she said. "Get a referral to a good psychiatrist. Not a psychologist, a *psychiatrist*. I really think you need to take some medication, or get some sort of thorough medical eval—"

"I'm not crazy," Simon said. "I thought I was going crazy, but now that I understand what's going on, I don't feel that way at all. Think, just think about what's been happening to me. The hearing. Wolves hear well. Or the hair growth. Wolves are hairy. Or, or, or how about all the meat-eating? Wolves eat meat. The changes aren't random; they're not a reaction to anything in my life. It's because I'm an animal now, or more of an animal, or . . . you know what I'm saying . . . I haven't been acting like myself because I haven't *been* myself."

"Mommy, I thought you were going shopping."

"One second, Jeremy," Simon snapped.

Looking at Simon intensely, Alison said, "I don't know why you're doing this to me, putting me on this emotional roller coaster."

"I'm sorry," Simon said. "I truly am. But the good news is, it's going to end. If what Michael's father told me is true, it's going to wear off. I'll be normal again soon."

"Daddy, can you play with me now?"

"One second," Simon said. Then to Alison, "Please give me another chance. I don't know how I'm going to handle all of this alone. I need you to be with me to help me through it."

"You want help?" Alison said. She checked to make sure Jeremy wasn't listening, then added to Simon, "Go see a shrink. Don't do it for me or for yourself . . . Do it for Jeremy." Then she said to Jeremy, "Bye-bye, sweetie," and marched away.

She reached the revolving doors leading to Forty-eighth Street, when she realized what she was doing—leaving her son with his father, who was obviously unhinged—and she returned and grabbed Jeremy by the arm and pulled him toward the elevator.

Jeremy dropped his crayons and was crying and screaming, "I want to play with Daddy! I want Daddy!"

Of course the elevator wasn't there, and Alison had to wait, trying to restrain her screaming three-year-old. Alison was facing the elevators, but she could feel the eyes of everyone in the lobby, watching the scene like it was great theater.

Finally an elevator came and they got on. Simon had remained near the couches and was looking right at her.

Jeremy let out his loudest wail, "Daddeeeeeee," just as the doors closed.

TWENTY-SIX

Walking uptown on Madison Avenue, Olivia called Diane and said, "I have some big news," and Diane said, "Me too."

"Really?" Had Diane's guy, Ramon, bitten her? Was she a wolf too? "Now we *have to* meet."

"But I'm on my way to see Ramon," Diane said.

"You don't understand, I *have to* see you right now. Where are you?"

Diane was just leaving work in midtown but agreed to meet Olivia for a quick drink at Brasserie, a bar/restaurant they sometimes met up at on Fifty-third Street near Park Avenue.

The host, a young blond guy, asked, "How many?"

She'd seen the guy there before but had never really noticed how incredibly cute he was. Eyeing him up and down, Olivia said, "One's enough for me." Then she spotted Diane waving to her from the bar and rushed over to her.

Olivia couldn't tell if Diane was a wolf as well, but she looked a hell of a lot happier than she'd ever looked before.

Olivia hugged her hello—squeezing her much tighter than she'd intended—and didn't let go until Diane said, "Ow, you're hurting me."

"Sorry," Olivia said. Then, checking the host out again, she added, "I want that guy."

"He could be your son," Diane said.

"Who cares about age?" Olivia said. "I just want his body."

"Okay, Demi," Diane said.

Olivia got the Demi Moore reference, but she didn't smile. She stared at the guy until he looked at her for a moment, and then he turned away quickly. Olivia had to work on this; whatever vibe she was sending out definitely wasn't helping her get laid.

"So," Diane said. "What's this big news you wanted to discuss? Ramon's waiting for me at his place."

"That's part of what I wanted to talk to you about," Olivia said. "How're things, um, going with him?"

"Amazingly well," Diane said, "and I owe it all to you. He's just so incredibly passionate, you know? He makes me feel so good, so *wanted*. I know I might be acting crazy, maybe I'm just rebounding from Steve, but I don't think so. I think we really have a real connection. I don't know where these guys've been hiding, but we're lucky we found them, right?"

Olivia was shifting her jaw around. After those wolf teeth receded her mouth had hurt like hell, and it still ached a little. But what was she supposed to do, call her dentist? Her dentist would say, "What seems to be the problem?" and she'd go, "I turned into a werewolf yesterday." Yeah, that would go over well.

"What's wrong with your mouth?" Diane asked.

"You mean it didn't happen to you yet?"

"What didn't happen?"

"He didn't bite you yet?"

"Bite me?"

"When you were having sex."

"Well, he kisses me really intensely, but I wouldn't call it *biting*."

"I mean did he bite your neck?"

"Like a hickey?"

"No, like an actual bite."

Olivia reached out and moved the hair away from Diane's neck but didn't see a bite mark.

"What are you *doing*?" she asked.

"Maybe it healed already," Olivia said. "He said it heals quickly. See? Mine is already gone and last night his teeth were deep inside me."

"Wait," Diane said. "Is this really why you wanted me to come meet you now? To talk about *biting*? When you called and said you had big news, I thought it was something dramatic. I thought you were pregnant or got engaged or something major happened at work. Didn't you meet with that big Japanese client today?"

"You mean you don't notice any weird physical changes?" Olivia said. "You're not faster and stronger and hairier? You don't crave meat and want to have sex all the time?"

"Hairier?" Diane asked.

"Oh." Olivia thought. "I just assumed since Ramon and Michael are friends and they act like they're from the same, well, tribe or whatever . . . I just thought he must've made you into a . . . never mind."

"Never mind what?" Diane said. "Please . . . just tell me what this is all about."

"You wouldn't believe me if I told you," Olivia said. "I didn't believe it myself at first. I thought Michael was just screwing with me, playing head games. But then I experienced it myself and it's amazing, it's empowering. You have to feel it for yourself."

"Seriously, are you feeling okay?"

"I know," Olivia said with renewed excitement. "Let's go to the ladies' room. I'll bite you there."

"Excuse me?"

"You didn't believe me about Michael, and then you met Ramon and you saw how amazing these guys are, right? So trust me with this too. . . . I promise it'll only hurt for a few seconds. You might black out for a while, but I'll take care of you, I promise. And when you wake up you won't believe how great you feel."

"I'm sorry," Diane said. She reached into her purse for a twenty-dollar bill and then put it on the bar. "Ramon's waiting for me, and I don't know what's going on, if this is some kind of joke or something, but this is getting a little too weird for me."

Suddenly craving the taste of meat, of raw human flesh, Olivia said, "You have to let me do this to you." Olivia grabbed Diane's hand, lifted her arm up to mouth level, then opened her mouth wide and closed her eyes, wanting to savor the taste of her flesh. She was about to clamp down when at the last moment Diane jerked her arm free and said, "Are you completely insane?"

"Don't worry, I told you . . . the wound heals."

"You're seriously scaring me now."

"You have no idea what you're missing."

"Just stop it, okay?"

"You don't understand. Before I went up to a bunch of guys at a construction site, you know, the type of guys who shout vile things at women, make them cower away in shame? Well, I used to be one of those women, I used to be a victim, but not anymore. Today I went up to the guys, right up to their faces, and took control, and *they* were afraid of *me*. You know how great that felt? It felt incredible, and you can feel it too if you just let me do this." Olivia grabbed Diane's arm and tried to bite Diane again, but her teeth only grazed her skin.

Diane broke free and left the restaurant.

Olivia followed her onto Fifty-third Street, saying, "Come on, you have no idea how great it feels to be a werewolf."

Diane's eyes widened. She said, "Okay, you're officially insane. You need help."

Olivia grabbed Diane's handbag from behind and pulled harder than she'd intended. Diane stumbled on her heels and fell onto the sidewalk on her side. People rushed over to help. She had a gash on her cheek. Seeing the blood made Olivia want her even more.

An older man was kneeling next to Diane, saying, "Are you okay, miss?"

Olivia shoved the man out of the way and licked Diane's wound. It was the most delicious taste in the world. She couldn't get enough of it.

"Please, just stay still," Olivia said.

Then Diane shoved her away and said, "Get the hell away from me, you crazy bitch!"

People were glaring at Olivia, and instinct kicked in—she was in danger, she had to flee—and she rushed away toward Lexington Avenue.

"Am I going to see Daddy tomorrow?" Jeremy asked.

In the middle of the Radisson's king-size bed, he looked so tiny and vulnerable, clutching Sam, his favorite stuffed bear, with the blanket pulled up to his chin.

"I'm not sure, sweetie," Alison said.

"Why not?" he persisted.

"Please just go to sleep now, okay?"

"But when am I going to see Daddy?"

"You just need to go to sleep, sweetie."

But Jeremy wouldn't go to sleep. He continued to ask about Simon until he realized he wasn't going to get a definitive answer; then he asked to go to the bathroom, and then he complained that he was hungry and thirsty and wasn't tired and that he was afraid there were bugs in his bed. It was almost like he had a list of things to ask for that would keep him awake as long as possible. Bugs, check; water, check; hugs and kisses, check. Alison was patient at first, but when it was nine o'clock and she'd put him to bed almost an hour ago and he was still awake, she couldn't stop herself from snapping at him and finally warning him that if he didn't fall asleep in five minutes she was going to take away Sam. Of course, that just made things worse, and Jeremy didn't cry himself to sleep until almost ten.

Alison felt guilty for raising her voice with Jeremy. She knew it was just the frustrations of this whole crazy day getting to her, but she also knew that was no excuse. Jeremy was already sad and confused, and she'd only made things worse.

She normally didn't drink hard liquor, but she needed something to calm herself down, so she went to the mini bar and poured out a little bottle of gin and mixed it with tonic. She drank most of it in one gulp and had the rest in the second gulp. Maybe it was psychosomatic, but she already felt more relaxed, a little less out of control anyway. What the hell? She opened another little bottle and poured a second glass.

She had a lot on her mind—like trying to figure out what she was going to do with the rest of her life—but she was mainly still trying to absorb the scene with Simon in the lobby earlier. What with all his erratic, eccentric behavior lately, she thought he'd gone as far as he could possibly go and he was finally ready to come back to earth, admit he was ready to deal with his problems, and then what does he do? He announces he's a werewolf. And the craziest part was that Simon hadn't seemed very crazy at all. He'd seemed sincere and rational and actually believed everything he was saying, the way a mental patient believes that he isn't mentally ill.

After knocking back the second drink, Alison felt rejuvenated, or at least determined to make some sense out of all of Simon's craziness—if not to help him, then at least to help herself. She went online on her laptop and Googled:

my husband thinks he's a werewolf

God bless the Internet. Just when you're at your lowest point, when you feel completely isolated and alone in the world and think no one could possibly be going through what you're going through, you can instantly find a community of co-sufferers. It turned out she wasn't the only wife who believed her husband was a werewolf. On various message boards and websites, women reported husbands who believed they were turning into werewolves, and there was even an account of one husband who'd begged his wife to have him arrested so he wouldn't hurt anyone. Okay, so some of the women posting seemed as crazy as their allegedly crazy husbands, but reading their posts was still reassuring.

Then Alison stumbled upon a search result that really got her attention. There was an actual psychological condition called lycanthropic disorder, in which a person had delusions of being a werewolf. One sufferer in northern England was so convinced that he was a werewolf that he'd developed actual wolflike features, including protruding teeth and—here was the big one—increased hair growth. Alison was buzzed, not only from the alcohol working its way through her bloodstream, but because she was convinced that she'd finally hit on the true source of Simon's problems, and she believed that with the right treatment he could be cured, or at least stabilized, and all of this craziness was temporary. Maybe she could find a psychiatrist, an expert in the field, and Simon could get the help he needed.

The drinks suddenly hit with full force; in an instant Alison went from pleasantly buzzed to verging on drunk. She couldn't focus on the Internet search results anymore. She got into bed with Jeremy, who was sleeping soundly but still frowning, and his pillow was moist with tears. Alison snuggled next to him and whispered, "I'm sorry, sweetie. Mommy loves you so, so much." She kissed him lightly on the forehead, but he remained fast asleep and didn't even stir.

TWENTY-SEVEN

Simon wanted to go after Alison and beg her to understand and to support him and to move back home, but he knew he was better off letting her go. She obviously thought he was insane, and could he really blame her? If the situation were reversed and she came to him with some story of how she had been turned into a werewolf, he'd probably do exactly what she'd done—tell her she was crazy and try to keep Jeremy as far away from her as possible.

So Simon left the hotel and headed back through the park toward the West Side. It was nearing dusk and there was a cool steady breeze. If it weren't for the way he felt, he would have thought he was crazy as well, but he knew that something beyond him had taken control of his body and the old Simon Burns was merely a passive observer.

Surrounded by all the trees and breathing in the fresher park air, he couldn't resist breaking into a full sprint. He ran along a path for a while, then veered into the Ramble, the woodsy and hilly area in the middle of the park, jumping over fallen branches and dodging trees effortlessly. His sense of smell seemed even more powerful, and although he was running randomly in every which direction, he always knew exactly where he was because he could orient himself by the smell of the algae on the lake and food odors wafting over from the Boathouse restaurant hundreds of yards away. He could also smell people and knew instinctively how to avoid them.

After running around for maybe a couple of hours, maybe longer, he continued to his apartment on West Eighty-ninth. It seemed noticeably quiet and bleak without his family there. His eyes welled up when he passed Jeremy's room and imagined him sitting on the floor, playing. Making it worse, he could smell Jeremy so distinctly, and Alison's scent was everywhere as well.

Simon took off his shirt and stared at the full-length mirror, shocked by how hairy he was. Maybe he'd been oblivious lately, or just plain ignorant, because he looked hairier than those Russian guys in the Coney Island Polar Bear Club who went swimming in the ocean in midwinter. He shuddered, the way you shudder when you remember that a loved one has died, as he thought, *This is real.* The entire day, since he'd spoken to Volker, he'd been so absorbed in worrying about finding Alison and Jeremy and trying to save his marriage that he hadn't fully realized the enormity of what had happened to him. This wasn't just about feeling great when he was running in the woods and having increased sensory perception. He'd actually changed, transformed somehow. Worse, it meant that his memories of killing Tom weren't just fantasies. He had actually murdered someone.

Looking in the mirror, Simon had no idea who this man was, but he wasn't Simon Burns.

He went into the bathroom, splashed warm water on his chest, and then spread on some shaving gel and started to frantically shave. He did it haphazardly, hating this person or *thing* he'd become, just wanting to get this hair off his body, to be his old self again. The razor quickly became clogged with hair, and he rinsed it and continued shaving, occasionally pushing down too hard and at the wrong angle and cutting himself, but not stopping. If anything he was getting more frantic, as he just wanted this hair off his body as fast as possible.

After about ten minutes, he'd shaved most of his chest. There were several cuts oozing blood, but he didn't bother to do anything about them. He shaved his shoulders and as much of his back as he could reach, cutting himself a few more times, and finally stopped, realizing how pointless this all was. His problems couldn't be resolved with a razor.

Or could they?

Maybe slitting his throat would be the best solution of all. Or taking pills, or taking a bath with the hair dryer, or jumping out the window. Even if what Volker had told him was true, and he really was only a temporary wolf and would revert to a normal human being if he wasn't bitten, would that really resolve his problems? He was a murderer, and that would never change. It seemed like it was only a matter of time until the police found the missing shoe, or another witness, or some evidence that proved he was at Tom's house that night. And even if the police were never able to connect him to the murder, how was he supposed to live with the guilt? Every day, for the rest of his life, he'd be haunted by his memories and have to live with the knowledge that he hadn't just ended Tom's life, but had ruined the lives of everyone in his family. And what about Alan Freedman and his wife? Simon might have been indirectly responsible for their deaths as well.

Simon might as well have been in a prison cell right then, because he already felt like he was in a virtual cage that was going to keep him confined for the rest of his life. There was no doubt about it—he was a horrible, dangerous person, and everyone would be better off with him dead.

Then he thought, *Why not just get it over with?* Trying to kill himself with a Gillette Mach 3 razor probably wouldn't work, but sleeping pills would.

His heart pounding, he dumped an entire bottle of Ambien into his palm. He was about to swallow all the pills at once when he thought about his family. He couldn't kill himself in the apartment—that would be too traumatic for Alison and Jeremy, and the last thing he wanted to do was to hurt them more than he already had. He'd jump—not from the building, from the Brooklyn Bridge. Nowadays there were cameras everywhere there and the cops might try to stop him, but if he moved quickly enough he could simply walk along one of the steel crossbeams to the edge of the bridge and fall swiftly to his death.

He got dressed again, figuring he'd just run downtown to the bridge and get it over with already. Within a half hour his misery would be over.

He left the apartment. On his way out of the building he said good-bye to James, the doorman.

"I just want to thank you for everything," Simon said.

"You going away somewhere?" James asked.

"Yeah," Simon said, and left the building.

He sprinted downtown on Columbus Avenue with the wind against his face, imagining how the wind would feel when he was falling to his death, soaring toward the dark river. Maybe he'd die before he hit the water, but he hoped he wouldn't. He deserved that final surge of pain.

He increased his speed and in a matter of seconds—well, or so it seemed—he was in midtown, approaching Times Square. It was late in the evening, but what with all the bright neon and hordes of people on the streets, it could have been midafternoon. A guy passing by shoved Simon and kept walking without looking back or acknowledging him in any way. Other people walked by without making eye contact or seeming to notice he was there. He might as well have already jumped off that bridge because as far as these people were concerned he didn't exist. His friends would miss him, and his parents, and some family members, but their lives would barely be affected with him gone either. The only two people in the world to whom his life really meant any-thing were Alison and Jeremy. Alison would be upset at first, but eventu-ally she'd meet someone else and start a new life, but Jeremy would feel the loss forever. When he was ninety years old he'd still be telling the story of how when he was three years old his father announced he was a werewolf and jumped off the Brooklyn Bridge. Was that really how he wanted his son to remember him? As a weak, troubled man? A coward?

Simon stopped on the sidewalk on Forty-fourth and Broadway. He

stood there for several minutes, practically oblivious to the people passing by in every which direction. Even if he spent the rest of his life in
jail, he wanted to be there for Jeremy in some way. And when he died
he wanted his son to remember him as a hero.

Looking up at one of the digital billboards, Simon saw the time:
9:42. In a little over two hours the guys would meet at the brewery and
Michael would bite them and maybe more people would die. Simon
had no idea if Volker was telling the truth about what was going to
happen tonight, but after what he'd experienced lately, he had no reason
not to believe all of it.

Simon felt for his cell phone, then remembered he hadn't brought
his phone or his wallet, figuring he wouldn't need them where he was
going. But didn't Charlie say he was going to the firehouse on Great
Jones Street for a birthday party before heading to the brewery later on?

Without giving it any more thought, Simon cut over on Forty-
fourth Street and then sprinted downtown.

"I'm looking for Charlie," Simon said to the balding fireman with
the tattoos all over his biceps.

Simon had just entered the Ladder 9 firehouse and approached the
three firemen who were hanging out in the back, playing cards.

"Who're you, another reporter?" the guy asked.

"No, just a friend," Simon said.

"Okay, hold on a sec."

The guy went upstairs, and a few seconds later Charlie, grinning
widely, slid down the pole.

"Hey, man, what a cool surprise."

He hugged Simon tightly but didn't maintain the hug for as long as
he usually did at the playground. Simon got the sense that Charlie was
modifying his behavior because he was at work.

"This is my buddy Simon," Charlie said. "Guy I hang out with at
the playground."

Simon and the other firemen exchanged hellos.

Then Charlie said to Simon, "So what brings you down here, man? You psyched for tonight?"

"I know what's going on," Simon said.

Charlie smiled, but Simon could tell he was concerned.

"Going on?" Charlie said. "Going on with what?"

"I know what Michael did to us," Simon said. "I know he changed us into werew—"

"Ha ha ha, that's really funny, man," Charlie said, louder and for effect, even though the other firemen were playing a new hand of poker, not paying attention. Then he said, "Come on, let's get some air."

Charlie let Simon walk ahead of him to the front of the firehouse. Then when they were both on the sidewalk, Charlie motioned with his head for Simon to follow him farther along toward Lafayette Street.

Then in a hushed tone Charlie said, "You can't come down here without telling me you're coming and start . . . This is my job, you understand?"

"So then it's all true," Simon said. "You knew about it all along, didn't you?"

Charlie looked away, shaking his head, then turned back to Simon and said, "We shouldn't be having this talk without the other guys around. There are no secrets in the pack."

"Oh, can you shut up with all that crap already. What do you know?"

"Hey, man, really, you gotta keep it down."

"Did Michael's father talk to you?"

"Seriously, you—"

"Answer me, damn it."

"Yes, he talked to me, all right?"

Simon just stared at Charlie for several seconds, then said, "So you lied to me. You knew all along about the beer and everything else?"

Charlie's inability to make eye contact was the answer.

"I don't get it," Simon said. "Why didn't you just tell me right away?"

"You didn't ask," Charlie said.

"You told me Michael is like a motivational speaker, that he's so captivating and inspiring."

"He is."

"Oh, give me a break, all right?" Simon couldn't help raising his voice. "You knew exactly what he did to us, what he did to me, and you acted like I was crazy, like I was imagining the whole thing."

Charlie took Simon by the forearm and led him farther along the street, away from the firehouse.

"Look," Charlie said. "I thought it was for the best, okay?"

"The best?" Simon said. "I killed my boss, I lost my family, my life is ruined." He was going to tell Charlie about how he'd even contemplated suicide, but then decided, why bother? Instead he said, "I have nothing."

"I'm sorry about your family," Charlie said. "But you'll work it out, I'm sure. And remember . . ." He rested a hand on Simon's shoulder. "You always have us."

As always, Charlie seemed sincere, but now the sincerity seemed so clearly to be an act designed to suck Simon in. How had he been so oblivious?

"I really thought you were different," Simon said. "Ramon is Ramon, he's always out there, but I thought you were . . . I don't know . . . grounded."

"I *am* grounded." Charlie kept his hand on Simon's shoulder for a few more seconds, then let go and said, "Believe me, I was like you at first. When I drank that beer I noticed the changes and I was like, what did this guy do to me? I was angry. I wanted answers . . . But then I saw all the positives. I saw how good it was, how much better my life was, and I realized Michael had given us this wonderful gift."

"Gift my ass," Simon said. "He drugged us, or infected us, whatever you want to call it."

"You can't tell me you don't like it. That you don't feel great. That it hasn't improved your life."

Simon remembered running in the woods earlier, how euphoric and alive he'd felt, and how he'd had the best sex of his life with Alison.

But he shook off these positive memories quickly, the horror of what he'd become taking over again, and said, "I committed a murder. I killed an innocent man because of what Michael did to me. How can you say that's great?"

"You're taking too much blame," Charlie said. "Like Michael says—it's natural to kill. Animals kill all the time and never feel remorse."

"So I shouldn't feel remorse for killing somebody?"

"You didn't kill him, an animal did."

"Listen to what you're saying," Simon said. "It's like Michael brainwashed you, or maybe it's the wolves' blood in your system affecting your behavior, but you're not thinking logically right now. Michael's a killer. He killed Alan Freedman and his wife last night. I think he killed others before us. There's this guy, Dave Doherty, he was killed last year. He had a kid the same age as our kids. And get this, the police found wolf bites on his body. Now how do you think that happened?"

"How?" Charlie asked.

"Michael, who do you think? Volker said that Michael bit others before he figured out how to put the wolves' serum into the beer. If Michael had met us last year we could be dead, and there are probably other missing dads in Manhattan, victims the police don't even know about."

"You don't know if any of that's true," Charlie said.

Simon realized Charlie was right but said, "Neither do you."

"Look, I really have to get back to the party," Charlie said. "I think the problem is you're afraid. You're afraid to admit how much you like this, afraid to admit how great this is, how much stronger and more confident you are, and how good it feels to have three friends, three *true* friends—friends who'd do anything for you. You're afraid to let go, to give in to it." He paused, letting his words sink in, then added, "Look, you make your own decisions, do what you gotta do; all I know is I'm happier than I've ever been. I'm a good father and women love me—

hell, even my ex-wife seems to like me lately. And you saw the paper, I'm a big hero now in the city. Guys in the department have respect for me like they've never had before, and when people and kids wave to me on the street, I feel like I can wave back to them with pride."

"It's not just about you," Simon said. "Other lives are affected by this. You're a fireman; your job is to protect people. You should understand this."

"Yeah, I understand," Charlie said. "I understand that if Michael didn't give me that beer and if I didn't put on all this muscle, if I wasn't so confident, I never would've pulled that woman out of that fire. She was trapped, a ceiling collapsed on her, but I got her out of there because of Michael. So you can't say this is all bad."

"So what're you saying?" Simon said. "If you save one person it's okay to kill somebody else? Lives cancel each other out?"

"No, I'm just saying just because you killed somebody doesn't mean I'm going to."

Simon absorbed this, knowing it could be true.

Then he said, "Maybe you're right. Maybe you won't kill anybody. Maybe you'll be the best, sexiest, most heroic fireman in the world. But right now I'm just going on what Michael's father told me, and he said if this spreads it's going to be the end of all of us. If you think about it, it's probably true. The police are already investigating me. What if they arrest me, do medical tests or whatever, and figure out what happened to me? Or what happens if you and Ramon get into some kind of trouble? Or what if other people are killed?"

"His father spoke to Ramon and me too," Charlie said. "We know the whole deal, okay?"

"If you know, then don't show up tonight," Simon said. "According to Volker, if Michael doesn't bite us it'll wear off eventually, and we can go on with our lives."

Charlie smiled, but it wasn't the way he usually smiled at the playground. It wasn't a friendly smile; it was a fake, distant smile, as if he were remembering a private joke. He said, "I don't think you've been listening to me. I don't want it to wear off. This is the best thing that ever happened to me, and as far as I'm concerned it can only get better."

The fireman with the tattoos on his arms came out and shouted, "Hey, Charlie, we're gettin' set to bring the cake out."

Charlie shouted back, "Thanks, bro, I'll be right there!" Then he said to Simon, "Look, man, I gotta go. I appreciate your concern, but I'm a big boy, I can make my own decisions."

"Then make the right decision," Simon said.

Charlie fake-smiled again, then said, "You do what you gotta do. I hope you show up tonight because I really do like you."

Without another word, Charlie returned to the firehouse.

Simon was frustrated that he couldn't get through to Charlie. He didn't see why he'd have any better luck with Ramon, but at this point what did he have to lose?

The other day Ramon had invited Simon to Diego's birthday party. Simon thought he remembered the address in Spanish Harlem, so he sprinted uptown on Third Avenue. This running-around-the-city thing was becoming a very efficient form of transportation. There was traffic in midtown and near the Fifty-ninth Street Bridge, but Simon ran by the bottled-up cars, going so fast he was able to time most of the lights, crossing the streets just as they were turning from red to green.

Simon turned onto 116th Street and slowed to a jog. Yep, he got the address right—Ramon Diaz, apartment 9. He pressed the buzzer. There was no response, and Simon realized it was very likely that Ramon wasn't home. He buzzed again and waited. Well, he'd given it his best shot.

He started away when he heard Ramon's garbled voice on the intercom: "Yeah?"

Simon rushed back and said, "It's me, Simon . . . Simon Burns from the playground."

A long—maybe ten-second—pause, and then Ramon beeped him in.

Simon took the stairs two at a time to the fifth floor. Ramon was waiting at the top of the stairs in a clean white robe. There was salsa playing—not in the living room, in another room in the apartment, or perhaps in another apartment. The music was probably low, but Simon could hear it clearly.

"Hey, man!"

Grinning, Ramon seemed truly happy to see him, but Simon knew that as with Charlie the warmth was fake, an act.

When Ramon extended his arms for an embrace, Simon said, "That isn't necessary," and walked past him and entered the apartment. There was a scent—a very flowery perfume. A woman either was here or had been here.

"Everything okay, man?" Ramon seemed hurt. Yeah, right. He sniffed. "I mean, I could tell you ran over here pretty damn fast. You got some good BO going on there."

Figuring he'd cut to the chase, Simon said, "You can't show up tonight. If you do, it'll be a big mistake and it'll be permanent; there'll be no turning back."

Ramon squinted, as if confused. "I don't know what you're talking about. We're just going to be hanging out tonight, chilling, throwin' back a few beers. But you don't gotta worry—no family recipe beers or nothin' crazy like that."

"I know," Simon said seriously.

"If you know, then what's the big deal?"

"No. I mean I know what's going on. I spoke to Michael's father; I know everything," Simon said. "I know what Michael did to us, and I know what the real meaning of the pack is."

Ramon absorbed this, then said, "If you know, what's the problem? I'll see you at midnight."

"You don't want to do this," Simon said. "You think you want to, but you don't."

Smiling widely, Ramon said, "I think I know what I want."

"No you don't," Simon said. "You're like an addict and Michael's like your dealer. He hooked you, made you think you need this to feel good about yourself, to improve your life. But you don't need it. And if you don't get out now, it's going to ruin our lives forever."

Ramon—his smile fake, like Charlie's—said, "Man, I don't know what's—"

"Stop the act, will you?" Simon said. "I'm trying to help you here. And if you don't want to save yourself, think about Diego. You don't want to go through your whole life with this crazy wolves' blood in you. What if you snap one day? What if you attack him?"

Then a female voice said, "You told me you didn't know anything about this."

Simon looked to his right and saw a slender woman, about thirty, with straight dark hair. She was in jeans and was finishing buttoning up her black blouse. She was definitely the woman he'd smelled.

"Back in the bedroom, baby," Ramon said.

"Who are you?" the woman asked Simon.

"Never mind who he is," Ramon said. "Just wait for me in bed."

"I'm Simon. Simon Burns."

"What's this about wolves' blood?" the woman asked.

"Baby." Ramon tried to take the woman's hand, but she slapped it away before he could.

"You told me you didn't know anything about this," she said to Ramon.

"I don't, baby, I—"

"What do you know?" Simon asked her.

"My friend was telling me she was a werewolf a few hours ago," she said. "She was acting crazy, trying to bite me."

"Does your friend know Michael Hartman, by any chance?" Simon asked.

"She's been dating a guy named Michael," the woman said. "Well, I don't know if you'd call it *dating*, but they've been hooking up practically every night."

"All right, you gotta go now," Ramon said to Simon.

"Where's your friend now?" Simon asked.

"I have no idea," the woman said.

"If she's trying to bite you, it sounds like she's extremely unstable," Simon said. "You have to stay away from her."

"I said it's time to go," Ramon said harshly.

Ramon, holding the door open, suddenly looked intense, on edge, as if he could lash out with violence at any moment. Simon had never seen this kind of anger from Ramon before, but somehow he wasn't surprised.

"I knew this would probably be a waste of time," Simon said, "but I like you and I wanted to help you. I still want to help you."

"I don't need help," Ramon said.

"See?" Simon said. "It's just like an addiction. You won't want help till you hit rock bottom, when it's too late." Then as he stepped into the hallway, he looked back and said to the woman, "Stay away from your friend," as Ramon slammed the door.

Simon went down to the street. Well, he'd given it his best shot, but you can't help people who don't want to be helped. The thing he didn't understand was why he didn't seem as far gone as they were. How come he could resist going to the brewery tonight but they couldn't? Did they have more wolves' blood flowing through their veins than he did?

Simon turned on the corner of Third, heading downtown, the hopelessness of the situation setting in. If the guys wanted to be bitten by Michael, and Michael was as powerful as Volker had claimed, how was Simon supposed to stop him? There was nothing else for Simon to do now except go home and wait for the rest of his life to go to hell. Even if the police never found evidence linking him to Tom's murder, he'd never be safe. After Michael turned Charlie and Ramon into permanent werewolves, there would be two more people out to kill him.

Then Simon heard, "Hey!" and turned and saw the woman from Ramon's apartment jogging toward him.

She caught up with him and slowed, walking alongside him, and said frantically, "I had to get out of there. Ramon's scaring me, *everyone's* scaring me with all this crazy werewolf crap."

"What's your name?" Simon asked, extending his hand.

She didn't shake, but she said, "Diane." Then she said, "So who are you? How do you know so much about all this?"

Simon knew that telling her he was a werewolf himself would freak her out and make it less likely that she'd believe anything he told her, so he said, "I know Ramon from the playground. We have sons the same age." Simon realized he'd answered the question elusively, the way Michael might've.

Diane seemed confused. "So Ramon told you about it?"

"He and his friends, yes."

"Why do they all think they're werewolves?"

Simon heard Michael's voice in his head: *She won't understand.*

"Look, they're seriously disturbed, okay?" Simon said. "You saw how your friend was acting. Did that seem normal to you?"

This seemed to have an effect on Diane. She said, "You should've seen her. She was trying to bite me, licking my blood, and now she's been sending me these crazy texts, saying she wants to come to my apartment."

"I think you might be in serious danger, Diane."

She looked truly terrified. "Why do you keep—"

"It might be worse than biting. What if she tries to kill you?"

"Why would she try to kill me?"

"Because she's out of control. She's insane."

Diane stopped walking and looked terrified, with her arms crossed in front of her chest. She said, "Please, just tell me what the hell is going on."

Stopping too, Simon said, "You have to trust me."

"Trust you? I have no idea who you are."

"I told you who I am. I'm Simon Burns. I'm an ad exec . . . I mean ex–ad exec. I'm a married man with a three-year-old son and I live on the Upper West Side. I know what's going on because they want to bite me too."

Diane glanced down briefly, probably at Simon's wedding band—this seemed to build her confidence in him. She was probably thinking, *Married guy? A kid? How dangerous could he possibly be?*

She asked, "So why don't you go to the police?"

"What are the police going to do when I tell them that I think people who claim they're werewolves want to bite me? Look, I know you have no reason to trust me, but I really am just trying to help you. They know you know about them, and that makes you a threat. You have to stay as far away from them as you can until this blows over."

Diane stared at Simon with very wide, incredulous eyes, and then she stepped off the curb onto the street and stuck her hand out, trying to hail a cab.

"Where are you going?" Simon asked.

"Home," she said. "I've had enough of this for one day."

A cab pulled alongside Diane.

"She could be waiting for you there," Simon said.

Diane hesitated with her hand on the door handle.

"You saw how crazy she is," Simon said. "Let me take you back to your apartment. Just to make sure it's safe."

"It's not necess—"

"Please," Simon said. "She texted you that she might be there, right?"

"You gettin' in or what?" the driver asked.

Diane, still thinking, didn't move for a few more seconds. Then she said to Simon, "Fine. Whatever."

Simon got in the back of the cab next to Diane. He could smell the odors of many people, Fritos, chewing gum, and urine.

As they headed downtown, Diane said to Simon, "You better not be some crazy stalker."

"I promise you, I'm not a crazy stalker," Simon said.

"Yeah, and that's exactly what a crazy stalker would say."

They almost smiled.

Then Diane said, "I'm sorry. Seriously, you seem like a good guy. It was just so scary before—I mean, to see somebody you know, somebody you trust, suddenly acting so completely insane. It was really like she'd become a different person."

"Yeah," Simon said. "I know what that's like."

"So what does her boyfriend have to do with all this?"

"Boyfriend?" Simon was playing dumb.

"Yeah, before, when I told you she told me she was a werewolf, you asked me if she knew Michael. What does he have to do with it?"

Trying to avoid the subject, Simon said, "I'm not sure. I just heard he's involved, that's all."

"You know, I warned her about him from the very beginning," she said. "The night they met, I didn't want her to go home with him, and then I tried to talk her into breaking up with him, but it was like he had some kind of spell over her. I thought he was crazy too, I mean, the way he was rough with her in bed and demanded sex and . . ." She shook her head, then said, "Listen to me, blaming her, when I did the same thing myself, falling so hard for Ramon. And to think, I used to complain about the crazy guys I've met on Match. At least those guys didn't think they were werewolves."

About ten minutes later, the cab slowed in front of Diane's apartment, a walk-up tenement on East Fourth Street between Avenues A and B. Diane paid the fare and then, as she and Simon got out of the cab, she was looking around in every direction, clearly terrified.

"You want me to check out your apartment for you?" Simon said. "Just to make sure all is well. She could've figured out a way to get in."

"You don't have to—"

"It's okay, I want to."

"Thanks," she said. "I am pretty scared."

They went through the double-door security and took the stairs up four flights. Diane was gasping a little, but Simon was breathing normally.

"Wow, you're in good shape," Diane said. "I've been living here five years and I'm still not used to the stairs."

She opened both locks and flicked on the lights. It was a narrow "railroad-style" apartment. There was a small kitchen to the left and a narrow living room leading to a narrow hallway and another room.

"I know I'm just being totally paranoid now," Diane said, "but would you mind just checking to make sure she isn't here?"

Simon went through the apartment, looking in the bathroom, including the shower, and then went into the small bedroom, which was barely wide enough to fit a double bed. He checked the bedroom closet and noticed the gate over the window that opened to the fire escape.

He returned to the living room, where Diane was standing, and said, "Coast is clear."

"Thank you," Diane said. "I admit I do feel much safer now. Want something to drink? I have cranberry juice and Vitaminwater."

Simon saw—and smelled—sliced turkey wrapped in deli paper in the fridge. He wanted the meat badly—he could practically taste it—but he resisted and said, "It's okay . . . I'm fine."

"I just want to apologize again," Diane said, taking the bottle of cranberry juice. "This has just been such a weird day and it keeps getting weirder. . . . I'm angry at myself too, for getting involved with Ramon. You said you're friends with him?"

"I'm not sure if *friend* is the right word," Simon said. "We're acquaintances."

"I can't believe I fell for a guy like that," Diane said. "He's so smooth and fake—I can usually see right through a guy like that. But there was just something about him. I was just unbelievably attracted to him, and I have no idea why."

"Yeah, Ramon seems to have that effect on people. It's probably the . . ." He was going to say *wolves' blood in his system*, but he didn't think that would go over very well, so he said, "It's probably just the way he is."

Diane poured herself a glass of juice. Simon noticed that her scent was much more pungent than before, probably because she'd been sweating coming up the stairs. He watched her suck down most of the juice in one gulp. He noticed the clock on the stove: 11:14.

Then she said, "But tonight he was really scaring me. The way he grabbed me when I said I was leaving, he was acting like Olivia was before."

"Do you have family in the city?" Simon asked.

"I'm from Michigan," she said.

"Well, I think you should think about going back home for a while," Simon said, "until things settle down."

"You're kidding, right?"

Simon's look said he wasn't.

"I can't leave my life," she said. "I have a job here. And why would I leave? Just because my friends are acting a little weird? Okay, a lot weird."

Simon was still very serious. "No," he said. "You'd be leaving to save your life."

"See? There you go, trying to scare me again. Do you get off on—"

She was looking downward toward Simon's waist, or at something slightly below it. At first Simon thought she was looking at his wedding band again, but then he realized something was amiss because she seemed shocked, even disgusted.

Then he caught on. "I'm so sorry," he said, turning away and reaching into his pants to adjust his erection. "That's never happened to me before . . . I mean it doesn't usually happen so . . . I'm really sorry."

Diane suddenly seemed horrified. "Ramon got sudden hard-ons like that too . . . Oh my God, you're one of them, aren't you?"

"No," Simon said. "Of course I—"

"Wait, let me guess, you think you're a werewolf too, don't you?"

"No, that's absolutely ridiculous; of course, werewolves don't actually exist." Simon was trying to make it sound absurd, but he was probably overdoing it.

"What do you want to do," Diane said, "bite me too?" She opened a drawer and took out a large steak knife. Sticking it out in front of her, she said, "Get the hell out of my apartment right now, you perverted son of a bitch!"

"Come on," Simon said, "just put the—"

She swiped the knife and it came dangerously close to Simon's face.

"Whoa," Simon said. "Are you crazy?"

"*I'm* crazy? Ha, that's a good one!"

She lunged at Simon with the knife, and he was able to back away in the nick of time.

"Okay, fine, I'm going, I'm going."

Simon went toward the door and was about to undo the locks when he smelled a woman. It wasn't Diane—though he could still smell her too. It was a different woman.

"I think she's here," he said.

Diane was confused. "Who's here? What the hell're you—?"

"There's a woman outside your door."

"How do you know that?"

"I can smell her."

Diane's look asked, *Huh?* Then the bell rang and Diane's eyes widened. She remained motionless, staring at Simon.

Then a female voice said, "Diane, come on, open up, and I know you have a guy in there, he smells absolutely scrumptious."

"Oh my God." Diane was horrified. "It's *her*."

TWENTY-EIGHT

"I heard that," Olivia said from the hallway.

Diane whispered to Simon, "How could she hear me? And how did you *smell* her?"

"Let her in," Simon said.

"Are you crazy? She'll try to bite me again."

"I won't let that happen."

"I should've just called the cops right away. You're all insane."

Simon grabbed Diane's hand—the one not holding the knife—and pulled her to the back of the apartment, to the bedroom. Then he leaned in very close to her ear and said in a voice so quiet it was barely audible, "Just let her in, okay? I'm here, I'll protect you, I promise."

"Let go of me."

Simon let go and whispered, "I'm not trying to hurt you, but your friend Olivia obviously is. I have to reason with her, make sure something bad doesn't happen tonight, something that would make this permanent. If that happens, you'll never be safe again, you'll always be in danger. Do you understand me?"

Diane seemed to be responding to Simon's intensity. She wasn't trying to stab him to death anymore, anyway.

"Fine," she said in a normal tone.

Simon made a face.

"Fine," she continued, whispering. "But if you can't convince her to
leave me alone, I'm calling the cops."

She took the knife with her into the bathroom and locked the door.

"Are you going to open up?" Olivia said. "I'm not leaving until I
can at least *talk* to you."

Simon opened the front door and was immediately mesmerized, the
way a dog on the street stops and stares at another dog of the same breed.

"Who are you?" she asked.

Simon knew she was feeling what he was feeling; she had to be
feeling it.

"A friend of Diane's," he said.

"She bagged another cute guy?" Olivia said. "Wow, she's really
cleaning up tonight and I can't even get laid."

"No, Diane and I just met, actually," Simon said.

"Oh really?" Olivia was in the apartment now, closing the door. "In
that case, fair game is fair game."

Suddenly she had her arms around his waist, pulling him against
her. He didn't want to be attracted to her, but he couldn't help it. She
smelled and felt so good; he wanted her as badly as he wanted a steak
dinner.

Her hands were on his ass now, pulling him up against her, and he
felt his hard-on pressing against the zipper of his jeans.

Then sanity returned as he thought, *What the hell am I doing?* He
had no real interest in any woman other than Alison. This was just the
wolves' blood messing with his brain.

"Stop it," he said, pushing her away with his hands.

"Why?" she said, panting. "I'm so horny for you, and I know you
want me too."

He watched her nostrils flare a little. He hated that she was right.

She unsnapped his jeans and slid her hands over his boxer briefs. He pushed her back again, a little harder this time, or at least with more intent, but then she shoved him hard against the wall. He was surprised how strong she was. He had to be sixty or seventy pounds heavier, but she was pushing him around almost effortlessly.

"Look, I know what's happening," Simon said.

"If you know, why don't you just take off your clothes?"

"No, I mean I know what he did to you. I know he gave you the beer too, but if you don't show up tonight you'll be okay, you'll return to normal."

She tried to grab his crotch again, and then, as if suddenly hearing what he'd said, she asked, "What beer?"

"The beer," Simon said, "at his brewery. That's what happened to you, right?"

"I have no idea what you're talking about," she said, lunging at him again.

Going around the small round kitchen table, barely avoiding her, Simon said, "I don't get it. If he didn't give you the beer, how did you get this way?" Then it hit him. "Wait, Michael didn't . . . bite you *already*, did he?"

Now she stopped and stared at him suspiciously. "How do *you* know about Michael?"

Then Simon looked at her neck and noticed a bite mark that seemed to be healing. Suddenly he sensed the danger he was in. Instinct shouted at him to run, get the hell away, but he couldn't leave Diane with her.

"Michael is just a guy I know," Simon said. "But I know what he did to you. I know how badly you want to bite Diane, but she won't survive if you do it. Do you really want to kill your friend?"

Olivia's expression softened. Was he getting through to her?

"Now I know why you're here," she said. "Because *you* want to bite her first."

Nope, wasn't getting through.

"No, I'm here because I know what's going on," Simon said. "I know how dangerous this is. We have to stop it now, before it gets out of hand."

"You know what I think?" Olivia said with a devilish grin. "I think I'll bite whoever I want to bite."

Olivia wasn't fooled. She easily intercepted him and pushed him back against the stove. He couldn't hold her back—she was way too powerful. To defend himself, he grabbed the only thing within his reach—a frying pan. He swung the pan as hard as he could, and it clanged against Olivia's head.

She keeled over, apparently stunned. Simon went to the bathroom and shouted to Diane, "Come on, let's go!"

Diane wouldn't open the door, so Simon stepped back, then bashed the door open with his shoulder. Diane, holding the knife in front of her, screamed for him to get the hell away.

Ignoring the knife, he said, "Just come on," and grabbed her other hand. He started to pull her toward the front door when they both stopped suddenly, horrified by what they saw in front of them.

Olivia was facing them, but it wasn't Olivia anymore. There was thick dark hair on her face, neck, and arms—some of the hair was still *growing*—and she had big sharp teeth and her hands were thick and hairy with large claws. Simon stared at her as if he were staring at a gruesome accident—with a combination of disgust, fear, and total disbelief.

When he was able to react, it was too late. Olivia had already leaped toward him, knocking him backward, and the back of his head slammed hard against the radiator. He was dazed, disoriented. Diane was screaming, "Help me!" Simon's vision cleared, and he saw that Olivia had tackled Diane, knocking the knife away, and was on top of her, about to bite into her neck.

Simon charged Olivia, his momentum toppling her off Diane. But she recovered quickly, unfazed, and came at Simon, her sharp claws extended. Simon tried to fight back, but it was pointless. She was pinning him down, digging her claws into his shoulders now. Her long sharp teeth glistened with drool as she growled. Even if Simon hadn't been completely overpowered, he would have been paralyzed by sheer terror.

When Olivia sank her teeth into Simon's neck, he didn't even try to fight back. The bite itself was painful, but the rest of his body was strangely relaxed, as if he were suddenly in a deep meditative trance. He wasn't experiencing his pain, he was *observing* it. But though he was extremely calm and unfazed, he was also hyper-aware of his surroundings and knew exactly what was happening to him. He knew that a crazed werewolf was biting into his neck, gnawing on him, and he could hear Diane screaming for her to stop, and there was another voice, a man in the hallway saying, "Hey, what's going on in there?" But despite all of the chaos surrounding him, Simon's mind was at rest and he didn't feel any anxiety or fear.

Only when Olivia ended the bite and looked down at him with blood—*his* blood—mixed with the drool on her teeth—did his rage return. He lashed out, pushing her away with his hands, and this was surprisingly effective, as she toppled onto the floor. Simon had no idea where this sudden strength had come from, but he loved the domination and control. For years the world had been beating him up, having its way with him, and now in a millisecond he'd gone from bullied to bully. He stood over her, panting, breathing, *really* breathing for the first time in years, or maybe ever.

Then, making angry, guttural sounds, Olivia—or the crazed wolflike version of her—got up and charged him again, but he grabbed her hair before she could scratch him and easily flung her away. She toppled over the table, falling hard onto the floor. This time she seemed dazed. She was about to come after him again, then hesitated, as if thinking better of it, probably realizing she was overmatched.

The guy outside was banging on the door. "Hey, Diane, you okay in there?" Then he banged some more.

For several more seconds, Olivia remained there—panting—trying to assess the situation, and then she started to transform back into her human form. Hair and teeth receding, she seemed terrified and confused.

"Wha-wha-what's going on?"

"Hello?" the neighbor said.

Then, as if instinctively knowing that she was in danger and had to flee, Olivia darted toward the back of the apartment. She unlocked the gate and went out the window to the fire escape. Simon considered going after her, but the neighbor was still banging on the door and Simon didn't want to leave Diane alone.

"Tell him everything's okay," Simon whispered to Diane.

Diane, who appeared beyond shocked, clearly traumatized by everything she'd seen, didn't answer.

Simon nudged her and whispered, "Come on, say it. Tell him everything's fine so he'll go away."

After a few more seconds of stunned silence, Diane said weakly, "Everything's fine."

"Louder," Simon whispered.

"Everything's fine!" she suddenly shouted.

"You sure?" the guy asked. "It sounded like there was fighting or something going on in there."

Simon nudged her again, and she shouted, "Yeah, I'm positive! Everything's totally fine!"

Long pause, then the man said, "Okay, if you say so."

But the man didn't leave. Simon's sense of hearing seemed even sharper now; through the door he could actually hear the man's shallow breathing. He could also hear music and TVs from other apartments, and street noise outside—horns honking, car engines. He could even make out conversations—a woman telling a man something she'd heard Jon Stewart say on *The Daily Show*, a guy talking about his wart medication, an old woman laughing.

Finally the man in the hallway walked away. Simon listened to his creaky footsteps, and then a door at the end of the hallway opened and slammed shut.

Looking around at the apartment, with chairs tipped over and the knife and frying pan on the floor, Diane said, "None of this actually happened, right?"

"You didn't call the police, did you?" Simon asked.

She shook her head.

"Good," Simon said. "If you told them about this, they'd probably want to send you to Bellevue. You have to leave New York immediately. Olivia's going to come back, and the others might come too. Especially now that you saw all this, they won't leave you alone, I promise."

"How . . . how is it possible?" Diane said. "How could she . . . change. . . . How could . . ."

Simon was terrified and in shock himself, but somehow he was able to stay calm. "That's not important right now. Just think about your own safety. That's all that matters."

Simon heard more of the conversation about Jon Stewart.

"Your neck," Diane said.

Simon touched his neck and then looked at the blood on his fingers. Since Olivia had bitten him, Simon had been in such a heightened state that he hadn't fully thought through the possible consequences of what had happened to him. He didn't know if getting bitten by someone other than Michael could make him into a permanent wolf, but something was definitely different about him. His senses of hearing and smell were even sharper than they'd been before, and what about his sudden incredible strength?

He went to the kitchen sink and rinsed the bite. It was a deep wound—she'd had her teeth deep inside him—but it wasn't bleeding as much as it should've been.

"You should go to a hospital," Diane said.

Simon knew that a hospital was out of the question. A visit to the hospital would inevitably lead to a visit from the police, which wouldn't lead to anything positive. Besides, if he was a permanent wolf now, there was probably nothing anyone could do to save him.

"Don't worry about me, I'll be fine," he said, realizing right away what a ridiculous statement that was; he'd be anything but fine. He added, "But promise me you'll leave New York now. You saw Olivia—now you know I'm not lying to you. The police will never believe you, and if you stay here, she's going to bite you one day and maybe even kill you."

Simon was giving her the hard sell because he didn't want her to mention his name to the police, and because he honestly believed it was in her best interest to leave the city.

"No," she said weakly.

"What?" Simon asked.

"No," she said louder, and picked up the knife from the floor. "Get the hell out of my apartment, right now, you crazy son of a bitch."

"I'm telling you," Simon said. "You're making a big—"

"Leave!" she shouted.

Afraid the neighbor was going to come over again, Simon warned Diane again not to call the police, then rushed out of the apartment.

He knew she was going to call the police, and he couldn't really blame her. She was terrified right now, and if he were in her position and had witnessed what she'd witnessed, he'd probably call the police too. If she mentioned his name—and he had no reason to believe that she wouldn't—in connection with a pack of alleged werewolves, it could cause problems for him, especially if the police decided to give him a blood test and they found wolves' blood. Then they'd link him to Tom's murder, and that wouldn't even be the worst of it. He imagined the media circus and news stories—a real-life werewolf discovered in Manhattan! It would cause the media frenzy to end all media frenzies, and Alison's and Jeremy's lives would be ruined forever.

He might have been contemplating suicide again if it weren't for one indisputable fact—he felt amazing.

Since Olivia had bitten him he'd felt a major surge of energy, and his senses of smell and hearing were incredibly sharp. As he went downstairs, he could make out conversations in every apartment he passed, and he also heard TVs, music, people having sex. And his sense of smell was incredible too. He could detect garbage, somebody eating shrimp with lobster sauce, somebody else eating roasted chicken and mashed potatoes, and the exterminator must have been to the building recently because the smell of insecticide on the first and second floors overwhelmed everything else.

He'd never been so attuned to his environment; he felt more alert and, well, more alive than he ever had before. Remembering his surge of strength after Olivia had bitten him, he wanted to test it, to see if it was a onetime thing—some kind of adrenaline rush—or if the effect was long-lasting. He looked around for something heavy to lift. A garbage can? Nah, that was too easy. How about a car? Or, better yet, an SUV.

There was an Explorer at the curb in front of him. He squatted behind the car, found something to grab on to below the license plate, and lifted. He wasn't using all his strength, so he didn't expect to move the car much, if at all. Yeah, he'd been able to push Olivia around, but there was a big difference between a woman and an SUV. So he was surprised, even shocked, when he not only moved the SUV, but easily lifted it several feet off the ground. It was so unexpected that he let go of it suddenly, and when it fell to the pavement the alarm started blaring. To Simon, the noise was excruciating and, partly because he wanted to get away from the noise and partly because a few people on the street were already looking over, he sprinted away toward Avenue A.

He was running much faster than he'd been able to run before, and he wasn't even pushing himself. Although he was soon twenty blocks from where the car alarm had gone off, when he focused he could still hear the alarm among the many other city sounds. If he could some-how avoid being arrested and could get used to the sensory overload, this didn't seem so bad. Nothing would ever undo what he'd done to Tom, but if the police didn't find enough evidence to arrest him, maybe he could put his new abilities to good use somehow. He didn't feel un-stable or homicidal, but the wolves' blood seemed to be having a much different effect on Olivia. She was clearly out there, capable of wreak-ing serious havoc. Maybe when Charlie and Ramon were bitten, they would become as crazy as Olivia. Or what about the people Charlie and Ramon might bite? It was easy to do the math—within weeks there could be dozens of homicidal werewolves roaming the streets of Manhattan.

But did Ramon and Charlie have to get bitten tonight? Though Simon hadn't been able to persuade them not to go to the brewery, maybe with his sudden new strength he could physically stop Michael from biting them. Then if, as Volker claimed, the wolves' blood eventually wore off or left their systems, maybe Charlie's and Ramon's rationality would return and they'd realize that living the rest of their lives as werewolves wasn't necessarily such a great thing.

Looking into the window of a closed clothing store, he saw a clock: 11:36.

He didn't know if he could possibly make it all the way to the brewery in Brooklyn in twenty-four minutes, or if he was strong enough to stop Michael from doing whatever the hell he wanted to do, but he was going to give it his best shot.

TWENTY-NINE

Sprinting downtown, Simon was amazed how fast he was going. Were these really his legs? He was probably doing four-minute miles, going so fast the wind was making his face feel numb, and people were stopping to watch and occasionally cheer him on as if he were running in the New York City Marathon. He zipped through the Bowery, Chinatown, and the City Hall area to the Brooklyn Bridge. It had stopped raining and the sky was clearing. The moon was big and full—maybe it was a harvest moon—and it seemed to be positioned directly over downtown Brooklyn.

Crossing the bridge, Simon slowed to a normal pace because he didn't want to attract attention from a few cops he passed. It was hard to believe that about two hours ago he'd been contemplating jumping from this very bridge. Now it was clear to him that suicide wouldn't only end his life, but would ensure the fate of any future victims of Michael and his pack. Okay, so maybe grandiosity was another side effect of being a wolf, but when he reached the Brooklyn side of the bridge, the idea that he was the last hope, a *savior*, gave him the motivation to run even faster toward the old Hartman Brewery.

Simon didn't need GPS anymore; he instinctively knew exactly which direction to head in, weaving through the dark, rain-slicked streets. He had no idea what time it was, but if it wasn't midnight already, it was damn close.

The door to the building was closed. He didn't have time to scream for someone to open it for him, so he rammed it with his shoulder, breaking through easily. He could smell the guys—Ramon's and Charlie's colognes and sweat, and Michael's much stronger scent; they were definitely here, but was he too late? Maybe he had another minute or two, but time was definitely running out.

He rang for the elevator, didn't hear anything, and then saw a doorway to his right. He creaked it open and saw a dark stairwell. He could barely see anything—just the bottom few stairs—but this didn't matter because his other senses overcompensated and he instinctively knew where he was going. He charged up, three steps at a time, ignoring the odors of urine and musk and feces. It wasn't human feces—it was animal feces, probably from mice and rats. Although he was in pitch-darkness, he didn't miss a single step and knew when the stairwell turned. He went up maybe ten flights. If the floors were marked, it didn't matter because he couldn't see them, but the smell of the guys' sweat was getting stronger, so he knew he was getting closer.

He went through the room he'd been in his previous times in the brewery. The odor of steak was prominent, and he didn't know if it was today or from previous days, but the odors of the guys were getting weaker. He went back toward the elevator and stairwell and down a hallway into an area of the brewery he'd never been in before. Well, he thought he'd never been there before, but then he passed a large pool table and remembered the guys telling him he'd played pool that night he'd blacked out. But, wait, was he losing the scent again? He stopped and inhaled deeply; the guys were close, and when he focused his hearing could make out the sound of Michael's voice. He rushed through the room and found another stairwell leading upward. Michael's voice was getting louder and the scents were getting much stronger, and then he came out onto the roof.

The moon was bright, like a giant spotlight, and the lights of Manhattan across the river seemed to be flickering like stars. Charlie and Ramon were standing near the ledge of the building, facing Michael, who had his back to Simon.

"Don't do it!" Simon shouted.

Michael looked back at Simon, typically expressionless. There was no way to tell whether he was shocked or surprised or couldn't care less.

"You came," Michael said.

"Yeah, I came," Simon said, "and I'm leaving right now with Charlie and Ramon."

"Hey, come on," Charlie said. "We talked about this already, bro."

"Yeah," Ramon said. "You gotta chill, man. If you don't wanna get your bite tonight, that's cool, but don't mess it up for us."

"Sorry," Simon said, "but I can't let him do this to you."

Simon knew Charlie and Ramon were thinking, *Yeah, and how are you going to stop him?* He knew this because he was thinking the exact same thing himself.

Then Michael's nostrils flared. "You have odor on your body," he said.

"That's a nice way to say hello," Simon said. Then he sniffed and said, "So do you."

Michael's scent had never seemed so dominating. It reminded Simon of the way some of the animals smelled at the Central Park Children's Zoo.

Michael's nostrils flared again, this time in a slower, more exaggerated way. He said, "You smell like the woman I've had sex with."

"Wow, you're good," Simon said. "I'm getting better at odor detection myself, but I have to say, that was impressive."

"You met Olivia," Michael said.

"Yeah, I had the pleasure of meeting your girlfriend this evening.

Small city, huh? She's a little on the, well, eccentric side, but I'm sure she has her strong points. I can see why you two are a couple—you have a lot in common."

No reaction from Michael, but Simon could sense fear in him. Charlie and Ramon looked clueless.

"Oh," Simon added, "and she gave me a little parting gift."

He pulled down his shirt collar a little and turned his head slightly to show Michael his bitten neck.

"Stupid little bitch," Michael said.

Simon had never seen Michael react so strongly about anything; he was usually so even-keeled. The guys noticed the change in behavior as well.

"What's going on?" Charlie asked.

"I was bitten tonight," Simon said, "by a woman who is clearly out of control and psychotic. If you get bitten, the same thing might happen to you. Do you want to roam around the city like lunatics trying to bite people?"

"Diane bit you?" Ramon asked.

"No, her friend did," Simon said.

Michael turned away from Simon, toward Charlie and Ramon, and said, "There is no time for discussion. I will now give you the ultimate gift—the power of the wolf." He said to Ramon, "Come forward."

Ramon hesitated, glancing at Simon briefly, then took a couple of steps toward Michael.

Wanting to get Michael's attention, Simon grabbed the object nearest to him—a picnic table with an umbrella—and easily lifted it above his head even though it must have weighed three hundred pounds. Then he flung the table and it crashed against the brick wall.

Michael turned toward Simon with an expression of—was it fear? He was at least startled.

"Let them go right now," Simon said.

He held his ground, trying to sound and act as menacing as possible.

"The pack is your family now," Michael said. "Let the others join us."

"I don't think you understand me," Simon said. "I don't care about you, and I don't care about the pack. I just don't want to see anyone else get hurt."

"You need to accept who you are," Michael said. "You have received a wonderful gift, and you must learn to cherish it."

"I didn't ask for any gift."

"A baby doesn't ask to be born."

"You're not God, you're just a psychopath."

"And you're exactly like me."

"I'm nothing like you."

Staring at the darkness in Michael's eyes, Simon couldn't help feeling intimidated. He knew he was overmatched, but he held his ground, refusing to show any weakness.

"You say that now," Michael said. "But wait till you experience the pleasure of killing for the first time. Then you will thank me."

"Actually I already know how it feels to kill," Simon said, "and I know I hate it."

"You haven't killed yet," Michael said.

"What do you mean? I killed my ex-boss, remember?"

"I killed him," Michael said.

Simon felt as if all the blood in his body had instantly rushed to his brain. He said, "That's impossible. I remember killing him."

"You fantasized about killing him. You wanted to be me."

"But I remember . . . being a wolf."

"When you were a temporary wolf, you couldn't transform yet," Michael said, "you didn't have that gift. But after you drank the family beer, you told me about how your boss fired you and how you wanted him to die. So later my driver took us to New Jersey. We drew him out of the house and you watched me kill him. You wanted to kill him and I wanted to help you. I wanted you to join the pack. The others joined the pack right away, but you were more difficult. If I didn't tell you you killed your boss, you might have never joined us. I did you a great favor."

Simon took a few moments to absorb all of this, then asked, "But how did I wind up naked?"

"When people receive the blood of our family for the first time, they have unpredictable reactions," Michael said. "Some die, some sleep, and some, like you, become euphoric. Perhaps it was because as a human you felt imprisoned by your life, and as a wolf for the first time you felt truly free."

It should have been a relief to find out he hadn't killed Tom, but Simon wasn't experiencing it this way. All he could think about was how believing he'd murdered Tom had almost ruined his marriage, and had made him contemplate suicide, and had led to his becoming a werewolf.

"If I didn't kill Tom, I can go to the police," Simon said. "I could tell them you did it, and I could tell them about Alan Freedman and his wife too."

"I have your shoe," Michael said.

"Shoe?" Simon said, but he knew exactly what shoe Michael was referring to.

Michael took out his cell phone and showed Simon an image of what was unquestionably the Rockport loafer he'd lost in New Jersey that night.

"It has the victim's blood on it," Michael said. "You don't want the police to have this."

If it really had Tom's blood on it—and Simon had no reason to believe Michael was lying—Simon might as well have killed Tom because the police would never believe he was innocent.

"Son of a bitch," Simon said, and he charged Michael and tried to tackle him, but he was like a jockey trying to pick a fight with a middle linebacker. Michael was so strong Simon could barely budge him, and then Michael shook back and forth very quickly, like a horse shooing away an annoying fly, and Simon fell hard onto the ground.

Simon came after Michael again from behind, wrapping his arms around his back and trying to tackle him. Michael struggled, trying to break free, but Simon, using all of his strength, wouldn't let go. From his angle, Simon couldn't see Michael's face, but Charlie and Ramon were both looking right at Michael like . . . well, like they were looking at a monster. Simon was losing his grip, as Michael seemed to be gaining strength, and Michael's neck was getting thicker and hairier. Then, with one violent shake, Michael knocked Simon hard onto the tar rooftop. When Simon looked up, he saw what had captivated the other guys—Michael had transformed. The thick white hair on his face contrasted with his dark eyes, and his nose was dark and wide and animal-like. As a werewolf, he looked more majestic than Olivia had, and much more menacing. He didn't have to growl to intimidate; his mere presence created an aura of fear. His thick, hairy hands had long claws, much longer and more lethal-looking than Olivia's claws, and as he breathed with his mouth open Simon could see his huge, very sharp-looking teeth.

Simon felt like prey, as if Michael could pounce on him and tear him to shreds at any moment. But then Michael shifted his attention back to Ramon.

"W-w-wait, h-hold up, man," Ramon said.

An instant later Michael had leaped onto Ramon and started to bite into his neck. At that same moment Simon felt pressure in his hands, feet, and gums, and his entire face was swelling. The pain was overwhelmed by a surge of confidence and strength. He knew what was happening, what he was becoming, yet he wasn't afraid. The transformation felt natural, as if he'd been this way for a long time, maybe forever, and he let himself go.

Olivia was dying to bite Diane. She'd been so close, her teeth had been almost through her skin, when that guy had pulled her away. The guy had tasted pretty good himself, but she was still craving Diane's flesh.

She hung out on the roof of Diane's building for a while until that guy left her apartment. She didn't have to see him leave; she could *smell* him leave. Then she tried to get back into the apartment through the window, but Diane had locked the gate. Olivia knew she could've broken the gate with one good pull, but the neighbors would probably hear it. She was

going to get into the building the same way she had earlier—through the
door on the roof leading to the stairwell—when she heard a police siren. It
was far away, but she could still hear it clearly. Then she went to the ledge
and saw the swirling lights of a police car, maybe ten blocks away, heading along Avenue B. Sure enough the car turned onto Diane's block and
stopped in front of her apartment building. Well, so much for biting her best
friend—at least for tonight. Olivia jumped from building to building until
she reached the top of the building at the end of the block. Then she went
down the fire escape and dropped onto East Fourth Street.

Olivia immediately detected the guy's scent. It was definitely his; it was
unmistakable. Biting his neck had seriously whetted her appetite; now she
wanted to finish her meal. She trailed the odor down the block, then downtown on Avenue A. She pulled off her boots and dropped them in a garbage can and continued barefoot. She started jogging, then running, then
all-out sprinting downtown. Weaving through the city streets, she didn't
know where she was going, but she knew that as long as she could smell
the guy she was going in the right direction. It was as if she were a rat in a
maze, except that at the end of the maze there wouldn't be a measly piece
of cheese—her reward would be a wonderful feast of raw human flesh.

The trail led her downtown, over the Brooklyn Bridge. The farther
she went, the hungrier she got. She'd been to Brooklyn only a few
times in her life, when she was dating that lawyer guy in Williamsburg.
She went through DUMBO into an industrial area in God knows what
part of the borough. She turned down a dark street—the streetlamp had
burned out—but she was following the scent, and if she had been blind
she would've known exactly where to go. The scent was the strongest in
front of a decrepit industrial-like building. Could this really be where he
had gone? Then she saw the words engraved above the entrance:

HARTMAN BREWERY

Didn't Michael once mention that he owned a brewery in Brooklyn? Why had the guy from Diane's come here?

The door had been broken open. Olivia entered the dark lobby, saying, "Hello? Anybody home?" but getting no response. The guy's scent was still very intense, and she tracked it to a dark stairwell. She said, "I know you're here, and I'm gonna find you no matter what, so there's no use hiding from me." Then she detected Michael's scent as well, and was that the scent of the Latino guy, Ramon, Diane had been dating? Yeah, it was definitely Ramon—she could tell him anywhere—and there was another strong male scent she didn't recognize.

In the pitch-dark of the stairwell, she knew exactly where she was going. She remembered being in the car with Michael, when he was driving with no headlights, and now she understood how he'd pulled that off. After she'd climbed a couple of flights the scents were more powerful, so she knew she was heading in the right direction. She could also hear sounds—animal-like growling and human screams—intensifying her desires for sex and blood. She exited into a large area that was surprisingly clean and well furnished, and then went past a pool table to another stairwell. As she went up, the sounds were getting louder and the odors of the virile men were intoxicating.

She emerged onto the roof and saw a powerful werewolf—by his smell, she knew he was Michael—with grayish hair, wrestling with a smaller, darker werewolf who she knew, by his scent, was the guy she'd been trailing. Michael was definitely getting the best of the battle—he was on top of the smaller werewolf, biting and clawing him—but then the smaller werewolf managed to free himself and swing his arm, like an awkward backhand in tennis, against Michael's face. Michael stumbled backward slightly, then regained his balance and charged again.

Watching the two werewolves was arousing for Olivia. She felt like they were fighting for *her* and she couldn't wait to screw or kill whoever won. Then she noticed the two men off to the side—Ramon and a big guy she'd never seen before but who also smelled incredible.

Olivia strutted toward them, swinging her hips and eyeing them seductively, "Hope you guys don't have other plans this evening," she said. "If you do, I have a hunch you'll be canceling."

"Who the hell are you?" the big guy asked.

"She's Michael's girlfriend," Ramon said. "The one who bit Simon."

"His name's Simon, huh?" Olivia said, watching Simon as a werewolf digging his claws into Michael's face. Some blood spurted and Olivia rushed over and licked it off the tar. She savored the taste, but it only whetted her appetite for a much larger meal.

As Simon and Michael continued to fight, Olivia got to her feet and eyed Ramon and the big guy. Ramon was sexier, but the big guy would be more satisfying, so she lunged at him, easily tackling him to the ground. He tried to get free, but his fighting back was just more of a turn-on. Despite his size, he was no match for her. She was about to sink her teeth into his face when she was knocked off him by something hard. She recovered fast and saw Ramon standing over her, holding a metal chair, about to hit her again. But this time she was ready and dodged it easily. Meanwhile she felt the change happening—the pain, but also the rush of confidence, and the feeling that nothing could ever hurt her, especially not some mere man.

Fully transformed, she glared at Ramon, loving how terrorized he looked and how powerful she felt. Knowing that she could pounce on this man, destroy him whenever she wanted to, was the most invigorating feeling she'd ever experienced, and she didn't want it to end. But her craving for flesh had intensified, becoming almost unbearable, so she lifted up the screaming and terrified little man, easily tossed him out of her way, and then went after the larger meal.

The big guy tried to flee toward the stairwell, but she grabbed him from behind. She tackled him and pinned him down and bit off a chunk of his cheek. His screaming was even more of a turn-on. She chewed on the tough, salty flesh, but it barely satisfied her. She wanted to eat his entire face, then work her way down to that big meaty chest and devour his whole body. She was going in for another bite when she felt a sharp pain in her back, claws tearing into her.

* * *

Simon saw Olivia attack Charlie, but Michael had him pinned to the ground and he couldn't get free. Simon was fighting Michael the best he could, but he was overmatched; besides Michael's advantage of strength and size, he had the major advantage of experience. Michael had been a werewolf all his life and had total control of his body, but Simon felt tentative in his werewolf body, as if he were driving a car he'd never driven before. His movements were awkward and he was afraid to take risks. When he tried to scratch and bite Michael, he mostly missed or stumbled, or just swiped at him gently. Meanwhile, Michael seemed to be toying with him, knowing he could put his adversary away at any time.

Still, the shock of seeing that Olivia had transformed into a werewolf and, oh Jesus, that she'd just taken a bite out of Charlie's face, gave Simon a surge of strength. He managed to free himself from Michael's grasp and went after Olivia, getting her attention when he clawed her back. She turned angrily and bit his shoulder. She had a wild, ravenous look and blood was dripping from her mouth. Simon groaned in agony while she resumed the attack on Charlie, biting off a chunk of his arm.

As Simon struggled to get to his feet, he wondered why Michael had given up on him, and then he saw why. Michael had pinned Ramon down in the corner of the roof and was biting into his neck. It was probably too late to save Ramon from becoming a werewolf, but Simon could still save Charlie.

From a crouched position Simon tried to leap onto Olivia's back. But he misjudged the leap, using too much strength, and went soaring toward the ledge of the building. He actually fell off the side, but at the last moment he managed to grab on with one clawed hand. It didn't matter, though—his grip was loosening. In a few seconds he'd fall ten stories. He tried to say, "Help me," but couldn't form the words. Besides, no one was going to save him.

He saw Olivia, baring her ugly teeth almost gleefully. He could tell she was milking this moment, enjoying his fear. She glared at him for a few seconds, then pounced on Charlie, biting his neck.

Simon's grip was slipping. He was about to just let go and end it all when he imagined he heard Jeremy say, "Daddy, don't," and fueled by the desires to live and fight and survive that he didn't know he had, he managed to hoist himself up with one hand.

But it may have been too late. Olivia was biting and clawing at Charlie, and Charlie was so out of it he was barely fighting back anymore. It was like Charlie had given in and was accepting his fate.

Simon charged Olivia, tackling her from behind. Olivia was able to use her strong wolflike legs to flip Simon off her, over her head. Simon landed on his knees, got to his feet quickly and turned, squaring off against her. Her face was covered in warm blood now and she growled, spraying saliva, trying to intimidate him with her prowess, but Simon, refusing to back down, growled even louder. When Olivia attacked him again he was ready. He went right for her head, managing to get both of his claws into her mouth. With his left claw he grabbed her upper jaw, digging into her gums, and with his right hand he grabbed her lower jaw, and then he pulled in opposite directions. Olivia roared with fury and tried to free herself, but Simon was determined and wouldn't let go. Telling himself he had to do this, that it was kill or be killed, he continued to tear Olivia's jaw apart until there was a loud crack. Olivia continued to fight back, choking on blood, but Simon refused to let go. Finally, after one last gargle, Olivia's body went limp.

The roof was suddenly quiet. Ramon was in the corner, holding his bitten neck, and Michael was still crouched over Charlie, his teeth deep in the other man's throat. Olivia was definitely dead, a dark pool of blood spreading around her.

Simon tilted his head up toward the giant moon and howled in despair.

THIRTY

"So let me get this straight," Officer Anthony Sanchez, a young NYPD cop with a freckled face, said to Diane. "You say you saw your best friend turn into a werewolf this evening."

Diane hated the way Sanchez was smirking, as if he were treating all of this as a big joke. Sanchez's partner, a stocky blonde named Cheryl Mullen, was also clearly getting a kick out of it.

"Look, I know it's hard to believe," Diane said, "it's hard for me to believe too, okay? But it happened—I saw it with my own eyes and I'm not crazy. Ask anybody. Ask my neighbors. Go ahead, ring their doorbells, and they'll tell you what they heard in here. Or bring some DNA people in. There must be DNA from her somewhere in here. Test the DNA, and then you won't be laughing anymore."

Diane realized that the more she denied she was crazy, the crazier she sounded, which definitely wasn't helping her cause.

"No one's laughing at you, ma'am," Sanchez said, straight-faced, but Diane could tell that underneath he was still smirking.

"Have you been using any drugs tonight?" Mullen asked.

"Of course not," Diane said. "Is that what you really think? That I'm on drugs?"

Mullen and Sanchez exchanged looks.

"Just talk to the guy next door," Diane said.

"We talked to him already," Mullen said.

"Great," Diane said. "And?"

"He said he heard some arguing and screaming from your apartment," Sanchez said, "but he didn't see a woman leave. He said he saw a guy leave."

"That's the guy I was telling you about," Diane said.

"The one who saved you who might be a werewolf now too," Sanchez said.

"Right," Diane said. "He went out the door, but she ran out onto the fire escape. But she wasn't a werewolf anymore when she ran away; she'd turned back into a human being again."

Mullen and Sanchez were looking at her deadpan, obviously not believing any of this.

"You think I'm lying to you, don't you?" Diane said. "You think that's what I do, how I get my kicks. I call cops and tell them lies about werewolves in my apartment. You think I have nothing better to do with my time. How come you won't look for evidence? There must be little hairs somewhere on the floor. Or there must be saliva or, wait, look at those spots on the floor, that's blood. Not her blood, *his* blood, but there must be more evidence somewhere if you'd just look."

The cops had moved toward the door.

"We're gonna have to go now," Sanchez said.

"You can't leave me here alone," Diane said frantically. "What if she comes back? What if she tries to break the door down? She's crazy. She wants to kill me. Or what if the others come after me? There's her boyfriend, Michael, he's the one who started it all. I knew he was trouble at that bar, but she went home with him anyway."

"If someone attempts to break into your apartment, you can call 911," Mullen said.

Diane grabbed Sanchez's arm and pleaded, "But you don't understand. They're after me, they're all after me!"

Sanchez freed his arm from Diane's grip and said, "We can call an ambulance for you, ma'am. Would you like us to do that?"

Backing away, her eyes darting back and forth, Diane said softly, "He was right."

"Who was right?" Mullen asked.

"Simon said you wouldn't believe me," she said. "He said you'd think I was crazy. He said you'd want to bring me to Bellevue."

"If you'd like us to call an ambulance for you, we can," Sanchez said. "If not, there's really nothing we can do for you right now."

"I'm not crazy," Diane said. "I don't care what you think. I'm *not* crazy."

When the cops left, Diane bolted the door with both locks and put on the chain, then made sure the lock on the gate on the window leading to the fire escape was secure. Still, she didn't feel safe, and she wasn't sure she'd feel safe ever again. Other than Olivia, she only had a few other close friends in the city, and they were all married with kids. She didn't want to call them up in the middle of the night and scare them with her werewolf story. Well, *if* they'd get scared. If the cops didn't believe her, why would her friends believe her? She considered calling her ex, Steve, and begging him to come over, but that seemed pathetic after he'd dumped her with a text message. She wanted to call her parents in Michigan—just hearing her mom's and dad's voices would have been soothing—but she didn't want to scare them, and what could they do to help her from a thousand miles away?

She'd never felt so thoroughly scared and so thoroughly alone. She sat on the floor in the hallway between the bedroom and the bathroom, holding her knees, rocking back and forth, sobbing. After maybe half an hour of that, she didn't feel any more relaxed, and she wondered if maybe the cops were right and she was crazy after all. How could she have possibly seen what she thought she'd seen? Maybe she'd somehow dreamed up this whole night. Maybe none of it had actually happened—

maybe the whole day hadn't happened. Maybe Olivia hadn't gone crazy and she'd never met that Simon guy. Maybe she was just hallucinating, on some kind of drug, or had a virus. Weren't there viruses that could make you hallucinate?

She called Olivia's cell and got her voice mail. She said, "Olivia, honey, it's me. Please tell me tonight didn't happen, please tell me there's some explanation for all of this. Please, *please* call me when you get this."

Making the phone call hadn't resolved anything, but at least it made her feel proactive. She didn't know what had actually happened, but she knew it couldn't be what she thought had happened, and knowing that some explanation existed, even if she didn't know it yet, gave her some comfort.

She lay in bed and, although it was still difficult to relax, she managed to sleep for a while. At dawn, the sunshine coming through the barred window into her room also gave her some optimism. Whatever had happened last night had happened in the past, and dwelling on the past certainly wasn't going to accomplish anything. She showered and got ready for work, eager to start her day and to get back into the safety of her routine. She would go to the office, go to the gym, meet a friend—maybe even Olivia—for a drink this evening, and everything would return to normal. The memories from last night didn't even seem like her memories anymore. They seemed like something she'd dreamed or watched on TV.

Leaving her apartment, she was cautious, looking both ways before she went out to the hallway, and then she went out to the street. It was a normal morning—people heading to work, listening to their iPods. She walked up the block, happy to be away from her apartment and back in a routine, and then she thought she heard something behind her and she turned around.

She didn't see anything unusual except a very old man standing near her apartment building. His face was extremely wrinkled and he had very dark eyes, and he seemed to be looking right at her. Just as his intense gaze was starting to make her uneasy, he turned and sprinted away from her toward Avenue B.

Diane didn't understand how an old man could run so fast. Was it possible that she'd dreamed up the old man, or that he was another hallucination?

Diane hurried away toward the subway, seriously worried about her sanity.

A lison made Jeremy his favorite breakfast—French toast and chocolate milk. Since checking out of the hotel earlier this morning, Alison had been trying to stay calm for Jeremy's sake, but she was actually terrified that something awful had happened to Simon. At first when she came home to the empty apartment she figured he was out for one of his long runs, but then she found his cell phone, and it was unusual for him to go anywhere without his cell.

If something had happened to him, it would be her fault. She felt guilty for turning him away yesterday at the hotel. What if the lycanthropic disorder was even worse than she'd thought? What if he was suffering from full-blown schizophrenia and he was confused, wandering the streets of New York City? He could even get himself killed.

"When's Daddy coming home?" Jeremy asked for the third time this morning, or was it the fourth?

"I don't know, sweetie." Alison felt as if she were using every muscle in her face to force a smile.

"But where did he go?" Jeremy persisted.

"He's just out running some errands," Alison said. Then before Jeremy could ask another question, she added quickly, "Why don't you finish that French toast before it gets cold, okay?"

After breakfast, she played with Jeremy and tried to keep him, and herself, distracted, but her mind kept thinking up worst-case scenarios. She imagined the police showing up and telling her Simon was dead. They would want her to go to the morgue to ID his body, and she'd be a widow and Jeremy would be fatherless. The scene seemed so real that she was contemplating calling the police to report a missing person, but was Simon actually missing? Didn't twenty-four hours have to pass before the police would bother to even look for Simon? It had only been about eighteen hours since she'd seen him at the hotel.

At noon Alison couldn't take it anymore. She had to at least get out of the apartment, because just hanging around, waiting, was making things worse. She was in Jeremy's room getting him ready to go out when she heard the key turning in the lock. She ran into the living room just as Simon entered the apartment.

"Thank God, you're okay," she said, and hugged him as if she hadn't seen him in years.

Then Jeremy came over shouting, "Daddy's home! Daddy's home! Daddy's home!" and rushed over and hugged Simon's leg.

"Hey, kiddo, it's so great to see you," Simon said. Then he said to Alison in a serious tone, "Is everything okay?"

"Everything's wonderful," she said.

"Oh, okay," he said tentatively. "Because yesterday you seemed so—"

"Yesterday was yesterday," she said. Then she winced. "Did you go running in those clothes?"

"Yeah," Simon said. "I—"

"Oh, never mind," she said. "I'm just so glad you're here."

Jeremy was squeezing his nostrils with his thumb and forefinger. "Daddy, you smell really bad."

"I know, kiddo, Daddy needs a shower," Simon said. "Why don't you go watch some TV for a few minutes, and then I'll come play with you, okay?"

"Okay," Jeremy said, and went happily to the TV.

Then Simon said to Alison, "So is this all for real? You're not angry at me anymore?"

"No, I'm not angry at all," she said. "I believe you now."

"You do?"

"Yes, and I don't think you're crazy. I would never judge you for something that's beyond your control."

"Wow," Simon said. "I really appreciate you saying that. But you're not afraid?"

"Why would I be afraid of my husband?" She hugged him and said, "I love you so much. And don't worry. We'll do whatever we have to do to cure you."

"Cure me? How do you think you can cure me?"

"Not me, but there's professional help you can get."

Simon stopped hugging her back and stepped back a couple of feet and said, "Wait, when you say you believe me. What do you believe?"

"What you told me yesterday." She whispered so Jeremy couldn't overhear, "That you think you're a werewolf."

"Look," Simon said, "I really appreciate you saying that, and I'm thrilled that you guys are back home, and I hope we can sit down and do whatever we have to do to work things out and get back on track. But that all said, I know how ludicrous this must've sounded to you. I didn't expect you to necessarily believe that this had actually happened to me, but I just wanted to be honest with you about what was happening, because I was tired of being deceitful."

"Oh stop," she said. "I said I believe you, okay?"

"You really believe that I'm a—?"

"Yes," she said. "If you believe it, then I believe it."

"But—"

"No buts," she said. "Marriage is a partnership. It's my fault, I guess, for losing sight of that. When I married you, it was in sickness and in health, and I'm going to help you through this, but you have to do your part too. I'll stay with you, but you have to deal with your problem, get the help you need."

"I don't think you understand exactly what—"

"I've already done some research online," she said. "There's a psychiatrist downtown, Dr. Milton Levinson, who's dealt with these sorts of problems before. I want you to see him and work on your problem. I just want to see you making an effort."

"Wait, a psychiatrist?" Simon said. "Why do you think I—"

"Because," Alison said. "I just think you're going through something very difficult right now, and you need someone to help you through it.

You won't be alone—I'll be there to give you all the support you need. And you don't have to worry, I've done a lot of research on your condition and it's very treatable."

"My condition?"

"Lycanthropic disorder," Alison said. "You know, when you believe that you're a . . ." She looked in Jeremy's direction again, then said, ". . . a you know what."

"I still don't think you under—"

"We can discuss it later," Alison said. "I'm not going anywhere, so there's plenty of time. Right now I have to catch up on some work, but you and Jeremy should spend some time together; he's been asking for you all day, and all day yesterday too." She winced again—he really did smell awful. "Why don't you go take that shower now, okay?"

Simon hated keeping secrets from Alison, but what choice did he have? He'd tried to tell her the truth yesterday and she didn't believe him, so, at least for right now, if letting her think he had a disorder was what it took to keep his family together, then so be it. Meanwhile, after what he'd been through last night, he was lucky to be here at all.

At the brewery Simon had washed up and cleaned Olivia's blood off his body, but he still needed a shower desperately. He ran the water as hot as he could stand it. He was hoping the pain would be a distraction, but he couldn't get the gruesome images from last night out of his head, and he doubted he ever would. Though he knew he'd killed Olivia in self-defense, and that she would have killed Charlie and maybe Ramon too if he hadn't stopped her, it was the sheer brutality of the killing that continued to shock him. He couldn't explain it away, tell himself it was the werewolf part of him that had done it, because he'd been completely aware of what he was doing. He'd killed her because he'd wanted to kill her; he'd made a choice.

Though Simon hadn't been able to prevent Michael from biting

Ramon and Charlie, at least Charlie's bleeding had stopped—apparently werewolves had a much faster recovery time than humans—and Michael claimed that Charlie would be okay. Simon hated how Michael had gotten exactly what he wanted—his pack of wolves—and Simon felt used and manipulated. He felt as if Michael had orchestrated everything that had happened last night on the roof, letting him go, knowing he'd wind up attacking and killing Olivia. Even worse, Michael had volunteered to get rid of Olivia's body and help cover up the incident, so now he had something else to hold over Simon.

With just a towel around his waist, Simon went into the bedroom, where Alison was working on her laptop at the desk.

"Nice shower, sweetie?" she asked.

Okay, her one-eighty attitude switch was a little freaky. It was hard to believe this was the same woman who'd seemed to hate his guts just yesterday.

"Pretty good," he said.

"Did you trim your chest hair?"

The hair he'd shaved off yesterday had already mostly grown back, making it look like he'd gotten a trim.

"Yeah, did a little manscaping," he said.

She smiled, then said, "About the psychiatrist. I just don't want you to think I'm threatening you, because that's totally not the case. I mean, getting professional help is your choice; I guess I just want to know you're willing to meet me halfway on this. And we can discuss this with Dr. Hagan too, of course."

"No, the psychiatrist sounds like a great idea," Simon said.

"Really?" Alison said.

"Yeah," Simon said. "I mean, you're right, I'm definitely going through something big. I mean, thinking I'm a werewolf—it doesn't get any bigger than that, right?"

"It's good that you can joke about it," Alison said. "It shows you have an awareness about your condition. That's probably very healthy." She looked at him seductively, biting down on her lower lip. "Come here."

He came over to where she was sitting, and she hugged him around the waist.

"Mmm, you smell great now," she said, and he said, "So do you."

It was true—she did smell amazing. He could tell she was turned on, and he was too, his sudden hard-on pushing out the towel.

"Ooo, look who's back." Alison massaged the bulge, getting him even harder. She said to his penis, "I missed you." Then to Simon, "Date in bed tonight?"

"Sounds like a plan," Simon said.

He got dressed and let her continue her work. He was amazed how his marriage suddenly seemed to be on the mend when he'd been so certain he was on the road to divorce.

In the living room, Simon picked up Jeremy and kissed his head, savoring the combined odor of his baby shampoo and unique bodily scent.

"Mmm, you have no idea how good it feels to breathe that smell," he said.

"What smell?" Jeremy asked.

"Never mind," Simon said, closing his eyes and breathing in more of it. "Never mind."

Jeremy sat on Simon's lap and they talked and watched some of *The Wiggles* together, and for a while he managed to forget that he was a werewolf and a killer and that the happy home life he was experiencing probably wouldn't last for long.

Alison came into the room and said, "Aww, look at you two. Wait, stay like that, let me get my camera." She returned and took a few photos. "You two look so, so adorable. I'm going to have to frame one of these."

They went out to dinner for hamburgers at Jackson Hole. One burger wasn't enough, and Simon couldn't resist ordering three more. At one point, Simon noticed Alison looking at him sympathetically and knowingly. Obviously she believed that the meat-eating was part of his "disorder" that she was going to help him "cure."

Later in the evening, after Jeremy went to bed, Simon was getting undressed when Alison sneaked up behind him and said, "Boo."

Simon said, "You surprised me," but of course he wasn't surprised. He'd heard her tiptoeing on the carpet and, if he focused, he could hear bits of conversations in the next apartment. Actually his hearing was so good that it was harder not to hear than to hear.

He could smell Alison too, and he knew she was naked before he turned around to hold her. They got into bed together and started making love. It was great to be with his wife, touching her and kissing her, and he'd never wanted her this much. He made her come a few times, and then it was his turn. He was on top, looking into her eyes. He felt the familiar build in his loins and rush of blood to his head, and his whole body tensed as he was on the verge of a powerful orgasm, and then it happened.

There was sudden pressure all over his body, especially in his mouth, and the bones in his legs and arms felt as if they were pulling apart, stretching his ligaments. Panicked, he said, "Oh my God," but Alison must have thought this was a precursor to his orgasm because she said what she usually said when he was about to climax—"Come for me, baby, come for me," and wrapped her legs around his waist, pulling him in closer. Simon knew that he had to get away, that in a few seconds he would turn into a crazed beast on top of his wife and do God knows what to her, and then, with the pressure building, he managed to break free and make it into the bathroom and lock the door.

He looked in the mirror. His teeth were jutting out slightly and his jaw was more prominent, and his eyes seemed bigger and maybe a shade darker, but there was no excess hair on his face—just his usual scruffiness—and the pains in his ligaments were subsiding.

"Simon?" Alison knocked on the door. "Simon, what's wrong? Are you okay?"

Simon splashed his face with cold water and looked in the mirror again. His teeth had receded, and except for some residual pain around his mouth, hands, and feet, he felt pretty much normal. He'd avoided disaster this time, but what would happen next time, and the time after that? It seemed that the change happened during times of extreme emotion—when he was angry or threatened or when he was having sex—but that didn't mean he'd ever be able to control it. Maybe he could avoid sex for the time being, but eventually, if he wanted to stay married, he'd have to have sex again, and what if he couldn't stop the transformation next time? He could snap and kill Alison the way he'd killed Olivia. Or what about the next time he lost his temper? He was normally an even-keeled guy but once in a while, like anybody else, he got upset and raised his voice. The next time he had a fight with Alison, was he going to turn into a homicidal werewolf? Or God forbid, what if he snapped at Jeremy one day for refusing to get into his stroller or taking too long in the bathroom? How was he supposed to stop himself from turning into a werewolf in front of his son? Even if he didn't injure Jeremy, the experience of seeing his dad turn would scar him for life.

Alison was banging on the door saying, "Simon, what're you doing in there? Simon, you're really scaring me now. Please say something."

"I'm fine," he said.

"What?" she asked.

"Fine," he said. "I . . . I said I'm fine."

His stayed in the bathroom for a couple more minutes, splashing his face with water, and then returned to the bedroom.

"What the hell just happened?" Alison asked.

"It must be part of the disorder." Simon didn't know what else to say.

"You're going to see Dr. Levinson as soon as possible," she said. "Maybe you can even get an appointment for tomorrow."

When Simon got back into bed, Alison was on her back with her eyes open, facing the ceiling. The room was dark except for some light from the nightlight in the bathroom.

He kissed her on the cheek and said, "Don't worry, everything's going to be okay. I promise."

He hoped he was telling the truth. He remembered Michael saying, *You're exactly like me now*, and Volker Hartman's warning that if the wolves' blood spreads, *It will be the end of all of us*.

"I know it will," Alison said.

Lying on his back, Simon could hear Alison's heart beating and, when he focused, Jeremy's soft breathing in the next room. At the moment the future didn't concern him; he just wanted to enjoy this time with his family, where he belonged. When Alison turned onto her side, Simon turned as well, holding her from behind, clinging to her, as they drifted into sleep.

AUTHOR'S NOTE

Many thanks to Gabriel Mason, Nick Harris, and Brian DeFiore; without their early support and encouragement, this novel wouldn't exist. I'm also fortunate to be part of a wonderful community of writers, including Alison Gaylin and Michelle Gagnon, who read early drafts and had many invaluable suggestions. Chynna Skye Starr helped me through several tough plot points and was a great sounding board. Susan Allison believed in *The Pack* from the very beginning, and her input improved the book in so many ways. And big, big shout-outs to the librarians, booksellers, and readers who have made my career possible.

Read on for a taster of the next
instalment in *The Pack* series:

The Craving

ONE

When Diane Coles heard the creaking footsteps in the hallway outside the bedroom she knew it was one of them coming to get her. She sat up in bed and screamed so loud it hurt her ears, but this didn't scare away the intruder. The footsteps got louder, and then the doorknob rattled and the door shook. Oh, God, this was it, the moment she'd feared since she'd left New York and moved back in with her parents in Grosse Pointe. He—well if it was a *he*—was going to break in and kill her. She had no idea how many of them there were. She knew there were at least a few, including her best friend—well, former best friend—Olivia.

Still shrieking, she grabbed the nearest object, a lamp, yanking the cord out of the wall. Yeah, like a lamp would protect her. Still, she raised it above her head, ready to fling it at whoever, or *whatever*, came inside.

"Diane, what's going on? What's wrong? Diane, open this door right now . . . Diane."

It took a few seconds before it registered that it wasn't one of *them* after all; it was just her mother.

"Diane, can you hear me?"

"I'm fine, Mom," Diane said, aware of her pulse pounding as if she were in an all-out sprint.

"You can't stay in there all day again," Barbara Coles said. "This is ridiculous. You have to get on with your life."

Diane remained with the lamp above her head for several seconds, then replaced it on the night table. She lay down again in bed and pulled the blanket up to her chin.

"Diane, will you please open the door?" Barbara shook the door a few more times.

"I'll be right down, Mom."

"What?" Barbara asked.

"I said I'll be right down."

Diane heard Barbara let out a long, frustrated breath, and then her fading footsteps as she marched downstairs.

Diane had been lashing out at her parents since she'd moved home, and she felt bad about it. She was thirty-two years old, but lately she'd been acting like a spoiled, angry fourteen-year-old. She'd thought moving back home would make her feel safe, protected, but if anything, being isolated in a small space had increased her paranoia.

If she knew who exactly was after her it would make things a little easier—at least she'd know whom to avoid—but it really could be anyone. Maybe it was the dark-haired guy in the black Honda that had been parked in front of her parents' house the day before, or that older, blond woman in the Delta terminal at LaGuardia who'd stared at her weirdly. Or maybe it was the very old guy, maybe ninety years old, who'd grabbed her in front of the apartment in the East Village one evening and said with a foreign accent, maybe German, "You must leave, before it's too late." The way the guy had looked at her with his intense dark eyes had scared the crap out of her. Before she could ask him who he was or any other questions, he ran away, with surprising speed for such an old man. Maybe he was one of them, or maybe there were others she didn't know about, but now she was certain of one thing—she wouldn't be able to avoid them forever.

Her parents, meanwhile, had no idea about the danger she was in, or the possible danger *they* were in. It would be so much easier if she were able to open up about it, get some genuine support, but she knew they wouldn't believe her. They'd have the same reaction as the police; they'd think she was crazy, disturbed, making it all up. Besides, they were getting older—both in their midsixties—and she didn't want to cause them any stress, especially since her father had had bypass surgery recently. So Diane had no choice but to keep all the stress to herself, and it had been taking its toll. She was losing weight and couldn't sleep, and her thoughts were so scattered it was hard to focus on anything.

She'd considered leaving Grosse Pointe, but where else would she go? If she stayed with another friend or relative, in Michigan or some other part of the country, she'd be endangering someone else, and she didn't have money to travel far or stay in a hotel. In New York, she'd been making decent money as a publicist for a financial services firm, but with rents the way they were, she had been barely able to save.

So, for better or worse, Diane was stuck at her parents' house. During the nearly three weeks she'd been here she hadn't gone outside at all. Her parents thought she was depressed—which was probably at least partly true—but as far as they knew she'd moved home because of a bad breakup with Steve, a jerk lawyer who'd dumped her with a text message, and because "the whole living-in-the-city thing just wasn't working out."

She shuddered as the memory nudged into her consciousness, but she refused to let her mind fully go there. Denial was her new mantra. Maybe it was a dysfunctional coping mechanism, but it had been working so far; after all, at least she wasn't in a mental institution. She wanted to believe that if she didn't think about what had happened in New York, the experience would eventually vanish, like a bad dream. Or, maybe if she just stayed in bed and hid her head in the darkness under her pillow, like she did when she was a kid on days she didn't want to get up to go to school, they wouldn't be able to find her and she would be safe, protected. The flashbacks—in vivid, horrifying detail—were still coming, though, but it had been only a few weeks. Maybe one day she'd wake up and it would all be gone, forgotten completely, as if it had never happened. She couldn't wait for that day.

Sitting at the edge of her bed, leaning over and kneading her scalp with her fingers obsessively, she'd never felt so out of control. She wondered if this was what insanity felt like. She didn't think she was insane, but wasn't that part of the definition of insanity? Didn't all insane people think they were sane? She was definitely *acting* insane—staying in bed all day, neglecting her appearance and hygiene, starving herself, virtually paralyzed by extreme paranoia. She had to admit, when she analyzed her behavior this way, as an outsider would, she didn't seem like a portrait of sanity. While she thought she had a very good reason to be behaving this way, if she was insane how could she trust her thoughts? Maybe nothing had happened to her in New York—maybe it seemed like a nightmare, because it had been an actual nightmare, or some kind of hallucination. It was true she'd been under a lot of stress lately and had never really adjusted to life in the city. Maybe the breakup with Steve had been the thing that had put her over the edge.

As she continued to rock back and forth, kneading her scalp with her fingertips, she whispered repeatedly, "New York never happened, New York never happened, New York never happened . . ."

Gradually, she started to believe that there was at least some chance that she'd made it all up, had had some kind of psychotic break, which gave her more hope than she'd had in days. Insanity was a good thing. Insanity could be cured. Insanity would mean that she could get through this. If she just pushed herself, if she stopped being the victim, she could snap herself out of this before it was too late and it took over completely.

She went downstairs, apologized to her parents, and ate all the food her mother put in front of her, even asking for seconds. Already she felt energized, convinced she could get through this.

Practically beaming, Barbara said, "I'm so happy you're finally eating."

"You and Dad are right," Diane said. "I can't live my life like this anymore. I need some things at the drugstore. Can I borrow your car?"

"Of course you can, sweetie."

Upstairs, Diane showered—unlike her other showers over the past few weeks, she managed to not see glimpses of that scene from *Psycho*—and then she put on clean clothes. She felt good. *This* felt good. If she could just get to CVS and back without having an attack of paranoia, it would be a great start, something to build on. She needed to prove to herself that the danger wasn't real.

The fear didn't set in until she was about to leave the house. At the front door she was so dizzy she almost lost her balance and had to grab on to the molding on the wall near the front door so she wouldn't fall down.

Her father was nearby and said, "Are you okay?"

"Yeah, I'm fine," Diane said, recovering quickly. "Just tripped on my heels."

She was wearing clogs, with maybe one-inch heels, so this didn't really make sense.

"Maybe I should come with you," Robert Coles said.

"Don't be ridiculous," Diane said, "it's a five-minute drive, maybe less. I'll see you soon."

Barbara came over and said, "Drive carefully."

"Don't worry," Diane said. "I will."

Diane went outside. It was a perfect November day—bright and sunny, about fifty degrees. Most leaves were gone from the trees and there was the smell of mulch in the crisp, cool air. She was enjoying being outdoors for the first time in days so much that she didn't get nervous and paranoid again until she was inside her mom's Ford Fusion. She felt like she was being watched. She looked around quickly in every direction, but that didn't mean they weren't there somewhere. Her heart was racing and she felt extremely dizzy, as if she'd just gotten off a merry-go-round. Her father was probably right—she probably shouldn't be driving a car right now—but she wanted to prove to herself that she could get through this, that this horrible paralyzing fear she'd been experiencing wasn't permanent.

She repeated out loud: "New York never happened, New York never happened, New York never happened, New York never happened. . . ." and she felt better—well, at least she didn't feel like she was going to pass out anymore.

She started the engine and backed out of the driveway onto the quiet, suburban street. Driving away, looking in the rearview mirror, she thought a black SUV, looked like a Lexus, was following her, but then the SUV turned down a side street.

In CVS, Diane hurried to get the things she needed, avoiding making eye contact with anyone. At the checkout line, someone bumped into her from behind and she turned around suddenly, maybe even cocking a fist, and said "Hey."

Then she saw that the person who had bumped her was an elderly woman with a cane, about eighty years old. The old woman could've been one of them, but it wasn't likely.

"Oh, sorry," Diane said. Then she closed her eyes and said, "New York never happened, New York never happened, New York never happened."

When she opened her eyes she saw that the girl working at the checkout counter was looking at her like . . . well, like she was a crazy person, but this was a good thing. Diane wanted to be crazy. If she was crazy, that meant she was safe.

Returning to the car, Diane was barely afraid. Her heart was beating much faster than normal and she felt clammy—especially the back of her neck—but she didn't feel dizzy or wobbly. She was proud of herself for doing so well. She realized a trip to CVS hardly constituted resuming her life, but it was a major step in the right direction. Maybe if, over the next week or so, she left her house every day to take a small trip somewhere—shopping, to the gym, maybe even see a movie— she'd get used to being around strangers again and eventually the fear—and the memories of New York—would vanish completely.

Driving home, she looked once or twice in the rearview mirror to check whether anyone was following her, but her paranoia had subsided significantly. At this point she didn't want to put too much pressure on herself, have unrealistic expectations. She needed to take it day by day and build on what she'd accomplished this afternoon, but it was hard not to fantasize about what a fear-free life in Michigan would be like. Maybe within a month she could move out of her parents' house into her own apartment. She had a lot of friends in the area. She'd fallen out of touch with some of them, and most of them were married, but she'd have people to socialize with. Eventually she'd be ready to date again and she'd meet a good, solid Michigan guy. He'd come from a good family and have a good job and, most important, he'd be normal. The idea of settling down in the suburbs used to terrify Diane; nothing had seemed more terrifying than living her parents' life. But now that was all she wanted—an easy, normal, safe life. And, really, was that too much to ask for?

She pulled into the driveway and parked in front of the garage. As she got out of the car she was absorbed in the fantasy of her future life—marriage, kids, a big house. It wouldn't be such an awful life. It would be a good, safe, easy life, and that was all that mattered to her now. She was through feeling that she had to be in the center of the action, that she had to be in a big city, going to the newest, hippest bars and restaurants and attending club openings and wine tastings. She didn't even like going to wine tastings, acting so self-important, having to think of new adjectives to describe the wine to whomever she was with. She was through trying to impress, being fake. She just wanted to go back to who she was—a simple, happy, laid-back Michigan girl. It would be so relieving to not feel like she had to go somewhere or transform into someone else in order to be happy. She could be happy being who she was and where she was. She could be happy right here, right now.

She was starting to smile, feeling better than she had in weeks, when she heard movement behind her. In the next instant there was a sharp pain in her head and she was falling forward into the darkness, and her mother was telling her to get her head out from under the pillow, it was time to get up to go to school, but she wouldn't go to school.

She would stay in the darkness forever.

He just wanted a decent book to read ...

Not too much to ask, is it? It was in 1935 when Allen Lane, Managing Director of Bodley Head Publishers, stood on a platform at Exeter railway station looking for something good to read on his journey back to London. His choice was limited to popular magazines and poor-quality paperbacks – the same choice faced every day by the vast majority of readers, few of whom could afford hardbacks. Lane's disappointment and subsequent anger at the range of books generally available led him to found a company – and change the world.

'We believed in the existence in this country of a vast reading public for intelligent books at a low price, and staked everything on it'
Sir Allen Lane, 1902–1970, founder of Penguin Books

The quality paperback had arrived – and not just in bookshops. Lane was adamant that his Penguins should appear in chain stores and tobacconists, and should cost no more than a packet of cigarettes.

Reading habits (and cigarette prices) have changed since 1935, but Penguin still believes in publishing the best books for everybody to enjoy. We still believe that good design costs no more than bad design, and we still believe that quality books published passionately and responsibly make the world a better place.

So wherever you see the little bird – whether it's on a piece of prize-winning literary fiction or a celebrity autobiography, political tour de force or historical masterpiece, a serial-killer thriller, reference book, world classic or a piece of pure escapism – you can bet that it represents the very best that the genre has to offer.

Whatever you like to read – trust Penguin.